The Lonely Hearts Dog Walkers

Sheila Norton

First published by Ebury Press in 2020

1 3 5 7 9 10 8 6 4 2

Ebury Press, an imprint of Ebury Publishing
20 Vauxhall Bridge Road,
London SW1V 2SA

Ebury Press is part of the Penguin Random House group of companies
whose addresses can be found at global.penguinrandomhouse.com

www.penguin.co.uk

A CIP catalogue record for this book is available from the British Library

ISBN 9781529103137

Typeset in 11.75/15 pt Berkeley
by Integra Software Services Pvt. Ltd, Pondicherry

Printed and bound in Great Britain by Clays Ltd, Elcograf S.p.A.

Penguin Random House is committed to a sustainable future for
our business, our readers and our planet. This book is made
from Forest Stewardship Council® certified paper.

For the dog walkers among my own family and friends –
and especially the very special humans belonging
to new puppies Dexter the labrador, Rosie the
cocker spaniel, Tess the labradoodle and
Rusty the border terrier.

PART 1

DOG DAYS

CHAPTER 1

I woke up suddenly, in complete darkness, wondering for a moment where I was, and what had woken me. The bed felt unfamiliar; the positions of the door, window and a wardrobe that I managed to make out as my eyes gradually adjusted to the dark, all wrong. Then the noise came again and there was a movement beside me and a quiet little whimper. It all came rushing back to me: the disturbed night, the tears, the protests, my eventual caving in to allow Mia to sleep in the bed with me, *just this once*, so that we could all get some peace. We were back in my mum's house in Furzewell – without my husband Josh, Mia's father. I'd left him behind, walked away from him, our home, our marriage and half my life history. Mia and I were here to make a new start.

It wasn't a spur of the moment thing; I'd thought it all out. But now, lying here in the dark, the doubts were threatening to overwhelm me. Especially after being woken by the cockerel – a noise I'd forgotten about from the years spent growing up here in the countryside, letting me know there'd be no more sleep for me now before daylight. I fumbled for my phone and glanced at the time, sighing when I saw the illuminated figures: 5:52. I groaned, and Mia stirred beside me again.

'The cock-a-doodle-do woke me up,' she muttered.

'Me too, sweetheart,' I said with a little rueful laugh as the cockerel crowed again, sounding for all the world as if it were just outside our window instead of at the farm down the road.

'When will it stop?'

'Usually they stop after it gets light. Or occasionally they carry on all day.' I yawned. 'We'll get used to it.'

'It's still night-time, though.'

'No, it's early morning. But they start when there's just a tiny smidgeon of light in the sky. We don't have to get up yet.'

It was the February half-term holiday. No school. A whole week for us both to get settled in – long enough, surely, I'd thought, overly optimistically, before we actually got here. Now, remembering the previous night's tears and tantrums, I wasn't so sure. 'We can just lie here and snuggle for a bit,' I said, pulling Mia's warm, sleepy body towards me and stroking her soft dark hair. 'Why don't you try to go back to sleep?'

I was aching with tiredness myself, and longing to close my eyes and drift back off, rooster or no rooster. But a few minutes later there was a clatter outside on the landing, the door was flung open – light suddenly flooding the room and making me groan again and cover my eyes – and Mum was standing in the doorway holding a tray.

'Morning, darlings!' she hollered. I felt like putting the pillow over my head. 'It's turned six o'clock. I knew you were awake – I heard you talking – so I thought you'd appreciate a nice cup of tea in bed on your first day. Nice glass of milk for you, Mia,' she added. 'And your favourite biscuits.'

'You shouldn't have,' I muttered. She really shouldn't. No chance now of getting back to sleep. My mother's voice was louder than the rooster's.

'Did you sleep well?' she boomed as she plonked the tray down on the bedside table.

'Not really. I—'

'And what time did *you* sneak into bed with your mummy?' she went on, directing this, in a disapproving tone, to Mia. 'Aren't you a bit too old for this?'

'She didn't *sneak* in, Mum,' I said quietly. 'I brought her in. At about two o'clock, when it was obvious neither of us were going to get any sleep otherwise.'

And she's only five, I wanted to add, but didn't, because I didn't want to argue, already, on our first day, in front of Mia. *And she's upset.*

'Oh,' she was saying, surprised. 'Was there a problem? I slept like a log.'

'Good. I didn't want to disturb you.'

Mum's bedroom was at the other side of the house, along the passage, down some rickety steps, through a heavy wooden door and round a corner. Nevertheless, I'd been conscious, every time Mia had started crying again, that it would be unfair if we woke her up – to say nothing of it being a bad start to our stay. I blinked back the memory of how Mum had been talking when she'd welcomed us the previous day, sounding for all the world as if we'd both agreed to spend the rest of our lives together.

'Welcome home, darling.' She'd been hugging me before I'd even crossed the threshold. 'It's so good to have you back.' She'd stepped aside so that I could shepherd Mia, who had her thumb in her mouth and Pink Bunny clasped tight to her chest, into the house ahead of me. 'And it's lovely to have *you* here too, sweetheart,' she added, bending to kiss the top of Mia's head. 'Come on, let's get the kettle on and find you a chocolate biscuit, shall we?'

'I'll just get the bags in from the car,' I said, but Mum hustled me through to the kitchen, shaking her head and smiling.

'There's plenty of time for that. We've got all the time in the world, now, haven't we? Just us three girls together.'

I took a sharp breath, slightly put out by the inappropriateness of her happy girly excitement. I supposed she was just trying to be cheerful for our sakes, but I'd been expecting a degree of sympathy, sadness, perhaps even a telling off for walking out on my marriage, rather than being greeted with the kind of enthusiasm that made me wonder if she'd secretly been hoping, for the previous twelve years, that it wasn't going to last.

I couldn't dwell on this for long, though. Before we'd even got our coats off, the mood was changed abruptly. Mia, still holding onto Pink Bunny, was looking around the kitchen, eyeing the cat basket, crouching to peer through the cat-flap in the back door.

'Where's Monty?' she said.

Mum stopped in the act of filling the kettle, letting the tap run and turning to give me an anxious look.

'Didn't I tell you?' Mum said more quietly.

'Tell me what?'

'He's gone.'

'Oh!' I gasped. 'No, Mum, you didn't say. When did he—? What happened? He was only young, wasn't he?'

'No, I don't mean that – well, I hope not. I mean he's gone, disappeared. A week or two ago now. I've looked everywhere, asked everyone. I keep hoping he'll just walk back in one day, but the longer it goes on…' She sighed. 'I do wonder if something's happened to him.'

'Oh, no.' I glanced at Mia. She was standing rigidly by the back door now, staring from one of us to the other. I lowered my voice, gave Mum a warning look and changed the subject. 'Anyway, did you say you had some chocolate biscuits?'

'Where's Monty gone?' Mia repeated in an accusing voice.

'We're not sure at the moment, darling,' I said. 'Perhaps he's playing hide-and-seek somewhere.'

'Can I go and look for him?'

'Not right now. Come on, let's get you a drink and a biscuit.'

'But I want to find Monty.' Her lower lip started to wobble. 'I wanted him to sleep on my bed.'

She burst into tears. And it was all my fault for making a promise I couldn't keep.

I'd come back to Furzewell, to my childhood home, to the village where I'd grown up and lived for the first twenty-three years of my life, because it felt like the only option. I was going to start again, return to my country girl roots, for Mia's sake as well as for mine. But five-year-old children don't always react to things the way we expect. I'd been prepared, of course, for Mia to cry about leaving our house in Plymouth, her school and her friends. I knew she'd be upset about all these changes. I'd uprooted her in the middle of her second school year, and I was aware that was potentially asking for trouble. But I'd done my best to handle everything carefully and sensitively, assuring her that she'd see Daddy regularly, that he'd pick her up and take her back to spend weekends in her old bedroom, and that her best friends from the old school, Polly and Jamila, could come to play with her during the school holidays. She'd seemed to accept all these reassurances calmly, without too many questions, but what I hadn't reckoned on was the fuss she'd make, at the last moment, about leaving our cat behind.

'*Why* can't Bella come to Nanny's house with us?' she'd asked sadly.

'Because she'd probably get lost,' I explained. 'She doesn't know her way around in Furzewell. And anyway, she's

Daddy's cat too, so wouldn't it be kind to let him have Bella to keep him company? Otherwise he'd be on his own.'

'Well if we don't go, he won't be on his own,' she pointed out. 'So let's just stay here.'

'We can't do that, baby. I've explained it all to you, haven't I? I've got a new job in Furzewell. We can't take Bella, can we – Nanny's cat wouldn't like it. He'd be jealous, and they might fight, and Bella might get hurt. But you'll be able to play with him – Monty – instead.'

She'd put her head on one side, considering this.

'He is a nice cat. He's got funny little twitchy ears. Will Nanny let him sleep on my bed?'

'I expect so.' I crossed my fingers. 'If you give him lots of cuddles as soon as we get there, he'll want to be your friend.'

'OK,' she conceded eventually. 'I'll ask Nanny if Monty can be my cat.'

I was so relieved this seemed to pacify her, that it didn't even occur to me talk to Mum about the cat. He'd always been there whenever we'd visited her, and had always been a friendly boy, so I'd had no reason to doubt Mia would be able to make friends with him again. Anyway, it had completely slipped my mind as I'd been so busy with the preparations for our departure: my job interview at Furzewell Primary School, the school visit for Mia, the packing, and the strained discussions with Josh about what was mine, what was his, and *why the hell we were going anyway*. These particular discussions would take place late at night, when Mia was asleep, the arguments hissing back and forth between us, and usually ending up with him sighing, shaking his head and saying he supposed I'd soon be coming back, and wasn't it about time I grew up and stopped thinking the grass was greener somewhere else?

I didn't rise to the bait. I just turned away, closing the argument, because I needed to keep our strained relationship as civil as possible, to keep things calm and especially not to wake Mia up. But I knew in my heart he was wrong. I wouldn't be back. My marriage was over, and I was starting again – back in Furzewell. I'd always loved it here, where I grew up. The quiet streets, surrounded by open countryside; the old grey stone buildings; the bench under the big old oak tree on the little village green, where as teenagers we'd gathered in the evenings to chat and flirt and drink cheap cider; the neighbours and local shopkeepers who'd known me all my life – I loved everything about it, even the bleakness and feeling of isolation that set in during the winters here. Now, in the middle of February, the lanes and fields and footpaths were full of mud, the sky grey and the nights often sharp with frost, but to me, it was still beautiful. I'd made up my mind, weeks before, that I was really going to do it – I was coming back to Furzewell for good. I'd stay at Mum's, but only until the marriage could be dissolved, the house sold, the mistakes of my life completely erased, and then I'd find somewhere permanent here, just for Mia and myself. Leaving Josh was one of the hardest things I'd ever had to do. But being back here in Furzewell was going to make it just that little bit easier.

CHAPTER 2

Eagle House, our family home, was named after the pub it once used to be. From old pictures I'd seen long ago, I'd deduced that The Eagle hadn't been a very big pub. But as a house, it had seemed enormous to me when I was a little girl, probably because it was detached, standing in its own grounds, and had five bedrooms. This was unusual enough for houses around here, even though none of the bedrooms were large. Neither of the two living rooms downstairs, which were originally the public bar and the snug, were particularly big either. But what had made it such a fun place to grow up in were the passages between the rooms – narrow, with uneven floors, steps and dark corners to hide in – and the big fireplaces. The fireplace in the lounge was actually so big that in the summer, when there wasn't a fire lit and it had been cleared, I could sit right inside it – something Mia still enjoyed doing now.

The garden was huge too, and that morning, after I'd brought in all our bags and boxes from the car and made a start on unpacking them, I put on my coat and joined Mia outside, where she was walking around the perimeter, searching shrubs and bushes and calling for Monty.

'He's hiding for a long time, isn't he,' she said, and then added more quietly, looking at the ground, 'do you think he's run away?'

'We don't know, Mia. Nanny says she's been looking for him, calling him every day, but he hasn't turned up yet.' I sighed. I knew it was always best to give children the truth rather than making things worse by fobbing them off, but at times it was so hard. 'You know what cats are like – Bella's the same – they do wander off sometimes. But it's been a long time now, and Nanny's worried that Monty might have got lost.'

'Nanny said something might have happened to him, didn't she? What, though, Mummy? What might have happened to him?'

I swallowed. 'Well, he might ... I don't know ... he might have wandered into someone else's garden, and been frightened by a dog, and climbed up a tree and got stuck. Something like that.'

'Or got run over by a car,' she said bluntly. 'That's what happened to Polly's old cat. Her mummy and daddy got a new one, though, and she likes it better than the old one because it's a kitten. It's ginger and white.'

Children can be tougher than we think. And fickle.

'But I want Monty to come back,' she added, putting a stop to the thoughts I was having about the possibility of going out to buy a ginger-and-white kitten. 'He was going to be my cat, and I wanted him to sleep on the end of my bed like Bella did. I couldn't go to sleep last night because I missed my other bedroom *and* I didn't have Bella. Mummy, please can we go and look for Monty? In case he is stuck up a tree. He might come down if we call him?'

'Yes, I suppose he might,' I agreed, to make her happy. I'd keep the ginger-and-white kitten option in reserve, though. Sadly I didn't hold out a lot of hope of finding Monty around the village after two weeks, although I guessed stranger things had happened. 'Come on, then, let's go out now, while it's not raining.'

'Can we go to Nanny's shop too?' Mia said, brightening up instantly. 'Can we get some sweets?'

'Of course.' I smiled at her. Mum worked part-time in one of the shops on Fore Street and it had always been Mia's treat, whenever we'd visited Mum in the past, to call in there while she was at work. Everyone in the shop would make a fuss of her, and her treat would be a children's magazine and a small bar of chocolate or packet of sweets. Right now, it didn't feel like much at all, especially to compensate for everything else.

A walk around Furzewell could never take very long. Leaving Eagle House, we strolled down Pump Lane to Fore Street, looking behind trees, in ditches and among brambles all the way and calling out for Monty. We passed a pair of thatched cottages, two cul-de-sacs of modern houses, then the entrance to School Lane, which, needless to say, led to the primary school where both of us would soon be spending our days. Next came the village hall opposite the little church, and then we arrived at the three small shops, of which Furzewell was justifiably proud. In these days of internet shopping and retail parks, it was quite something for such a small village to still boast a privately run greengrocery, butcher's shop and general store. How they'd survived was frankly beyond me, unless it was simply because of the distance to the nearest town and the lack of a bus route. Mum had explained that quite a few of the residents were now getting on a bit, and preferred not to drive too far. But I'd also noticed that the managers of the shops had kept up with new demands, so that they appealed to the younger families too. As well as the old favourites – cabbages, swede and turnips, Granny Smith apples, plums – the greengrocer's had very prominent displays of the more fashionable items like Swiss chard, kale, avocadoes and guava, all organic of course. The butcher's shop was so well known for the quality and value of its locally sourced meat that people drove to Furzewell from bigger towns just to stock up their freezers. And I'd yet to discover all the items sold by the enterprising owners of Furzewell General Store, which was a grocery shop, bakery, newsagent's, sweetshop, draper's and hardware shop all rolled into one. The same family also owned the property next door to the shop, which I remembered as a nice little house when I was at school here, but which had now been turned into quite a trendy café, simply called *Smiths* after the owners. It was much loved by the young parents who congregated here after dropping off their children at school, to chat over their macchiatos and their flat whites.

As Mia and I walked into the shop, Mum looked up in surprise from her position at the till.

'I thought you'd be busy all morning unpacking and sorting everything out,' she said.

'We're looking for Monty,' Mia told her, and Mum gave me a quick nod of understanding. 'We're going to try the park next.'

'And we also, obviously, need chocolate and magazines,' I said with a wink. 'To keep us going.'

These necessities having been chosen and purchased, we said goodbye again, promising to be home by one o'clock, when Mum finished her shift, to have lunch together. We carried on down Fore Street to the little village green, where the remaining village pub, the Fox and Goose, stood on a small gravelled forecourt, with wooden benches and tables against the cream stone walls. Josh and I had often sat here in summertime to enjoy a pub lunch. I sighed to myself as I remembered those happier days, but tried to push the memories away. I'd never be able to get on with my new life back in Furzewell if I started getting sentimental about things like this – the memories were everywhere here.

As well as the pub, the village green was encircled by half-a-dozen pastel-coloured cottages known collectively and unimaginatively as The Houses on the Green. Number Four had been the home of my childhood friend, Amber. It was mostly in her company that I'd spent the early part of my teenage years, and these were the memories I was happy to indulge now, looking back fondly on our evenings of illegal booze, cigarettes and giggling with the local boys who gathered, like us, under that big horse chestnut. I was smiling to myself as we turned into Furzewell Park Lane opposite the green.

'We need to keep looking for Monty, Mummy,' Mia reminded me, bringing me back abruptly to the present. 'Do you think we'll find him in the park?'

'I don't know, sweetheart. Don't get your hopes up.'

'But my hopes *are* up. I don't want them to go down.'

I smiled. 'OK. Come on, then, let's have a good look round the park.'

Furzewell Park, like the three shops, was something of an anomaly for such a small village. It had once, apparently, been the grounds of a big old mansion, which had long ago been demolished, and two small cul-de-sacs of 1960s semi-detached houses and bungalows now stood on its site. The local council, which must have had more funds back then than it seemed to have these days, had bought the mansion's parkland and turned it into a recreation facility for the area. Like the village green, it had served the purposes of generations of raucous teenagers and courting couples, but these days there didn't seem to be much evidence of football or cricket being played here, the tennis courts had returned to nature and the children's play area had seen better days.

Mia and I were just scrabbling about in some hedgerow at the far side of the park, calling out 'Monty! Monty!' as if our lives depended on it, when from behind me a voice suddenly said: 'Nic! I *thought* it was you.'

I swung around.

'Amber!' Straightening up and pushing my hair out of my eyes, I waded out of the bushes and gave her a hug.

She was laughing. 'You've got twigs in your hair! What are you doing here?'

'Searching for Monty.' I nodded at Mia, who was still in the bushes, peering around. 'Mia's desperate to find him, but—'

'I mean, what are you doing here in Furzewell? Visiting your mum, are you?'

'Um . . . yes. Kind of. Well, actually, it's more than just a visit. But what about you? Are you visiting your family too?'

Amber and I had been best friends, back in the day, but I hadn't seen her for years. The last I'd heard, she was living in a flat share in Bristol. I sometimes saw her posts on social media, and I knew she was still single but had moved around a bit since, like me, she'd left Furzewell during her early twenties.

'I moved back here, just before Christmas, actually. Bought myself a starter home on the new estate. I decided it was about time, at thirty-five, I grew up, got on the housing ladder and stopped living like some kind of ageing hippy.'

I laughed. 'Hardly! But good for you. And it's lovely that you're back here as well as me.'

She looked at me with her head on one side.

'What do you mean? Have you and Josh moved back too?'

'Not Josh. Just me. And Mia, of course.'

There was silence – apart from the forlorn cries of 'Monty! Monty!' coming from the shrubbery.

'What's happened, Nic?' Amber said at length. 'Have you split up? You two ... you go back forever.'

'Mm. Perhaps that's half the problem,' I said wearily. 'Look, I'd better not go into it all right now. But let's get together for a drink sometime – soon! I'm *so* pleased we're going to be able to spend time together.' Carried away by the welcome thought of having fun with my old friend again, imagining us both as some kind of born-again teenagers, I added: 'Where does everyone hang out around here these days?'

'Hang out?' she said, giving me an amused look, eyebrows raised. 'Come on, Nic, this is Furzewell, and we're both practically middle-aged. We can have a beer in the Fox and Goose if you like. I haven't been in there for years. Or we could go for a coffee in Smiths.'

'Right.' I felt a bit silly. Of course, we were a bit past giggling together on the village green. 'Well, yes, a beer in the Fox and Goose would be nice. I could ask Mum to babysit one evening. I'm off all this week, starting my new job next Monday. What about you? What are you up to these days?'

'I work from home. Editing scientific journals.'

'Blimey. You always were good at that kind of stuff. You got a degree in – chemistry, wasn't it?'

'Yes...' She looked at her watch. 'Look, sorry, Nic. It's great to see you, but can we catch up properly another time? I've only come out because I've got a dentist's appointment, and then I need to get back to walk my dog before I get on with my work.'

'Oh! I didn't know you had a dog.'

'Yes – Benji.' She smiled. 'We have got a lot to catch up on, haven't we?'

We made a date for the following evening, and were just saying goodbye when Mia stomped out of the shrubbery again, looking cross.

'You're not helping to find Monty, Mummy.'

'Who is Monty?' Amber asked, looking puzzled.

'My mum's cat.'

'Oh, I see.' She shrugged. 'Well, good luck. I'm not a cat lover myself.' She pulled a face. 'Don't like what they do to the bird population. Prefer dogs.'

'Fair enough.' I shrugged. 'I like both. Well, let's chat some more tomorrow night. Bye, Amber.'

Mia and I continued on our way round the park. She'd practically lost her voice by now with her calls for Monty, which I joined in with less and less enthusiasm. This search was never going to end well.

'We can try again tomorrow,' I said as we left the park and headed up the hill, past the entrance road into the new estate being built on High Meadow, past the farm, and turned into the other end of Pump Lane to complete our circuit of the village. I wondered how on earth I was going to console Mia when she finally had to accept that we weren't going to find the cat. Perhaps Mum would agree to the ginger-and-white kitten idea.

'I met Amber Stowell in the park,' I told Mum when she arrived home for lunch. 'She's moved back to the village – bought one of those new houses on the High Meadow estate.'

'Oh, I didn't realise any of them were occupied yet.'

'Yes: I walked past on my way back. There are a few with curtains up now, and cars parked outside.' I shrugged. 'It'll be good to have some new young families in the village, won't it?'

'Yes. And nice that Amber's moved back here. Is she married now, then?'

'Seems not. We said we'd meet for a drink tomorrow night. Is that OK?'

'Oh, yes – lovely, I'll join you! I do like a girls' night out.'

I blinked. 'Mum, I was going to ask if you'd mind babysitting. I won't make it late. But—'

'Oh. Yes, of course. Fine.' She turned away. 'I'm going out the next night anyway, with Angie and Sue.'

'Are you sure you don't mind?'

'No, no, it's fine.' She gave me a look. 'But you know, you could always ask Amber round here for an evening instead. It would save your money. And we could all have a nice glass of wine and a chat. All girls together – it'd be fun.'

I didn't quite know how to respond. I knew perfectly well I had to be careful about my money, but I was looking forward to having a drink with Amber, and this would be the first time I'd met a friend for a drink for years. Mum's little hint about cosy nights in – all girls together – made me feel slightly queasy. I hadn't *wanted* to be single again. It wasn't something to be cheerful about. Being back here in Furzewell was the only good thing about it. But I did appreciate how good Mum was being to me and Mia. So I just smiled and said I'd consider it another time.

CHAPTER 3

Mia slept a little better that second night, tired out from her disturbed sleep the night before. But we were both woken by the rooster again before dawn, and she'd climbed into bed with me, talking about renewing the search for Monty, before I'd even got my eyes open.

'It's pouring with rain outside,' I muttered, listening to the patter on the windows and pulling her close to me, stroking her soft dark curls, so like her father's, in the hope that she might drift back off to sleep.

'Poor Monty. He'll be all wet and cold.'

I sighed. Josh had called the previous evening, wanting to talk to Mia. She'd brightened up when she heard his voice, smiling at something he said, but then fell silent and handed the phone back to me.

'Daddy says Bella misses me,' she said mournfully, and I cursed Josh for his lack of tact. I knew I'd have to have a serious conversation with her about the fact that – let's face it – Monty was unlikely to turn up now. Perhaps after breakfast, I thought as we cuddled up together and listened to the rain beating down and the cock crowing.

But after breakfast, and after Mum had left for work, just as I was loading the dishwasher and thinking about how to broach that conversation, there was a ring at the doorbell and there on the step, shaking her spotty umbrella and kicking off her purple welly boots, was my grandmother.

'Gran!' I gave her a hug. 'I was going to come down and see *you* later. You shouldn't have come out in this rain.'

She gave me a look. 'You think a drop of rain's going to keep me indoors, Nicky? What am I, a lump of sugar, now, that's going to melt in the wet?' She shrugged herself out of her mac and hung it up, turning back to grab hold of Mia as she ran towards her. 'Look at you!' she said, laughing. 'You're so tall now. So grown up. I suppose you'll be thinking about going out to work, driving your mum's car and getting married soon?'

'No, Granny Helen!' Mia giggled. 'I'm only five!'

'But you're going to be eighteen on your birthday, isn't that right?' Gran teased her.

'*No*! I'll be *six*, and my birthday is on April the twenty-eighth.'

'Oh, is that right?' She winked at me. 'Well, I'd better start saving up for a *big* birthday present, then. Six is a *very* special age.'

'That's what you said last year about five.' Mia giggled again.

'Did I? Dear me. I must be getting muddled in my old age.'

I laughed. Muddled was the last word I'd use to describe my grandmother. At eighty-one, she was as sharp and bright as ever, as capable, sensible and intelligent as anyone half her age. On her eightieth birthday, in front of the family gathered here for a celebratory lunch, she'd announced that she was moving out of Eagle House – where she'd lived with Mum since my granddad died – into one of the little bungalows in Nightingale Court, a sheltered complex for elderly people opposite the village school. Mum had put up a barrage of protests.

'But why on earth can't you stay here? There's so much room! What's the point of paying rent on a bungalow? You don't need to. You don't need *sheltering* – you're still as fit as a fiddle!'

Gran had waited until she'd finished, and then, calmly but firmly, explained that she'd thought it all through, that although she was lucky enough to still be fairly fit, she was beginning to find the stairs a bit much and it would only get worse, that she wanted to move now, while she could cope with the upheaval, before it got too difficult or her health deteriorated. Besides, it'd be a nice change, and she'd only be just down the road. And yes, she could afford the rent, she'd worked out her finances, she had enough money, she'd never been a big spender, so even if she lived to a hundred there would still be a bit left for Mum after she'd gone.

At this, Mum had reacted indignantly, saying she hadn't meant anything of the sort, she didn't want Gran's money, she could spend it on whatever she liked – throw it all away, give it all to a cats' home, chuck it in the sea for all she cared. And if a change was what she wanted, why didn't she bugger off to *Ireland*, like every other bugger in this family seemed to do.

At the mention of *Ireland* we had shifted in our chairs, looking at each other, panic in our eyes. It could have escalated into something very unpleasant at that point, but Gran simply got on with her lunch, without responding.

'Mum,' I warned, shaking my head at her. 'Perhaps you and Gran should talk about this another time.'

Josh, who tended to be the conflict-avoider, had said, 'Yes. It's a birthday party. Let's all have some cake.' Everyone quickly started to talk about the birthday cake, the cards and presents and flowers that Gran had been given by her friends in the village, and the subject of her move was dropped. But it did go ahead, a couple of months later. Gran quietly stuck to her guns. Even now, there was still a bit of tension between her and Mum on the subject.

'So...' Gran began as she sipped the coffee I'd made her, giving me a look over the top of her glasses. 'Your mum says you're staying here for good.'

'In Furzewell? Yes. I'm starting work at the school on Monday.'

'And is Mia happy about that?' she said quietly, glancing through the door into the lounge where Mia was engrossed in a kids' TV programme. 'Leaving her old school, starting somewhere new?'

'Well, obviously not *happy* exactly.' I sighed. 'This situation ... moving her in the middle of the school year, leaving her friends, her home … her dad. Well, it isn't ideal, obviously.'

'But necessary.'

'If I didn't think so, Gran, I wouldn't be doing it.'

'Fair enough.' She nodded. There was kindness, understanding, in her eyes, as well as sadness.

I swallowed. 'You haven't asked why.'

'None of my business. Whatever the reason, you wouldn't make the decision lightly, I know that. It's not easy being a single parent. Your mum knows all about that.'

'Yes. That's why it wasn't what I wanted. Why I tried to stick at it – my marriage. But…'

I shook my head, couldn't go on. I'd been putting a brave face on it for a long time, for Mia's sake, but talking to my lovely grandmother now, the misery and unfairness of it all had suddenly risen up and threatened to overwhelm me.

She covered my hands with hers – hands that were worn thin, gnarled and weather-beaten but still strong despite the arthritic changes to her knuckles that had bent and distorted some of the fingers. The hands of a working woman. She'd grown up on a farm, milked cows, scrubbed out milking sheds, raised four children and then, when they were about forty, she and Grandad suddenly changed direction. They sold the farm, moved here to Furzewell, and while he ran a garden centre just outside the village, Gran fulfilled her ambition to train as a teacher. She'd finished up as deputy head of the village school, and was still – twenty years since her retirement – a respected member of the community. I'd always intended to follow in her footsteps, but I'd been in too much of a hurry to get married and throw myself into domesticity to bother going to university. Josh and I had wanted a family quickly, but as things turned out, it was several years before I had Mia, and we hadn't had any more. By the time I started to regret not fulfilling my own career ambitions, the best I could do was to follow Mia to school when she turned four, working as a teaching assistant. I'd been happy in my work at the school in Plymouth and I was looking forward to taking up a similar post here at the village school.

'You'll be fine,' Gran was saying to me now. 'You're tough. You're your own person. You've made your decision; now you have to get on with it. Just keep looking to the future. Don't look back and ... *wallow*, will you. Wallowing makes people bitter.'

I knew she was referring to my mum. To *Ireland*. I knew she was right – Mum had wallowed about it for as long as I could remember, and although I didn't really blame her, it wasn't the way I intended to live.

'Don't worry,' I said, wiping my eyes and straightening my shoulders. 'I'm not going to wallow. I'm meeting Amber for a drink tonight – she's moved back here too. I'm looking forward to it.'

'OK.' Gran smiled. 'Baby steps, though, eh, my lovely? It's going to take time to adapt. Especially for Mia.'

With Gran's warning very much on my mind, I set off to meet Amber that evening. I was keen to catch up and renew our friendship. But as soon as we'd got the first drink in front of us and started to chat, a wave of exhaustion suddenly came over me like a fog.

'Are you OK?' Amber asked, as I sat back in my chair, yawning, running a hand across my eyes.

'I'm fine. Sorry. It's just that it's all been a bit … full on, you know. All the upset of moving out, doing my best to make it OK for Mia, leaving most of my things behind until I can get a place of my own. And then Mum being, well, *Mum*. All false cheer and chirpiness, saying how much *fun* it's going to be, having me living with her – as if it was a matter of choice—'

'And it wasn't?'

I frowned. 'No. I wanted my marriage to work – doesn't everyone? I never wanted it to end up like this.'

'I'm sure you didn't,' she soothed me. 'But at least your mum's happy to have you, till you can get somewhere of your own.'

'I know. She's been very good. I'm not complaining, I'm just tired. I shouldn't have promised Mia Monty would be able to sleep on her bed – it was just something I went along with, to help make the move easier, but now it's ended up with Mia getting really upset over it. I've had to talk to her this afternoon, try to make her understand that he's probably not coming back. Let's face it, a fox might have got him, or anything.' I sighed. 'I haven't told Mia *that*, of course. Considering he's not even her cat, she seems to have made a huge trauma out of him being missing. I'm thinking it's a kind of displacement from all the other worries: leaving Josh, changing schools, and so on.' I stopped and glanced at Amber. 'Sorry. This must all be dead boring for you, not having kids. Or liking cats.'

She smiled. 'Don't be silly. I can appreciate what a tough time it is for you. It'll get easier, though, won't it? Children adapt quickly, so they say.'

'Yes, I hope so. I'm thinking perhaps I'll ask Mum if we can get a new kitten.'

'Why not a dog?' She grinned. 'I know I'm biased, but they're such good company. Didn't you used to have a dog when we were kids back here?'

'Yes, *Jake* – he was a setter, a complete nutcase! He was already getting old when I was living here. And before him, we had a spaniel, Penny. But Mum didn't want another dog after Jake died.'

'Do you think she'd consider one now, though? She only works part time, doesn't she?'

'Yes. Maybe – I'd have to talk to her. I hadn't thought of it, but I suppose, with all the countryside around here for walks...'

'Exactly. Honestly, there's nothing like getting out in the fresh air with a lovely dog for company. It cheers you up no matter how stressed you feel. It's really helped me to settle back into the village. People always stop and talk to you when you're walking a dog. There's actually a little group of us here now that have started walking our dogs together.'

'Really?'

'Yes. Not all the time, of course. Mostly evenings and weekends, sometimes early mornings. It varies, depending who's free, who's at work, obviously.'

'Where do you meet?'

'At the park. We have an arrangement now that anyone who can make it meets at the park gates with their dogs at set times of day. We all have different commitments, so none of us are there every time, but there's usually at least one other person to walk with and talk to. The dogs love it, too.' She smiled. 'But of course I take Benji for walks on my own, at other times – through the copse, or along the stream.'

'It sounds a great idea. Do I know any of the others?'

'Yes, you do, actually. Sara.'

'Sara?' I questioned, frowning.

'Sara Buckingham. Remember her? From our class at school.'

'Not Snooty Sara? Oh my God. I bet it's a barrel of laughs walking with *her*.'

Amber chuckled. 'Oh, she's not so bad now. Come on, Nic, we've all grown up a bit since those days! Anyway, I've told her you're back in Furzewell and she said it'd be nice to meet up. In fact, she wanted to come tonight but I wasn't sure how you'd feel about that.'

'Huh. Thanks.' I drained the rest of my beer. 'My mother wanted to come tonight too, believe it or not, and I think even that would've been preferable to spending an evening with Snooty Sara.'

Amber laughed again. 'She's all right, you'll see. She broke up with her own partner a year or so back, so you'll have something in common. Want another drink?'

'OK, thanks. Just one more. Perhaps it'll help me sleep,' I joked.

I watched her as she stood at the bar, chatting with the barmaid. She seemed to have slipped back into village life happily enough. I supposed it was easier, being single and not having a child to worry about. And perhaps she was right – perhaps the dog did help, too.

'Who are the other dog walkers, then?' I asked as she came back with our drinks and dropped two packets of crisps on the table.

'You might not know them. There's Craig; he went to our school, but he was a few years below us. And Simon's quite a bit older than us – his wife died a few years back, very tragic, very sudden...'

'Oh dear.'

'He's lovely, though. And Craig's single too. Well, he usually seems to be seeing someone, but never anything serious, you know the type...' She stopped, her head on one side, thinking for a moment. 'In fact, none of us in the group have got partners. Isn't that strange? So you'd fit right in,' she added with a smile.

I didn't smile back, though. Suddenly, the thought of *fitting right in* with a group of lonely hearts dog walkers felt so sad, so completely *not* what I'd imagined for myself all those years ago when I'd walked out of Furzewell church, newly married to the love of my life, that I just wanted to put my head down and cry big fat tears into my beer.

'Well, it does sound like a nice group, although I haven't even got a dog at the moment,' I said, swallowing and staring out of the pub window into the darkness. 'I'll just have to see how things work out.'

CHAPTER 4

As that first week passed, we settled in at Eagle House as well as could be expected. It still felt odd, and slightly unreal, as if we were just there for a holiday.

'Nothing wrong with having a bit of a holiday, is there?' Mum said when I told her how I was feeling. 'You'll be starting your new job on Monday. *Then* you'll start to feel like it's real life, won't you, once you get into more of a routine. Make the most of it in the meantime.'

'I wish you'd let me cook, or do some of the housework, though,' I said. 'I can't go on like this, having you wait on us hand and foot, if we're going to be staying for some time.'

'*If*? Of *course* you'll be staying. This is your home now, just as it always used to be. And there's plenty of time for you to help with the cooking and so on. Just enjoy spending time with Mia, get settled in.'

'Thanks, Mum. You know I appreciate it.' I gave her a hug. 'But please, there's no need for all this.' I waved my hand around the kitchen, where she was busy preparing a huge chicken dinner with about six different vegetables and an apple pie for dessert. 'We'd be happy with sausages and chips, or a takeaway – you shouldn't be going to all this trouble.'

'Nonsense! I *love* having you both here to cook for and look after,' she sang back in the same overexcited tone she'd been using since we'd arrived. 'And some good home cooking will do you both the world of good. Now, go and sit at the table, I'm just dishing up.'

There had still been no sign of Monty – not that I was expecting it. Mia and I had made some posters, which we put up on lamp-posts and telegraph poles around the village, but nobody had come forward with any sightings of him. It felt too soon to broach the subject about a new kitten, or dog, with Mum. Despite the fact that she seemed so excited about having us staying with her, I still couldn't help thinking it was, really, enough for now that she had two extra humans in the house, making a lot of extra mess and noise, without being asked to take on a new pet too!

To try to take Mia's mind off the situation, Mum and I filled the remaining afternoons of that week with some fun activities. One dark, drizzly day we had lunch as a picnic on the lounge floor, with a tablecloth spread out, sandwiches cut into fancy shapes and all of Mia's dolls and soft toys seated around on the carpet with us. Then we made cakes and decorated them with our names. Another afternoon when it was cold but bright, we wrapped up warmly and went for a walk through Cuckoo Copse, teaching Mia the names of different trees, birds and plants, and playing I-Spy as we walked. On the Saturday, when it poured with rain, we all snuggled down on the sofa and watched one of Mia's favourite films. I'd like to say I was adjusting to life as a single parent, but to be honest, Mia and I had always done things like this on our own, so the biggest difference was that Mum was with us. I'd become used, in recent years, to Mia and I being a little twosome, and despite the sadness of our situation now, it was admittedly quite nice that we were now part of a trio again – as we'd been, originally, with Josh. Before things changed.

On the Sunday I talked to Mia again about the new school, telling her how exciting it would be, how much fun she'd have making new friends. She listened in silence, holding Pink Bunny, her thumb in her mouth – a habit she'd given up when she was three.

'Of course, it's always a bit scary too,' I added gently. 'Anything new can feel quite frightening, but as soon as you meet your new friends you'll forget about feeling scared.'

No response. I hung up her new uniform while she lay in bed, waiting for her story, and when I turned back to smile at her, she was looking like she was going to cry.

'I don't like red,' she said in a little voice. 'I want to wear my blue uniform.' There were tears in her eyes now, which I wiped away gently as I pulled her close for a cuddle. 'And why hasn't anyone found Monty yet?' she added. 'It's *not fair*.'

*

In the morning, the sun was shining, the sky as blue as a summer day. Mia dressed in silence, an unhappy expression on her face as she pulled on the red uniform. Mum and I, exchanging knowing looks, chatted chirpily over breakfast about the beautiful day, the birds singing, the fact that it would soon be March and spring would be on the way.

'I've got a tummy ache,' Mia said, pushing her cereal bowl away.

I knew it was due to anxiety. She was too young to invent an illness to avoid going to school. Having finally encouraged her to nibble half a slice of toast by adding her favourite chocolate spread, and chasing her off to clean her teeth, we were then in a rush to leave on time. Although it was still cold outside, the sunshine made me feel more optimistic, and I kept up the one-sided, excited chatter as we walked the short distance to the little village school.

Furzewell Church of England Primary School was in a tiny, old-fashioned building and was so small that most of the classes combined two school years each. Mia was used to being in a large class of children all the same age, but would now be in a smaller one, mixed with the children from the year above. My own post was with the reception class who, as they tended to need extra help, were the only ones taught on their own. When I'd brought Mia for her visit to the school a few weeks previously, her new teacher, Mr Gregory, had appointed two little girls to look after her. I'd been pleased and reassured when she skipped out of her classroom after the visit, telling me about Olivia S and Olivia P, and how funny it was that they were both called Olivia but one had dark hair and one had fair hair, and they were both on the same reading book as she was, at her *other school*. Looking back now, I realised that she really hadn't taken on board, back then, that this was going to be her new school, permanently. Her new reality.

Today, she clung to my hand at the classroom door, looking at her feet, her lip wobbling.

'I don't want to go in,' she whispered. 'I want to stay with you, Mummy.'

'Hello, Mia.' Mr Gregory was smiling down at us. 'Come on in. Olivia P – why don't you come and show Mia where to hang her coat, in case she's forgotten. We're starting a new project today, Mia. I think you'll enjoy it. I'll be telling everyone all about it after assembly.'

With some subtle encouragement, she was eased over the threshold and into the classroom. I hesitated, aware that I needed to be reporting to my own classroom. Mr Gregory gave me a smile.

'Probably best if you leave her with the two Olivias,' he said. 'She'll be fine. They've been looking forward to helping her settle in. Say goodbye to Mummy, Mia.'

'I'll only be in the room next door,' I reminded her as I gave her a hug. 'I'll see you at lunchtime, remember. Have fun!'

And with a last mock-cheerful wave at the door, I turned away, doing my best to hide my own nervousness. The day passed slowly. My little class of reception children was delightful, as was their teacher, Mrs French, and I was kept busy. But I still couldn't stop glancing at the clock and wondering how Mia was getting on in the next room. I saw her briefly at lunchtime, but my little charges were let out to play at a different time from the bigger children, so my playground duty was over by the time Mia's class came out.

'Well, how did it go? Did you have a lovely day?' I asked her when we finally met up at ten past three.

She shrugged.

'What did you do?'

'Nothing.'

Her face was white with tiredness. I could understand it. I felt tired myself, just from the effort of learning my new children's names and getting used to the way they did everything. I decided not to press her, but I had made a promise as a reward for us both after our first day.

'Come on, then,' I said, taking her hand. 'We're going to the café, aren't we? What sort of cake do you think you'd like?'

This kind of occasional after-school treat had been a highlight of our week back at the old school. I'd been thinking about it all day, certain it would cheer her up and help her settle into the new routine. But Mia looked up at me wearily, shaking her head.

'Mummy, I just want to go home,' she said sadly.

'Oh. Really? Are you too tired even for a cake? OK, then. Maybe another day. Perhaps we'll have hot chocolate back at Nanny's house instead.'

'I mean, I want to go to our *other* home,' Mia said, her voice scratchy with unshed tears. 'I want to go back to my other school. I don't want to stay here, Mummy. Why do we have to? I want to see Bella. Why did you tell me I could have Monty instead? Where has he gone? Why can't we *find* him?'

I tried to put my arms round her, tried to tell her that it would all be OK, she'd soon be happy here, soon get used to the new school, but she just shook her head, trying not to cry.

'I knew it was going to be hard,' I said to Mum as Mia went up to her bedroom as soon as we got home, saying she wanted to play on her own. 'But this constant thing about finding Monty – it's so wearing. She's obviously using it to deflect from the things she's really unhappy about.'

'Well,' Mum said, putting a cup of tea down in front of me and smiling. 'Give her time, I'm sure she'll be OK, love. But in the meantime, if the cat is really such a big deal for her, why don't we get a new one?'

'Would you mind? Would *Monty* mind, if he does come back?'

'I can't see that happening,' she said, shaking her head sadly. 'Poor thing, I do hope he's with someone, being looked after, and not – well, that nothing horrible happened to him. But I'm happy to get a new kitten, of course. Especially if it will help Mia. What do you think?'

'It would be lovely,' I agreed. 'Or ... I was wondering ... Amber suggested we might get a dog. I mean, *I'd* get the dog, it would be my responsibility. I'd look after it and walk it and everything, and take it with me when we eventually get a place of our own—'

'You don't have to sound so apologetic about the idea, Nicky.' Mum smiled. 'Of course you can get a dog. We always used to have dogs when you were younger, didn't we. It'd be nice to have one around the house again.'

'Yes,' I said, and then, my enthusiasm for the idea of a new dog overcoming my worries for a moment, added: 'Do you remember that spaniel we had when I was quite little? Penny, we called her, didn't we? It was such fun, growing up with a dog.'

'She was good company for you,' Mum said. 'You being an only child.' She sighed. 'Funny how history's repeated itself – with Mia.'

The smile dropped from my face. Yes, like me – and like Josh too, as a matter of fact – Mia was an only child. But however long Mum waited, with that meaningful look on her face, she should know perfectly well by now that I wasn't going to talk about the reason for that.

'I'll go and talk to Mia now, about the dog idea,' I said, getting to my feet abruptly. 'Hopefully it'll cheer her up and give her something nice to focus on.'

Mia was lying on her bed, holding Pink Bunny and staring at the ceiling.

'Are you OK, baby?' I asked her gently. I sat down on the bed next to her, stroking her face. 'I know it must have been a hard day for you. But it's going to get easier, I promise. Can you think of anything that might help you settle down here?'

She sighed. 'Only if Monty came back.'

'I know,' I said. 'I wish we could find him, too. But what if we got a *new* pet, to keep us company here and make it feel more like home?'

'A new kitten?' she asked, opening her eyes a little wider. 'Can we get a ginger-and-white one?'

'Maybe. Or . . . what about a dog instead? A puppy?'

'A dog?' She looked at me in surprise. 'A real one?'

'Of course!' I laughed. 'Why don't you come downstairs and look at some pictures with me. If we're going to get a puppy, we'll need to decide which type would be best for us, and we can choose together.'

And thankfully, as soon as she was cuddled up with me on the sofa, looking at doggies on my laptop, school seemed to be forgotten. For now, anyway.

CHAPTER 5

'Labradoodle, labradoodle!' Mia sang to herself over and over, giving little skips of excitement as she went to wash her hands for dinner later. 'Isn't it a funny name, Mummy?'

It hadn't taken us long to settle on our chosen breed. And once Mia was tucked up in bed, I called a dog breeder near Exeter who I'd found on the internet. As luck would have it, he had just one male puppy still available, of a litter of caramel-coloured labradoodles that were ready to be rehomed ten days later.

'I'd sold them all,' he explained. 'But the lady who was taking this little chap has changed her mind. Wants something smaller.' I heard the exasperation in his voice. 'You'd think people would work out what they want before they choose, wouldn't you.'

'Yes,' I agreed, secretly pleased about it. 'Well, we're *certain* this is what we want.'

'Good. Glad to hear it. Well, why don't we arrange a date for you to come and meet the puppy – and for me to meet you, too.'

With the thought of the puppy and a day arranged for meeting him firmly in her mind, Mia seemed to have cheered up a bit. She reluctantly got herself through her school days, without too much more crying or obvious distress, although she still wouldn't really talk to me about it. I took her with me for the visit, and the breeder encouraged her to carefully handle and stroke the friendly little puppy, while politely asking me some searching questions about our home, how experienced I was with dogs, and whether I understood the latest advice about caring for puppies. The interrogation made me feel quite nervous, but apparently I did OK, and we were soon making another date – for coming back to collect our pup.

I took a photo of our 'new baby', which Mia then kept by her bed, and I marked the 'puppy collection' day on our wall calendar so that she could see how soon it was. We agreed to wait to choose a name until we brought the puppy home, but when we were finally in the car, coming home with our eight-week-old bundle of fluff and mischief, Mia announced that she'd already decided his name should be Smartie.

'Because they're my favourite sweets,' she said. 'And he's my favourite puppy.'

'Fair enough!' Mum laughed.

Even while I was dishing up his first meal in Eagle House, Mia was trying to cuddle him, telling him she loved him and that he was her best friend. I smiled, pleased at how quickly he seemed to have cheered her up. But my smile soon dropped when she added wistfully:

'Can we take him back home to our other house, Mummy?'

Although she continued to be very quiet and withdrawn on the subject of school, and the renewed habit of thumb-sucking seemed to be here to stay, Mia did at least seem more settled now at home in Eagle House. She was all smiles whenever she saw the little dog, and spent hours running around the house playing with him, or sitting down with him on her lap, cuddling him and, I suspect, whispering her secrets to him.

The following weekend she went back to the old house for the first time. Josh collected her on the Saturday morning, sweeping her into his arms on the doorstep of Eagle House and hustling her into his car, pretty much ignoring me and Mum. 'Are you sure you don't want me to come and pick her up tomorrow?' I said, following them down the path, trying to get Mia to turn back to me for a last goodbye.

'No. I'll bring her back after her tea,' was all he said.

He strapped Mia into her car seat and started the engine. She gave me a little wave, the car disappeared down the lane and I stood there, hugging myself against the cold, feeling bereft. I tried, all weekend, to keep myself busy. I cleaned all the windows, ignoring Mum's squawks of protest. I met up with Amber again for lunch in the pub, and did a lot of mostly unnecessary washing and ironing. By the time Josh brought Mia back on the Sunday, on the dot of six o'clock as agreed, I was almost breathless with the need to see her and hug her. It was the longest she'd ever been out of my sight.

'Hello, sweetheart.' I pulled her into my arms, kissing her face and the top of her head. 'Did you have a nice time?'

I'd been so worried that she'd have found it strange, being with her father for so long. It hadn't exactly been the normal pattern of her childhood, especially in recent years.

'Yes,' she said, her eyes bright. She struggled out of my embrace. 'Daddy took me to the Soft Play *and* the cinema *and* bought me some new trainers – look!' She lifted her feet to show off the sparkly silver shoes. 'When can I go back again? I like it better at our other house.'

'Don't react,' Mum warned me, after Mia had settled down in front of the TV with a sigh, as if it was already boring to be back with us. 'And don't try to compete.'

Compete? I'd wanted to yell. As if I could! There were no soft play centres, cinemas or shops for buying sparkly trainers anywhere within miles of Furzewell. But what hurt me most was the fact that Josh was now playing the bountiful father, whereas when we were together he was normally too busy to take his daughter anywhere or do anything with her. And now the weekend was over, I was having to deal with the hangover from it.

*

We were well into March now, with its promise of spring, which never quite seemed to be fulfilled. Daffodils nodded in the chilly breeze, and after a few milder, sunny days we noticed the occasional primrose daring to spring up in the park and meadows. Then the wind would whip up again, whistling through the valley where the village was situated; the clouds would gather and we'd have two solid days of heavy rain. I was fed up with wearing my boots to negotiate the muddy puddles in the country lanes and my heavy waterproof coat because of the unexpected downpours. I couldn't wait for the weather to improve.

'But this is my favourite time of year,' Gran said when Mia and I popped over the road to see her, as we often did, after school. 'So much nicer to be looking forward to summer than looking back on it, I always think.' She rummaged in her cupboards for a packet of biscuits. 'Ah, here they are: your favourites, Mia. Take two, go on. I've been keeping them specially for you. Want a drink of milk with them?'

'Thank you, Granny Helen,' Mia said.

Gran raised her eyebrows at me. 'Quiet, isn't she,' she whispered.

'I know. School seems to be tiring her out,' I whispered back. 'But when we get home to Smartie, he always cheers you up, doesn't he, Mia,' I added out loud, and Mia nodded.

'He's my best friend,' she told Gran. 'I really love him.'

'And is your mum OK with having a puppy around the house again?' Gran asked me. 'I must admit I was a tad surprised. She said she'd never get another one.'

'She seems to be enjoying him. But I'll be doing everything for him – walking him and so on, and of course he'll come with me and Mia when we move out.'

There was a silence. 'You think she'll let you move out?'

I laughed. 'Of course she will! By the time I'm in a position to get my own place, she'll have had enough of us cramping her style.' I paused and glanced at Gran before going on, 'Mum has quite a social life these days, doesn't she?'

'That's one way of putting it,' Gran said. 'I know what Ros is like. Can't bear to be on her own. Always off out somewhere, with one of her friends or another. Or one of her boyfriends.'

'Boyfriends?' I nearly choked on my biscuit. 'Since when has Mum had boyfriends?'

'Oh, there have been a few, over the years. Never anything serious, though. I suppose she doesn't tell you. The last one seemed quite a nice chap, good-looking, too. Can't think of his name – he's a local. He lasted longer than the others. Mostly she only sees them once or twice, from what I can make out. She comes out with that same old line every time about enjoying being a *single girl*.' Gran snorted. 'Anyone would think she was twenty-five, the way she talks – not coming up for sixty.'

'Well, good for her, I suppose, if she's enjoying her life.'

'Hmm,' said Gran enigmatically. 'That's as may be. Anyway, drink up, both of you.' She got to her feet and looked for her shoes. 'I'll walk back round to Eagle House with you and say hello to that little doggy – and your mother, I suppose! I need to stretch my legs.'

Gran and Mum had a strange relationship. I knew they loved each other really, but the way they spoke to each other, and about each other, you might not have guessed it. They were quite different: Gran was small and wiry, with a tough, calm, no-nonsense attitude and a wealth of common sense, whereas Mum had always been the big, cuddly, emotional type. I wasn't sure whether I took after her or not; from the physical point of view I was more like Gran. I hadn't inherited Mum's generous figure, or her rounded face and thick, wavy hair. When I was at the most emotionally fragile stage of growing up, I'd been called *Nic the Stick* by some of the boys at school, which might have traumatised me for life if I hadn't, instead of her curves, inherited Mum's fiery nature. I was perfectly able to answer my tormentors back, calling them worse and more humiliating names than any of their unoriginal 'stick insect' and 'beanpole' taunts. And luckily for me, as I grew older and taller, my skinny figure and straight blonde hair became the must-have look. Despite the fact that I had this look by accident rather than by design, the boys were suddenly staring at me in a different way, and the teasing stopped. Through it all, it was Gran, even more than Mum, who'd given me the constant reassurance I'd needed that I looked perfectly fine.

'*Sticks and stones may break your bones* ...' had been Gran's favourite quote to help me understand that the teasing didn't matter, and it always made me laugh, in the circumstances.

'But *Stick* is what they call me!' I'd remind her.

'Well, there you are, then,' she'd say, with a satisfied nod, as if it explained everything.

Gran had already become as charmed by Smartie as Mia and I were. She loved to sit with the little pup by her feet, rubbing his tummy, or rolling his ball along the floor for him to catch and bring back to her. He showed signs of being a happy and energetic little dog, and we'd started teaching him some basic commands like *Sit, Stay* and *Leave it*, right from his first day with us, so that he would learn quickly.

'He'll be a big dog, won't he, when he's fully grown?' Gran said.

'About medium size, really, we think. He's a second-generation labradoodle, and the breeder said neither of his parents were exceptionally big,' I explained.

'Mummy says Smartie's going to need lots of long walks, once he's allowed to go out,' Mia told Gran. 'We're going to walk him in the park with Mummy's friends.'

I explained about Amber and her dog-walking group.

'That's nice,' Gran said approvingly. 'Glad you've met up with Amber again. She was always a nice girl, wasn't she? I'm surprised she's never got married.'

'Maybe she had more sense,' I muttered under my breath.

The next time I met Amber at the Fox and Goose, she'd invited Sara to join us.

'Hope you don't mind,' she whispered to me as Sara went to the bar to get the first round of drinks. 'She was keen to meet up with you.'

'Can't think why,' I said with a shrug. 'We were never friends at school.'

Sara had clasped me in an embrace as soon as I'd arrived in the pub, kissing me on both cheeks and exclaiming that I hadn't changed a bit – which of course was ridiculous – and I had no intention of saying the same thing back to her. In fact, annoyingly, she'd changed very little over the years. Since having Mia I'd put on some weight – no longer quite such a *stick* – and I now coloured my hair blonde, because, if I left it to its own devices, it was a dirty shade of mouse rather than the natural blonde of my younger years. But Sara still had the same slim figure, the same long, glossy, chestnut hair, and was wearing heels and full make-up just to have a drink in the village pub. Needless to say, most of the men in the pub were eyeing her up surreptitiously over their pint mugs.

'How did she walk down the lane in those shoes?' I muttered, with a touch of bitchiness, as Sara tottered back towards our table with the drinks balanced on a tray.

'Try to be nice, Nic,' Amber whispered back. 'It won't hurt you to smile.'

I felt rebuked and I supposed she was right, I had to make an effort, especially if I was going to join their dog-walking group. Just because I'd become the kind of person who slopped around in jeans, boots and anorak, and had the type of flyaway hair that stood on end as if I'd had an electric shock whenever I went out in the wind, didn't mean I couldn't look at someone who dressed so much more glamorously without turning up my lip in a sneer. If I wasn't careful, it could be misconstrued as envy.

'So! How are things with you, Sara?' I said, trying to adopt a more interested tone 'What have you been up to over the last ... um ... fifteen years or so?'

She took a sip of her sparkling water – no wonder she was so slim – patted her scarlet lips gently with a serviette, and gave me a beaming smile.

'Well, after graduating from Oxford – I expect you heard I got a first in law? – I passed the LPC with flying colours—'

I tried to stifle a yawn. I was tired, and although I was trying to pay attention, needless to say I didn't know what the LPC was. I was beginning to regret asking the question.

'Then I took up a training post,' she was going on, 'with, well, you won't have heard of them, but one of the best law firms in London. Daddy had a connection there luckily—'

'Of course,' I said mildly, lifting my glass to hide my grin. Amber nudged me.

'And after completing my training period—' Sara was saying, smiling benevolently at us. I wondered how long this was likely to go on.

'So: you're a solicitor,' I interrupted her eventually. 'That's great, it must be ... um, fun. And is that how you met your husband ... partner?'

Her smile disappeared. 'Keith worked for the same company, yes.' She took a big gulp of her water. 'I don't work there now, of course. After we split, I was headhunted by a company back here in Devon – in Tavistock, actually – so it made sense to move back.'

I tried to imagine the difference between a prestigious law firm in London and one in Tavistock. The difference between the potential salaries. Of course, I really had no idea, but I couldn't help thinking it would have been a comedown. *Headhunted* didn't quite seem to fit. I actually felt a bit sorry for her, for a fleeting moment. But when she continued, in the same self-aggrandising tone, to describe how important her job was, how busy, how stressful, how much her company relied on her and valued her – my sympathy went straight out of the window again. Same old Sara.

This was exactly how she'd been at school. When the rest of us were comparing notes after our GCSEs, commiserating with each other about how hard the maths questions were or the fact that we'd revised *all* the wrong stuff for history, Sara would smile that infuriating superior smile and say that, *actually*, she'd found it fairly easy. We didn't care that she passed them all, mostly with A grades. She'd flouted the unspoken rule: you were supposed to complain about them. You weren't supposed to say you'd found them easy, when everyone else was crying on each other's shoulders about the ridiculous and unfair questions. But that was typical of Sara. She was the girl who, even at the age of about fifteen when most of us delighted in being different from our parents' generation, prefaced almost every opinion she voiced with '*Daddy says*—' or '*Mummy thinks*—'.

'So anyway,' I interrupted her again, mid-monologue about her unbelievable volume of work, 'I hear you've got a dog now. What sort of dog is it?'

'My *petite Babette*?' she said, brightening. 'She's such a precious girl – my little princess. I adore her. She's a bichon frise.' I nodded. She would be. 'And Amber says you're going to join our little dog-walking group, Nic. You've got a new puppy? How wonderful.'

'Yes. He's called Smartie,' I said, suddenly feeling like the parent of a new baby, attempting to keep up with the other mums in the cute kid stakes. 'He's a labradoodle.'

'Oh, a *cross*-breed. Very *à la mode*.'

I sighed and drained the rest of my beer. What was the point? I didn't even want to try to compete with her. What I really wanted to hear was the goss on this Keith, her ex, but although I tried several times during the next hour or so to lead the conversation back in his direction, Sara was obviously determined not to discuss him.

'Perhaps he had an affair with another solicitor,' I said to Amber as, outside the pub afterwards, we watched Sara climb into her rather smart BMW to drive the short distance home. Of course – couldn't get those shoes muddy.

'It's none of our business, really, Nic, is it, if she doesn't want to talk about it,' Amber rebuked me gently.

I shrugged. 'Sorry. She's just *so* bloody irritating.'

'I think she's insecure, actually.'

I snorted. 'If that was insecurity, I'd hate to see her when she's feeling confident.'

Amber sighed. 'Well, I wonder if all that showing off was just her way of trying to impress you and make you like her, as she obviously realises you weren't friends at school. Anyway, I hope you're going to try and get on with her if you join us for dog walks, when Smartie's old enough.'

'Of course I will. Sorry.' I gave her a hug goodbye, feeling mean now for spoiling the tone of the get-together. 'It will be nice to get to know more people. I'm looking forward to it.'

Smartie was having his second vaccination the following day and would soon be able to start short walks outside. The prospect of joining the others to walk our dogs round the park together in the sunshine, the thought of long light evenings ahead, and warm days when we might not need our coats and welly boots, made me suddenly feel more cheerful. I certainly wasn't going to let Snooty Sara spoil it for me!

CHAPTER 6

March soon became April, but the weather was still something of a disappointment so far. Every now and then there were some mild, sunny days; my little charges at school would be allowed to play outside without their coats, everyone would be smiling and pointing out the early blossom in the trees, the primroses by the roadside – and then the next day we'd be back to dark skies, drizzle or gale-force winds.

'Is this winter never going to end?' I complained to Gran when she called round one Saturday morning in the first week of April. Mum was at work in the shop and Mia was playing in her bedroom. 'It's Easter next weekend.'

It would be Mia's weekend for staying with Josh, and we'd agreed that he'd keep her for Easter Monday too. It had seemed only fair when we'd agreed on it, but the nearer it got, the less I liked the idea. Every time she was with him, she came back with expensive gifts – toys, clothes, little purses, bags and trinkets that she treasured – and tales of extravagant outings and treats, like going to the cinema or theme parks. I had really mixed feelings about this. On one level I was glad Josh seemed to be making the most of his time with Mia, and glad she was enjoying being with her dad, but I couldn't help worrying that he was trying to buy her affection. I couldn't afford to buy her lots of extra treats like this myself, and I was frankly surprised he was able to find the money for them too. I didn't like the idea of Mia becoming used to this kind of indulgence, taking it for granted and becoming spoilt. I tried to explain this to Gran, but she just sighed and shook her head.

'It must be quite hard for him only seeing her every other weekend. He's bound to miss her and maybe he's frightened of losing her.'

'He won't lose her. I'd never try to stop him seeing her. I get that he wants to make their weekends together as nice as possible. But it's a pity he didn't make more effort with her like this when we were together.'

'People don't appreciate what they've got till it's gone,' she pointed out.

'Well, he didn't appreciate *me* and he still doesn't, now I'm gone,' I said. Then I sighed and added: 'Sorry, Gran. I'm being a grump. This dreary weather probably isn't helping either. If we'd just get a good long spell of sunshine I'm sure I'd feel more cheerful.'

Smartie, who'd just woken from a nap, suddenly stood up on his sturdy little paws and trotted over to me, giving a yawn so wide it nearly made him topple over. I laughed and rubbed his head, making his ears twitch.

'That little chap should make you happy,' Gran pointed out.

'He does. And today's going to be our first time out with the dog-walking group! We're really looking forward to it, aren't we, Smartie?'

He gave a little yelp and ran to look for his favourite toy, a red plastic thing that made a noise when he chewed it, like a demented budgie squawking.

Gran laughed. 'Well, I'll be getting home, then.' She hauled herself out of her armchair with difficulty. 'My dog-walking days are over, that's for sure. I'm grateful enough that I can still walk myself. When the day comes that I can't do that anymore, you can take me to the place in Switzerland where they do the euthanasia.'

'Gran!' I protested. 'Don't talk like that!'

'Why not? You'd do it for this little fella, wouldn't you, if *his* life wasn't worth living?' She grinned. 'Don't look so worried, girl. I'm good for a few years yet, all being well.'

'Of course you are.' I gave her a kiss goodbye. 'Mind how you go.'

'And you have fun with those dog walkers. It'll cheer you up, being out in the fresh air, and the two of you making new friends.'

Half an hour later, Mia and I, togged up in our warm fleeces against the chilly wind, were walking to the park with Smartie on his lead. It wasn't his first time out since his vaccinations were finished – we'd already been giving him short walks on his lead on our own, to get him used to the idea – but it would be his debut with the dog-walking group. I was so excited, and a little nervous, about how he might react to the other dogs that I hadn't had time yet to think about how I was going to get on with the rest of the group.

Amber was waiting for us at the park gates, her dog Benji straining on his lead beside her. Waiting with her was a tall, good-looking guy in a chunky navy-blue sweater and smart jeans.

'Nic, this is Craig,' she said. 'And Judy.'

Judy, a border collie, was sitting obediently next to her master, looking up at him adoringly. Her lead was draped casually around Craig's shoulders, as if to draw attention to the fact that she was so well behaved, she didn't need it.

'Nice to meet you, Craig,' I said. I pointed to my two little companions. 'This is my daughter, Mia, and our new puppy, Smartie.'

Hearing his name, Smartie immediately stopped sniffing the ground around him, looked up and trotted excitedly towards the group, wagging his tail with delight as he noticed two potential new doggy friends. Benji seemed somewhat perturbed by this small newcomer, backing up closer to Amber's legs as Smartie approached. But Judy remained dutifully frozen to the spot, watching for Craig's instructions. Smartie sat down and, seeming unsure how to deal with the situation, gave himself a good scratch with his back paw. We all laughed, and the ice was broken. Craig began to talk to me about which years we'd been in at school – I didn't remember him at all but he said my name was familiar – and nobody actually noticed Sara arriving until her bichon frise, Babette, began to sniff around Smartie, and Smartie stumbled to his feet, tail wagging again. Friend made – if only it was that easy for humans!

'It doesn't look like Simon's going to make it today,' Amber said, looking at her watch. 'Come on, let's get going. He'll catch us up if he does come. He's a landscape gardener,' she explained to me as we began to walk along the path into the park. 'He often has to work Saturdays. He'll probably turn up tomorrow, and he usually makes the evening walks.'

Mia was quiet as we walked along. I let her hold Smartie's lead for a while, hovering close beside her in case the puppy suddenly got spooked by one of the other dogs and tried to run off.

'Sorry,' I said to the others as Smartie kept stopping to investigate new scents, skipping delightedly from tree to tree, sticking his nose into flowerbeds and patches of weeds, while Mia and I gently encouraged him to keep up. 'I think we're going to slow you down.'

'Only for a little while,' Amber said. 'When he's a bit bigger he'll probably outrun them all. Well, maybe not this one,' she added with a grin, at which she let Benji off his lead and stood back as he took off like a rocket, running across the grass in huge circles, his tail flying behind him.

'Oooh!' Mia said, her eyes wide with surprise. 'He's like a superhero dog.'

'Well, I know you said he was a whippet cross,' I said to Amber, laughing. 'But I reckon he could race greyhounds! Look at him go.'

Smartie, too, was transfixed by the sight of this superfast dog rushing past him like the wind. He stood motionless, staring at him, before turning to me and giving two little barks of consternation.

'Does he want to run around with Benji, Mummy?' Mia said.

'No, he's too little, and he's not well trained enough yet,' I said. 'We're not going to be letting him off his lead until we're sure he'll come back.'

Judy, obedient and responsive to every click of her master's fingers like most border collies, spent the entire walk running after the ball Craig threw for her, bringing it back and running for it again – a routine which Smartie seemed to find as baffling as Benji's furious racetrack performance. Instead, he contented himself with trotting along beside little Babette who, despite now being off her lead, seemed reluctant to run too far off, continually coming back to sniff Smartie and walk close to him.

'She's looking after him,' Mia said happily.

'Like your new best friends when you started at the school,' I said. Her smile dropped and she fell quiet again, so I instantly wished I hadn't said it.

We walked for about half an hour that first day. When we'd crossed the whole of the park, round the abandoned tennis courts and the disused paddling pool – now drained of water – and came to the other entrance at the far side, the others were going on to follow the stream out along the lane and as far as Cuckoo Copse and back.

'It'll be a bit too much for Smartie,' I said, 'as it's only his first time.'

'Of course,' Amber agreed at once. 'He's still only a baby, you don't want to tire him out.'

Sara, who'd spent most of the walk telling me about her recent outing to a swanky new restaurant with her boss, said she hoped we'd come out with them again soon, and Craig gave me a slightly flirtatious smile, and treated Mia to a funny little bow and shook her hand, making her giggle. We headed back across the park and home, where Smartie, exhausted by his exciting morning, went straight to his drinking bowl and then collapsed on the floor next to it and fell asleep.

'Did you enjoy your walk?' Mum asked when she arrived home from her shift at the shop at lunchtime.

'Yes, it was fun,' I said, realising I was looking forward to the next time already.

'Benji is a superhero dog,' Mia told Mum. 'And Babette is Smartie's new best friend, and Judy's so clever, she knows exactly what Craig wants her to do even when he doesn't say anything.'

'Wow!' Mum gave me a look, her eyebrows raised. It was the most excited Mia had sounded about anything since we'd moved into Eagle House. 'It sounds like you've met some *very* interesting dogs. Let me take my coat off and you can tell me all about them.'

That afternoon Mia drew a picture of the dogs with their owners – stick men and women with long arms and legs, and stick dogs of varying sizes wearing big red smiling mouths – which she announced was a present for Daddy. And for the first time, she went to bed without complaining about the loss of Monty. I had a hopeful feeling in my heart. Perhaps she was beginning to settle down.

A little later, I poured myself a glass of wine and found an old film to watch on TV. Since we'd been at Mum's, and although I did enjoy her company, I quite liked the occasional evening on my own when she was out with her 'girlfriends'. It had been strange, getting used to being two women in the same house, both using the kitchen and sometimes getting in each other's way. After all, we'd both been used to being in charge of our own homes. It sometimes felt awkward, being in my mum's house again now that I was an adult, and having to adapt to her routines. And I was well aware that, despite her insistence that she loved having Mia and me there to look after, Mum must sometimes find the chaos in her previously peaceful and tidy house a bit trying. It was good for her to be out with her friends.

Tonight she'd spent longer than usual making herself up, trying on various outfits and asking me if her hair looked OK. At fifty-nine, Mum was still undeniably attractive, but I secretly thought she looked nicer when she dressed in her everyday clothes. On these nights out, it seemed to me that she was competing with her friends – all of a similar age – to see who could look the youngest, wear the shortest skirt or the lowest neckline.

'Is this a special occasion?' I asked, trying to be tactful, as I watched her putting on long, high-heeled boots and more lipstick than usual.

She looked back at me and winked. 'Well, you never know: it might be.'

And she gave a suggestive little giggle, making me recoil, my eyes wide with surprise. Was my mother actually going out on the pull? I remembered Gran's comment about boyfriends. Was this what Mum and her friends did on their nights out – flirt and chat up the men? Perhaps I was naïve, but it had never occurred to me that Mum might want to find herself a new partner. Her marriage to my dad had ended acrimoniously when I was quite young, and she'd spent most of the years when I was growing up complaining about him and about men in general, giving me the impression that she wouldn't care if she never had to speak to another male member of the human race for the rest of her life, never mind become intimately involved with one.

Even if I'd wanted to ask her more, which, to be honest, I didn't – who wants to hear about their mother's sex life or even believe such a thing exists? – there wasn't any opportunity that evening, because one of her friends called for her at that moment and they set off, giggling together in a way that made me feel even more uncomfortable, to pick up the other friend and head off to the bright lights of Plymouth. At least I knew they took it in turns to drive and Mum told me all of them were very responsible about not drinking when they were the designated driver. It would have come to something if I'd had to lecture my own mother about drink-driving!

'But what if she brings a boyfriend home?' Amber said when I told her all this on the Sunday morning. Mia and

I had left Mum to sleep off her late night, and had come to meet up with the dog walkers again at the park. Mia had run a little way ahead of me with the puppy on his lead, giving us a chance to chat without little ears flapping with curiosity. 'I mean – what if they stay overnight?'

'Oh, God!' I groaned. Memories of my younger years – of creeping quietly up to my bedroom in Eagle House with Josh, both of us trying to avoid the creaky stairs, and smothering giggles – came flooding back to me. Was I really going to be faced with an ironic role reversal, pretending not to hear my mum sneaking men into the house? 'Surely she wouldn't do that? While I'm there? While *Mia's* there? How could I explain that to Mia – suddenly finding a strange man making toast in the morning?'

'No. You're right,' Amber said at once. 'She wouldn't, would she? Of course not. But … on the other hand,' she added with a grin, 'what about the weekends when Mia's with Josh?'

'Oh my God,' I groaned again. 'The sooner we move out, the better.'

'You've only just moved in!'

'I know. And I've no idea how I'm going to afford a place of my own, even after the divorce, and after the house has been sold.' I sighed. Saying this out loud suddenly made the whole thing – divorce, house sale – sound so serious and final. It *was* what I wanted, I reminded myself, what I'd decided was the only way forward. But that didn't make it any less sad.

Amber put an arm round my shoulders. 'It'll be OK,' she said gently. 'You'll see, it'll work out, somehow. Things always do.'

'Do they?' I said. I watched Mia, skipping along in front of me with Smartie, chatting to Craig about how clever she thought Judy was. Was she happy? Would everything work out OK for her – for us both – back here in Furzewell? I hoped Amber was right, but at the moment I felt like the jury was definitely still out.

CHAPTER 7

During the following week, I met up with the dog walkers every day for their early evening walk. As it was now the school Easter holiday and she didn't need to be in bed until a bit later, Mia normally came with me. Smartie already seemed to be enjoying the company of the other dogs and we were gradually taking him further before turning back, so that we could get him used to longer walks. The weather had finally started to improve, too, and we'd had a couple of days that week that were really warm. I'd forgotten how suddenly the countryside sprang into life during a spell of good weather at this time of year. Hedgerows looked fuller and greener. The grass in the park, and in cottage gardens, had started to grow faster, and was sprinkled with daisies. Footpaths were becoming less muddy, the country lanes were full of the rustle and scurry of birds foraging for insects, and everywhere seemed to smell of spring.

'I think winter's finally over, thank God,' Simon remarked as we set off across the park on Good Friday, and I smiled and said yes, I hoped so.

Simon, who was the oldest member of our little group, in his fifties, was a big, likeable bear of a man. He seemed to be popular with all the others, as he was a good conversationalist who had a cheerful smile and a hearty laugh, but was also a sympathetic listener, as I soon discovered when he asked politely what had brought me back to live in the village. Encouraged by his attentiveness and put at ease by his kind nature, I poured out the story of my marriage breakdown, Mia's difficulties adjusting to the new school, and my worries about the future. He listened quietly, nodding and giving me sympathetic looks of understanding. His dog Max, a big soppy black cross-breed with an affectionate nature and bright intelligent eyes, seemed perfectly suited to Simon.

'He was my wife's dog really,' he said, waving aside my sympathy when he explained that Jane had died suddenly of a heart condition and that their only son lived abroad. 'Max was devoted to her. But he seems to have accepted me happily enough as a replacement. And he's been a life saver for me. He's such good company. But then, you'd understand that, wouldn't you.' He nodded at Smartie, who was gambolling playfully between my feet and Mia's. 'Four legs and waggy tails make the best companions.'

'They do,' I agreed. 'And I'm hoping and praying Smartie turns things around for Mia. She seems a bit more settled since we've had him.'

In fact, although Smartie had made a big difference, I suspected Mia was only happier because it was the school holiday. School, for now, was a taboo subject. I'd expected her to have some homework to do – a little holiday project of some sort, or at least a couple of new books to read, but the same two relatively easy-reading books she'd brought home over a week ago were still in her bag.

'No spellings to learn?' I asked her – as I'd done every week since she'd started at the school, but she just shook her head, and the usual search of her school bag produced nothing other than her reading record book, where my counterpart in her class had written encouraging comments about her reading.

I guessed her teacher had, in view of her anxiety about the new school, decided to go easy with her schoolwork for the first half term. I made up my mind to have a chat with him after the holiday, though, as I knew it was important to back up the school lessons with help at home.

I'd already asked Mia if she'd like any of her new friends who seemed limited at the moment to the two Olivias – to come and play at Eagle House during the holiday, but she'd insisted she only wanted her friends from the old school. So I'd arranged for Polly and Jamila to come one day the following week. In the meantime, she had her prearranged long weekend with Josh to look forward to. I remembered how, to my complete astonishment, he'd announced in a phone call a few days earlier that he was taking her away.

'Away?' I'd said. 'Where to?'

'Only down to Torquay. I'd like to take her further afield, but that'll have to wait for when I have her for my two weeks in the summer. But I've booked a place near the beach, and if it rains we can go to the caves and the Dinosaur World place, or Paignton Zoo.'

'But…' I struggled to speak, too shocked to get my words out properly. 'But you've never wanted to go anywhere! All these years, whenever I suggested we had a few days away—'

'Yes, well, things seem to be different now, don't they,' was all he said in response. It wasn't *just* that I resented him – too late – spoiling Mia with all these treats and outings. It was also, much as I hated to admit it, that I felt kind of left out. Left sitting at home like Cinderella while Josh and Mia had happy days out and seaside breaks together. I knew it had been my decision to separate, but as far as I was concerned we'd reached the stage where it was pointless staying together any longer, because Josh quite simply seemed to have no feelings left either for me or, as it had seemed at times, for Mia. So for him, now, to want to spend time with her and spoil her so much was doubly hurtful. At the same time, I felt really silly and cross with myself. How could I be jealous of my own child? And was I just jealous because of all the fun she was having, or because it was *Josh* who was showering her with affection and special treats? My mixed-up emotions were making me feel tired and miserable. But what could I say? Mia was so excited about the proposed trip, I couldn't let her see how miffed I felt. Remembering Mum's advice, I made up my mind to keep myself busy and refrain from saying anything detrimental. I packed Mia's bag that evening when we got home from our walk, and Josh picked her up early on the Saturday morning.

'Have a lovely time, sweetheart,' I said, hugging her tight. 'See you in a couple of days.'

'I'll bring her back after tea on Monday,' Josh said, without looking at me. And he shepherded Mia – who was chatting so excitedly about the beach and the sea, she didn't even say goodbye to Smartie – out to his car without another word.

Three whole days without my baby girl. It was going to feel like a lifetime.

'No good having that long face, it won't make the time go any sooner,' Gran told me firmly. She'd come round early the next morning to bring an Easter egg for Mia, having forgotten that she was away for the whole weekend with Josh, and had found me moping as I sorted the washing. 'It's good you've got your new friends, anyway,' she added more gently. 'Just enjoy having the weekend to do whatever you want.'

'Yes, I suppose you're right. I can have an evening out with Amber without having to ask Mum to babysit. Especially as she likes to have evenings out herself.'

'Yes, with those so-called friends of hers,' Gran said, raising her eyebrows.

'So-called?' I looked at her in surprise. 'Don't you like them?'

'Oh, they're all right, I suppose – what's their names? Angie and Sue, isn't it? They dress like they're still in their teens – make themselves look proper daft. The Gruesome Twosome, I call them.'

'Oh, Gran! That's awful!' I laughed. 'Anyway, Mum's just as bad.'

'Yes. Your mum's always been like that – following the crowd. Even when she was a girl. I used to tell her: *Ros, you don't always have to do what your friends do. Try and be your own person.* But she never learned.'

'You told me she's had a few boyfriends,' I said cautiously. 'Is there anyone at the moment? I don't like to ask her. She gets all giggly and weird – it freaks me out.'

'Not as far as I know,' Gran said with a shrug. 'I think the three of them just go around together. I don't think they're really as interested in men as they make out.'

Sara and Craig were already waiting at the park gate when I arrived a bit later, their dogs panting with enthusiasm to get started on the walk, and within a few minutes Simon and Amber joined us and we all set off. Sara, walking nearest to me, suddenly turned to me and said:

'Nic, did you ever find your poor cat?'

'Oh, he wasn't my cat, he was my mum's, but no – he's still missing.'

'Such a shame, poor thing,' she cooed.

'Yes. Somehow I don't think we'll find him now.'

'Well, it might just be a coincidence,' she went on, 'but I was talking to Craig about it just now while we were waiting for you—' she turned to give Craig a smile and took the opportunity to flutter her eyelashes at him in such a suggestive way that his eyebrows nearly hit the top of his head, '—and guess what? His next-door neighbour's cat's gone missing too.'

'Yes, well, cats do—' I began, but Craig nodded and picked up the story:

'My neighbour's been frantic. Her cat's a pedigree of some sort and she's contacted pretty much every police station, vet and animal charity in Devon, trying to find him. Not only that, she says a friend of hers who lives in one of the Houses on the Green has lost her cat too. Seems they've all gone during the last few months.'

'That's very odd,' Simon said, looking back at us. 'I called at one of the new houses up at the High Meadow estate last week, to quote the owners for sorting out their garden, and they were saying the same thing. Their cat went missing soon after they moved in. They'd tried to keep her in for the first couple of weeks, like you're supposed to, but she made a dash for it when they opened the door and they haven't seen her since. They just assumed the poor cat didn't know her way around the area yet, but then they got talking to someone else in the village shop whose cat had disappeared too.' He paused, shaking his head. 'It's beginning to sound like more than a coincidence, isn't it?'

'Well, cats *do* wander off,' I said again, reluctant to believe it was anything more sinister, but Sara shook her head.

'Not as many as this, in such a short time, Nic. And you do read some *awful* stories in the papers, don't you.

Cats being poisoned and all sorts. There are some nasty people around. People who don't like cats.'

I shook my head, uncomfortable with the idea.

'Maybe we should do something?' Craig said.

'Like what?' I sighed. 'I've already put up notices about Monty on lamp-posts and so on. And it sounds like your neighbour has tried everything.'

'Well, maybe all the people who've lost a cat could get together and compare notes,' Simon suggested quietly. 'I'm not saying it *has* to be anything more than a coincidence,' he added, giving me a sympathetic look. 'But, well, perhaps if there were to be a bit in the local paper about it—'

'Yes, that's definitely worth doing,' Sara agreed. 'Actually, I know the editor of the *South Devon Recorder* personally.' She made it sound like being on first-name terms with the prime minister. 'Robert and I were at Oxford together. He's actually a millionaire, you know, he owns a chain of hotels here in the West Country, but he still likes to edit the local paper; he says it gives him an interest. I'm sure he'd give me a front-page slot if I asked him nicely.'

I felt an instinctive dislike for Mr Millionaire hobby-editor. Just the sort of person who Snooty Sara *would* suck up to, I thought, trying not to scowl.

'Well, what do you all think?' Simon asked. We'd stopped at the far side of the park, where hardly anyone else seemed to venture, to let the dogs have a run. He looked around the group. 'We could put up a poster on the notice board outside the village hall, asking anyone who's lost a cat recently to get in touch? Find out exactly how many have gone missing? And go from there?'

'I suppose it wouldn't hurt,' I said with a shrug. 'If there are a lot, we could have a meeting and see if they all want to do the newspaper thing. The *Recorder*'s online too – that might be more worthwhile than the actual paper. Nobody reads them now, do they?'

'Oh, round here they do, trust me,' Sara said, laughing. 'They're a very traditional bunch in Furzewell, remember? I bet half of the residents aren't even online.'

'Only because the internet connection's so bad,' Simon said mildly.

We called the dogs and moved on, and the conversation turned to other things. After a while, though, Sara tore herself away from Craig for a moment and walked next to me again, nodding in Amber's direction as she said, quietly:

'Did you notice how one member of our group stayed out of the *cat* conversation completely?'

I shrugged. 'Amber probably wasn't that interested. She doesn't really like cats.'

'Oh. Right.'

I looked at her sharply, wondering about the tone of her voice.

'Not everyone is a cat lover,' I pointed out.

'No, OK, fair enough. I just would've thought she'd be more supportive.'

'She is! I mean, she was, when I first told her about Monty. She just prefers dogs herself, and she probably didn't have anything to add to what we were saying earlier.'

'Yes, you're probably right,' Sara nodded thoughtfully.

Something about the conversation niggled at me. But that was typical of Sara – making irritating, oblique comments and then just leaving you hanging, wondering what she was on about. I tried to shrug it off, and went to walk with Amber for the rest of the way. Sara had got on my nerves enough for one day, with her name-dropping about her millionaire newspaper editor friend. To say nothing of her oh-so-obvious flirting with Craig, which was making me cringe. She was walking close beside him now, nudging him and giggling.

It hadn't taken me long to realise Craig was the joker of the group – he liked a laugh, and normally had us all laughing along with him. But with Sara monopolising him like this, it was impossible for the rest of us to join in with the banter. We were having to leave them to it, and start our own conversations while we listened to them laughing together. It felt awkward and uncomfortable. I might have been the newbie in the group, but I already found myself wishing she'd stop it.

CHAPTER 8

As promised, Josh brought Mia back in time for bed on Easter Monday. She'd fallen asleep in the car on the journey back and was tired and fractious. I sat with her on the sofa, cuddling up, wanting to hear all about her weekend, but she complained that her tummy hurt.

I felt her forehead. She wasn't hot, but looked a little pale.

'Do you feel sick?' I asked her, hoping she wasn't coming down with a bug.

'No.' She lay back against the cushions, looking like she was struggling to keep her eyes open.

'I'll just get you a nice warm drink then, and you can go straight to bed.'

'I don't want a drink, Mummy. My tummy's too full up. We had burger and chips for tea, and ice cream. And Daddy bought me a *huge* Easter egg and I ate it all up.'

No wonder she had a tummy ache, I thought crossly. She eventually fell back to sleep in my arms, clutching

Pink Bunny, her thumb in her mouth, and I half-carried her up to bed and tucked her in, wishing crossly that Josh would realise it wasn't good for her to feed her junk food, on top of tiring her out so much.

The next morning she'd recovered, though, and couldn't wait to tell me all about her little holiday. The beach was *amazing*, the caves were also *amazing* and, best of all, there had been a fair on, on the seafront, and the rides were even more *amazing*.

'Daddy let me go on *loads* of rides, and he let me stay up really late. Why don't you let me stay up late?' she enthused. 'Why don't we hardly ever have burger and chips?'

I had to swallow back my irritation and resist, with difficulty, the temptation to criticise Josh.

'Those sort of things are OK for occasional treats,' I explained. 'They wouldn't be treats if you could do them all the time.'

Daddy had also, apparently, let her choose whatever she wanted from the gift shop at the caves. Luckily for him she'd only picked a cheap-looking purple plastic dinosaur. And Daddy had bought her a new bucket and spade, but he was keeping it at his house because there was no seaside here in Furzewell. (This last comment was added with a tut and a sigh.)

'But there's no seaside where Daddy lives, either,' I pointed out.

'I know. But he's going to take me to another seaside soon. The *really* nice one we used to go to *before*,' she added.

'Bigbury-on-Sea. *I* can still take you there, you don't have to wait for Daddy,' I said, aware that I was sounding petulant and childish.

'Daddy says it's miles and miles from here, and it's too far for you, and you won't want to bother.'

'No it's not, and I *will* want to,' I said, and then stopped, aware that I really shouldn't rise to Josh's bait. 'I know how much you liked it there,' I added more quietly.

Mia shrugged. 'I liked it then because Daddy came too,' she said. I sighed. It was probably the *only* time Josh had *ever* come on a day out with us. No wonder she had such fond memories of it.

I knew it was childish of me but I didn't see why Josh should now have all the fun parts of parenting while I just got the tears and the tantrums. Where had he been during so much of the previous six years? During the really hard parts – the night feeds, constant nappy changes, colic, sickness, night terrors, sticky fingers into everything, screaming fits for no apparent reason, food being thrown out of the highchair, cups of milk turned upside down, bumps and bruises during those first baby steps? Where was he then, eh? Hardly ever at home, that was for sure. Not around to share the responsibility, to help, to commiserate, to support me. And *now* he got to be Mister Perfect Father? He got to make me feel guilty because he didn't see her often, so he could spoil her rotten and leave me to deal with the consequences? Well, he didn't used to see her often when we were living together either, but that was *his* choice, not mine!

'He's doing it deliberately,' Mum said, after I'd repeated all this to her when she came home from her shift at the shop. 'Trying to wind you up. Don't rise to it.'

'Easy for you to say,' I retorted, a bit too crossly.

'I know. But I've been there myself, don't forget.'

'That was different, though. Dad never even bothered to keep in touch with me, never mind taking me on holidays and buying me treats!'

'No, but I did have to bring you up on my own.'

'I know.' I sighed. I shouldn't have snapped at her. She'd been through a worse situation than mine. I reached out and took her hand sympathetically. 'We were OK, though, weren't we? We managed fine, just the two of us. You brought me up brilliantly and I never wanted for anything.'

Mum nodded and smiled at me. 'In some ways perhaps it was easier, your father being out of the picture completely – at least I didn't have to share you with him. I just pretended he didn't exist, and you and I got on with our lives.'

Mum was right. We'd been particularly close back then, on our own.

'You made it a happy childhood for me, despite Dad not being around,' I said now. 'I'm grateful for that, Mum. And I know it was really hard for you, after what happened. But in my case, how can I pretend Josh doesn't exist? He's still there, in our house. He's seeing Mia, giving her a better time than I can afford to, even though he's never done anything with her before.'

'And that's not helping her to settle here in Furzewell, is it,' Mum sympathised.

'No. But I can't say anything, because Mia's obviously loving all the treats, and suddenly getting some attention from her dad after all this time.'

And besides ... I thought to myself miserably, *he's Josh! Josh, the boy I fell in love with when I was still at school*. I was disappointed in him, resented him for how things had turned out, but I didn't want to hate him, the way Mum hated Dad. I couldn't pretend he didn't exist. Despite everything, I missed ... not *him*, exactly, as I'd got used to him not being around ... but the way we used to be, back in those early days together. Like everyone, when I got married – here in the village church – I believed it would be forever. We'd moved to our little terraced house in a suburb of Plymouth soon after the wedding, glad to leave behind the furnished flat above the greengrocer's shop here that we'd been renting together previously. It had been fun, exciting, filling our new house with second-hand furniture, cheap rugs, bits of crockery and utensils donated by our families. Playing house. I often looked back to those happy early days, wishing everything hadn't changed so much over the years since Mia was born. Even so, I'd hoped we could manage this separation sensibly, like mature adults, and maybe – eventually – recover an amicable relationship. Maybe after a while he'd stop with the big showing-off gestures. He surely couldn't afford to keep splashing out on Mia like this, any more than I could.

Mum gave me a hug as she got up to make us both a cup of tea, and I swallowed back tears, telling myself crossly to get over it. I had to try to move on from my annoyance about the way Josh had spoilt Mia this weekend. I did want us to be grown up about this separation and not be constantly criticising each other, but it was hard sometimes. It helped that Mum understood how I felt. I was glad we'd had that little chat.

That Friday evening, the other dog walkers and I had arranged to meet up at Smiths to discuss the wording of the notice we were going to produce about the missing cats. Sara was very friendly with someone on the parish council, who'd offered to put it up on the notice board at the village hall for us – the one place everyone in Furzewell was bound to see it. Mum was going out with her friends that night – the Gruesome Twosome, as Gran had unkindly christened them – but Gran had offered to come round to babysit.

'Go out as early as you like, love,' she'd told me. 'Mia and I are going to play some games together and then when she's in her jamas I'll read her a bedtime story.'

'Are you sure?' I said, a little anxiously. I gave Mia a warning look. 'No nonsense about going to bed, then – OK? Granny Helen doesn't want to keep coming up and down the stairs after you.'

'Think I'm too old for the job?' Gran challenged me with a grin. 'Go on, go off and meet your friends. I need to talk to Mia about this birthday of hers that's coming up. We've got secret birthday business to plan.'

'I'll leave you to it, then.' I kissed them both, and called out goodbye to Mum, who was, of course, upstairs in her room making herself glamorous, ready for God-Only-Knew-What she and the others were going to get up to in the pubs and bars of Plymouth.

It was a pleasant evening, not at all chilly for April, and not yet dark. I walked slowly down Pump Lane and along Fore Street, enjoying the sound of the birds beginning their evening chorus. I waved to people working outside in their front gardens as I passed, and smiled to myself at the thought that I was, albeit gradually and not entirely painlessly, slipping back into village life.

'Mind theself, my lovely,' an elderly man called out as, too interested in admiring the tulips, hyacinths and lily-of-the-valley he was lovingly tending in his cottage garden, I nearly stumbled into the ditch at the side of the road. 'Don't 'ee go a-tiss-toss down thar, mind!'

'I won't!' I laughed. 'I was being too nosey, that's all. Your garden looks so lovely.'

'Oh aye, thank'ee.' He leant on his fork and wiped his face with his handkerchief. 'It be the divil's 'ard work, though, truth to tell, what with th'ole snails an' slugs an' all.'

'I'm sure it is,' I commiserated. There weren't too many people now, even here in the back of beyond on the edge of Dartmoor, who spoke in a Devon dialect. Most of my own generation had only a slight twang, especially those who'd been away to university, or worked up-country for any length of time. So it was nice to hear the dialect still spoken by some of the older folk. I stayed for a while, reintroducing myself to the old chap, whose name I remembered was Tommy Burrows. He knew my Gran well, having been a drinking buddy of my grandad's, and soon remembered me as the *liddle maid who wed young Joshua Pearce, backalong*.

'That's me,' I said with a sigh. 'I'm back living at Eagle House now with my mum, and my little girl.'

He nodded, two or three times, giving me a long look but saying nothing, and after watching in silence with him as a robin (*liddle rabbin urdick* as he called it) hopped unafraid around his fork, picking up worms for an evening snack, I said goodbye and went on up the street to the café.

Smiths – popular as a coffee shop during the day – became a surprisingly busy wine bar in the evenings, visited by people from outlying villages as well as locals. But it was only open on Friday and Saturday nights, the owners having experimented with the opening hours and finding too few people in these parts tended to come out for drinks when they had work the next day. Sara was already seated at a table in the window, and while I went to get a drink, Craig and Simon both arrived together.

'Amber can't make it,' I said. 'She messaged me to say her mum's not well and she's gone round to keep her company.'

'Oh dear,' said Sara.

I gave her a sharp look. There was something sarcastic in her tone that I didn't like. But I didn't have time to challenge her on it: Craig was opening his laptop and asking us all to move closer so that we could see the screen, as he played with text sizes, colours and fonts, and we discussed the wording for our poster. By the time we'd finished our first drinks, we were happy with the result, and taking advantage of the café's Wi-Fi, Craig saved it to the cloud so that Sara would be able to pick it up, print it and pass it to the woman on the parish council.

'It'll be interesting to see if we get any responses,' Craig said as we settled down with another round of drinks, Sara shuffling closer to him on the bench seat they were sharing.

'Well, from what you've all said, there definitely seem to be a few people around here looking for lost cats, so I'm sure we will,' I said. 'I'd love to get Monty back for my mum. Although I'm not sure how he'd react to Smartie.'

'Pity Amber couldn't make it,' Simon said, taking a mouthful of his wine. 'Something tells me she's not altogether on board with this?'

'Yes, she is, I'm sure,' I said. 'She's just not particularly a cat person. So it doesn't really affect her. And her mum's in bed with the flu, so she's round there helping out. That's all.'

'Fair enough.' Simon smiled at me, but once again I caught a strange, knowing look on Sara's face. And I didn't know whether that irritated me more, or less, than the open and ostentatious flirting going on between her and Craig – little semi-accidental touches of their hands, little cheeky smiles and nudges. Were they getting together? And if they were, why should I care? Just because I'd come to think of it as a *lonely hearts* group, didn't mean none of them were allowed to go out with each other, did it? Surely I didn't expect everyone else to be lonely and alone forever – just because I probably would be?

Perhaps it was simply that Sara tended to irritate me anyway, and I felt that she monopolised Craig when we were all together. He seemed a bit immature but was undeniably very charming and handsome, and was good fun, so it would have been nice for us all to join in with the jokes. I couldn't possibly be jealous, I told myself as I walked home a little later. Not when I'd pretty much decided I was through with men and had absolutely no intention of getting together with another one as long as I lived!

CHAPTER 9

As promised, I'd invited Mia's two best friends, Polly and Jamila, from her old school to stay for a sleepover during the second week of the Easter holiday. Mia had got herself so overexcited, she was bouncing off the walls by the time they arrived, and although it was lovely to see her so happy, I had had to warn her several times to calm down. I'd decided to take the three of them to Dartmoor Zoo for a special treat. The other two girls were as good as gold – on their best behaviour, quietly enjoying our day out. But Mia, now she was back in the company of the children she'd been friends with since preschool days, became so shrill and hysterical with excitement that, if she'd been anyone else's child, I'd probably have said she was behaving like a spoilt brat. Even Polly and Jamila seemed taken aback by the change in her.

'Stop being so *naughty*!' I hissed at her at one point at the zoo, pulling her aside briefly from her friends. 'If you keep running off, answering me back and showing off like this, we'll go straight home.'

By the time we did finally drive home, I was exhausted from the strain of dealing with her behaviour. The girls had stroked alpacas, laughed at the meerkats, watched the wallabies and stared in fascination at the spiders and bugs – but there'd hardly been five minutes when I hadn't had to tell Mia to quieten down and stop being silly. She didn't really calm down until, after they'd all demolished the pizzas I'd got them for their tea, I put on a film for them to watch before they went to bed. By then she was so tired she could hardly keep her eyes open, and I felt the same!

Jamila's and Polly's mothers, Gita and Jen, had been my own two closest friends in Plymouth, and it was really nice to see them both when they came to collect their daughters the next day.

'We miss you!' Gita exclaimed. 'When are you coming back to see us?'

'I don't know,' I admitted. We'd kept in touch on the phone and on Facebook, of course, and their calls and messages had been a great source of support to me. But I didn't feel as if I was really part of their lives anymore. We'd belonged to a group of mums who went out for lunches and treats together in the school holidays, and now that these social occasions were continuing without me, I felt like an outsider. It had already become a bit awkward, anyway, when I'd started working at the Plymouth primary school our daughters went to. I couldn't discuss the confidential things I knew about other children or their families, so I always used to feel on my guard during those get-togethers. Gita and Jen were lovely, but they felt, now, as much a part of my old life as Josh was. And this realisation felt like another loss, to go with the bigger ones.

But once Mia and I were both back at school after the holiday, I made up my mind to take some positive steps to move on with my life. I needed to get myself into a routine with the dog walks. Smartie was growing fast, and would soon need more exercise to keep him fit and happy. The most important thing was a good walk in the mornings before we all went out, so that he wouldn't be restless and miserable on his own. Mum was normally home in the afternoons to keep him company, and now that Mia was back to an earlier bedtime I usually joined the dog-walking group on my own for the evening walks, Mia just coming along at weekends when she wasn't with Josh. I decided I'd walk Smartie very early on school day mornings, leaving Mia in bed. By the time I got back, Mum would be giving her breakfast, and I'd just need to chase her up to get into her school uniform while I swallowed a cup of tea and slice of toast and changed for work myself.

The system worked well. Now the mornings were light, I didn't mind being up and about early. I'd throw on trackie bottoms, boots and an old anorak, and set off for a circular walk of the village. This was still normally enough for the puppy, but if it was dry and bright, I sometimes took the footpath across High Meadow too, skirting around the new housing development. I walked briskly, breathing in the freshness of the morning, while Smartie trotted ahead of me, sniffing the scents of the hedgerows, alert for evidence of other dogs, curious and still slightly wary if we encountered horses.

In fact, the morning walks in the fresh air were helping me as much the puppy. They were putting me in an energetic and positive frame of mind, and I needed that, to cope with Mia's continued reluctance where school was concerned. The first day back had been awful. She'd clung to me and cried again at the classroom door, and Mr Gregory had had to gently peel her off me. When I saw him in the staffroom at lunchtime he assured me that she had soon calmed down, adding that she still wasn't finding things easy.

'I thought she was getting better,' I said. 'She's been here a whole half term now.'

'Yes, well. . .' He hesitated. 'Some children do find change harder to cope with than others. She'll adjust, but it might take more time. How's her behaviour at home?' he added quietly.

'Well, she's being a bit babyish, really,' I admitted. 'She's either quiet and moody – sucking her thumb like she did as a toddler – or having temper tantrums.'

He nodded. 'Yes. That's what we're seeing in class, too. I was planning to have another chat to you about it if it didn't improve.'

We'd already talked a couple of times about her unhappiness at school, but now I was far more concerned. 'You don't mean she's having tantrums in class?' I said, shocked.

'No, but she does still sometimes get really upset.' He looked apologetic. 'Mostly she's just quiet and withdrawn, though, as you say. Look, don't worry, I'm sure she'll gradually settle down this term. We want her to be happy at school, obviously – and to achieve her potential.'

I nodded. 'She keeps bringing home the same reading books for whole weeks at a time. I presume you're letting her take things slowly at the moment? They do seem quite easy for her.'

Mia had now been refusing to read them, complaining that they were boring.

He cleared his throat and looked at me apologetically again.

'Actually, Nicola, it's because she still isn't really making any progress at the moment. In fact, she seems to be struggling a bit with those books we're giving her.'

'But … they're easy!' I said again, staring at him. Mia had been doing so well at her previous school, and even though Mr Gregory had already warned me that being unsettled and unhappy could hold her back a little, I hadn't expected it to last this long.

'As you probably realise, a brief spell of regression isn't unusual, if a child's going through some emotional difficulties,' he said gently. 'As I said, I'm sure she'll soon catch up again. Just keep encouraging her to read as much as possible and to practise her spellings—'

'But she's told me she hasn't been given any spellings to learn,' I said.

He raised his eyebrows. 'Leave that with me. I'll make sure her spelling book goes into her bag every night – and stays there!'

To say I was mortified was an understatement. As an experienced teaching assistant, I was used to the accidental, or sometimes deliberate, forgetfulness of small children. Why hadn't I checked with Mr Gregory before about the spellings? And about the books I'd assumed were too easy? Mia had been one of the best readers in her class at the previous school. I was upset that she'd lied to me about having no spellings to learn. And I was ashamed to realise I'd been too caught up in my own worries, my own problems adapting to my new life, to take on board the signs that Mia wasn't just struggling with the emotional issues of starting a new school, but with the learning too.

'I'm so sorry. I should have talked to you again sooner,' I said. 'I just thought she was being a bit babyish, and that you were giving her time to settle in.'

'Don't worry, she *will* settle. I'd have told you sooner if I thought things were really serious,' he reassured me. 'And try not to let Mia see that you're too concerned. She's obviously anxious enough already, that's why she's retreated into this … kind of toddler-like behaviour. Just take it slowly, gently, OK?'

'Of course. Thanks, Mr Gregory.'

'Mike,' he corrected me with a smile. 'You're welcome. Try not to worry, Nicola, she'll be fine.'

But of course, I *was* worried. Since that first day back, I'd thought of little else. I was cross with myself for not raising the fact that some of my reception children were attempting books that were more challenging than those Mia had been bringing home, and for not questioning the lack of spellings or homework. Now that it had been flagged up, the result was instant: a list of spellings to learn every week, some maths or writing to do every weekend. And I was even more concerned when, tested on the spellings, Mia seemed less able to put the phonics together to build her words than she'd done during her reception year. When I sat with her to encourage her to write a few lines about her weekend, about the weather, or about Smartie, she struggled to form her letters correctly and, more often than not, ended up crying, and shouting in frustration that she *couldn't do it.*

'Of course you can,' I tried to reassure her, doing my best to stay calm. 'You just need to keep practising. It'll all come back to you – you could do it before.'

'That was at my *other* school,' she sobbed. 'I'm *no good* at this school. Please can we go back?'

Easy for Mr Gregory – Mike – to say not to worry. I lay awake at night, sometimes hardly sleeping at all between getting into bed and the unearthly hour that the cockerel began to crow, thinking about the disruption and upheaval I'd put Mia through – the one person I loved more than my own life. I'd done it with the best of intentions, convinced I was doing the right thing, even if not the easiest, for us both, and that Mia would thrive in a happier home atmosphere – but it seemed I'd just ended up making her more unhappy after all. Well, it was too late now to have regrets. I had to stick this out, I told myself as I tossed and turned and looked at the clock again, longing for sleep. It could only get better.

Walking little Smartie was my escape from all this anxiety, and as April sped past, he gradually grew stronger, enjoying longer walks that really tired him out. Sometimes only one or two of the other dog walkers turned up for the evening walks. On one occasion it was just Amber and me, and inevitably I found myself moaning about Sara again as we walked through the park – in particular her outrageous flirting with Craig.

'So what's the problem?' Amber said, laughing, when I'd finally run out of steam. 'They're both single, after all. You're not jealous, are you?' she added, nudging me. 'Do you fancy him too?'

'No!' I denied hotly. 'Absolutely not! I've had enough of men, frankly.' I walked on in silence for a while, thinking about it. 'Although I suppose he is quite good-looking,' I admitted grudgingly. 'And he's good fun, isn't he – always makes us laugh. Why? Are *you* interested?'

'Not at all,' she said, laughing some more. 'He's not my type.'

'Well, he's obviously Sara's type. He's a bit young for her, though, isn't he? And from what you've said, not exactly the settling-down sort.'

'Maybe she just wants to have some fun, Nic,' Amber said, with a shrug. 'I guess that's fairly normal after you've been through a break-up—' she tailed off, giving me a sympathetic glance. 'Well, it's too soon for you, of course, I get that.'

'Yes, it is,' I said with feeling. 'And I'm sorry for going on like that about Sara. She just gets under my skin sometimes, that's all.'

'I know what you mean. But while she's spending all her time fluttering her eyelashes at Craig, she's leaving us alone. Ignore her.'

Amber was right, of course. She always was the sensible, nice-natured girl, even back at school. And anyway, it had to be said, Sara had made a good job of producing our poster. It had appeared on the parish council notice board a few days previously, outside the village hall, and we were now waiting to see if there would be any response. With everything that was going on with Mia, I hadn't given it too much thought, but it would definitely be interesting to try to get to the bottom of the missing cat mystery. Whatever the reason, I had to admit it did seem too much of a coincidence that so many cats had disappeared recently.

CHAPTER 10

One evening a few days later, I'd waited at the park gates for several minutes, Smartie becoming restless on his lead beside me, before deciding that nobody else was coming for the dog walk on this occasion.

'Come on, Smartie. Looks like just you and me tonight,' I said, starting off into the park. He trotted along happily beside me, stopping occasionally to sniff the air, skipping a little way in front and then looking back to wait for me, his tail wagging happily. Suddenly he gave a little bark of excitement, and I was almost knocked over from behind by Simon's dog Max, who'd bounded up the path after us, Simon running behind to catch him up.

'Sorry about that,' he said. 'I saw you and Smartie from the gates – I'm a bit late tonight – and I was just about to call you but Max spotted Smartie first!'

I laughed. 'Glad you could make it. I thought I was on my own. Nobody else has turned up.'

'Happens sometimes. All busy with other things, I suppose. Anyway, it's nice to chat to you on your own for a change.' He gave me a smile. 'How are you? Settling down back here now?'

'Well, yes, it's easy enough for me, really. It was just like coming home.' I sighed. 'It's Mia I'm worried about.' Encouraged by his usual sympathetic expression, I told him briefly about her problems at school, and her regression into babyish behaviour. 'I suppose I shouldn't worry: her teacher says it will sort itself out in time. But—'

'But of course you're worried. You're her mum,' he said gently, and I smiled at him gratefully.

'I feel so guilty for disrupting her life like this,' I said. 'Maybe I shouldn't have left—'

'Stop it. You shouldn't think like that. If your marriage wasn't happy, that would have been having an effect on Mia, whatever you think. And how long would you have been prepared to put up with it? Until she started senior school? Until she was a teenager? I doubt there's ever a good time, Nic. Better to make the break before things just got worse and worse, surely – and everybody's life got more miserable?'

'That's what I thought, at the time.'

'And it's not all about Mia is it? You deserve to be happy too.'

I felt tears come to my eyes and couldn't respond. It was a comfort to be able to confide in someone so kind and understanding, but no matter what he said, I knew that as a mother, I should have put Mia's happiness before my own. Mine shouldn't matter – I couldn't be happy anyway, if Mia wasn't. I already felt like a failure because I hadn't realised quite how badly the move was affecting her schoolwork.

'Oh dear, I always seem to have that effect on women,' Simon joked lightly, noticing me wiping my eyes. 'Sorry. Shall we change the subject?'

'Yes.' I tried to smile again. 'I feel like you always end up listening to my problems. Let's talk about you instead. You're not from round here, are you?'

'No.' He shook his head and stared ahead of us across the park as we did the usual circuit of the disused paddling pool. 'Jane and I lived in Dorset. I needed to make a big change after she died: everything around there reminded me too much of her. Not that I wanted to forget her,' he added quickly. 'I brought the memories of her, of course, but I knew I'd never be able to move on if I stayed there.'

'How long has it been, now?' I asked, looking at him with concerned affection. He was such a nice man, it seemed cruel that he'd been left on his own like this.

'Oh, long enough: nine years now. She was only forty; it was such a shock when she died. We'd been planning a big holiday to celebrate our twentieth wedding anniversary, but we never even reached it.' He shrugged and smiled now. 'We were one of those couples who married stupidly young.'

'Us too. But in our case, it actually *was* stupid.'

He laughed, and to my surprise, grabbed my free hand with his and gave it a squeeze.

'You'll be fine, Nic, and so will Mia, I'm sure of it. Don't be sad. Life can still be good, even after sad things happen. I should know.'

He gave my hand another little squeeze before letting it go, putting on a spurt and hollering for Max, who'd run into the bushes and was barking at something – probably a squirrel or some pigeons. I followed him with Smartie, my hand feeling warm where he'd held it so briefly, wondering what it meant – and then quickly rebuking myself for thinking it meant anything at all other than caring, friendly concern. And reminding myself of how lucky I was to have made these new friends, particularly this one, who, more than all the others, seemed so kind and wise.

That Saturday was April the twenty-eighth, Mia's sixth birthday. It happened to be her weekend for being with Josh, but he had been quite reasonable about it. We'd agreed that she could stay with me for the Saturday, in case she wanted to have a little party with her new friends from school, and Josh would just have her on the Sunday. As it happened, she was quite insistent that she didn't want a party, didn't want any friends home for tea and in fact she now denied having any friends at all at the school. Of course, this just added to all my concerns about her.

'What about the two Olivias?' I prompted her. 'I thought you liked them.'

'They only like each other,' she said, pouting. 'They don't like me.'

'I'm sure that's not true,' I said gently, but she refused to discuss it any further. Feeling even more like a terrible mother who'd ruined her child's life, I made a mental note to ask Mr Gregory about this next time I spoke to him, but I didn't want to make an issue about it right now. Mum had offered to take the morning off work, and if Mia would be happier celebrating her birthday with just me, Mum and Gran – and Smartie of course! – that was what we'd do.

The night before, after she'd gone to bed, Mum and I put up some balloons, and piled up her presents on the kitchen table ready for the morning. I was almost as excited as Mia. I'd promised her a special treat: with Josh's challenge about the seaside still burning in my mind, I'd decided we would drive down to Bigbury-on-Sea, taking a picnic lunch with us, including the chocolate birthday cake I'd bought. To show I was being reasonable too, I'd suggested we could drop Mia off with Josh on the way home in the evening, ready for his Sunday with her. Mia seemed happy with this plan too, her only gripe being that it would have been even nicer if Daddy had come with us to the beach.

'He can't,' I said. 'He's working.' I didn't feel bad about saying it. After all, it was the excuse he'd usually used himself, before the split, for not spending any time with Mia. Or me.

On the day, Mia was awake as soon as the cockerel uttered his first half-hearted crow, and she was in my room, jumping on my bed, before I'd even opened my eyes.

'Happy birthday, darling,' I muttered, putting my arms around her. 'Six years old today!'

I sighed. It seemed like only yesterday that she was a newborn baby. Where had the time gone?

'Can we get up now, Mummy?' Her voice was high with excitement. 'I want to start my birthday!'

As soon as she saw the presents piled up on the table, Mia's eyes widened and she did a little dance on the spot.

'Are they all for me? Can I open one?'

'You can open them all, sweetie. Which one first?'

Within five minutes they were all unwrapped, paper and ribbon strewn around the room. I'd strained the balance on my credit card to buy her the battery-operated walking, meowing, purring toy cat she'd been pleading for, ever since we found out about Monty going missing. Despite the fact that we now had Smartie, and despite me warning her that it was a toy intended for younger children and she'd soon get bored with it, her longing for it had remained unchanged and I'd reasoned it was a small thing to make her happy. She was already on the floor with it, giggling as it ran around, meowing, and Smartie followed it at a trot, his tail wagging, sniffing it and jumping back with surprise when it moved again.

Mum had bought her a new dress – purple with pink hearts – and two pairs of pyjamas and a dressing gown, all of which she'd needed desperately since she'd grown another inch taller. A couple of smaller presents had arrived in the post – a colouring book and pens from Polly, and a sticker book from Jamila. I was touched that their mums had remembered the date; I'd have to get back in touch with them and thank them. But it was Gran's present that surprised us all the most. It was a huge box of garden games, including child-size golf clubs with bright-coloured balls and plastic ramps for designing a crazy golf course, a skipping rope, a hoopla set with four rings and a football with the kit to construct two goals.

'Looks like we're all going to be keeping fit this summer!' Mum laughed.

'It's a great idea. There's so much space outside, it'll be lovely to have some games to play.'

I was touched by Gran's thoughtfulness, and wondered how on earth she'd managed to get such a big present home from town by herself. She didn't drive, and normally relied on Mum to take her into Plymouth for anything she couldn't buy from the village shops – but the present had been a complete surprise to Mum as well as to me.

'Ordered it on Amazon, of course,' she responded when I asked her about it a little later, when we picked her up for the day trip to Bigbury. 'Don't look so surprised. How else do you think I manage anything these days?'

I gave her a hug. It was always a mistake to underestimate my gran!

The sun came out as we headed through the country lanes towards the main road, Mia singing happy little songs about the seaside to Mum and Smartie in the back seat as I chatted quietly with Gran in the front. Mum had found an old bucket and spade in the shed, which, although Mia had looked at them somewhat critically and declared them *not really as nice as the new ones from Daddy*, had been accepted as a good substitute – possibly because the bucket was her favourite shade of purple – and she was clutching these excitedly on her lap in anticipation of sandcastle building.

'Are you sure dogs are allowed on the beach?' Mum said.

'Yes, I checked. But we'd better keep him on his lead. I'm not sure what he's going to make of the sand, or the sea.'

We hadn't been to Bigbury since the previous summer and I'd almost forgotten how lovely it was here. It was still early in the season, so there was only a scattering of people on the beach. It was breezy, but sunny, and the sea looked beautiful.

We all got out of the car, breathing in the sea air, laughing at little Smartie's nose twitching. I took Gran's arm, despite her protest that she was *perfectly fine,* as we made our way slowly across the fine golden sand to a nicely sheltered spot. Mum was carrying a fold-up chair for Gran and a blanket for the rest of us; I held the picnic basket, and had some towels flung over my arm. Within two minutes Mia was out of her new dress and into her swimming costume.

'The sea's going to be absolutely freezing, Mia,' Mum warned her. 'It might be sunny but it's still only April.'

'Don't worry, she'll only paddle, but at least she won't get her clothes wet. Come on, Mia, I'll race you down to the sea,' I said, rolling up the legs of my jeans.

I ran down to the water's edge, taking Smartie with me, Mia racing ahead of us. She was soon jumping over the shallow waves, squealing with excitement, splashing me thoroughly and making us both giggle as Smartie jumped back, yelping with surprise.

The day passed happily. Relaxing there on the beach in the sunshine, I felt my worries and anxieties slip into the back of my mind for the first time in months. At midday we ate our sandwiches and enjoyed the look of surprise on Mia's face when I opened the tin containing the chocolate cake – complete with six candles. I'd even remembered matches, but the difficulty of lighting the candles in the breeze off the sea gave us plenty of laughs, until Mum hit on the idea of holding up the big beach towel to shelter us, just long enough for all six candles to be alight so that Mia could blow them out. As we sang 'Happy Birthday', Mia was overcome with shy delight to realise other families nearby on the beach were joining in, finishing off with a round of cheers and clapping for the birthday girl.

When we'd had enough of the beach, we left Gran sitting contentedly on a bench overlooking the sea while the rest of us took Smartie for a brisk walk along the coast and back. Finally we rounded the day off with fish and chips.

'It's been my best birthday *ever*,' Mia proclaimed as we all climbed back into the car later in the afternoon.

Mum and I exchanged glances. Her best birthday ever? Had she, for a moment, actually forgotten that Daddy hadn't been with us and that everything had changed, in ways she still hadn't really been able to accept? It was good that she'd enjoyed her day so much, and perhaps – like me – she'd simply been able to put all the other stuff out of her mind for a while. She rubbed her eyes with tiredness as I strapped her into her car seat.

'Where's Pink Bunny?' she asked sleepily, her thumb going into her mouth.

I looked along the back seat. On the floor of the car. Checked the boot, the picnic basket, under the blanket, even under the car.

'Mum,' I said quietly. 'I'm just going back to the beach for a minute.'

Mum nodded at me, understanding at once, and kept Mia chatting while I ran, looking frantically in every direction, out of the car park, down the slope, back to our spot on the beach. No Pink Bunny. I stared up at the road. It would take me at least half an hour to retrace our earlier walk – but then I remembered telling Mia, when we took the picnic basket and beach things back to the car, to leave Pink Bunny there rather than carrying him with us on the walk. *He might get lost*, I said. *He'll be safe here in the car, waiting for you.* She hadn't been carrying him with her on the walk.

I rushed back to the car, checking again in all directions as I went. He *must* be in the car! I got everyone out, searched under all the seats again, emptied the boot, turned the bags upside down. By now Mia was crying, of course. She'd had Pink Bunny since she was a baby, and had always taken him everywhere with her. She'd started to grow out of the obsession slightly during the last year or so – until the move, the separation, everything that had happened to disrupt her little life recently. Since then, she'd become completely dependent on him again. She wouldn't be able to sleep without him. I couldn't imagine how she was going to cope. But it was no good. I'd looked everywhere. We even drove slowly along the route we'd taken for our walk, checking, although I knew she hadn't taken it with her. Pink Bunny had vanished, and the *best birthday ever* looked like ending up as a disaster. If I'd felt like a bad mother before, right now I felt like the worst one in the world.

PART 2

PAWS OFF OUR PARK

CHAPTER 11

It was strange being back at the old house for the first time since I'd left, over two months before. And it was even weirder being castigated by Josh, of all people, for my careless parenting – even if I did think I deserved it.

'How the hell did you manage to lose it?' he hissed at me when Mia, who'd tired herself out even more by crying about Pink Bunny all the way back to Plymouth, had gone into the lounge and collapsed miserably on the sofa. I'd stayed by the front door, out of her earshot, to tell Josh about the missing toy. 'Didn't you go back and look for it?'

'Of course I bloody well did!' I retorted, exasperated.

'Well, it's nice of you to bring her over to me so upset, I must say,' he went on sarcastically. 'Especially on her birthday, poor kid.'

'Poor kid? She's had a fantastic day – ask her! She said it was her best birthday ever.' I was aware I was sounding childish again, trying to score points. Was this what we were reduced to now? I sighed. 'Look, it's no use us arguing about it. She's exhausted, she'll fall asleep as soon as her head hits the pillow, bunny or no bunny.'

'Hopefully.' He was still frowning at me. 'You never know, it might even get her out of the habit. I thought she'd grown out of it already – it's so babyish. Why did you let her get so dependent on it again?'

'I didn't *let* her, it just happened,' I said wearily. I'd had enough of this. Mum and Gran were waiting in the car with Smartie, and I just wanted to go home. 'I'm sure Mia will be fine without Pink Bunny. She's just tired.'

'Well, maybe I'll give Mia her birthday present now, instead of leaving it till tomorrow.'

'No, Josh, she's so tired I think it's better to wait until the morning. We told her she was having two celebrations anyway.'

'Yes, but now she needs cheering up after her day's been spoilt like this.'

I glared at him. 'Please don't turn it into a blame game. Or let Mia hear you talking like this. She's upset enough, she just needs us to stay calm and carry on as normal.'

'Normal?' he shot back. 'And what exactly *is* normal now, Nic? Mia's life was perfectly normal until you took it into your head to move out and turn everything upside down for her.'

'It stopped being normal long before that! How *normal* was it for her father to never be around? How normal is it, come to that, for you to start spoiling her rotten now, every time you see her?' I closed my eyes, annoyed with myself, as soon as the words were out of my mouth. I'd promised myself I wouldn't bring this up – but I'd been too angry to help it.

'Oh, I see,' he said, folding his arms across his chest. 'So first I don't spend enough time with her, and now I spoil her. I can't win, can I, Nic?'

I shook my head. 'Forget I said anything. I'm tired, and we're both upset for Mia.' I felt my eyes sting with tears for a moment. 'She had a lovely day until the bunny went missing. I'm doing my best, Josh, whatever you think.'

'So am I,' he retorted. 'Even if you think I'm spoiling her.' I turned and walked away. I'd already kissed Mia goodbye and promised her a new Pink Bunny, even though I knew it could never be the same. I got in the car and started the engine, neither Mum nor Gran saying anything. They could probably see from my face that I really wasn't in the mood to chat.

I was so upset with myself for ruining our nice day, but I was consoled by the thought that Mia had enjoyed it so much until the Lost Bunny situation. We dropped Gran home and by the time we'd unpacked the picnic things and sat down with a cup of tea, Mum and I were both so tired ourselves that we were almost falling asleep on the sofa.

The next day when Mia arrived back from her father's, her eyes were shining with excitement again. His present to her had apparently been a brand-new purple bike. It was being kept at his house, for her visits there. I thought she might have been disappointed by this and I couldn't help wondering if Josh wanted to keep the bike there so that Mia preferred being with him, to being at home with me. But she was so thrilled with the bike, I couldn't be anything other than happy for her, especially as I couldn't afford to buy her a new one myself. But I did feel sad, and a bit resentful, that he seemed determined to outdo me in every way, making it feel like the day out and all the treats we'd given Mia on the Saturday hadn't even happened. He'd even managed to get in before me to buy her a new Pink Bunny – nothing like the original, of course – which she held defensively, saying it was *nice*. When I later found it discarded under her bed, I was just a tiny bit gratified that she wasn't carrying it around everywhere with her. It didn't stop her missing her old babyhood comfort toy, however, which she continued to ask for every night in much the same way she'd kept on about Monty the cat when we'd first arrived.

As always, my walks with Smartie and the other dog walkers took my mind off my worries and frustrations. And within a few days we were into May, making me feel that summer was just around the corner. It wasn't, of course – the weather was still as changeable as it had been throughout April – but the blossom on the trees, the hedgerows filling out and blooming, buzzing with bees and chirruping little birds, together with the occasional days of blue sky and sunshine, were helping to give us a taste of it.

'Somebody's decided we're having a heatwave already,' Amber said on one of our evening walks that first week of

May – nodding at the rather pleasant rear view of Craig, who was striding ahead of us in his shorts, Judy as always trotting alongside him, constantly attentive for his commands.

I laughed. 'Yes, and somebody else can't take her eyes off him!'

Sara might have been making it more obvious, but I had to admit I wasn't immune to the sight either. OK, so I might have sworn off men for life, but there was no harm in looking, was there! And there was no denying Craig was worth looking at.

Smartie had bounded off in front of us, chasing something in the undergrowth, and after a minute or two I called him, to make sure he'd come trotting back. He was becoming more reliable now, the training classes paying off. Mia and I had been going together to the classes once a week after school, in a neighbouring village. I'd been enjoying these outings, for the time out with Mia, as much as for Smartie's training. The fifteen-minute drive there and back gave us a rare opportunity to talk on our own. Mia seemed to feel more inclined to talk to me about her feelings while she was sitting on the back seat with Smartie, addressing the back of my head. Just the previous day, she'd suddenly burst out that she didn't like being 'naughty' at school. Managing somehow to keep my voice calm and my eyes on the road, I'd done my best to assure her that she hadn't ever been naughty at school – just upset and a bit scared – that everybody understood, and that she'd soon be doing just as well as she did at the old school.

When we got out of the car I'd hugged her close as we walked Smartie to his class and as usual the training session cheered us both up.

So we felt confident enough now to be able to let him off his lead for a run in the park with Benji and the other dogs. Sara, who of course had been walking ahead of us with Craig, suddenly turned back, almost falling over Babette, and called out to me:

'Craig and I were just comparing notes on the missing cats. Between us, we've had six responses now.'

'Oh, and I had another one last night,' I said. 'So seven calls altogether now. That makes eight cats including Monty. And they're all from Furzewell? And all disappeared recently?'

'Within the last few months, yes.' She glanced at Amber, who'd bent down to refasten Benji's lead and didn't appear to be listening. 'It's *definitely* not a coincidence, Nic. I suggest we get all the owners together for a meeting this weekend and move forward with contacting the Press. How's Friday night for you?'

'Fine, yes.' I sighed. Eight cats missing, from such a small village. Sara was right, it couldn't be a coincidence. Something was happening to them, or someone surely must know something about it. Well, if a story in the paper could help, then the sooner the better.

Once again we met in Smiths that Friday evening. We were a strangely mixed group: Sara, Craig, Amber and myself – Simon was held up in Cornwall where he'd been working – plus a selection of villagers whose cats were missing. As well as Craig's neighbour – a very anxious and distressed lady who described her missing Devon rex cat as *my little baby* – and her friend from the Houses on the Green, we met the young couple from the new estate, whose garden Simon had agreed to landscape, an elderly lady who lived next-door to the school and a burly-looking youngish guy covered in tattoos who told us his kitten, *Petal*, had gone missing on her very first time outside. He'd presumed it had been his fault, that he'd let her out too soon, and was surprisingly and touchingly upset as he described how guilty he felt. We were just about to start the meeting when the last two people turned up – the vicar, Reverend Timms, who explained apologetically that he'd only realised one of his five cats was missing when he saw our poster and went home to have a count up ('They're in and out all the time, you know how it is, so I don't know exactly how long he's been gone') – and old Tommy Burrows whose front garden I'd recently admired. His own ginger tom, he told us, had been gone since soon after Christmas and he'd presumed he'd never see him again, until he saw the poster.

I was glad Amber had turned up, despite her professed dislike of cats.

'Well, I wanted to support you all,' she said with a shrug. 'But I will have to dash off early, I'm afraid. I've got work to finish.'

Sara stood up and called for silence so that she could take charge of the meeting.

'Thank you all for coming,' she said. 'As I'm sure you realise, of course, we can't promise anything. But I think you'll all agree with us that this is really too much to be a coincidence.'

There was a murmur of agreement, and a stifled sob from the owner of the Devon rex.

'What we're suggesting,' Sara went on, 'is getting the local media on board with this. The editor of the *South Devon Recorder* happens to be a personal friend of mine.' She paused, patting her hair, waiting for this supposedly impressive fact to sink in. 'So if you all agree, I'm going to talk to him about getting a story in the paper. He'll want to interview some of us, of course.' She paused again. It seemed to have only just occurred to her that she wouldn't need to be interviewed herself, not having a cat, never mind one that had gone missing. That must have been a disappointment! 'I mean, interview some of you who have lost cats,' she amended quickly. 'If you're happy to be interviewed, perhaps you'd like to confirm that now, so that the reporter will know who to get in touch with.'

Several hands were raised and Sara nodded at me.

'Make a note of their names, Nic,' she said.

Craig raised his eyebrows at me. Even he must have wondered who had suddenly made me Sara's secretary. But I did as I was told. It was all for a good cause.

'And of course,' she went on, 'photos of the missing cats would be very helpful. If you're interviewed, please see if you can have a good clear photo available to go in the paper. In fact, ideally, we'd like one of each of the missing cats.

We can then write a post for various local social media sites, with all their names, photos and dates of disappearance. Far more people view social media than read newspapers,' she explained patiently, presumably for the benefit of the rest of us poor ignorant yokels who couldn't be expected to keep up with the times. 'Craig,' she said, her tone of voice and facial expression suddenly softening as she turned to him, 'I'll leave the social media side of things to you.'

'Thank you,' he said, without a trace of sarcasm, but giving me another amused look. That quick smile, those raised eyebrows – they could be the undoing of a girl, if she hadn't already sworn off men for life.

'Now,' Sara was concluding, 'over to you, everyone. We're open to any other practical suggestions, obviously.'

She sat down, and immediately there was bedlam – everyone calling out their ideas at once.

'OK, shall we take one at a time?' I suggested, getting a stare from Sara who must have thought I was taking over her chairing of the meeting. 'Reverend Timms? Your thoughts?'

'I hope we're not forgetting the power of prayer in all this,' he said, smiling around at us all benevolently.

'It ain't done much yet, Reverend,' Petal the kitten's multi-tattooed owner retorted.

'Tha' be right,' Tommy Burrows agreed. 'I done a fair ol' bit of praying mesel'. *For the love of God All-bliddy-mighty, Ginger, where ye be gone then?* I been saying, but 'e bain't come back yet, be 'e?'

There was smothered laughter, and the Reverend sat back in his chair, looking disappointed.

'I reckon we should talk to someone on the radio,' said the woman from the Houses on the Green. 'You could do that, couldn't you, what's-your-name – Sara. You've got a posh voice. You could explain it all proper-like.'

'Yes, thank you, that's a good idea, I'll look into that,' Sara said, beaming. 'Write that down, would you, Nic?'

And so it went on, with various people suggesting talking to the police, someone else saying we should knock on every door in Furzewell to ask the residents if they were cat lovers or not, and variations on the theme of more posters. And each time: *Write that down, Nic.* And Craig giving me that raised-eyebrow, slightly amused look – until eventually neither of us could keep a straight face any longer and both burst into giggles, unfortunately at the inappropriate moment of the Devon rex's owner wiping her tears after suggesting we get all the vets in the area to check their records for recently deceased cats.

'I'm sorry,' I said, hot with embarrassment and something else I couldn't quite identify. 'Craig and I both … just saw something … a bit funny … in my notes…'

The stern look of admonishment from Chairperson Sara was something neither of us would forget for quite a while. And after that, the meeting gradually broke up.

'I think it was worthwhile, don't you?' I said to Sara as we left the café – trying to make up for my earlier faux-pas.

'Definitely,' she said, 'I hope you've got all those points listed accurately, Nic. I'll be needing them emailed across to me.'

I just about managed to stop myself from saluting and saying *Aye-aye, Cap'n.* I was glad Craig had already left, or we'd probably both have started giggling again! Although I was determined not to give any more thought at all to those funny little smiles of his, or that feeling that we'd been kind of *together* in our amusement at Sara's bossiness. I was pretty sure no good could come from thinking too much about things like that.

CHAPTER 12

It was the early spring bank holiday that weekend, and as it wasn't Josh's turn to have Mia, I'd promised her a quiet, relaxing few days, taking Smartie for extra walks. She was still finding school challenging and tiring, but at least she was beginning to open up to me a bit about it. I really wanted her to have some breathing space without too much stuff going on.

'We could play some of those garden games Granny Helen bought you for your birthday,' I suggested. 'That would be fun, wouldn't it?'

'Yes,' she agreed, brightening up. And then, to my surprise, added: 'Can Eddie come and play the games too?'

'Eddie?' I queried.

'You know. I told you about him. He's the new boy in my class. He's my friend now.'

To say I was surprised would be an understatement. I was aware of a new boy who'd started after the Easter holiday, and although Mia had mentioned him once or twice, I'd had no inkling that she thought of him as a friend. I questioned her gently about him a little more now, and I got the impression they'd been drawn together because both of them had been new and felt lonely.

'Of course he can come and play,' I said, pleased with this development. I'd been disappointed that the two Olivias didn't appear to have worked out as potential friends. I'd been trying to hide my anxiety, hoping that eventually Mia would make new friendships – and it seemed this one had been developing gradually without me really being aware. When I met Mia at the classroom door the next afternoon, I asked her to point out Eddie, and together Mia and I approached his mum to ask her if he could come round at the weekend. She seemed really grateful. She hadn't met many people yet since moving into one of the new houses, and had been worried about Eddie settling in at school. Mia was more cheerful than usual on the way home, and I wondered if it was too much to hope for, that this might be a turning point.

When we woke up on the Saturday morning, the sun was shining.

'Is Eddie coming round today?' Mia asked.

'No. Tomorrow afternoon. What would you like to do today?'

'Can I go for a ride on my bike, and can you take off the stabilisers please, Mummy?' she asked excitedly.

Apparently, the new purple bike at Daddy's house was bigger than her old one, and had no stabilisers. Since we'd moved to Eagle House, she'd shown no interest in the old bike, which was languishing in the shed here. But the prospect of being able to ride the new one seemed to have changed all that. To be fair, I was pleased to see her so animated and excited. She watched while I took off the stabilisers, and after doing a few circuits of the garden, with me running after her, holding the back of the saddle whenever she wobbled, I suggested she could ride it to the park when we took Smartie out. There was a path around the park's perimeter, so she could pedal alongside us while I walked with the other dog walkers. The bike was small enough for her to manage well, despite being a stabiliser-free novice. But the first part of the walk was a bit of a challenge: holding onto Smartie's lead with one hand, I had to run all the way down Pump Lane and along Fore Street to keep up with Mia, my other hand outstretched in case she overbalanced. Smartie seemed to find the whole thing hilarious, bounding along next to me, his tail and ears flapping up and down, woofing at Mia every now and then as if he was warning her to slow down. It was much easier once we were in the park, though, and I could let her cycle up and down the path in front of us, her balance and proficiency improving amazingly fast.

'She's practising for riding her new bigger bike. Birthday present from her dad,' I told Simon when he commented on her excitement.

'Oh, good, at least he's doing his bit, then?'

'Yes.' I sighed, and he looked at me questioningly. 'You're right,' I went on after a moment. 'I'm glad he's ... buying her things, and taking her to places. I suppose I sound ungrateful, but, well, he never showed this kind of interest in her before. Or in me,' I added quietly. 'If I'm honest, I never thought this would last – all the presents and treats he's been giving her. I thought he was just showing off, to get back at me. But it seems like he really does want to be there for Mia now, be a part of her life.'

'So perhaps this separation has been a wake-up call?' he suggested.

'No.' I sighed. 'I've walked out before, twice actually. Both times it was only temporary, but I was hoping it would shake him a bit, make him sit up and take notice. It didn't. Nothing changed. In fact, things just got worse. The thing is, Josh is married to his job. He works for an advertising agency. He always loved the work, but whereas when we were first married he talked to me about his projects – shared his enthusiasm with me – eventually the job completely took him over, like a drug, so that it was all he thought about, day and night. He was always either in the office or out with clients, and it didn't even seem as if the enjoyment was there anymore – just the addiction. And Mia and I didn't seem to matter. He was hardly ever home in the end. Not even Christmas day.' I swallowed. 'That was the most hurtful thing. How could he not want to spend Christmas with his daughter, even if he didn't care about me? That was when I made up my mind – when I sat down to eat Christmas dinner with Mia on our own – that the marriage wasn't worth trying to save anymore. That there wouldn't be any going back this time.'

I took a deep breath. I hadn't told anyone else, here in the village, this much about my break-up with Josh before. It had felt painful to say it all out loud, but Simon was so easy to talk to.

'So it's doubly galling that he's now doing more for Mia than he did when you were together,' Simon said, giving me his sympathetic look.

'Exactly. He took her to Torquay over Easter, and he's talking about taking her abroad somewhere in the summer holidays. Abroad! We never went abroad, not in the whole time we were married.' I stopped, looking at Simon apologetically. 'Sorry. You don't need to hear all this.'

'It helps to talk to someone, Nic. That's what friends are for.'

I nodded gratefully, strangely touched that he thought of us as friends. Because he'd already confided in me about his wife and how long it had been since she'd died, I felt able to ask him whether he thought he'd ever settle down with anyone else. He seemed to consider for a while before answering.

'I don't know. I have dated a couple of women during the last few years. It felt strange at first, but there was one I became quite close to. I did start to wonder if it might become more serious. But it turned out she wasn't the settling-down type.' He laughed. 'Either that, or I just wasn't the right one for her.'

I found myself wondering what on earth that woman could have been looking for that she didn't find in Simon. He seemed to be that perfect combination of rugged and strong, but kind and gentle.

'Her loss. She must have been daft,' I said lightly, touching his arm.

He laughed again, shaking his head. 'So must your ex, if you ask me.'

Simon really did have a habit of always making me feel better about myself and cheering me up.

It stayed sunny and really quite warm for the rest of that weekend. People were outside in T-shirts, smiling at each other and commenting that the weather surely couldn't last. But I was just glad it lasted for Sunday. Mia had been so excited about her new friend Eddie coming to play. We invited Gran to join us for the day, and when the fabled Eddie turned up, I chatted to his mum, Louise, for a few minutes and discovered that she was a single parent herself, having brought up Eddie on her own since he was a baby. I suggested she might like to stay for the afternoon and join us for the barbecue we'd planned later, and she accepted gratefully.

'I haven't had a chance to make friends in the village yet,' she admitted. 'This is so nice of you.'

'It's nothing, I know how it feels. I'm just grateful that Mia's made a friend,' I said, and went on to explain that Mia was new to the school too.

'Yes: Eddie told me that. It's hard for them, isn't it, starting somewhere new. Especially if they're a bit quiet and shy. Eddie says Mia's only just turned six? She's quite a bit younger than him, then. He was seven in January.'

'Oh, I see.' Eddie wasn't much taller than Mia, but he was obviously in the school year above her. 'These mixed-age group classes are a bit hard to get used to, aren't they. But there's no alternative really in such a small school.'

We chatted together over a cup of tea while the two children ran around the garden playing with Smartie. It was the most relaxed I'd seen Mia with anyone from her new school. She and Eddie seemed comfortable in each other's company, but neither of them were getting silly and overexcited. I wondered if Eddie, being more than a year older than her, was a calming influence on Mia.

'He cried on his first day at the school,' Louise admitted. 'He told me afterwards that the other boys laughed at him.'

'Poor Eddie,' I said. 'Mia's been quite unhappy too. She's taking longer to settle than I hoped.'

'Oh, but apparently when Eddie got upset, Mia told him not to worry, that she'd be his friend and look after him.' Louise smiled. 'I thought that was so sweet. I think he's in love with her now.'

I looked at her in surprise. 'Mia hasn't told me any of this,' I said. 'But honestly, I'm so glad they've become friends. Perhaps that was what they both needed – another newcomer so that they didn't feel so alone.'

'What I needed too, actually,' she said shyly, giving me another smile. 'This is so nice, Nic. Thanks again for inviting me.'

Mum and Gran came out into the garden then, announcing that it was time to try out the new games, and the rest of the afternoon was spent happily competing against each other in crazy golf, hoopla, bat-and-ball and kicking the football into the net (or in my case, around it – I was hopeless). By the time we'd had the barbecue, it was early evening and cooling down. When Louise and Eddie left, she suggested a return visit another weekend.

'We've just got one of the little houses on the new estate, though,' she said. 'Tiny garden. Nothing grand like this.'

'Oh, we're not grand at all,' I laughed. 'The difference is, at least you've got a place of your own.'

'Yes. It took a long while, though. But you're right: it's all mine, and it feels good.'

'I really like Eddie. He's nice to me,' Mia said after they'd gone. 'He doesn't think I'm a baby.'

'You mean because you're younger than him?' I said.

'No. Because I cry sometimes at school,' she said, very quietly. 'And some of the other children laugh and call me a baby.'

This was a first. She was actually talking to me about it. I pulled her onto my lap and gave her a hug.

'I bet that feels horrible,' I sympathised. 'But Eddie doesn't laugh?'

'No, because he cried too, on his first day. So that's why we're friends.'

'He seems like a really nice boy. I'm glad you're friends. And you *will* soon make others.'

'I don't care now. Eddie's my best friend ever. When can we go to his house?'

'Soon,' I promised her. Satisfied, she jumped off my lap and ran to play with Smartie again. I felt a lightness in my heart that hadn't been there before, a feeling that everything might work out OK after all. And just to round off the day, a little later I went to get something from my car – my insurance documents, which I kept in the glovebox, and which I wanted to check as the policy was soon due for renewal – and found something in there that we'd all given up for lost.

'Pink Bunny!' Mia squealed in surprise as I held it out to her.

'Where on earth did you find that?' Mum asked.

'In the glovebox. I'm *sure* I didn't put it there,' I said, shaking my head, puzzled.

'Surely we checked in there when it went missing?'

'Well, no, I don't think I did, because I so rarely even open it.' I thought back to Mia's birthday. 'Gran,' I said, turning to her. 'You were in the front seat, weren't you? You wouldn't have put—'

'Mia's bunny – in the glovebox,' she interrupted me. 'Oh dear. Yes, maybe I thought it would be safe there, and then ... well, I must have completely forgotten about doing it. I'm so sorry.'

'It doesn't matter, Gran. At least we've found it.'

'Well, yes, I'm glad about that but poor Mia was ever so upset. What a daft old thing I am,' she added, with a self-deprecating laugh. 'I'll be forgetting my own head next.'

'Your own *head*?' Mia squawked, staring at Gran in surprise. 'But it's stuck onto your body, Granny Helen!'

We all laughed, and the incident was smoothed over happily. Mia cuddled Pink Bunny for a while, and took him up to bed with her that night, but the ironic thing was that over the course of the next few days, it became obvious that she didn't care so much about him anymore. Now Furzewell was beginning to feel like home, she didn't need the comfort quite so much. What a relief.

CHAPTER 13

I don't know if it was the sunny weather, the feeling of summer just around the corner, or the fact that Mia was beginning to look happier, but during those first weeks of May I felt much more content myself. Fruit trees in the orchard next to the park were full of pink and white blossom. All along the lanes, hawthorn and blackthorn scented the air, and the hedgerows were sprinkled with the pinks and reds of ragged robin and red valerian, the creams and greens of wild garlic and cow parsley. Daisies and buttercups spread across the meadows by the stream; and Cuckoo Copse, where I sometimes walked Smartie, became carpeted, almost overnight, with the delicate blues and whites of bluebells. Smartie would scamper ahead of me, sniffing in delight at all the new, unfamiliar scents, and looking back at me from time to time, his eyes bright with excitement, his tail wagging with pleasure.

At school, I was getting to know the teachers better, and enjoying the banter of the staffroom again as I had in my previous job. I was pleased and relieved when Mr Gregory took me to one side and confirmed that Mia had definitely 'turned a corner'.

'She's much more settled,' he said. 'It'll take time for her to catch up again, but at least she's happy now. We want her to be enjoying school and the progress will come.'

'Yes.' I nodded. 'I've noticed it at home, too. She brought me a book yesterday – one she'd had as a birthday present – and said she wanted to read it. It was a bit too difficult for her but she sat with me and we read it together. She was really trying hard. She says she wants to move on from the easy books she's been bringing home from school.'

'And she will do, very soon, but I don't want to rush her and make her lose heart again.'

'Thank you,' I said, glad Mia had such an understanding teacher. 'I think it's made all the difference that she's got a new friend in the class now.'

'Yes.' He smiled, but went on to warn me: 'Eddie will be in a different class, though, from September – he'll be in Year 3, and that's mixed with the year above.'

'Of course.' I nodded. I knew that was going to happen but I didn't want to give too much thought to it yet, especially with Mia only just starting to feel comfortable.

In my reception class, the four- and five-year-olds were used to me now, and I'd got to know which among them needed gentle coaxing, who might respond well to lots of praise and encouragement, and who required firmer handling. I'd always loved my job, but at this little school – with all its memories of my own childhood – I felt as if I'd really found myself at last. Mrs French, the reception teacher, had told me several times how pleased she was with me, and I was beginning to envisage my role being a long-term career choice, rather than just a convenient job while Mia was so young. My self-esteem might have taken a big knock in my personal life, but here at work I was feeling more confident and happier day by day.

After school, Louise and I often chatted together as we waited for Mia and Eddie outside their classroom, and it was gratifying to see the two children come out together, talking happily and pleading to be allowed to play at each other's houses. On the Friday of that first week after our bank holiday together, we took them both to Smiths for an after-school cake as a treat, while we talked over a cup of tea, and we agreed it was something we could repeat whenever possible. I was enjoying Louise's company. She understood my anxieties about being a single parent in a way that Amber probably couldn't, and hearing how Louise had coped with the difficulties of bringing up Eddie herself made me feel a little less afraid about the future.

But it was the times I spent with my fellow dog walkers when I felt the most relaxed. Despite our different situations and characteristics, we did seem to have a lot in common – we were all dog lovers, after all – and there was always plenty to talk about as we walked. On one occasion, when Amber happened not to have joined us for the walk,

Sara was giving us an update on the interviews that had been carried out by the reporter from the *South Devon Recorder*.

'Apparently he's got enough for his story now,' she said. 'It'll be going in this week's paper.'

'Great.' I nodded. 'Well, let's hope it does some good. *Somebody* must know what's happened to all these cats. They can't all have just vanished into thin air.'

'Hm.' She raised her eyebrows. 'Trouble is, Nic, somebody might know perfectly well what's happened to them but have good reason for keeping quiet.'

'You really think someone's taken the cats?' Simon said, frowning.

'Taken them, or done something to them, yes. I think it's a very strong possibility, don't you?' she retorted.

We all walked on in silence. We were probably all thinking the same, but didn't want to say it. It was too horrible to contemplate.

'Let's be honest,' she resumed after a few minutes, 'we all know people who don't like cats, who complain about other people's cats digging up their gardens and frightening away the birds.'

'Yes,' I said, 'and they're entitled to their opinion.' I shrugged. 'Personally, I don't like mice. Or spiders. But I wouldn't hurt them. I just try to keep out of their way.'

'And what happens if you find a mouse in your kitchen? Or a spider in your bath?' Craig teased.

I laughed. 'Well, of course, I do a lot of squealing and hopping around!'

'And scream for a man to take it outside?' he said, grinning.

'No. I do it myself,' I protested.

'Squealing and hopping all the way?' Craig persisted.

'Nothing wrong with a bit of squealing and hopping, is there, Nic,' Simon said. Everyone had been laughing at Craig's teasing – including me. We always enjoyed the way he joked with us, and I had to admit it was one of the things I found ... quite attractive about him. It cheered me up and distracted me from my own worries. 'I do some of that myself,' Simon went on, 'if I put my hand on a slug when I'm working. Yuck!'

'But you're a gardener,' I laughed. 'You must have to deal with slugs and snails and worms all the time.'

'Yes, and I'm fine with snails and worms. And caterpillars, and pretty much anything else I might come across. It's just *slugs* – I can't bear them. Slimy, squishy things, ugh! I know they're all God's creatures, but even so...'

'They're revolting,' Craig agreed. 'I bet Nic would squeal and hop about if she had to touch one of *them*.'

I laughed again, but Sara interrupted, sounding a bit tetchy now that we'd all changed the subject from what she'd wanted to discuss:

'Well, maybe that's how *some* people feel about cats.'

I'd got used to this. If Craig started chatting to me or Amber – teasing us, in that friendly, flirtatious way of his – she made it fairly plain that she didn't like it. It was becoming more and more obvious to me that she liked him and didn't want to have to share his attention. I wished she'd just get on with it and ask him out or something. I was sure he'd be up for it. Although he often showed off a bit about the women he'd supposedly been seeing, none of us had ever actually met any of them. Amber reckoned he must live his life as a series of one-night stands, whereas my personal theory was that he might be inventing them all. Although, to be fair, it was hard to believe he *wouldn't* be successful with women.

'People don't squeal and hop around when they see a cat, Sara,' Simon pointed out reasonably, 'however much they might dislike them.'

'No. They just kidnap them, or put poison down for them.'

'Ouch!' I pulled a face. 'Don't say that.'

'Why not? It's what we're all thinking, isn't it? We should face facts. We're not going to find these cats alive. The whole point of the newspaper article, the posters and everything, is to try to find the culprit.'

None of us responded this time. We walked on, calling to the dogs, who'd been running madly in circles around each other on the grass of the park, and the subject was dropped.

The culprit, I thought to myself. Was that really what we were looking for? Was Sara right – was there actually a crazed cat-hater in the village, kidnapping or exterminating them all? It was a truly horrible thought.

Within a few days, Sara had more news for us, not particularly good news either.

'I spoke to Robert last night.' Her newspaper editor friend. 'He can't run our story on the front page after all.'

'Well, I suppose it doesn't matter if it's inside, does it?' Simon said. 'If it's a full page, as you said, with pictures of the cats and a big catchy headline...'

Sara shook her head. 'Front page is what we need. People look at the headline when they're browsing in the paper shop or the supermarket, even if they're not intending to buy the paper. It won't have half as much impact if it's inside.'

'So why can't he do that now? I thought he'd promised you,' I said. Maybe her relationship with Robert wasn't as close as she liked to think.

'He will, but it's got to wait another week. He's got a bigger story this week. He wouldn't tell me what it was but he said it affects Furzewell in particular, so he wants it to headline for our local edition.'

'Well, I guess another week won't hurt, will it.' Simon said. 'Some of the cats have been missing for months now, anyway. I wonder what the big story is. Affecting Furzewell? I didn't think there was ever anything exciting going on in the village.'

'Maybe someone's tractor got vandalised,' Craig joked.

'Someone heard the first cuckoo,' I suggested.

'Or there was a riot at the pub because they ran out of cider.'

We spent the rest of our walk joking about the potential newspaper headline, each suggestion more ridiculous than the last. But a couple of days later, when we found out what the front page of the *Recorder* was really about, it wiped the smiles off all our faces.

FURZEWELL PARK 'TO BE SOLD FOR HOUSING DEVELOPMENT'?

'Unused and unloved' says council spokesman, of the once-popular open space.

'Unused?' Amber shrieked, stabbing the words with her finger. Alerted by Sara, who had, needless to say, been the first to read the paper, we'd gathered at the pub that evening, leaning over each other's shoulders to read the story spread out on the table. 'What are they talking about? *We* use it!'

'Everybody uses it,' Simon agreed. 'Don't they?'

'I don't know. Do they?' Sara shook her head, sighing. 'How many families with children do we see in the park?'

'Well, *we* always used it when we were kids,' I said. 'All the time.'

'I know. But that was then, and this is now. Kids spend more time indoors playing games on their phones and tablets. And let's face it, there's nothing much to attract even the youngest children to the park. The paddling pool's been empty for years, and the playground equipment is so old and rickety nobody wants to use it.'

'Well, then, they ought to put that right, instead of just selling off the land. More housing? How can Furzewell cope with more housing? We've already got the estate going up on High Meadow.'

Sara sighed and folded up the paper. She looked around at us all.

'Leave this with me,' she said solemnly.

I wanted to laugh. Leave it with her? Who did she think she was now? Leader of the opposition?

'What are you going to do?' Amber said.

'Well, first off, I'll talk to someone at the district council, and find out how far along they are with these plans. If they've only just voted on it, there may be time to do something about it before they actually put the land up for sale.'

'But do *what*?' I insisted. 'What can we do?'

'Protest, of course,' she said with a smile. 'Get the rest of the village on our side, and fight this thing. Come on, all of you, stop looking so beaten and negative. We can do something about this; we don't have to lie down and accept it. It's *our* park – it's an important resource for Furzewell. If it's been neglected, that needs to change. We pay our council tax, *and* a parish council precept, and God knows we get little enough for it.'

'That's true,' Simon agreed. 'How often do the public footpaths get tended to?'

'Or the potholes in the roads,' Craig pointed out. 'Just because we only have minor roads around here doesn't mean our tyres are any less likely to be damaged.'

'Well, some of these issues are the responsibility of the *county* council, not the district,' Sara said. 'We have to make sure we pick the right fight with the right people.'

I watched her face, animated and determined. *She loves this*, I thought to myself. *Taking charge, telling us all what to do, getting us motivated.* Well, fine; we were all agreed that this needed fighting and if Sara, with her legal hat on, knew the best way of going about it, I guessed we'd all be happy to follow her lead, however irritating I might find her bossiness.

'OK,' I said. 'If you find out what you can from the council, Sara, then we can talk about it some more and maybe organise a petition.'

'Good idea, Nic,' Sara said, giving me an approving look.

'I'll do whatever I can,' I said. Sara obviously enjoyed being in charge, but it didn't seem right for her to be the only one being proactive around here. Besides, I wanted to get stuck in and fight this thing, as much as anyone did. 'But for now, who wants another drink?'

I had the feeling this was going to be a long battle. And also that, if we weren't careful, it might very well take over from our concerns about the missing cats.

CHAPTER 14

Things seemed to have settled down a bit with Josh recently. To be fair, he was always an easygoing, amenable sort of guy in the beginning. Even when we started arguing, it was normally me ranting and raving at him, while he would just sigh and tell me to calm down, even choosing to walk away from me rather than fight – which just added to my impression of how little he cared. I wouldn't go so far as to say he was now back to his old self, but since our argument on the evening of Mia's birthday, we'd managed to be civil to each other when he picked up Mia or brought her back. That weekend, after the dog-walkers' meeting about the park, he even managed to make eye contact with me and be quite friendly, asking me how I was. I assumed he was beginning to come to terms with the fact that the marriage was over and this was how things would now be between us.

I, on the other hand, still had evenings when I felt so sad about the whole situation that I'd burst into tears over something as silly as hearing one of our favourite songs on the radio or seeing an old film listed on Netflix and remembering enjoying it with him. It was worst when Mum had gone out with her friends, Mia was asleep in bed and I was alone with the TV. Then the black moods would sometimes come over me like clouds and I'd hug little Smartie and cry into his fur until he whined in sympathy. I hated to admit it, but at times like this I still missed Josh – missed having someone coming home to me (however late and however infrequently), someone sleeping next to me at night. I wished I still had a partner, but then that's what I'd wished for even when we were together, because he hadn't been around much in the end. Those early days of our marriage when we'd had so much fun setting up home, laughing and singing together, enjoying every moment of each other's company, seemed like a lifetime ago. I had to remind myself that I was getting on with my life now, and was bound to have the odd bad day and wobble. But overall I was more content than I'd been for some time, settling down to single parenthood, enjoying being back in my home village. And I still had so much to be grateful for: my darling Mia, my mum and my gran, my new friends and of course our new little puppy who always managed to cheer me up. I knew the best thing I could do was to stop looking back and focus on the future. But it wasn't always easy.

Gran came round for Sunday dinner that weekend, as she often did, and while we were eating she told us she'd missed a doctor's appointment during the week.

'I've never done anything like that before in my life,' she said, sounding cross with herself. 'It was only one of those routine check-up things, but even so, I'd *never* want to miss an appointment. I know how busy they are. I felt dreadful when the receptionist called me.'

'Was she annoyed?' I asked.

'No, not at all, luckily. She said these things happen, and that she'd only called to make sure I was all right. I suppose she thought I might have dropped dead,' she added with snort of laughter.

'Oh, don't say that,' I protested. 'Did she make you another appointment?'

'Yes, and I wrote it down in big letters with a red pen.' She paused 'I'm getting so damned forgetful. Anyone would think I had dementia, or something.'

'Of *course* you haven't,' I retorted. I wasn't sure if she was just joking, but I wanted to reassure her anyway. 'Everybody forgets things occasionally. I do all the time. I nearly missed a staff meeting last week—'

'Yes, and I left my washing on the line for three days, didn't I,' Mum joined in.

'I know, but you're both busy people, with jobs and commitments. Of course you're going to forget things. I haven't got that excuse, have I.' Gran sounded more serious now. Was she actually worried about this? 'I had nothing else to remember last week apart from the doctor's appointment, and still I managed to miss it.'

'Honestly, Gran,' I said gently. 'I'm sure it's not a big deal, forgetting something once in a while.'

'Yes, I'm just an absent-minded old woman, I suppose,' she said, smiling back at me as if it was a joke. I wasn't fooled. 'What with that, and forgetting I'd put Mia's bunny in the glovebox – maybe I should start writing down everything I do in future.'

'Gran, there's nothing wrong with your memory,' I insisted.

'You remembered to come round for dinner today, didn't you,' Mum said. 'Nicky's right, you're fine.'

Mum led the conversation around to other things: the weather, the news about the park that I'd already shared with her, and Smartie's latest misdemeanour of running off with a half-full bag of crisps Mia had left on the coffee table and hiding behind the sofa to eat them all. The forgetfulness wasn't mentioned again. But I talked to Mum about it later, when we were on our own.

'Do you think Gran's really worried about her memory? It's hard to tell with her – she pretends to make a joke of things, but—'

'But she was looking for some reassurance, wasn't she,' Mum agreed. 'I really don't think it's anything to worry about. Everyone forgets things, don't they? It's because she's living in that complex with all those other elderly people, if you ask me. I expect your gran sees some of them starting to suffer with dementia and she imagines she's going the same way.'

On occasions like this, I noticed Mum was still harbouring some resentment about Gran moving out to live in her bungalow. I couldn't understand it. You'd think, really, that she'd be glad her mother was still fit enough to want to live independently.

'I wouldn't like to think she was really worried, though,' I said, choosing not to rise to the bait about the bungalow on this occasion.

'Well, hopefully we've talked her out of it. She's OK, Nicky. She's a tough old bird, you know, and her mind's as sharp as needles.'

I nodded. It was true, Gran always *had* been tough – and sharp. And I really didn't like to think that would ever change.

As for Smartie, that crisp-eating episode was just one of many little adventures our growing and increasingly mischievous puppy had been getting up to. We'd had to fit a wire basket below the letter box in the front door after he'd chewed up Mum's credit card bill. Another day, I'd been in the kitchen when Mia had screamed out to me that he'd got into her school bag and was running around the lounge with her homework in his mouth. Luckily it was none the worse apart from a few dribble marks, and Mia had found it funny.

'Why has he started being so naughty?' she asked, giggling.

'Well, I suppose he's a bit like a toddler now – getting into everything,' I said. 'You were the same when you were smaller. Smartie doesn't know he shouldn't eat your home-work. So keep your school bag out of his way.'

'OK.' She looked at me, her head on one side. 'What was the worst thing I ever did, Mummy, when I was a toddler?'

'Let me think.' I smiled at her. 'Well, there was one time when I put you to bed for your afternoon nap, and instead of going to sleep you found a red colouring-pen you'd dropped on the floor, and you started scribbling all over the wall next to your bed, and all over one of your books.'

'Ooh!' She covered her mouth with her hand, her eyes round with shock. 'I'd *never* do anything like that now, would I, Mummy.'

'Of course not,' I said, giving her a hug. 'You're a big girl now and much more sensible. You definitely wouldn't scribble on a book.' I looked at her thoughtfully for a moment. I didn't want to push my luck but I thought I should try to bring up the subject of reading now we'd mentioned books. 'You love books, don't you, Mia?'

She nodded, but her thumb went into her mouth and she looked down at the floor.

'You're a good reader,' I went on, very gently. 'You were one of the best in the class at your other school.'

She took her thumb out of her mouth again.

'I know,' she said eventually in a little voice. 'But I didn't like doing reading, or anything, at this school.'

'Because you were unhappy?' I suggested quietly.

She nodded again. 'I didn't like being there, so I didn't want to try. But I am now.'

'That's really good,' I said, my heart giving a little leap. 'I can see you're happier now. And you're already reading your books so much better again.'

It was as if a barrier had lifted from between us. Suddenly she was smiling at me eagerly, her voice more animated.

'You know what, Mummy? I'm actually starting to like the new school now. I had to pretend to like it, to help Eddie, when he first started, because he was upset and I felt sorry for him. And now we're *both* getting better at liking it. Eddie's a *really, really* good reader,' she said. 'He's *miles* ahead of me and I want to catch him up.'

'Good for you!' I laughed. 'But he's older than you, isn't he. He's in Year 2. So you mustn't worry that he's ahead of you.'

'I'm *not* worried. I just want to be as good as him,' she asserted.

It seemed her old spark was back. I hugged her again, breathing in the floral scent of her shampoo, and the smell of her skin, still exactly the same as it was in her baby days. I remembered how I used to bath her, then wrap her in a fluffy white towel and hold her close, so close to me it felt like we were breathing the same breaths, her soft, downy head resting against my arm, her eyes gazing into mine as I wondered, as all mothers must do, at this miracle, this precious life I'd given birth to. My precious only daughter. Even more precious because of . . . the thing I never talked about. Mia and I had always shared such a close, special bond. Thank God – and I supposed, thanks to Eddie – she was going to be happy again. Perhaps I could dare to hope that I hadn't ruined her life by moving her here to Furzewell, after all.

'I'm glad you're getting better at liking school,' I said. 'And that Eddie is, too. His mummy's getting more used to living here too, you know. It's hard when you start somewhere new and miss your old friends, the way you missed Polly and Jamila. You know their mummies, Gita and Jen, were my best friends before we moved, and I missed them both a lot at first. But now Louise and I are getting to know each other, and like you and Eddie, we're good company for each other. It really helps to have a friend who's in the same boat.'

'The same *boat*?' she giggled. 'What boat?'

And by the time I'd explained the expression to her, we were laughing out loud together and I could almost believe the sulks and tantrums of the last few months were a figment of my imagination. I wasn't going to get carried away, though. I knew perfectly well that children's moods could change inexplicably in a moment, much like the Devon weather – from sunny and warm to stormy and dark. Just as, in fact, the weather in Furzewell, sadly, suddenly changed only a few days later.

CHAPTER 15

It rained so heavily the whole of that week in the middle of May that all the blossom came down from the trees and went brown and soggy on the ground. We trudged to school in macs and welly boots again, Mia splashing through the puddles, and my reception children's coats and boots made pools of water in our little cloakroom. By the Thursday, it felt as if it was never going to stop.

'Maybe we should start building the ark!' I joked to Louise as we waited, huddling together under her umbrella, for Mia and Eddie to come out of their classroom after school.

She laughed, then went on: 'Talking of building, did you see the piece in last week's local paper about the council wanting to sell off the park for more housing?'

'Yes.' I hesitated. The last thing I wanted was for Louise – who was a new resident of Furzewell herself – to think I was opposed to newcomers being housed here. *Not in my backyard* wasn't a stance I'd ever take, and that wasn't the point of our objections to the council's plan. 'Some of us who like walking our dogs in the park aren't very happy about it,' I said carefully.

'Nor am I,' she said vehemently, to my surprise. 'I bought my little house on High Meadow because I was told it was only ever going to be a small estate. I can't see how a village as small as Furzewell can possibly cope with another big development, and it is bound to be big, isn't it, if they're talking about selling off the whole park.'

'Yes, exactly. The council doesn't seem to consider the infrastructure when they come up with these ideas. The school couldn't possibly cope, for a start.'

'Nor could the doctors' surgery. When I went to register myself and Eddie there, the receptionist said they're pretty much at full capacity now. There's only one full-time GP and one part-time, and she hinted that one of them might be considering retiring soon.'

'And we know all about the shortage of GPs,' I agreed. Louise worked as a receptionist for a doctors' practice herself, in another nearby village, so she was all too aware of the difficulties.

'Also, have they considered the roads?' Louise went on. 'Furzewell Park Lane isn't exactly a major route. It's not suitable for such an increase in traffic.'

'I agree.' It was in fact a single track road bordered by high hedges, with very few passing places. 'I suppose they'd have to widen it. It couldn't even cope with the construction lorries, as it stands.'

The children came out of the classroom at that point, and for a few minutes we were busy making sure they had their hoods up and their book bags fastened against the elements, but as we began to walk out of the school playground I said:

'I didn't realise you'd be as opposed to the council's plans as we are. We're against the whole principle of the park being sold. One of our dog walkers is a lawyer, so she's good at dealing with stuff like this. She's been talking to the council about it on our behalf. We're meeting in the pub tomorrow evening. Would you like to come?'

'Yes, I'd like that, but I haven't got a babysitter here yet. I was thinking of asking my neighbour, but—'

'Well, the meeting won't go on late, and there's no school the next day. Mum will be looking after Mia. I'll ask her if she'd have Eddie too.'

'She surely won't want both of them!'

I laughed. 'I think, actually, it'll make it easier. The two of them will occupy each other and Mum can watch her own TV programmes.'

As I'd predicted, Mum was fine about having both children for a few hours.

'Eddie's a nice boy. And after all, Louise is a single mum, like us, so I'm happy to help out. We have to stick together, don't we, us girls.'

'Thanks, Mum.' As usual, she had to get in that bit about us all being single mums together, as if it was a jolly little club where we all had great fun. That might be true for Mum these days, with her giggly nights out with the Gruesome Twosome, and I couldn't begrudge her that enjoyment, after all the years of struggling to bring me up on her own. But it certainly wasn't true for me or I suspect for Louise. As far as I was concerned, being a single mum was scary and quite overwhelming, and although arguably it had been my own decision to become one, it certainly hadn't been my plan.

But when, the next evening, Louise brought Eddie round to Eagle House, and Mum got out crisps and fruit for them, put on a film they'd both been asking to watch, and told them she was excited about seeing it herself so they could all three have a nice *cinema night* together and stay up late, I felt a rush of love and gratitude for her. Not all mothers, especially those who'd become used to enjoying an active social life, would be quite so happy at being landed with a prodigal daughter returning to live with them, let alone babysitting for her granddaughter *and* friend. I was aware that at times she'd appeared a bit fraught and tired since we'd arrived to stay with her, and I tried to do my best to minimise the disruption. But it did seem that for her the pleasure of our company outweighed the natural irritations, and I was grateful for that.

Louise and I walked down to the Fox and Goose sharing an umbrella. The others were already gathered around a table by the window, and after I'd introduced Louise and explained why I thought she'd be interested in being involved, Sara took charge of our gathering. I wouldn't have expected anything else, of course, given that we'd asked her to liaise with the council, but as usual it was evident that she relished her position as chairperson and if she'd only had a gavel, she'd have been banging it on the table for silence every time any of us dared to utter a word.

'Right, well, the good news is that the plan to sell the park is still exactly that – just a plan. Nothing's actually happened yet. And the gist of the council's position is this,' she said in that self-important way of hers. 'They say the park is underused, that valuable resources are being wasted in looking after the site—'

'Looking after it!' Simon interrupted. 'Have they even looked at it recently? When did the grass last get mowed? Has anything been planted there in the last ten years?'

Sara sighed. 'I'm just telling you what their argument is, Simon, I'm not saying I agree with it.'

'OK.' He shrugged. 'Point taken, go on.'

'So their position is that as things stand, it's a waste of ratepayers' money.' She held up her hand before anyone could interrupt to protest. 'They say they've looked at the park's viability as a leisure resource, decided it doesn't meet their criteria, so to save money—'

'Whose money?' I retorted.

Sara sighed again and closed her eyes as if in pain. 'Let me finish, Nic, please. Naturally, they're trying to make it sound as if they're saving us – the council tax payers – money. But of course, our council tax is hardly likely to go down as a result of this plan, we all know that. Like all councils, they're cash-strapped—' she totally ignored the next attempted interruption from Amber and ploughed on, merely raising her voice '—so from their point of view, the obvious solution is to sell off the land for housing. One hundred per cent profit.'

'Without considering the infrastructure, of course,' Craig said.

'Exactly, Craig.' Funny how she didn't snap *his* head off for interrupting. Teacher's pet!

We all started muttering among ourselves about the roads, the healthcare facilities, the environment, the school and the lack of public transport. Louise was just explaining that even she and her neighbours on the new High Meadow estate were worried about the consequences of another big development in the village, when Sara called us to order again.

'I agree with all of that,' she said somewhat dismissively. 'And it definitely should make up part of our argument. But I think it's more important to tackle the issue from the other angle.'

'What other angle?' I said.

'The suggestion that the park's underused. This, to me, is the crux of the matter.' She was really getting into her stride now. 'If it *weren't* underused, they wouldn't have a foot to stand on. They can't sell something that can be shown to be a valuable community asset.'

There was a puzzled silence. Probably none of us wanted to be the one to say it, but eventually Amber did:

'But, Sara, it *is* underused. We all had to agree on that, didn't we, when we talked about it last week. Kids don't play in the park now, families don't go there at weekends—'

'Of course they don't. There aren't any facilities. Even the toilets have been padlocked.' Sara looked around at us all now, smiling, evidently pleased with herself for what was coming next. 'But we need to convince them that it *is* being used. Used, enjoyed and appreciated not just by a few of us who walk our dogs there but by everyone in the village. Not just in the village,' she went on with the fervour, now, of a preacher on the point of converting a roomful of non-believers, 'no, we need to make them aware that it's not just a valuable asset to *us,* but to outsiders too. That people come here from all over Devon. That tourists come here from up-country.'

'To do what?' Simon asked sceptically. 'Walk their dogs?'

She gave him a look, but the gleam of victory was still in her eyes.

'For outings. To bring their kids, enjoy the play equipment, sail their toy boats in the pond, feed the ducks, have group picnics, but most of all, to take part in *events* here.'

There was silence again now. The rest of us exchanged glances. I guessed they were all, like me, beginning to wonder if Sara had lost the plot.

'Er ... there isn't a pond,' Simon pointed out. 'Or ducks.'

'And the play equipment's all rusted up or vandalised,' I said.

'And as you said yourself, there aren't any toilets,' Louise said.

'Or events,' Craig added. 'What events?'

Sara beamed. 'The events we're going to organise, Craig. We, the Friends of Furzewell Park.'

'*Friends of Furzewell Park*?' Amber muttered.

'Yes. I've looked into this. It's quite common practice these days for community groups to take over the running of parks rather than face them being closed. I'm not suggesting we take over the whole thing, although as a last resort, if the entire village were to be behind us and willing to help, it could be a possible option. But for now, what I propose is this. First, as Nic suggested at our last meeting, we should set up a petition – not that I expect the council to take any notice, but it needs to be done. I'll write a letter to every resident of Furzewell, which we can distribute ourselves. I'll briefly outline the situation, give them a date for a meeting for anyone who's interested in supporting us and tell them what we're planning to do.'

'Which is. . .?' I said, shaking my head. I couldn't work out where we were going with this.

'I've already told you!' Sara said, sounding exasperated. 'We're going to hold events. Bring people in, people from the village, people from outside—'

'And the council's going to allow that?' Simon asked.

'Yes. They've given permission for the first one already,' she replied. There was a smile of satisfaction on her face now. 'Why would they refuse? It won't cost *them* anything. We advertise it, organise it, tidy up afterwards—'

'Hell of a job that's going to be,' Craig objected.

'So we get more people involved.' Amber suddenly sounded more excited. 'Sara's right. If we want to save the park, we've got to work for it. Get all the village on our side, get everyone helping. It'd be great for the village community if everyone pulls together on this. If lots of people help, it could be fun. And after all, if we manage to save the park it will benefit everyone.'

'We can't hold an event there, though, not without toilet facilities,' Simon said.

'They've agreed to unlock them and send someone in to make sure they're in working order.' Sara shrugged. 'We may have to clean them ourselves.'

I caught Craig's eye and we both grinned. I wondered if he was thinking the same as me. It was worth coming tonight, just to hear Snooty Sara suggest she might be prepared to clean public loos. But almost immediately she went on, quickly, to say: 'I mean, we'd get a team of willing helpers from around the village to do it, obviously.'

Obviously!

'OK,' I said, cautiously. 'Well, it all makes sense, I suppose, although who knows whether all this effort will get us anywhere? If we're going ahead with it, we need to discuss what sort of event we're proposing to hold.'

Frankly, it sounded like such an enormous undertaking. I felt exhausted just thinking about it. I'd never had any experience at organising any sort of event, and had no idea whether any of the others had. 'Oh, didn't I tell you?' Sara said. 'That's all decided.'

'Decided by whom exactly?' Amber shot back, sounding annoyed, and we all stared at Sara. It was good of her to take the lead, and I supposed on one level I admired the way she was getting stuck in and organising all this. But who gave her the green light to make a decision like this on behalf of everyone else?

'Well, sorry, but I had to pretend I'd already got something lined up, in order to get their permission,' she said, sounding slightly less arrogant now. 'In fact, I had to tell a *teeny* white lie and say it was already at the planning stage. I've filled in all the application forms they gave me, and made sure there aren't any legal loopholes to worry about. I had to presume you'd all be in agreement – sorry – there wasn't really time to consult.'

We all looked at each other warily.

'And what exactly is it that we're supposed to be already planning?' Simon asked.

'A pet show,' Sara said. 'It'll be a doddle, won't it – we're all animal lovers. We can all work together to publicise it. The first ever Furzewell Pet Show, to be held in Furzewell Park on August Bank Holiday Monday.'

There was a collective gasp from the group. It was the middle of May, and we had only until the end of August to organise and publicise a pet show, to say nothing of somehow making the park fit for purpose.

'Well that does sound like a great idea,' Amber said eventually, 'If it's all been decided, we need to roll up our sleeves and get on with it.'

'Yes.' I nodded agreement. 'It'll be a rush, but if we pull together and get everyone on board, it's got to be worth a try. I'll do whatever I can to help, Sara.'

'You're right. We can do this, guys,' Craig joined in. 'Let's give it our best shot.'

'I'm in,' Simon agreed. 'We need to share the work, all of us, so that we can be ready in time.'

'Count me in too, absolutely,' Louise said. 'A pet show is a brilliant idea.'

'Well done, Sara,' I conceded.

'We're all in agreement, then,' she said, sounding relieved. 'So let's get started on our plans.'

She raised her glass. 'Here's to the Friends of Furzewell Park.'

Slightly dazed, we all raised our glasses and repeated the toast.

'And,' I said, having taken a long swig of my beer and lifting the glass again, 'here's to us, the Lonely Hearts Dog Walkers!'

I'd christened them by this name in my own mind for so long now that it didn't occur to me that any of them might be offended. Fortunately, there was an immediate burst of laughter, and they all raised their glasses again.

'The Lonely Hearts Dog Walkers! May our hearts not be lonely forever!' joked Craig, giving me a wink.

By the time I'd finished my third beer that evening, I was feeling quite excited about the whole thing. And more than ready to get stuck into our scheme for protecting our park. It was good to be working with my new friends on something so worthwhile. And even quite good to have been winked at by Craig. Of course, I wasn't the least bit taken in by his flirty chatting, teasing and winking – even if Sara so obviously was. But it did help my battered self-confidence – just a tiny bit.

CHAPTER 16

My cheerful mood didn't last long after Louise and I arrived home and saw the state of the house. Smartie had helped himself to half a dish of crisps and an unknown number of strawberries while Mum and the children had been engrossed in *The Greatest Showman*, and he had been thoroughly sick all over the rug. Mia, hyped up with excitement, told me in horrible detail about the amount and colour of vomit poor Mum had had to clean off the rug, whereas Eddie, who was quieter than usual, said the incident had made him feel sick himself and he wanted to go home. I suspected it was more likely he'd also overindulged on the strawberries, but I had to admit he did look a bit pale.

'I do hope he'll be all right,' I said to Louise, after we'd both apologised to Mum about the rug and the vomit, and I'd made her a well-deserved cup of tea.

'Oh, he's probably just tired. He was so excited about this evening,' she said. 'Come on, Eddie, home to bed. You'll be fine in the morning.'

But he wasn't. The next day Louise messaged me to say he'd come out in spots, and the emergency doctor had diagnosed chickenpox.

'I'm sorry, he's probably passed it on to Mia,' she said.

But luckily Mia had already had the virus so, much as I sympathised with poor Eddie, the only concern I had in relation to Mia was how much she'd miss her new friend. He was obviously going to be off school now for a while, and I couldn't help wondering if without Eddie, she'd be unhappy there again.

'Has Smartie got the chicken-spots too?' she asked me when I told her about Eddie. 'Is that why he was sick?'

'Chickenpox,' I corrected her with a smile. 'No. Smartie just ate too much, of things he shouldn't be eating at all. Puppies do that.'

'I know.' She put her arms around Smartie, who responded by licking her hand and making her giggle. 'Like when he ate my pen top.'

About a week previously, we'd had the unpleasant job of inspecting his poo to make sure the top of one of her colouring pens had passed safely through. Mia had made a big show of her disgust about this, and I hoped it had been a good lesson for her, about ensuring in future that she didn't leave things lying around where he could chew or swallow them.

It wasn't until that Saturday morning that I had a chance to buy the new edition of the *South Devon Recorder*. I was pleased to see that, as promised, Sara's editor friend had devoted a large part of the front page to our missing cats problem. There were quotes from several of the villagers who'd contacted us, together with photos of their cats. The young guy with all the tattoos who'd come to our initial meeting had submitted a picture of himself holding his kitten, Petal. *She's such a little sweetheart*, he was reported as saying. *It would break my heart if anything has happened to her*. Reverend Timms was quoted as saying that his remaining four cats were pining for their missing companion, adding that there would be *much joy in heaven* if Pussy Willow came back home. And Tommy Burrows, whose cat Ginger was pictured asleep on his bed, brought a tear to my eye with the plea for his *best friend in the whole world* to be returned to him. The piece was well written, and finished by asking for anyone who had any information at all about any of the missing cats to get in touch with Sara or myself. I showed Mum before she went off to work, and she seemed very impressed.

'Well, if that doesn't get poor Monty found, nothing will. And all the other cats, of course. Let's hope someone knows something or that somebody somewhere has seen them.' She sighed. 'I do miss Monty. He was very affectionate, you know, and good company for me, before you moved back.'

I put my arm round her. She'd never actually complained about being lonely in the past, but I suddenly realised that of course sometimes she must have been – especially since Gran had moved out. I supposed I should have been more understanding about the fact that she'd seemed so inappropriately excited when Mia and I arrived. And about her nights out with her friends. When she complained bitterly about Dad – about *Ireland*, as if everything that had happened to upset her was the fault of the country rather than the man – I'd only ever seen the hurt and bitterness, never the loneliness it had caused. Of course she would have missed Monty. He'd been her only companion here at Eagle House before we came.

'I'm sure *somebody* must know something,' I said. 'Even if it turns out to be … well, bad news—'

'It's better to know,' she finished for me. 'Absolutely. Not knowing is horrible. For all these other people, too. Poor Tommy Burrows, he doted on that Ginger. And the vicar. He might still have his other cats, but you know, it doesn't make any difference. The loss of just one is still a loss.'

I nodded, unable to speak, suddenly overwhelmed by the memory of a loss of my own, the terrible loss I never mentioned, to anyone, because the pain of it still took my breath away. Mum was looking at me, aware of what she'd said and the effect it had had on me.

'You *can* talk about it, Nicky,' she said gently. 'You never have, not really, and it might help, even now—'

'No,' I said abruptly. 'I'm fine.'

I turned the pages of the paper, quickly, to distract myself and get my thoughts back to everyday things. Away from the darkness, the unspeakable. Mum was wrong. I was fine as long as I didn't dwell on it. Dwelling on things never did any good. Move on, be fine, be normal – that had been my mantra for all these years and I'd coped perfectly well. The pages of the paper blurred before my eyes for a moment and then, suddenly, something caught my attention. On the Letters to the Editor pages, there were … I counted quickly … ten, no eleven letters responding to the previous week's front-page story.

Park sell-off plan is unfair, one letter was headed.

Greedy council has got it wrong, screamed another.

Hands off Furzewell Park! a third began.

My eyes widened as I sat back in my chair and began to read them all. Every single writer was not only against the proposal but absolutely furious about it. They accused the council of caring more about money than people, and of being blind to the lack of facilities in Furzewell for a proposed huge influx of new residents. *Disgusted Furzewell Ratepayer* challenged the council leader to come to Furzewell and look at the village himself *as he's probably never even been here*, while *Mr A. P. of High Meadow estate* made the point that even the new residents were shocked at the plan. *The park was one of the reasons we decided to move here, as we have two small children and loved the fact that they'd be able to play there safely*, he wrote. There were even letters from people in neighbouring smaller villages, who'd been in the habit of driving to Furzewell to walk their dogs or just to enjoy the wide open space. *If the council had bothered to look after Furzewell Park and maintain its facilities, it wouldn't have been 'underused', as they claim*, a Mrs Duggan of Little Blackmoor ranted. *Lots more people would want to come and enjoy this lovely park if the grass was cut, the toilets were open and the play equipment was in better condition.*

Don't tell us you can't afford to do that, not when our council tax goes up every year.

'Look at this,' I called to Mum, who'd started to walk off to the kitchen. 'All these angry letters about the park. I must tell the others.'

We'd set up a WhatsApp group for the dog walkers, and I used this now to message them all.

I know! Sara's reply came back almost instantly. *And there are even more on the Recorder's website!*

We need to act quickly, Amber messaged, *while people are so worked up about it.*

By the time the other two had responded, Sara had replied that she'd already drafted her letter to all the residents and was now emailing it to us to make sure we were happy with it before getting it printed off so that we could deliver a copy to every house in Furzewell. When I read her draft a few minutes later, I had to admit I was impressed. She had quite rightly asserted that most people never bothered to plough through too much text and in just a few lines had summed up our intention to fight the proposal, urging people to sign the online petition I'd now set up, to attend a public meeting the following week in the village hall, and meanwhile to make as much use of the park as they could, to prove the council wrong. Also to keep Bank Holiday Monday free if possible for a major event there – more details to be revealed at the meeting.

'That was clever of her,' I said to Craig later when we were walking the dogs. 'Holding back some of the information, to keep them interested.'

'And more to the point,' he said grimly, 'we haven't *got* any more information yet. Getting this thing off the ground is going to be one hell of a rush.'

'I know. But Sara's really got the bit between her teeth. She already knows exactly what we have to do to conform to all the council's rules and regulations about holding public events,' I said. However reluctant I was to admit it, I couldn't help admiring her for the way she was handling it. But Craig just laughed.

'Yes, but all this – looking at council regulations, legal stuff, writing documents – it's her forte, isn't it. She's in her element, if you ask me. And of course, she just *loves* to be in charge.'

I looked back at him, somewhat surprised. The teacher's pet, criticising the head girl? Surely not. I only just stopped myself from saying, with childish glee, *Oh, and here was I thinking you liked her*.

Sara wasn't with us on the walk that day. She'd said in one of her messages earlier that she'd be too busy *progressing our campaign*. Mia had come with me on her little bike, as she often did now on Saturdays, and was riding ahead of us on the wide paths through the park, stopping every now and then to look back and wait for us to catch up, calling out to the dogs and laughing as they trotted up to her, wagging their tails. Amber was walking just behind us with Simon, and I could hear them discussing, loudly and animatedly, the various posts people had left on the *Recorder*'s website about the park proposal.

Smartie was still on his lead – I never let him off until we were in the furthest area of the park, away from the paths and the areas where children might be playing. I looked down at him trotting along beside me, and smiled to myself, enjoying the way he kept a watchful eye on his doggy friends, as if he were aware that they were older and wiser than him and he should learn good canine manners from them. He was growing fast, his little legs now quite stout and sturdy, but he still had that adorable puppy fluffiness about him that melted my heart.

'Cute little chap, isn't he,' Craig said, noticing my smile. He glanced from Smartie to his own Judy, walking obediently at heel with no need for a lead and a superior expression on her face. 'Are you going to get him neutered?'

'Yes, of course. The vet says six months is a good age for it.'

'Good.' He laughed. 'Judy's been spayed, but I'm not sure about Babette. We don't want any shenanigans going on in the group, do we? Not among the dogs, anyway.'

I looked up at him – he was so tall I almost had to crick my neck to do so, despite my own height – and couldn't help noticing how his laughter caused little creases around his eyes and mouth. He really was a very attractive man. Realising I'd been staring at him, I felt myself blush and looked away quickly, but not before he'd given me another little grin and added in that teasing voice of his:

'Shenanigans among the humans, on the other hand, are fine, of course.'

'You think so?' I countered, keeping my eyes fixed firmly on Smartie now.

'Of course. Human shenanigans are much more civilised than dog shenanigans,' he said. 'Humans do at least get a room.'

'Well, I'd hope so.' I smiled. I'd recovered slightly now from my embarrassment and was beginning to enjoy the banter. 'It wouldn't do for humans to start *shenanigan-ing* in the park in broad daylight, would it?'

He chuckled again, more softly this time. There was something very suggestive about that laugh. He leaned a little closer to me as we walked, close enough to speak straight into my ear, in little more than a whisper:

'Haven't you ever done that, then? I bet you have.'

'No, I haven't!' I protested, laughing back at him. My ear was tingling from his whisper, from his breath.

'You've never lived, then,' he said. 'Not that it'd be a very pleasant proposition in this kind of weather.' The rain of the preceding days had lessened to a miserable, persistent drizzle, and even as I giggled and shook my head at the whole silly turn of conversation, I could see that he had a point. 'No,' he went on, 'it's a summertime activity, that's for sure, although May *is* actually the traditional month for such things, of course.'

'Is it?' I was still giggling. 'Why?'

'You don't know?' He made a great play of staring at me and shaking his head. 'Nicola Pearce, I'm surprised at you. You grew up around here, in the countryside, and you've never heard that famous old country rhyme about the first of May?'

'No, I haven't,' I said. 'Tell me.'

His smile broadened. He leaned closer again, and this time, I swear his lips were actually touching my ear as he whispered huskily:

'*Hooray, hooray, the first of May. Outdoor sex begins today*!'

'Oh, *that*!' I laughed out loud, pushing him away, not wanting him to notice that he'd actually made me shiver. It was just his breath, his mouth, tickling my ear, that was all. 'That stupid verse the kids at school used to say. I thought you meant something *serious*.'

'Of course it's serious,' he replied, but he was laughing too. 'What goes for the birds and the bees – and the dogs, I suppose, unless they've been neutered – surely goes for humans too. May is the month, mark my words.'

'Well, there's not too much of May left,' I said.

'No.' He sounded regretful. 'You're right. Oh well, there's always next year, I suppose.'

We'd reached the far side of the park, and I was glad in a way to drop the subject, to pick up Mia's bike from where she'd left it lying on the grass when the path ran out, call her back from the tree she was attempting to climb, let Smartie off his lead and watch him jump and skip through the long, wet grass after Judy and the other dogs. As we all stood for a while to wait for them to have their play, we went back to discussing the park, in particular how much it needed tending to, if we were going to be ready for a pet show at the end of August. Simon started to tell us that, if the council refused to tidy up the park, he'd tackle the job himself, as long as he had a few volunteers helping. He had all the equipment, after all, and could do the work on Sundays.

'I'd give you a hand with that, mate, no worries at all,' Craig said. 'Not that I know one end of a lawnmower from the other, but if you need some muscle—' he flexed his arms, and grinned at me, '—I'm your man.'

'What a show-off,' Amber whispered to me behind her hand, tickling my ear in a way that reminded me uncomfortably of how Craig's lips had felt. 'He so loves himself, doesn't he?'

'Oh, he's harmless, isn't he? He just likes a joke,' I whispered back. 'He's fun.'

'Mm. I noticed the two of you *joking* just now. Careful, Nic. As you know, he's a bit of a ladies' man.'

'What?' I took her by the elbow and moved her further away, to make sure we weren't overheard by Craig and more importantly by Mia, who rarely missed a trick. 'Amber, I'm not *interested*. Not in him, not in anyone. For God's sake.' I stared at her. 'It's Sara who likes him, unless I'm missing something? Are *you* interested in him?'

'No, absolutely not.' She snorted and shook her head. 'As if! I've told you already, he's not my type.'

'Well, OK, but look, we were just having a laugh and being silly together, that's all. Anyway, I realise he and Sara might be—'

'Not as far as I know,' she said sharply. 'But I doubt that'd stop him, even if they were having a thing together. He's only ever after a hook-up, take my word for it.'

'Has he tried it on with you, then?' I said. I was starting to get a bit irritated, feeling like I was defending myself and Craig. I was thirty-five, for God's sake, and if I wanted to have a few jokes with Craig what did it matter? It was none of Amber's business or anyone else's.

'No,' she replied, abruptly. There was a silence. I was just about to shrug and walk back to join the group when she added: 'Look, sorry, Nic. It's just that I know how much you've been hurt. Splitting up with Josh – it's still so recent, isn't it? I don't want you to make any disastrous mistakes right now, just ... I don't know ... just because you're lonely, or to get back at Josh, or whatever.'

'Well, I'm sorry you think I'm so pathetic but I'm not lonely,' I said quietly. 'And I'm not trying to get back at Josh. It was just quite nice, for a few minutes there, to forget about everything and have a bit of a laugh.'

'Point taken. And again, I'm sorry if that came out all wrong.'

She smiled and linked her arm through mine. I gave a grunt of acceptance. If she was only looking out for me, fair enough, that was what friends did and I should be grateful. But she had been quite forceful in warning me off Craig. I still had a sneaky suspicion that she liked him more than she was letting on. But as she'd denied it, I'd just have to take her word for it.

CHAPTER 17

Amber had been my best friend from our very first day at Furzewell Primary. She was cleverer than me, better at exams, more sure of herself, but neither of us seemed to care about any of that. There was no jealousy between us. When she was eleven and already wearing a bra, I was going through the worst of my *Nic the Stick* phase. I'd have loved to have had her shape instead of being straight up and down, but whenever I said so, she'd pull a face and tell me it wasn't actually very nice to have boys smirking and gawping at her chest. A few years later, when other girls suddenly started to compare me to the latest stick-thin, long-blonde-haired models in the celebrity magazines, Amber hadn't grown any taller, but had filled out to the point where she was teased for being little and round, and it was my turn to remind her that boys preferred girls with boobs and bums. To say nothing of brains, which she had in abundance.

In fact, we both ended up getting our fair share of attention from the opposite sex. Because there was nowhere much to go in Furzewell, all the kids hung around in the only available places – the village green outside the pub and the park. The playground equipment was properly maintained in those days, and after the younger children for whom it was intended had gone home to bed, then – as with every generation before us, I'm sure – it became the province of us teenagers. It gave us girls the perfect opportunity to squeal and scream, pretending to be nervous when the boys pushed the swings too high or the roundabout too fast, and the perfect place for the boys to hold onto us, pretending to protect us but really just wanting to put their arms around us and try their luck. And, of course, if their luck was in, the park was deserted on winter nights, the corners behind the toilet block dark and sheltered. On summer evenings the grass in the wooded area was soft and scented, the shadows long and forgiving. So despite my heated denials to Craig, by the time I was seventeen I knew all about what was meant by the first of May. By then, Josh and I were already an item. Already talking about being together forever.

After that, there was never anyone else for me; my days of squealing on the swings and fumbles with various boys under the trees were over. But I'd still enjoy a laugh and joke with Amber, pretending to indulge in light flirtation when we were out on our own, or together with the other girls, just for her sake – because there never seemed to be anyone serious for Amber. Nothing that lasted longer than a few days, a few weeks, occasionally a month or so, before she dumped them with no sign of regret. After Josh and I married and moved away, we stayed in touch for a while, sometimes getting together at weekends. But eventually she moved to Bristol and our communication dwindled to the occasional text, Facebook message and comments on each other's Instagram posts. It was through these that I knew she'd remained single, with hardly ever a mention of anyone else in her life, never a photo or reference to anyone apart from various friends.

From our first accidental meeting back here in Furzewell, I'd wondered if she'd perhaps been hurt by someone and didn't want to talk about it. If I attempted to reminisce with her now about our teenage years – about those nights in the park, the boys we kissed and teased, the fun we had with them – she seemed to close up, making it clear it wasn't a memory lane she wanted to walk down with me. So now I normally kept off the subject of relationships when I was with her, which made it all the more surprising that she'd decided to lecture me about Craig.

Her interference had felt unnecessary – and a bit humiliating. If she *was* nursing a secret desire for Craig herself, maybe she was feeling resentful about him flirting with me as well as Sara. But because we'd been friends for so long, I wanted to believe her. She was just looking out for me.

On the Monday, I thought it best to remind Mia while we were getting ready, that Eddie wouldn't be at school that morning. Her mouth turned down a little but she nodded and said, very seriously:

'I know, Mummy. But I want to make him a get-well card. Can we go and see him after school so I can take it to him?'

'Of course we can. That's a lovely idea.'

I was so relieved that she seemed to be handling the temporary absence of her new buddy better than I'd expected, that I almost forgot, when I was saying goodbye to her outside her classroom, that I'd planned to warn her teacher that today might be a little difficult. But I needn't have worried. Mia was already telling Mr Gregory, in quite a calm, grown-up way:

'Eddie can't come to school today. He's got the chicken-spots. I'm going to see him after school, so I can take him a new reading book if you like.'

'Thank you, Mia,' Mr Gregory said, raising his eyebrows at me and giving me a smile. 'That's very helpful of you.'

I went into my reception class feeling almost euphoric with relief. My little girl was growing up, and as long as I managed not to think about the fact that Eddie wouldn't be in her class any more from September, I could believe that she was going to be happy and thrive in Furzewell.

When I collected her after school, she'd made, as promised, a get-well card, with a picture of a dog on the front and *Dear Edie I hop you sone feel beter luve from Mia x x x* written inside. I'd bought some chocolate for him and a football magazine he liked, and we took these round to Louise's house, together with his new reading book. He seemed well enough, although his itchy spots were causing him grief, and he and Mia immediately ran off to play, while Louise put the kettle on.

'How are you managing about your work while he's off school?' I asked her.

She normally worked part-time hours to fit in with school times.

'I've had to take some of my annual leave. Unfortunately, I'd already booked a week off next week for half-term, so that will be another chunk of it gone.' She sighed. 'I'm a bit worried about the long summer holiday, to be honest. My mum's offered to have him for a week – she lives in Cornwall – and I'm taking the following week off myself to stay down there with him. Other than that, I've been looking at holiday childcare – you know, activity clubs and so on – but I worry that Eddie's going to struggle with it, especially if he doesn't know anyone there.'

'Oh, he can come and play with Mia,' I said at once. 'Sorry, I should have thought of it before. I'm lucky, working at the school I don't have to worry about holidays. Let's compare our diaries. Mia will be going to Lanzarote with her dad for ten days in the middle of the holiday, but the rest of the time she'd be pleased to bits to have Eddie with us.'

'Are you sure? I'll pay you whatever the holiday clubs would have charged me—'

'Don't be silly. It'll keep Mia happy. I'm sure you'd return the favour if I needed it.'

'Of course, and you're an angel. It'd be a weight off my mind, even if it's just for one week.'

'I'm sure we can do more than that. If you can work it that you, or your mum, has Eddie for the weeks Mia's away with Josh, we can cover the whole holiday between us.'

She paused. 'But aren't you going away yourself at all?'

'No.' I shook my head. 'Can't afford it, to be honest. I don't mind. It still feels a little bit like a holiday, being back here in Furzewell.'

'Then you and Mia must come to Cornwall with us. Yes, really, I insist. Mum and Charles – my stepdad – would be happy to have you, I know. They've got lots of room, and they live near the beach. It'll make me feel better about you having Eddie for the other weeks.'

By the time we left for home, we had our holiday all arranged, and although I wasn't going to tell Mia about it yet, I felt a lightness in my heart just at the thought of it. At my insistence, Louise had called her mum while I was still with her, to make sure it really was OK with her. And as soon as I got home, I checked with Mum that she could look after Smartie for the week. A week by the sea with our new friends really was an unexpected bonus.

Already I'd come to think of Louise as a good friend. We might not have known each other for long but we'd developed such a strong bond. We understood each other's problems, both being mums bringing up our children without their fathers. I had to admit, I had more in common with Louise now than I did with Amber – who suddenly didn't seem to understand me quite so well at all. The realisation made me feel a bit disloyal; it had been so exciting to be reunited with my old friend, and already I was drifting closer to someone new. Well, there was room in life for more than one good friend, I told myself firmly. Nothing to feel guilty about. Amber and I still enjoyed our walks together with our dogs, and we went back a long way – even if our lives were now so different.

Eddie was back at school for the last two days before the half-term holiday, and as school broke up, the weather changed for the better again, filling us all once again with the optimism of summer. The trees that had been beaten down by rain were now shining in the sunshine with their fresh green leaves. Fields were scattered with cornflowers and by the end of the week, as we turned into June, even the first poppies were beginning to appear.

Mia had an extended stay with Josh during that holiday week, from the Saturday to the Tuesday, and to my surprise I found that it didn't hurt so much now when she ran out to his car, waving goodbye. I was slowly getting used to it. Even more surprisingly, Josh waved to me himself as they drove off, and when he brought her back on the Tuesday evening, we chatted for a few minutes on the doorstep. In fact, I'd found myself thinking, afterwards, that the conversation had been quite nice: he'd sounded genuinely interested when he'd asked how I was settling down in Furzewell; he'd smiled and nodded and seemed in no rush to leave. It was nice that we could be like this with each other, for Mia's sake, although it had left me feeling a bit wistful, and almost lonely, after he'd gone.

I still found it hard, though, to accept the way he took Mia out for expensive treats and brought her home, every time, with presents. Was he *bribing* her to look forward to seeing him? I tried to put myself in his shoes, to imagine how he felt, but every time, it just came back to this: he'd never made any effort when we lived with him. It was too late to start now.

For the remainder of the week, Mia and I went for long walks with Smartie, sometimes with some of the other dog walkers, sometimes with Louise and Eddie, who also often came to play with us in the garden at Eagle House.

'You're welcome to come to mine instead, obviously,' she said, 'but it's so lovely here, with all this lawn and trees, and shrubs, compared with my little postage stamp of a garden.' She laughed. 'And anyway, until I get around to doing something with it, it's just an empty space. I really need a gardener to put in a few flowerbeds. I'm clueless myself and I haven't got a lot of spare time.'

'Actually, one of the dog walkers – Simon – is a landscape gardener. If you like, I'll ask him to call round and give you a quote. He's been doing quite a few gardens on your estate.'

'That would be great. Thanks, Nic.'

On the last day of the holiday we took the two children to the Fox and Goose for a pub lunch, sitting outside in the sunshine. I asked Mum if she'd like to join us when she finished at the shop, but she said she was going straight to Plymouth after work to meet a friend for lunch.

'It's so nice here,' Louise sighed as we enjoyed our drinks and sandwiches at a table in the shade of the big oak tree.

'Yes. It was our favourite thing – me and Josh – back when we lived here before. We were still kids, really. We lived in the flat over the shop, and there wasn't much money to spare after we'd paid the rent, but once a week, on a Saturday, we came here for lunch like this. Funny, I don't remember it ever raining or being cold enough to sit inside the pub. It must have been, obviously, but in my memory it was always sunny.' I glanced across the table at Mia, but she and Eddie were chatting and laughing so loudly I didn't think she'd overhear. 'And we were always happy,' I added quietly, feeling my eyes smart with unshed tears.

Louise put her hand over mine. I hadn't really talked to her much about Josh before.

'And you'll be happy again,' she said. 'I'm sure of it. You've got Mia, and Smartie, and your mum and gran here in Furzewell. And you love it here, don't you. You belong here.'

'Thanks, Lou.' I smiled at her. 'I know, you're right, I'm lucky, really. Things could be much worse.'

'Yes.' She laughed. 'You could have had a whole brood of kids – imagine how hard *that* would be, on your own. I must admit I'm glad now that I only had the one.'

I nodded and took another bite of my sandwich. Louise couldn't possibly have known why I had a lump in my throat at the mention of that.

CHAPTER 18

Mum didn't come home from Plymouth until halfway through the evening. Mia was in bed, Smartie asleep at my feet and I was dozing in front of the TV when I heard her key in the door.

'Hello!' I said, jumping up as she came in. 'Did you have a good time? Want a cup of tea?'

'Yes, please.' She yawned and smiled. 'Sorry I'm a bit late.'

I laughed. 'It must have been a good pub lunch.'

'Yes. It sort of ... turned into dinner.'

I looked at her. She had a kind of glow about her, a contented smile on her face and her eyes were sparkling. She was wearing a new dress, too, and I couldn't help noticing how nice she looked – not overdressed with too much make-up, the way she sometimes was when she went out with the Gruesome Twosome. This was no girly get-together she'd been to, that was for sure!

'So it was nice?' I asked again carefully as I filled the kettle.

'Very nice, thank you. And before you ask – or try to avoid asking, because I can see you're dying to know – yes, it was a date. But don't worry, it's nothing serious.'

'Why would I worry? You have to live your own life, Mum, and if you meet someone, and it's serious, well—'

She held up her hand to stop me.

'That's not going to happen. I don't want a relationship with a man. Going out for lunch, for dinner, whatever, is fine. But I'm never living with anyone again.'

The kettle boiled, I poured water on the teabags and it wasn't until we sat down together that I'd worked up the courage to ask her why.

'You know why,' she retorted – as I knew she would.

'Because of Dad. Yes, but not every man you meet will be like him, or behave like him. There are good men out there, Mum.'

'I know. I just had dinner with one of them.' She smiled. 'But that doesn't mean I want to live with him.'

'Fair enough. I feel the same way myself so I don't blame you.'

'Well, there you are, then. Once bitten, and all that. And anyway, I like my life just the way it is. I want to have fun, go out with whoever I want, and enjoy myself. Not be shackled to someone again and have to wash his smelly socks.'

I laughed. 'So there's never been anyone serious for you, all these years, since Dad left?'

'No. Well...' She hesitated for a moment, and I looked up at her, surprised. 'Well, not really. There's one person, only one, who I was seeing for quite a while. I could have been tempted, I suppose.' There was that little sparkle in her eyes again, just for a moment. 'But no, it's not what I want, Nic. I've made up my mind. I don't want to be tied down.'

'But did he – this man – want it to be more serious?'

She smiled again. 'He still does. He's the one I saw today. We still see each other sometimes – we're still friends. He's a lovely man, but he understands and respects my feelings about it.'

'But he'd jump like a shot if you changed your mind?'

She shrugged. 'I won't.'

And with that it was clear that the subject was closed. But it was the most Mum had ever told me about her feelings regarding relationships. And I couldn't help feeling a bit sad about this mystery man who seemed to mean so much to her – but not quite enough to melt that bitterness in her heart about my dad.

It happened when I was only eleven years old and we were on a family holiday. Mum had always wanted to visit Ireland. Her ancestors, several generations back, had come from Dublin, and it had always held a fascination for her. Seeing the place for herself had been a kind of romantic dream, and I can still remember her excitement that summer as we packed our cases. That was what made it all the harder.

On about the second or third day, we were strolling around the Temple Bar area when it began to pour with rain. We dived into a pub. It was lunchtime, and luckily they served sandwiches, so we settled at a table and I sipped my orange-juice while Mum and Dad had a pint of Guinness each.

'Oh, lovely, they're going to play some traditional folk music,' Mum said delightedly as we noticed a group of people at a nearby table picking up their instruments – a bodhran, tin whistle, banjo and fiddle.

The girl playing the fiddle was tall, slim and beautiful. She had waist-length auburn hair, bright green eyes, and a smile that lit up the room. To me, a skinny, awkward girl on the cusp of adolescence, she looked like a fairy-tale Celtic princess. I couldn't take my eyes off her, watching her every move and carried away by imagining how it would feel to be like this vision of perfection myself. I was so entranced by the lilt of her accent as she announced each song and thanked us for our applause, by the way she looked and the way she played, tapping her foot, swinging her body as her bow flew across the strings, her short blue dress swaying with the rhythm – that I didn't even notice my dad's face, his mouth dropping open, his eyes out on stalks as he stared at her so intently, until I heard Mum say, laughing:

'Stop slobbering, Phil!'

Mum wouldn't have laughed if she'd been able to see into the future. When the band stopped for a break, Dad was instantly up on his feet, heading to the bar to buy them all a drink. He perched himself on a bar stool next to the auburn-haired girl, and within minutes they were chatting and laughing together.

'Look at him,' Mum said, mildly amused. 'Silly old fool.'

Dad wasn't old, of course. He was thirty-seven at the time, and (from what I remember, and from looking at old photos), a charming, good-looking man. Siobhan was twenty-two. And although Mum had been condescendingly tolerant of him *making a damned fool of himself* over her that lunchtime, teasing him about it when we left, what she didn't know was that they'd already exchanged contact details. That they'd arranged to meet up that evening, when Dad went out from our B&B after dinner for his usual *quick stroll and a pint.* Or that within days, he would have told Siobhan he was besotted with her and nothing was going to stand in the way of the two of them being together. And then he told Mum the same thing.

It was horrendous for both of us. Mum went into a kind of catatonic state of disbelief. At first she thought he was joking and was in denial about it, then convinced herself that it was just a silly infatuation, that he'd come to his senses by the end of the holiday. But he left us immediately, moving out of the B&B and into Siobhan's flat, phoning his boss to resign from his job, getting work as a barman in the very pub where he and Siobhan had met. At only eleven, I couldn't appreciate the full extent of what was happening, and didn't have the maturity or the words to comfort my mum – I just felt bewildered and frightened by her distress. At the end of the week we flew home, just the two of us, and that was when it really hit me what was happening. My own state of shock and grief, now I understood that Dad was actually staying behind, was almost as deep as Mum's. We both kept trying to tell ourselves that he'd soon be back, begging for forgiveness. But the weeks went by and at first there were terrible rows over the phone, then his number was abruptly changed, Mum's angry letters started coming back stamped 'gone away', and then there was nothing. Nothing, ever again. Nothing for her and nothing for me, his only daughter, either.

Gran and Grandad urged her to hire private detectives to try to track him down, and her friends felt she should talk to solicitors and try to get money out of him – maintenance payments to help with my upbringing – but she refused. She cleared out all his stuff, and at the same time seemed determined to wipe out his memory. He simply disappeared from our lives. The whole thing was horribly distressing and confusing to me. It felt almost as if he'd died but worse, in a way, because then at least we'd have talked about him. We'd still have had his photos around the house, instead of them being taken down and torn up. We'd have shared happy memories of him and eventually that could have eased our grief. But this felt almost as if he'd never existed, as if I'd never had a father at all, one who'd appeared to love me and love my mum, and act like a normal dad, like other people's dads – until Ireland happened.

So yes, I could understand Mum's bitterness, her refusal, even now, to talk about him. I could easily have grown up hating him myself, but instead I only ever thought of him with bewildered puzzlement, regret and a sense of loss. How could he have done that? Did he really feel *nothing* for us? Even now, I could understand the falling in love, the crime of passion as it were – not condone it, but understand it – but I couldn't understand the complete shrugging off of a wife and child as if they were nothing. Within the family, he was never even mentioned now.

The next day was Saturday and that evening we were hosting our public meeting about the park at the village hall. Mum had offered – despite the rug disaster on the previous occasion – to look after Mia and Eddie again, so that Louise could come. Like before, I felt a bit guilty about her having to cope, not only with the extra noise and mess involved in having a small child and a puppy in her house, but also our increasingly frequent guest in Eddie. But she was insistent.

'You and Louise both need to be there. You can fill me in with all the news, whatever gets decided at the meeting,' she said. 'I'm just as keen as you are to stop this nonsense about selling the park.'

It seemed, as we sat at a table on the stage, facing the crowd gradually filling the little hall, that everybody in Furzewell felt the same way.

'We've run out of chairs,' Louise reported back to us, having gone down into the auditorium to see how Simon and Craig were coping, ushering people in at the door.

'Well, that can only be a good thing,' I said. 'As long as people don't mind standing.'

On the dot of eight o'clock, Sara stood up and greeted everyone.

'It's fantastic to see so many of you here. I'm sorry some of you are having to stand at the back,' she said. She had no need of a microphone. Her voice could have carried all the way to the park. 'Perhaps you'd like to raise your hand if you really do need a seat, and maybe if there's anyone young and fit sitting down they might be kind enough to give theirs up for you.'

'Nice touch,' Craig, sitting next to me, muttered. 'Showing her human, compassionate side at the start of the meeting. Didn't realise she had one.'

Once the seat-shuffling had finished, Sara swiftly outlined the most important points of the meeting. First of all, the petition: it was on a clipboard on the table at the back of the hall for anyone who hadn't signed it online, so that the council could receive it as soon as possible. Secondly, the use of the park: imperative that we all increased this, despite the state it was in, and the lack of facilities. We should think of ways to make the most of the open space. Hold family picnics, kids' activities – didn't we all need to get them away from their screens, especially now summer was here? – and perhaps the leaders of local clubs like the Brownies could hold fun sports days there. And finally – she'd built up to this with increasing volume and passion as she waved aside interruptions, promising everyone a chance to have their say when she'd finished – the main event. The *committee*, she announced – and the rest of us up on the stage looked at each other in surprise at having been called something so official – were arranging a pet show, to be held in the park on Bank Holiday Monday, and we needed all the support we could get, to make this a success.

Needless to say, as soon as Sara uttered the words 'Any questions?', we were deafened by people calling out, and Simon then took over, asking for raised hands, and calmly took one question at a time. Most of the questions concerned the council's response to our plans, whether they'd approved of what we were doing and whether we'd checked all the legal requirements – Sara came into her own again here, of course. And when these had all been dealt with, she closed by asking for anyone who was prepared to lend a hand with a tidy-up of the park, to please come up and give us their names. Reverend Timms, acting as a spokesperson for the audience, stood up to thank us and led a round of applause, and the meeting finally closed, with an excited queue of people wanting to add their names as helpers, and another queue to sign the petition.

'Wow,' said Louise, as by mutual agreement, we, 'the committee', retired to the pub after everyone had gone. 'That was amazing. Everyone in the village must have turned up.'

'Not quite,' said Sara, who'd apparently done a quick headcount tonight, having already obtained the exact up-to-date population figure from her friend on the parish council. 'But definitely a very large majority.'

'Well, we've got a really good number of people prepared to help with the clear-up,' said Simon, who'd already volunteered to be in charge of this. He had all their phone numbers or emails and was going to contact them to make a start the following weekend. 'If we can get the grass cut, the flowerbeds and shrubberies tidied up, the park will already start to look more welcoming.'

'The vicar told me he'll organise a Sunday school picnic there next month, with races and games for the kids,' Amber said.

We all reported back, telling each other about people who'd approached us at the end of the meeting with their ideas. Brown Owl was going to take the Brownies there for a nature ramble and treasure hunt. The parent-and-toddler group would consider shifting their meetings from the village hall to the park on sunny days. The youth club leader – who turned out to be none other than our friend with the tattoos and desperate love for his missing kitten – offered his gang of teenagers, and some youth club funds, to reinstall white lines and goals to the long-neglected football pitch so that they could hold some local friendlies in the park.

'If we have enough helpers, we could weed the tennis courts, too,' Craig said.

'The nets need replacing,' Sara pointed out. She put her glass down and added, looking around at us all: 'Ideally, we need to raise some cash. The youth club shouldn't have to pay for the football goals. It should be a community cost.'

'But the council have told us they won't fund any of this,' I said.

'Exactly. Not until the final decision's been made about the sell-off, anyway. So, *ideally,*' she repeated, 'we need to raise the funds ourselves. What I'm thinking is, we should ask all these people who are supporting us to become Friends of Furzewell Park too. We – the six of us – can't do it on our own. They all then pay a modest amount every year, which goes towards upkeep and costs. We can have family memberships, of course, and reductions for pensioners—'

'We don't even know if the park will stay open for another year,' I protested.

'No. But if the council knew we were considering doing this, there'd be a much better chance that it *would* stay open.' She paused, looked down for a minute, as if she wasn't quite sure whether she ought to be telling us this, and then went on: 'I've been looking into it.' *Of course she had*, I thought. She was so fiercely determined and organised that I couldn't help admiring her. 'It's not a new idea. In fact, it's becoming more and more common for community groups to help meet the financial cost of keeping parks and green spaces open. I've seen an estimated annual figure of thirty million pounds quoted, as the amount raised by groups like this around the country.'

There was a stunned silence.

'Thirty *million*?' Craig repeated, with a whistle.

'Yes. Nationwide that is,' she repeated.

'So why didn't you suggest this at the meeting?' I asked, and she looked at me, eyebrows raised.

'Why do you think? People are on our side at the moment – one hundred per cent. They want the park kept open, even if they've never used it in their lives, because they don't like the council taking something away from them that they consider they're already paying for. Introduce the idea of paying – even a small amount – on *top* of their council tax, for the same purpose, and we risk losing the support of half of them.'

We all nodded, in agreement. I took a gulp of my beer. Although we could see the sense of what she was saying, we probably all realised it would be tricky to persuade people to contribute financially.

'So you think we *shouldn't* even ask them, then?' Simon asked.

'Actually, I definitely think we should. But let's keep it to ourselves for now. Meanwhile, if you're all in agreement – think about it overnight, if you like—'

'Gee, thanks,' Craig muttered.

'—then we can start to think about *how* to encourage people to join. Probably the best incentive would be to suggest the kind of facilities we might be able to fund, if we're successful in keeping the park open.'

'That sounds sensible,' I said. 'But there's no point asking people to pay an annual membership now, when the park still might be closed by the end of the year.'

'We wouldn't take any money from them until we know the answer to that, of course,' she agreed, giving me a look that implied I must be stupid. 'But we'd need to know if the majority would be in favour of the idea. Meanwhile, we'll be getting the work started on tidying up the park and organising our pet show anyway, which will hopefully continue to get everyone fired up with enthusiasm.'

As far as Sara was concerned, I thought as we walked home from the pub later, the decision was already made – and she was probably quite right, as always, I conceded reluctantly. The council were less likely to sell off the park if we showed how serious we were about helping to maintain it. I still wasn't really too fond of Sara. I couldn't help it; her bossiness and self-important manner got to me. But on the other hand, I could see that these were the very qualities that made her a born leader. And although she'd been delegating various tasks to the rest of us – tasks she apparently felt we were just about capable of taking on – there was no doubt we needed her leadership. I might not have liked her, but I had to admit to a growing respect for her.

CHAPTER 19

The half-term holiday was now over, Mia and I were back at school, and 'flaming June' was living up to its promise, as we woke up every day to sunshine, and a warmth in the air even first thing in the morning. The grounds of Eagle House, so easy to care for because they were mainly laid to lawn, broken up only by a few collections of mature trees and shrubs, were at their best now, with our late-flowering azaleas and rhododendrons fully in bloom, giving us a fabulous display of colour. Gardens along the lanes were overflowing with roses and lilies, camellias and peonies, and one of the fields on the edge of the village was a sea of the stunning bright blue of cultivated linseed.

'June is such a beautiful month,' Simon said, when one evening that week we were the only two to turn up for the dog walk. It was such a lovely evening and we'd walked on, beyond the park, down the lane to Cuckoo Copse where the birds were still singing, and tiny insects darted about in the sunshine filtering down between the branches of the trees. Max bounded ahead of us, pushing his way through the undergrowth, with little Smartie trotting faithfully behind him.

'Yes, it is,' I agreed, sighing with contentment. It was still so warm that we were both in T-shirts and shorts. 'But not always. This weather is pretty unusual.'

'That's why we have to make the most of it.' He glanced at me. 'Are you in a rush to get home?'

'Not particularly.' Mia was already in bed, and Mum was watching one of her favourite soaps.

'Shall we do a circuit of the copse and head back via the pub for a quick one?'

'That sounds good,' I smiled. Simon was, I'd already decided, probably the nicest and most uncomplicated member of our little group. Kind, considerate, always with a good word to say about everyone and with a sort of old-fashioned courtesy about him.

We caught up with the dogs and walked on through the copse, returning them to their leads at the far end, where Cuckoo Lane joined Fore Street. Smartie was slowing down, looking weary from trying to keep up with his bigger friend, and while I found a table outside the pub, Simon went inside to order our beers and bring a bowl of water out for them both. For a while, we chatted some more about Sara's ideas for the park, and he told me how many people he had lined up to help him with the first gardening session that coming weekend.

'I'll be able to help, too,' I said. 'It's Mia's weekend for seeing her dad, so I don't have anything planned.'

'It must seem quiet without her,' Simon sympathised.

'Oh, it's not so bad now. I'm getting used to it,' I said, sitting up straight and trying to sound positive. 'Josh was hostile at first but now we're managing to get on OK, it isn't quite such an ordeal as it was.'

'Good.' He gave me a half-apologetic little smile. 'Maybe his hostility was because he was so hurt – about you leaving? It must have been hard on him too.'

I stared at him. 'Hurt? Hardly! He didn't even care.'

'Perhaps he regrets that now, then. If, as you say, things have improved between you?'

'I doubt he regrets anything,' I retorted. 'And I wouldn't say things have improved *that* much. He's just ... more civil.'

'So do you see yourselves ever managing to get back together?'

'What?' I looked at him again, quite shocked now. 'No! Definitely not. I wouldn't have moved out – put Mia through all this – if I'd had any doubt that this time it was final.'

'I see.' He nodded. His expression gave nothing away, but it had given me a start of surprise that he'd asked something quite so personal. It wasn't like him, not like his usual way of keeping a polite, thoughtful but considerate distance. And it felt weird that he had, in a way, tried to defend Josh. 'Well, it's good, at least, that you have your mum, and your gran, here in the village,' he said now. 'That must be a great help.'

'Yes, it is.' I smiled, glad the conversation had moved away from Josh.

We went back to discussing how he was planning to start tidying up the park, the grass cutting and weed clearing, and all the work to be done. When we'd eventually finished our drinks and got up to leave, I had to wake Smartie, who'd fallen fast asleep under the table, with Max lying protectively next to him.

'Poor little soul looks half drunk on his feet!' Simon laughed as Smartie staggered upright, blinking in the sunshine.

'He did well to keep up with Max in the copse,' I said. 'Come on, Smartie. Let's get you home.'

As we prepared to part company – Simon turning off Fore Street towards his own house before I did – he turned to me, smiling.

'I've enjoyed this evening, Nic. It makes a change, being just the two of us.'

'Yes, and a very welcome drink at the end,' I agreed.

'We should do it again.'

'Well, yes, no doubt we will,' I replied, slightly puzzled. There were often times when only a couple of the group turned up for the walk, so it was inevitable it would happen again.

'See you soon, then, Nic,' he said. 'Come on, Max.'

I watched them go, thinking again about what a lovely guy he was, and trying to shrug off the odd feeling it had given me when he'd seemed – just slightly, there – to take Josh's side. I supposed he couldn't help but see the male point of view, however sympathetic he'd been to me – but he didn't even know Josh. He might see things differently if he did.

*

The next afternoon, after school, Mia and I tried to call on Gran, as we often did on our way home, but there was no answer when we rang her doorbell.

'Maybe she's round at our house with Nanny,' Mia said. I was pleased, and relieved, that she'd started to call it *our house* now. The house in Plymouth had finally been relegated to *Daddy's house* and, most surprising of all, despite having spent an afternoon with them during her recent stay with Josh, she didn't talk much at all now about Polly and Jamila. We were moving on, slowly but surely.

'Yes, maybe she is,' I agreed. And sure enough, when we arrived home, Gran was there, sitting on the sofa with a cup of tea, looking unhappy as Mum fussed around getting biscuits out.

'Hello Gran,' I said, giving her a kiss. 'Fancy you being here – we just called at your place to see how you were.'

'Well, I'm not there, am I,' she said, surprisingly sharply. 'As you can see.'

'No.' I sat down next to her. 'Are you OK?'

'I'm fine. Stop fussing.'

'She's not fine, actually, Nicky,' Mum said, coming in with the biscuit tin just at that minute. 'She's locked herself out.'

'Oh dear. Well, it's not a problem, is it? We've got your spare key—' I began, but Mum interrupted me:

'She's locked herself out for the third time this week. It's getting to be a habit.'

'Oh.' I looked from one of them to the other, slightly puzzled by the tone of the conversation. It was hard to tell whether Mum was worried or annoyed, whereas Gran was definitely on the defensive.

'Twice already this week she's had to come back to the shop, leaving her bags on her doorstep, to borrow the spare key from me,' Mum explained. 'Lucky I carry it around with me, isn't it?'

Actually, I'd have thought it was obvious she'd always have the spare key on her. What else would she do, other than keep it on her own keyring in case she needed to let herself into Gran's bungalow in an emergency? But I sensed I'd better stay out of it until I understood exactly what was going on here. I just shrugged and said something to the effect that these things happen.

'Not three times in a week they don't,' Mum retorted. 'Now it turns out she never found her own key after she locked herself out yesterday morning, but still she went out this afternoon, shut the door behind her and toddled off to her Knit & Natter group in the village hall without a thought of how she was going to get back in.'

'I knew you had the spare key,' Gran muttered. 'I gave it back to you yesterday.' But I caught a flash of something in her eyes. She wasn't cross with Mum, or me. She was upset with herself.

I took hold of her hand. 'Never mind, Gran. I'll come back with you now and we'll look for your key together. It must be indoors somewhere, mustn't it?'

'That's not the point,' she said. 'As your mum says, it's ridiculous – three times in a week. I'm getting forgetful, aren't I. Old and daft and forgetful.' She glanced up at

Mum, who was standing beside her, shaking her head. 'Don't try and pretend that's not what you're thinking, Ros. I know damned well you think I'm losing my marbles and can't cope on my own. Well, maybe I am. Would that satisfy you? You'd be happy then, I suppose, if you were proved right – if I couldn't manage on my own anymore and you had to look after me? You never did want me to move out.'

'Don't talk like that, Gran,' I protested, as Mum gasped and actually took a step back in surprise at this outburst.

'Of course I don't think you're *losing your marbles* – what a horrible expression, anyway,' she said. 'I just think you're being a bit careless, that's why I'm ... well, frustrated with you. If I really thought you were too forgetful to manage on your own, I'd be worried, not happy about it. Honestly, Mum, do you really think I'm that heartless?'

Gran seemed to deflate. She leaned back against the sofa, sighing, and closed her eyes as if in defeat. 'All right, all right, I shouldn't have said that. I apologise. I'm just ... not ready, you know? Not ready to go into one of those bloody dementia homes.'

'Don't be silly, Gran,' I said, feeling a lump come to my throat. She was not only upset, she was frightened. That was what this was all about.

'You haven't got dementia,' Mum said, dropping the biscuit tin and sitting down on the other side of Gran on the sofa to put her arms around her. 'For God's sake, you've just forgotten your key. I shouldn't have got annoyed about it – Nicky's right, it doesn't matter, that's why we keep the spare one. You just weren't concentrating, that's all. You just have to make sure you put it back in your purse as soon as you've unlocked the door.'

'If you had dementia, Gran, you wouldn't just be forgetting your key. You wouldn't be able to remember what a key is, or what it's for,' I pointed out.

'But this isn't the only thing, is it,' she murmured. 'First I forgot were I'd put Mia's bunny, then I missed that doctor's appointment—'

'And we told you at the time, didn't we, that everybody does things like that. It doesn't mean you've got dementia,' I said.

She sniffed, not saying anything. Mum turned to pick up the biscuit tin from where she'd dropped it on the floor, and gave a shout that made both me and Gran jump.

'Smartie! Leave them, Smartie! Bad dog! Go to your bed.'

Smartie, his ears and tail drooping, looked up at us, his shiny black eyes round with surprise at this scolding. The lid of the tin had come off, and to be fair, how was he supposed to have known that biscuits thrown on the floor weren't meant for him?

'Ah, don't shout at the poor dog,' Gran said, sounding more like herself again. 'It's not his fault if you drop the bloody biscuits, Ros.'

'And whose fault was it that I dropped them?' Mum shot back. 'You with all your talk about dementia.'

And suddenly, just like that, all three of us were laughing.

'Daft old woman,' Mum muttered to Gran, wiping her eyes, still laughing.

'Silly old bat, yourself,' Gran retorted, chuckling.

'Honestly, you two!' I smiled, relieved that we were back to normal. I looked round at Smartie again. Having ignored the rather confused signals he'd been getting from the two older humans who were now, bafflingly, both convulsed with laughter, he was sniffing around on the carpet, hoping to hoover up any remaining biscuit crumbs, while Mia sat on the floor with her arms around him protectively.

'Poor Smartie,' she said, giving us all an admonishing look. 'He wasn't being naughty.'

'No. Sorry, Smartie,' Mum admitted, reaching out to give him a stroke.

There was a silence, a more comfortable one this time. We took a biscuit each and had just begun to relax when Mia piped up curiously:

'What's dementia, Gran?'

'I didn't realise she was listening,' Gran apologised later after, between us, we'd managed to give Mia a brief explanation that was neither fudging the truth nor too unnecessarily detailed, and Mia, seeming satisfied by our reassurance that none of us actually had it, had run off outside to play. 'I thought she was doing her homework.'

'A six-year-old can learn her spellings *and* earwig adult conversation at the same time,' I reminded her ruefully. 'We all should have realised that.'

Gran ended up staying for dinner and afterwards, with Smartie in tow, I walked back to Nightingale Court with her. Once inside the little bungalow, I helped her search for her own key, and eventually found it in the bathroom, on the shelf over the sink.

'Oh, I remember what happened now,' she said. 'The other day, I met Marion Potter for a coffee in Smiths before I did my shopping. By the time I got home, I was in a hurry for the toilet, so I ran straight into the bathroom. I must have still had the key in my hand, put it up there, and then forgot all about it.'

'Perfectly understandable,' I said. 'Now, look: there's no way you'd have been able to remember that, and work out what happened, if you had dementia. Are we in agreement?'

'I suppose so,' she said. 'I'm sorry, love. Sorry for causing all that fuss, getting your mum all agitated. What a nuisance I am to you both.'

I gave her a kiss. 'You're never a nuisance, Gran. And didn't we all have a good laugh in the end? And Mia's even learnt a new word!'

'Yes.' She gave another little chuckle now. 'I just hope she doesn't go into school talking about it tomorrow. Asking all her friends whether their grandparents have got dementia. Oh dear, it isn't really funny, is it. Not a subject for laughter at all, really.'

'No, not for the poor people who do have it. But we're not being disrespectful to them, Gran. And you know what they say: laughter's the best medicine.'

I was still smiling as I set off for my walk with Smartie. It helped me to forget the unease I'd felt, at the back of my mind earlier on, when I'd seen the fear in Gran's eyes.

I hoped to God, however forgetful she might become, that she'd never lose the sharpness of her wit, the clarity of her thoughts – everything that made her who she was. But I knew only too well, perhaps better than most, that life held no guarantees for any of us.

CHAPTER 20

The weather was still warm and fine, luckily, for Simon's gardening weekend at the park. There were about twenty of us meeting in the car park beside the park entrance. Some had brought garden tools with them and Simon, who'd arrived with his assistant, Terry, in their van, unloaded two ride-on petrol lawnmowers, and an assortment of their heavy-duty industrial tools for serious digging and cutting back.

We were all assigned jobs, in pairs, according to our experience, strength and fitness. I was paired with Amber to do some hoeing of the flowerbeds, which were so full of weeds it was hard to discern which flowers were struggling to survive in their choked environment. Between us, Amber and I just about managed to agree on which were weeds and which weren't – neither of us being particularly knowledgeable in horticulture – but Simon had reassured us that it wouldn't be the end of the world if a few flowers were culled by mistake.

'The beds have been neglected for so long, quite honestly they need to be dug up and replanted,' he said with a sigh. 'Not many of the flowers or shrubs look particularly happy or healthy. But until we have the funds to do it – or the council changes its mind and decides to fund the work themselves—'

'And pigs take off and fly across the park,' Amber put in, sarcastically.

'Quite. Until then, this just has to be a tidy-up. So be ruthless, girls. Hoe away.'

We did. We hoed until our arms ached, we threw huge clumps of weeds (we hoped) into the wheelbarrow and barely stopped to draw breath, never mind talk. I'd never done much gardening. At our house in Plymouth the garden had been tiny, and mostly laid to lawn with a little patio where we simply had a few plants in pots. Since I'd been back at Eagle House I'd helped Mum with the garden, but the biggest job was keeping the grass cut. That Saturday, after she'd finished at the shop, Mum turned up unexpectedly at the park with Smartie.

'I promised you I'd walk him this afternoon, didn't I,' she said. 'So I thought we'd come and see how you're getting on. Is that all you've done?' she added teasingly.

'*Thank* you!' I straightened up, rubbing my back. 'It's hard work in this heat, you know.'

'I know. And there's so much to do.' She looked around the park. Smartie, straining on his lead, was whimpering with excitement as he spotted all his favourite people – not just Amber and myself but Simon, away in the distance, riding one of the lawnmowers, Craig lopping dead branches off some sad-looking bushes near the disused pool, and Sara, dressed more casually than I'd ever seen her, walking around the perimeter, picking up litter and dropping it into a sack. 'I'll take Smartie for his walk, leave him back at home and come back to give you a hand,' Mum said decisively. 'At least I can tell a weed from a flower, which from the look of what's in that wheelbarrow, neither of you have quite managed to work out.'

'Simon said not to worry too much,' I laughed.

'OK, but it'd be nice if one or two of those poor astrantias were allowed to survive.'

She walked off, with Smartie trotting along excitedly beside her, and Amber and I looked at each other.

'Those poor *whats*?' she asked me.

'Search me,' I admitted. 'It sounds like we'll definitely benefit from Mum's expertise.'

By the time Simon called a halt to the work at lunchtime on the Sunday, we were all exhausted, especially those of us unused to that kind of labour.

'We've made a fantastic start,' he said. 'But it's been hot work, and you'll be wanting to get back to your families – or maybe just to the pub! Thanks again, all of you. If anyone is up for another go at it next week, we'll meet at the same time in the car park meeting point.'

I stared around me as we packed up the tools. Already, the park was looking better. Just having the grass cut to a decent length was a huge improvement. There was still work to do, and even after the tidy-up was finished, we'd need regular working sessions to keep it tidy if it wasn't going to revert to a jungle over the summer.

'I won't be able to do next weekend – I'll have Mia,' I said when, together with the other dog walkers, we retired to the Fox and Goose for a quick drink.

'Not being funny, Nic, but your mum would be more useful than you anyway,' Craig joked, and I gave him a shove, making him slop some of his beer down his T-shirt, and some of the others laughed.

'Sorry,' I said, with a grin. 'Hope it's not your best shirt.'

Like all of us, he was wearing old clothes, which were now streaked with dirt.

'Cheeky,' he replied, smiling back at me. 'I know you can't keep your hands off me, Nic.'

I felt myself flush as they all laughed again. It was probably just a touch of sunburn, I thought. Then I caught Amber frowning at me, and I hid my face behind my drink.

What's her problem? I thought, crossly. We were only joking around. Amber had told me she wasn't interested in Craig herself, and although I'd accepted that she'd been worried about me getting hurt, I didn't see why I should stop enjoying our little flirtations. It felt nice to be paid some attention for a change.

Our park campaign, in general, seemed to be gaining momentum at an unbelievable rate. Everywhere I went in the village, people were talking to me about it. Teachers and parents at the school were asking what they could do to help. Whenever I went into the shop, Mum's colleagues would ask me how it was going, and as I walked Smartie around the village, I'd have people coming up to me, asking if I was one of the group organising the pet show. I'd sent off the petition to the council now. Sara had warned us that it was unlikely to make any difference on its own, but did at least show them that we were by no means alone in wanting the park kept open.

The day after that first tidying-up weekend, I happened to see old Tommy Burrows working in his front garden again.

'Lovely morning, ain't it,' he called out to me, resting on his garden fork. 'I hear you young folk be fighting that darn council over their silly buggerin' idea of selling off the parkland.'

'We are, Tommy. Are going to support us?' I asked him.

''Course I am. Good for ye. Don't 'e go forgitting 'bout our cats though, will 'e? Fair breaks my heart to think of ol' Ginger lying in some ditch hereabouts. I bin out looking for 'e meself, every bliddy night, calling 'e till me voice is darn' near gone, but...' He sighed and shook his head. 'I reckon you young folk has got more chance. What with your newspaper and your buggerin' social media and all that.'

I nodded. I'd already mentioned to the others that I was worried we'd overlook the search for the missing cats now that we were so busy fighting for the park.

'I won't forget, Tommy. You know my mum's cat Monty is one of the missing ones, and I really do want to find out what's happened to him.'

'Thank 'e, young Nicola. Tis good to have you back in Furzewell, though we were all sorry about your marriage. But truth told, I can't see meself coming to the pet show without 'aving Ginger back.'

'Of course not. I understand.' Seeing other people's cats on show would just make his loss feel worse. I wondered if the owners of the other missing cats would feel the same. I hoped it wasn't going to be seen as a tactless move – putting on a show for those lucky enough to still have their pets, while so many villagers were missing their beloved cats.

'I don't know what else we can do,' Craig admitted when I put this to him that evening. We were the only two, on this occasion, who'd gone on to do a longer walk with the dogs. Simon had messaged us to say he wouldn't be back from work in time to meet us that night. Sara had excused herself after giving Babette a quick run at the back of the park, saying she wanted to spend some time designing posters for the pet show. We'd all offered to help, but she seemed to delight in doing a lot of these things on her own. And Amber said she had some work for a client that she needed to finish by the next day – giving me a warning look, as she left me and Craig together, that made me feel irritated all over again.

'I know,' I said now. 'But I do feel bad about it. We promised to try to help find the cats—'

'We *did* try, Nic. And we can keep trying, even if we're concentrating more on the park at the moment.' He paused, looking at me sympathetically. 'I know you'd like to find your mum's cat. Maybe we could devote a page of the pet show programme to a reminder about it? Put in pictures of all the missing cats?'

'Actually, that's a really good idea,' I agreed. I was touched at how thoughtful he was, considering he didn't have a cat himself. Under all his banter and joking, he was a nice, caring guy, I thought to myself. 'Everyone who buys a programme will be an animal lover. Perfect place to remind them about it. We could head it something like *Enjoy the pet show today – but please spare a thought for these missing cats*.'

'Yes – brilliant.' He gave me a smile. 'Let's suggest it to the others.'

He pulled out his phone and typed a quick message to our WhatsApp group, before looking back up at me and saying:

'I think we ought to get a move on. Look at that sky.'

While we'd been strolling at a leisurely pace through Cuckoo Copse, allowing Smartie and Judy to run ahead through the bracken, sniffing into the undergrowth, the bright evening sky had slowly darkened, and not in a good way.

'Yes. The air does feel suddenly really close and heavy,' I agreed. I've always been one of those people who can sense a storm coming. My head felt tight, as if I had a headache brewing.

We walked on more quickly, the dogs bounding ahead of us. We came to the far end of the copse and called the dogs back to put them on their leads. Judy had turned obediently towards Craig, with Smartie following, when there was a flash of lightning in the sky above us. Judy stopped dead, sniffing the air, looking around her anxiously, while Smartie bounded back to me and I fastened on his lead.

'Here, Judy,' Craig said, walking towards her.

She took a tentative step closer, but at that moment, there was a crash of thunder, so loud that even I nearly jumped out of my skin. Smartie yelped, shaking and running behind my legs – but Judy, completely spooked, gave a terrified whimper and bolted straight back into the copse.

'Judy!' Craig and I both yelled – making Smartie yelp again in fear.

I'd never known Judy not to come back at her master's command. But, having yelled her name again, with no response, Craig simply turned and started to walk back into the copse.

'Sorry,' he called back over his shoulder. 'I'll have to go after her. She's probably just sheltering somewhere. She's terrified of storms.'

There was another flash of lightning and almost instantly an even louder crash of thunder – and it began to rain, suddenly, violently, as if the heavens were emptying. The storm must be directly overhead. I'd started to follow Craig, keeping poor shivering Smartie close to me on his lead, but he called back to me again:

'Go home, Nic. You'll get drenched. Smartie's scared.'

'I'm drenched already.' The worst of the soaking had happened while we were at the edge of the copse, almost in the open; now we were back under the tree canopy it wasn't quite so bad, although it was surprising how much of the downpour was still finding its way through. And Smartie wasn't going to get any less scared, walking all the way home, than he was now. 'I'll help you look for Judy, it will be easier with two of us,' I insisted.

The next fifteen or twenty minutes were panic-stricken. We separated, ploughing our way back through the copse by different paths, both of us walking slowly and calling softly to Judy, rather than startling her further by running or shouting. The rain came down relentlessly, beating on the trees, trickling down the neck of my T-shirt, and the thunder crashed again and again above me. Smartie whined and yelped a couple more times but then seemed to fall into silent misery, plodding along beside me, as close to my legs as he could get.

'It's all right, Smartie,' I tried to reassure him above the noise of the thunder and the sound of the rain on the leaves. In actual fact, I knew it wasn't all right at all. We shouldn't be under trees during a thunderstorm, everybody knows that, but what else could we do? 'We've just got to find Judy, then we can go home. Where's Judy gone, Smartie?'

He pricked up his ears at the sound of his friend's name, and gave another quiet little whine.

And then, just as I thought we were going to reach the other end of the copse without finding any sign of Judy, Smartie stopped in his tracks, giving two sharp little barks.

'Come on, you're OK,' I said, giving a gentle tug at his lead. But he was trying to pull me in a different direction. 'What is it, Smartie? Did you hear Judy?' I looked around me. I was pretty sure we'd already covered the section of path he was pulling me towards. But it was worth a try. 'OK, then. Let's go.'

Nose to the ground, whimpering, Smartie ran ahead of me now in the direction he'd chosen. Too afraid to let him loose in case another clap of thunder made him bolt too, I gave him the length of his lead and ran after him, stumbling over roots, slipping now and again on wet leaves where the rain had got through a gap in the trees and soaked the ground. We turned off the path and dived through thicker undergrowth. Twice I almost let go of the lead as Smartie ran faster and faster, tugging me behind him. And there, suddenly, in a dense, dark part of the copse far from all the well-trodden paths, where I couldn't remember ever venturing before, we finally found poor Judy, lying exhausted under a clump of ferns, panting silently in fear.

'Quiet, Smartie; well done,' I said, as the pup immediately started to bark with excitement. 'OK, Judy. It's all right, girl, stay still. Good girl, stay, stay,' I went on, gently, as I walked closer. 'That's right, stay, here we are now. Are you hurt?'

Looping Smartie's lead around my arm, I squatted down and stroked Judy's head, trying to calm her. She nuzzled under my free arm and I quickly threaded my end of Smartie's lead through her collar so that both dogs were tethered to me.

'Craig!' I yelled, now that I'd got Judy under control and knew she couldn't bolt again. 'Over here! I've found her!'

There was a faint answering call, and for the next few minutes I kept shouting so that he could find us. The thunder was now coming less frequently, rumbling off into the distance, and the rain had eased off slightly. When Craig finally came crashing through the undergrowth, his hair plastered to his head, his clothes clinging to him, he was out of breath and almost on the verge of tears.

'I ran right back down Cuckoo Lane, almost back to the park,' he gasped. 'I'd just turned back again and started another search of the copse when I heard you call. Judy! Thank God. Are you hurt, baby?'

I'd never doubted his love for his dog. But now, watching as he threw himself down onto his knees on the damp ground, putting his arms around her as he gently felt her, checking for any injuries, I felt a lump in my throat. Amber was wrong about him, I thought. He was a far more sensitive, caring man than she'd been giving him credit for.

'Smartie led me to her,' I told him. 'Is she OK?'

'Clever dog,' he said, getting up and patting Smartie on the head. 'Yes, I think she's fine.' Judy had staggered up onto her paws now, and her tail was beginning to wave very gently in response to her master's caresses. 'She was probably just too frightened to run any further.' Murmuring quietly to Judy again, he fastened her lead to her collar, handing me back my end of Smartie's lead. Then he straightened up, sighing with relief, and finally turned to me. 'Thank you so much, Nic.' He enveloped me in a hug, taking me completely by surprise, and kissed me on the cheek. 'I might never have found her if you hadn't stayed to help.'

His face was wet, rainwater still running from his hair, and his shirt soaked through – I could feel it, through the clammy dampness of my own T-shirt. He held me for longer than would have been necessary for a simple thank you, and I found I didn't mind. There in the dripping, steaming copse, with the heat of the summer evening beginning to build again already as the storm passed, he held me, and I didn't pull away. I didn't object, either, when he kissed me again, or when this time, his lips found mine. And to my own astonishment, as the dogs lay panting at our feet, recovering from their fright, we kissed with an intensity I'd never imagined kissing anyone with, ever again. It felt like a long time before, eventually, we stopped, out of breath, and he looked down at me, and traced the shape of my mouth with his fingers.

'It must have been the storm,' he muttered, with that smile of his that never failed to make me shiver. 'Something to do with electricity.'

Electricity, I thought to myself as eventually, we led Judy and Smartie back out of the copse. That was exactly how it had felt. Just before we reached the road we stopped and kissed again, more slowly this time.

'We should do this more often,' he said, looking directly into my eyes.

'Yes,' I found myself agreeing, wondering if I was going to regret this after I'd got home, dried off, changed out of my wet clothes, washed away the traces of his kisses and the memory of how close he'd held me.

But I didn't. Slightly shocked though I was by this new, reckless me, this still-officially-married, brazen hussy of a woman who'd shared passionate kisses with a rain-soaked man in the middle of the wood, I couldn't bring myself to regret it. It had been hard, loving Josh for so long when he'd stopped loving me back. It had made me feel unwanted, unattractive; I'd wondered what was wrong with me, and my self-esteem had been left in tatters. Now somebody seemed to like me. Somebody young, good-looking and charming. I pushed aside thoughts that it was shallow of me to be gratified by that. Josh hadn't been interested in me anymore, but it seemed Craig was. He wanted *me*, not Sara, after all, and not Amber either. Why shouldn't I be pleased about it? And why shouldn't I admit that, in fact, I wanted him too?

PART 3

HEAD OVER TAILS

CHAPTER 21

I didn't see Craig again until the end of that week, by which time a few doubts had, needless to say, started to creep in. What on earth was I thinking of to have kissed him back? Why was I even considering getting involved? And anyway, he probably regretted saying anything to me about *doing it more often*. Probably regretted kissing me at all. It was just the euphoria of the moment – finding his beloved Judy – and now he was worried that I might get the wrong idea and read too much into it, so he was going to keep his distance.

But on the Friday evening walk, there he was again, giving me that cheeky grin and – when he found a moment to walk close enough to me for none of the others to overhear – whispering that he was looking forward to another walk in the woods some time, just the two of us.

'Or maybe you'd just settle for a drive and a meal at nice little pub,' he added, suggesting a spot in the middle of Dartmoor. There was no need for him to explain why it wouldn't be a good idea to be seen out together in Furzewell. The whole village would be buzzing with gossip within an hour.

'OK,' I said. 'Yes. That sounds good.' I smiled. It *would* be good to be taken out for a meal by an attentive, good-looking man. Although I did feel a bit strange about going out with another man after being married for so long, I supposed it was natural. 'Can I ask Mum when she's free to babysit, first?'

'Of course. Don't make me wait too long, though,' he teased, making me giggle.

Then I looked up, to see Amber frowning at me.

'What's the matter?' Craig asked, following my gaze.

'Amber,' I whispered. 'She keeps watching me, around you. She looks like she disapproves.'

'Oh, she's always like that,' he retorted scathingly. 'Doesn't seem to want anyone else to have any fun. Probably hasn't had any herself for years.'

'Don't be like that. She's my oldest friend,' I said. Despite myself, I felt disloyal for talking about her like this. 'We always used to be so close and get on so well together. I wonder what's happened. I mean, perhaps she's had her heart broken badly somewhere along the line.'

'Well, don't look at me!' he said vehemently. 'She's not my type and she quite clearly doesn't like me.'

I shook my head. 'No. I think she's probably just trying to protect me. From getting hurt again, you know.'

He looked at me for a minute, his head on one side, and went on, sounding more serious than usual: 'It's knocked your confidence, hasn't it – your husband cheating on you.'

'Oh, he didn't cheat on me,' I said. 'Well, not as far as I know. He didn't have time for anything like that. Our marriage just broke down. All he did was work, it felt like we barely spent any time together anymore.'

'Silly man,' he said more softly, his eyes caressing me now.

I felt myself blushing. 'Well, you're right, anyway – I have to admit it did knock my confidence. I don't feel ready for another relationship, that's for sure. Not now, possibly not ever.'

I didn't know why I felt I had to give him that kind of warning. After all, I'd already heard enough about him to know he didn't seem to be relationship material himself.

'But we could still go on a date?' he persisted.

'Yes. I'd like that. I think it's probably best if we don't mention it to the group, and especially to Amber, though.'

'You're right,' he agreed at once. 'No point starting gossip, is there.'

That weekend Mum duly came along to help at the park – mainly to give advice about flowers versus weeds – and I only stayed for a little while with Mia, until she got bored. It was the last weekend in June. Time seemed to be rushing past. School was busy, with sports day and the end-of-term 'talent show' to prepare for, and my reception class children were becoming overexcited already. Meanwhile, August

Bank Holiday, the date of the pet show, felt worryingly close. We'd put posters up around the village, and Sara had arranged for adverts to go in the local paper and on local radio during the preceding few weeks. Although there was no doubt Sara was brilliant at organising it all, and we trusted her, I still found it irritating that she seemed to want to do everything – except, perhaps, the gardening – herself. I'd have liked to contribute more to the campaign myself, and much as I appreciated her leadership qualities, it was frustrating only being allowed to take on a few minor tasks.

'Don't forget we wanted to put a page in there about the cats,' I reminded her during one of our evening walks, after she'd shown us what she'd drafted out, so far, for the programme.

'I haven't forgotten. I asked all the owners of the missing cats for photos, but I'm still waiting for some of them.'

'Well, let me chase them up,' I offered.

'It's OK, I'll do it. We've still got plenty of time.' She shrugged. 'Not that I really believe it's going to make any difference.'

'Maybe not, but it's worth a try, isn't it? We did promise we'd do all we could.'

'If someone's taken those cats,' Sara said, dropping her voice, 'or done something to them, I'm sorry but an advert in the pet show programme won't make any difference—'

'But obviously we're still hoping it *wasn't* somebody taking them,' I said.

'Then you're being a bit naïve, Nic. Sorry,' she said again – and this time she couldn't seem to help herself, as she looked directly in Amber's direction, 'but I think we all need to accept that this is what's happened. There's a cat-hater in the village, and you know it as well as I do.'

'I don't *know* it,' I retorted, rattled. 'I'm still hoping there's a less sinister reason, and if that makes me naïve, I don't care. And stop staring at Amber,' I added in a sharp hiss. Amber was walking some way in front of us, but I'd have hated for her to turn round and see Sara giving her that look.

'Well, there's only one person among us who openly says she doesn't like cats. Only one who hasn't been particularly enthusiastic about the idea of the advert in the programme.'

'You don't sound particularly enthusiastic yourself,' I pointed out.

'Only because I think it might raise false hopes. Yours included.'

'Well, I'd rather have my hopes raised than start suspecting one of our friends.'

I naturally sprang to Amber's defence, despite our friendship having become a bit strained recently. It was completely ridiculous to imagine she'd do anything to hurt a cat, or any animal. But I was aware that I was particularly determined right then to defend her and show I still thought of her as my friend – because I felt guilty for how I'd been thinking about her recently, and how I'd talked to Craig about her. She had no idea, of course, that I'd agreed to go on a date with Craig, and I had no intention of telling her. And, ridiculously, that just added to my feelings of guilt. We'd spent so much of our lives sharing our most intimate secrets, and even though it wasn't the same now and we'd drifted apart in the last few years, those childhood and teenage memories weren't something to be ignored lightly.

Louise and I, on the other hand, were spending more time together than ever after school. I'd even agreed to be her contact and nominated person to collect Eddie if she was ever late getting home from her work, which she said was a huge weight off her mind. She finished at three every afternoon, and it normally took her exactly fifteen minutes to drive back to Furzewell, just in time for school finishing, but she only had to find herself behind a tractor on one of the country lanes, and the whole thing came unstuck.

'I've … got a secret,' I confided in her, one afternoon when we were sitting in the sunshine in the garden of Eagle House, watching Mia and Eddie play. 'I haven't told anyone.'

Not even Mum. I'd decided my date with Craig was going to be the following Saturday evening, when Mia would be with Josh again. Mum had already told me she'd be out with her friends that night. I'd have the house to myself while I got ready, and nobody to care what time I got home. Nobody need know. But … I was just itching to share it with someone.

'Oooh,' Louise said. 'That sounds intriguing. Come on, spill the beans. I promise it won't go any further,' she added when I hesitated.

'I've got a date. With a man.' I bit my lip. Saying it out loud had suddenly made it feel real, and more nerve-wracking. What was I doing? I wasn't even sure I wanted to go anymore. 'Do you think it's too soon?' I asked anxiously.

'Why? You're separated, aren't you? Good luck to you, Nic. Who is he? Has he got a friend, or a brother?'

I laughed. 'Well, it's one of the dog walkers—'

'Oh – Simon?' she guessed, with a smile. 'Ah, he's such a nice guy.'

I felt my face flare with heat. I supposed that was what anyone would assume. Nice, kind, Simon, the gentle giant, the lonely widower – why wouldn't anyone want to go out with him? Anyone, perhaps, who wasn't so pathetically immature that they preferred a young, good-looking, smooth-talking guy with a reputation for being a ladies' man.

'*Craig*?' Louise questioned, seeing as I hadn't replied – and immediately burst out laughing.

'Is it that ridiculous?' I asked, feeling mortified. Perhaps I should cancel. It wasn't too late, and he wouldn't care, anyway.

'Of course it's not ridiculous,' she said at once, putting an arm round me. 'I'm laughing because I'm so impressed. A younger man – good for you.'

'Only by a few years.'

'But even so. He's . . .' She grinned. 'Have fun, you deserve it.'

'You don't think I'm being really stupid? Amber would. She's warned me off already, and she doesn't even know about us kissing in the copse last week.'

'Kissing? In the—?' Louise's eyes were out on stalks now. 'Hey, you've been holding out on me. Come on, I want all the details. What happened? Who made the first move? What was it like?'

And within seconds, we were giggling together like schoolgirls. Like Amber and I used to do, I thought afterwards with a bit of a pang. I did miss being able to share things with her. But instead of feeling judged, talking to Louise had made it all feel OK. Better than OK – she'd reassured me, agreed with me that it was perfectly fine for me to throw caution to the wind, have a bit of fun and enjoy myself.

'I did something similar myself soon after my marriage broke up,' she said. 'He was a football player – good-looking and a bit conceited—'

'Like Craig.'

'Well, yes, there's a type, isn't there.' She nodded. 'It didn't last long. I knew it wasn't going to go anywhere, and I didn't care. I guess I was just looking for reassurance, that someone still wanted me. Since then, though, I haven't bothered looking for another relationship. I'm happy to be on my own, at least while Eddie's still young.'

'I can understand that. I don't want another serious relationship either. I'm not sure I ever will. I'll probably end up like my mum – pretending to be a good-time girl, going out and having fun even when she's a grandmother.'

'You think she's only pretending?' Louise asked me in surprise.

'Hard to know, to be honest. She's still so bitter about my dad. She keeps up this *life is fun* thing, almost as if she's trying to prove to him that she's happy without him. But he'll never even know, or care, whether she's happy or not. He's lived in Ireland ever since they split up.'

I hadn't told Louise about Ireland. How my dad had torn our family apart, about my poor mum's humiliation all those years ago, which seemed to have followed her down the years, hanging over her like a cloud of shame – when of course, none of it was her fault at all. Even now, she couldn't hear an Irish accent without flinching. She'd recently turned the radio off with an angry click and a face like thunder because the words of Ed Sheeran's 'Galway Girl' were so close to the mark, and she muttered that he must have written the song about Dad and *that woman*. And in some unfathomable way, over the years the shame seemed to have seeped into my own consciousness too, so that I didn't want to talk about it to anyone. *He's lived in Ireland ever since they split up* was my standard response, if anyone asked me about Dad, which was usually enough to answer their questions and quickly change the subject.

'My parents split when I was quite young, too,' Louise said. 'But I was pleased when she met Charles and got remarried. He's lovely.' She shrugged. 'It seems like a genetic disorder, doesn't it, handed down from one generation to the next. And yet I tried so hard to make a go of my own marriage. I really didn't want to be a single parent. I'd seen how hard it was for Mum.'

'Me too.'

We sat in silence for a while. Then she nudged me and started laughing again.

'Never mind. Come on, tell me what you're planning to wear for your date.'

'God knows.' I laughed too. 'I haven't bought anything new for ages. I'll probably try on everything in my wardrobe and end up in jeans.'

It was good to be laughing. Good to have a friend to share this with. I thought, guiltily, of Amber again, but dismissed the thought straight away. It was hardly my fault that she'd made it impossible for me to talk to her like this. But I wasn't going along with Sara's stupid cat-napper theory. At least I wasn't *that* disloyal.

As it happened, it was Amber who had news for us all at our next scheduled meeting about the pet show.

'I've been talking to Kelly, one of the nurses at the vet's,' she said. 'You know I've had to take Benji a few times about his skin recently.' Poor Benji had developed horribly itchy skin, which the vet had diagnosed as an allergy, and was trying to determine the cause. 'She's really excited about the pet show – she's going to enter her own two rabbits – and she's got Mr Brent's agreement to put posters up in the surgery.'

'That's great' Simon smiled enthusiastically.

'And also she says she can ask him if he'll be one of the judges if we like.'

Mr Brent was the senior vet at the practice. To have him on board, especially as a judge, would be really helpful. We were all enthusiastic, and went on to discuss who else we could ask to be judges.

'Ideally we need three,' Sara pointed out. 'So that there can be a majority verdict, if there's any disagreement about the best in any class.'

'And they need to be unbiased,' I added. 'Someone who knows about pets, but isn't entering one.'

'What about the lady who runs the boarding kennels?' Craig suggested. 'She's looked after Judy sometimes when I've gone away. I'll give her a call and ask her, if you like.'

'Good idea,' Sara approved. 'And, to be honest, there's no reason why one of us can't be a judge. We can't enter our own pets – it would be seen as unfair.'

'That's a shame,' I said. 'I suppose you're right, but Mia was hoping to enter Smartie in the *best children's pet* class.'

'Oh, that's fine, surely?' Simon said, and the others nodded agreement. 'This isn't exactly Crufts. I don't think anyone's going to take it *too* seriously.'

'Actually,' Sara said, 'I hope they will. It needs to be taken seriously, if we're going to have any chance of changing the council's mind about the park. So we all need to pray for nice weather, a good turnout, and lots of interest and enthusiasm from the press, the people of Furzewell – and the wider Devon population. This is our chance to show them what we can do. We can't afford to treat it as if it's just a bit of fun.' She looked around at us, her face deadly serious. 'This is war, guys. And the pet show is only going to be the first battle.'

CHAPTER 22

The first week of July seemed to pass slowly and I knew, without wanting to admit it to myself, it was because I was counting the days until my date with Craig. Since the storm, our surprise heatwave had eventually fizzled out, replaced with warm but dull weather and the occasional summer shower.

'Typical!' Louise said, as we put up our umbrellas once again on the way home from school on the Wednesday. 'As soon we get anywhere close to the big summer holidays, the weather changes.'

'Well, there's still more than two weeks – plenty of time for it to change again,' I said, trying to be optimistic. 'It's sports day tomorrow, though. I hope it doesn't rain for that.'

'Oh yes. I've got the afternoon off work to come and watch it.'

Mia and Eddie were looking forward to it. They were both in Purple Team, and were chanting *Purple are the best, Purple are the winners* together as they walked along in front of us now. I just hoped they weren't going to be disappointed. Mia wasn't a fast runner, but Eddie was. He was also, apparently, the best in his year group at throwing beanbags into a hoop, and at kicking a football into the net, which were two of the planned activities. I'd had a lot of fun helping my reception class children practise these, and soothing the tears of some of these little ones when they dropped their beanbags, missed the goal, or fell over in the attempt. I knew there would probably be several more tearful episodes the next day when they faced the more stressful situation of competing in front of the parents. But it was all part of the steep learning curve of growing up. By the next year's sports day, most of them would be marching onto the playing field like confident mini athletes, and I'd have a new class of nervous little ones to help. I loved helping to bring out the best of them, especially on special occasions like this.

'After sports day,' Mia said when we arrived home that afternoon, 'it's only one more day and then I go to Daddy's house again.'

'Yes, that's right.' I smiled at her, but felt my stomach give a lurch. One more day until I went out with Craig.

'Good, I can't wait,' Mia went on, giving herself a little hug. 'I love going to Daddy's house.'

My smile dropped. My stomach was now lurching for a different reason.

'Well, that's nice that you enjoy seeing him,' I said carefully, trying to be grown up about it and ignore the pain stabbing me in the heart.

'We always have fun,' she said.

Go on, twist the knife, I thought. I couldn't ignore the stabbing anymore.

'More fun than you have here at home?' I found myself saying. I was doing my best not to sound like a pathetic, needy, jealous, resentful person, but it wasn't easy. 'With Smartie? And Eddie? And ... and me?'

'Oh, it's OK here too,' she said thoughtfully. 'I mean, I didn't like it when we first moved here, but I've got used to it now. It's just that I've got my new bike at Daddy's house. And Daddy takes me out to places. Cafés, and soft play, and the cinema, and the swimming pool.'

'I know,' I said, in my pathetic, needy, jealous, resentful voice. 'But he didn't used to, did he? When we all lived together? You hardly ever saw him, then. He didn't come home until you were in bed asleep. Even at weekends, he was never there.'

I stopped. What was I doing? I'd never done this – I'd *prided* myself on never doing it. Criticising the father to the child, it was almost the worst sin a separated parent could commit, everybody knew that. OK, it hurt, hearing her talking about Josh and his programme of fun outings. It was really upsetting that she seemed to prefer her weekends with him, to the time she spent with boring old me. Me, the parent who'd always been there for her, perhaps a little taken for granted as I'd always had to be the one to get her up for school, make sure she ate healthy meals, did her homework and went to bed on time. No wonder she was now enjoying her weekends with Josh, who just got the fun bits: taking her out for day trips and fast food. It didn't seem fair. But of course, Mia was just a young child, and any child would be the same – easily won over by treats and presents, whereas I was – or was supposed to be – a sensible, rational adult who ought to be mature enough to swallow her own hurt and keep nodding and smiling.

'Still,' I said, forcing the nod and the smile, 'it's really nice that you get to spend more time together now. And he does really spoil you too.'

'Yes. Daddy says he wishes he'd done it then – when we all lived together. He says we might have still been living together *now*, if he'd done it then.' She paused, looking up at me, her innocent expression melting my heart. '*Would* we, Mummy?'

It took me a few moments to answer as I was so taken aback. It was something of a shock to hear that Josh had been saying these things to her. After all, when I'd left him, he'd claimed to have absolutely no idea what my problem was.

'No, sweetheart,' I said eventually. 'It wouldn't have changed anything. Mummy and Daddy weren't getting along together. We didn't love each other anymore. It wasn't anything to do with you. We both love you, and we both always have done.'

She nodded. Of course it was what I'd told her from the start and I'd continually reinforced – that she was our priority. It was one of the most difficult things to try and make her understand, bringing up painful memories for me.

'Well, I don't really mind now, anyway,' Mia said, turning back to the drawing she was doing – a picture of herself, to give Daddy. 'At least I get to go to the soft play. And the cinema.'

'Yes, you do,' I agreed, biting my tongue. She was six. Of course these things would be her priorities. I had to get over it. Even if I could afford them, there was no cinema, soft play centre or swimming pool anywhere around Furzewell to take her to. Driving her back to Plymouth on my weekends, to visit the same places that Josh took her to, would be a tad ridiculous, and he'd rightly see it as undermining him and being confrontational. 'And there *are* fun things happening here in Furzewell. We've got the pet show to look forward to, haven't we?'

'Mm,' she said, going back to concentrating on colouring her self-portrait.

Clearly the pet show was no competition for the cinema and the soft play centre.

School Sports Day, however, was a hit. All the children seemed to enjoy it, with the inevitable exception of a few of my reception children, one of whom – a shy little girl who'd only just turned five – spent most of the time gripping my hand and crying, only cheering up when she won her race (with me running beside her). When the goals and points scored by everyone were added up at the end of the afternoon, it was announced that Purple Team were, indeed, the winners of the day – narrowly beating Yellow by only two points.

'We are the champions!' Eddie sang as we walked home later, throwing his arms in the air. Mia laughed and joined in. It was lovely to see them both so happy. They'd become even closer, to the point where Mia now referred to him as her best friend *and* her boyfriend, and had even mentioned that they would probably get married when they grew up.

'It seems like only yesterday,' I said to Louise, 'since she was crying at home – and at school – because she was so unhappy here. Making friends with Eddie has made such a difference.'

'She'd have settled down eventually,' Louise said. 'Eddie was miserable at first too. It's good that they had each other to help.'

But now we both had to face the fact that they'd be separated, in different classes, when they came back to school after the summer holiday. I don't think either of us wanted to talk about that. It would spoil the mood.

On the Saturday morning, after Josh had picked Mia up, Smartie and I went out for a long walk with Simon and Sara. I was relieved, to be honest, that Craig didn't turn up on this occasion. Tonight was our date and it was hard enough to keep myself from feeling jittery about the evening ahead. I was heading home down Fore Street afterwards when Amber came out of the village shop, looking preoccupied and anxious.

'Hello!' I called out. 'Are you OK? You missed the walk this morning.'

'Yes. I'm not walking Benji for a few days. He's really not well.'

'Oh no! What's wrong?'

'It's this skin condition he's got – it's really troubling him. He's scratching so much, his skin has started getting infected. The vet's given me some medicated shampoo for him, and he's got to have special therapeutic dog food, at least until it settles down. It looks like there's something in the new food I've been giving him that's triggered the allergy.'

'Oh, poor Benji. I didn't realise dogs could be allergic to their food.'

'Me neither. At first I thought it must be fleas, although I do treat him regularly for those, of course. But now he's got diarrhoea too, so the vet is pretty sure it must be something in the food. I feel really guilty now for changing the brand. It was a bit cheaper and I didn't think it would matter,' she admitted.

'You weren't to know he'd be allergic to it,' I sympathised. 'Can't he just go back on the other brand?'

'Yes, hopefully, once this has all settled down. The skin infection from all the scratching, and his poor tummy.' She sighed. 'I'd better get back to him, Nic. Sorry. See you soon.'

'OK. I hope he gets better soon.'

I could imagine how Amber must be feeling. Even though it wasn't her fault, she must be blaming herself for it. Benji was such a sweet-natured, gentle dog – I hated to think of him suffering, not even being well enough to come out for his walks. I'd be just as upset if it were Smartie. Thinking this now, I looked down with a smile at my little dog, trotting obediently along beside me on his lead. He was growing up fast; he was nearly six months old, and I needed to book him in at the vet's for his neutering operation. We didn't want to breed from him or enter him into shows – apart from our own Furzewell pet show, of course – so it was the right thing to do.

'Sorry to leave you on your own tonight,' Mum said as she came out of the bathroom later with a towel around her, preparing to dress up ready for her night out with the girls. 'What will you do – watch a film? You could always ask your gran to come round and watch it with you. You know how she likes a good rom com.'

'No,' I said hurriedly. 'It's OK, I'm going out myself, actually. With Amber,' I added when Mum stopped dead in her bedroom doorway, giving me an appraising look. 'We're … um … going for a drive, as it's such a nice evening. Probably we'll find a nice country pub somewhere and have a bar meal.'

I felt guilty and silly about lying to her, as if I were a teenager again, needing an excuse to be out late with my boyfriend. This wasn't at all where I'd expected to find myself at this age – living in my mother's house, sneaking out on a date. It was embarrassing. But I really didn't want an inquisition into it. I'd had to think on my feet, because even if I'd said I was going to one of Furzewell's only two drinking establishments, she just might have taken it in her head to suggest she and the Gruesome Twosome joined us.

'Oh, that'll be nice, then,' she said now, but she was still looking at me somewhat critically. 'Are you sure you can afford to go out for meals like this, though?'

'It's not like I do it all the time, Mum,' I protested, the feeling of being a teenager, still living at home under Mum's scrutiny, intensifying now. 'It'll just be something cheap at a pub, anyway.'

'Well, I suppose you deserve a treat now and then,' she conceded.

I half expected her to tell me not to be too late, not to talk to strangers and look both ways before crossing the road. It was so weird being in this situation. If I ever did decide to start dating other men seriously I'd definitely have to move into a place of my own!

After Mum had gone out, I went through my wardrobe, tossing items onto the bed as I gradually discarded them all as too old, too casual, too *middle-aged.* At the back of the wardrobe was a dress I'd last worn years ago – pre-Mia. It was red, sleeveless, shortish without being tarty and, I thought, would have been perfect if only I wasn't now a size bigger than I was back then. I remembered wearing it to go out with Josh for one of our early wedding anniversaries, how happy and confident I'd been, wearing it then and how he'd smiled, saying I looked good. I sighed. Those days were gone.

Nevertheless, on a silly whim to try to recreate that feeling, I tried it on, and was surprised to find it still fitted.

I was aware that I'd lost a pound or two of my excess weight since the separation from Josh, probably, as everyone had said, because of the stress, or maybe because of all the exercise involved in walking Smartie. But nevertheless the dress was a bit … snug … where all those years ago it used to be comfortable. I looked at myself in the full-length mirror, turning one way and then the other, trying to make up my mind. Although I was never likely to become exactly curvaceous, I did have more of a figure now than back when I used to be Nic the Stick, and the dress certainly clung in all the right places. Could I carry it off? Well, I didn't have time to dither. It was either this dress, or – as usual – skinny jeans and a baggy top. I kept the dress on.

When Craig arrived to pick me up, I knew, as soon as I opened the door to him, that I'd made the right choice. His eyes widened as he looked me up and down. Bearing in mind he'd only ever seen me before in my dog-walking gear or usual pub outfit of … well, jeans and a baggy top … he seemed almost to do a double-take.

'Wow. You look stunning,' he said, giving me a kiss on the cheek. I couldn't keep the smile off my face. I couldn't remember when I'd last had a compliment like that. 'If I wasn't such a gentleman,' he went on, 'I'd have trouble keeping my hands off you.'

A gentleman? I doubted that! But as it happened, the evening did prove me wrong in some of my preconceptions about him. For a start, as it turned out, Mum needn't have worried about the expense. Not only did the little pub

Craig had chosen, in a fairly remote part of Dartmoor, serve fresh pub grub at reasonable prices – but he completely refused any suggestion of splitting the bill.

'I asked you to come out with me – I'm paying,' he insisted. He then reverted to type somewhat, looking at me with that twinkle in his eye that made me go a bit weak at the knees. 'What's the matter? Are you worried I might want something in return?'

'On a first date?' I countered, trying not to blush. 'I'm not that kind of girl!' We both laughed. I actually had no idea what kind of girl I was these days. It had been so long. 'Well, I'll pay next time,' I added. 'If there is a next time, of course.'

'I hope there will be,' he replied at once. 'And if *you're* going to want something in return, I'd be more than happy to oblige. It won't be our first date then, will it?'

It was difficult to concentrate on my food after that. But in fact he was surprisingly considerate and attentive, listening with every sign of interest to my chatter about my job, about sports day and Mia being so happy about her team's victory, and how she hadn't cared at all that she, personally, had come last in her own race, had missed the goal every time with the football and dropped her beanbag. He laughed in all the right places, and we were halfway through our main course before I thought to apologise for hogging the conversation.

'You must find this really boring,' I said.

'Not at all. I do *like* kids, you know. I just don't happen to have had any myself. Not as far as I know, anyway.'

'And what would you do if you found out you *had*?' I teased. 'Leave the country?'

He laughed. 'I seem to have this reputation for being shallow.'

'Oh, really?' I smiled. 'And why would people have that impression of you?'

'I don't know.' He shrugged. 'I guess it's because they think that by now I should be in a serious relationship, settled down with someone, planning a family and all that stuff.' He turned those eyes on me again. 'Perhaps I just haven't met the right person – till now.'

I gave an awkward little laugh, suddenly uncomfortable. He was just teasing, obviously, or – as Amber had, with her veiled hints, been so anxious to warn me – was he just flattering me, pretending to be serious, when all he really wanted was to get me into bed? I'd already told him I wasn't looking for a relationship, so I was sure he *wasn't* being serious. Or was he? That look in his eyes ... the way he was smiling at me, so wistfully ... the fact that he'd sounded genuinely hurt by the fact that people thought him shallow ... was there an honest, serious side to him behind that façade after all?

By the time we'd finished our meal and he'd driven me home, kissing me comparatively chastely in the car ('unfortunately it's not as private as the middle of the woods'), and insisting on fixing another date before we parted, I was actually beginning to wonder if I, and possibly everyone else, had got it all wrong about Craig. Apart from a little bit of innuendo and teasing, he *had* been a perfect gentleman.

Mum came out from the kitchen as soon as I closed the front door. She'd got home before me after all.

'Amber dropped you off, did she?' She blinked as she looked me up and down. 'You're dressed up, aren't you, for a night out with your friend?' She corrected herself at once, smiling and adding, 'You look very nice.'

'Thanks, Mum.' Again, I had to look away, the ridiculousness of lying to my mother at the age of thirty-five making me feel like a child and lessening the excitement of the evening.

'Like a coffee?'

'No, thanks. I think I'll go straight to bed.'

I wanted to run through the whole evening again in my head. It had been . . . different from what I'd expected – in a good way. I'd enjoyed our date, and I was looking forward to doing it again. But as soon as I got into bed and closed my eyes, I found myself thinking, not about Craig, but Josh, an annoying little voice in my head insisting on reminding me that he was still my husband. Despite the fact that, as far as I was concerned at least, the marriage was over in all but name.

What about your marriage vows? the annoying little voice said. *Remember how sure you were on your wedding day that you'd never want another man as long as you lived?*

But that was then, I told the annoying voice. *This is now. Things have changed.*

Think how devastated Josh would be, though, if he knew you were dating someone else.

I turned over, giving the pillow a shake and a thump, trying to silence that stupid voice.

Would he? I retorted inside my head. *I don't actually think he'd care less. And anyway, he should have thought about that, shouldn't he. He should have cared about me more, shown me more love and affection when he had the chance. It's too late now. Josh is in my past, we're separated and eventually we'll be divorced. Craig's making me feel good about myself again. Now, shut up, irritating little voice, and let me get some sleep.*

I was still awake for half the night, though. And it was only when the morning light began to stream through the curtains and the cockerel, as usual, started crowing his head off down the lane that I managed to banish those thoughts of Josh, and enjoy the memory of the previous evening.

CHAPTER 23

I purposely didn't walk next to Craig when we met for the dog walk that morning, conscious that I didn't want any of the others to pick up on anything between us and become the subject of gossip. But I couldn't help sneaking glances at him as I walked next to Sara, discussing the latest news about the park campaign. And whenever he caught my eye he gave me a little grin and a wink.

'It's great to see people taking the situation on board like this,' Sara said, glancing over to a group of children enjoying a picnic spread out on blankets, while the parents of one little boy, whose birthday it evidently was, were pouring out drinks and handing around cakes for them all. 'The use of the park has increased massively since we had the public meeting.'

It was true. At one time, we rarely saw anyone else when we walked our dogs through the park, apart from an occasional jogger or a family out for a stroll together. Now, there were always groups like this birthday party having picnics, and families getting together to organise games of rounders or races for the children. Because the grass had been cut, on hot weekends there were teenagers lying on the grass sunbathing, looking at their phones, chatting, laughing and flirting, reminding me with a pang of my younger days. Amber and I used to lie here in the sun like this, on hot days in the summer holidays when we were teenagers, talking about our plans and dreams for the future. I wondered, now, how many of those dreams had come true, for either of us.

'Are you all right?' Sara said, somewhat sharply, and I realised I hadn't replied to her.

'Sorry. Yes, I'm fine. You're right, there are lots more people here now. Let's hope it continues like this.'

'Well, we're doing all we can, aren't we, but to be honest I'm still not particularly optimistic about it. In fact,' she looked around at Craig and Simon, to include them in the conversation, 'I've got to let everyone know there's been further communication from the council. As we expected, our petition has merely prompted a standard acknowledgement. But meanwhile we've had a formal letter, stating the council's reasons for wanting to close the park. Apart from the fact that they claim it's under-used, of course.'

'Go on,' said Simon, frowning. 'What else?'

'Well, firstly the play equipment is in a dangerous condition…'

'It's been like that for years,' I said. 'It's their fault for not maintaining it.'

'Quite. But they're obviously not intending to either and they don't want to be sued if a child gets hurt on it.'

'Nobody ever uses it,' I said scathingly. 'It's rusting and falling apart.'

'Yes. As we know, the playground's now been fenced off. And the equipment's been scheduled for removal. It's an eyesore as well as being dangerous. But of course, they'd prefer to sell the whole park for housing.' She sighed. 'And then there's the paddling pool. They say that's a hazard too.'

'There hasn't been any water in it for years,' I protested.

'Exactly. It's a dirty great hole, and *that's* fenced off because someone might fall in it and break their leg. Their point is, you see, that the whole park is hazardous so they're better off selling it than spending money on it.'

'Unless *we*, as a community, as Friends of the Park, spend our own money on it.'

'That's right. So they're giving us the rest of this year to come up with the dosh to make the park safe, prove it's being used as a valuable community asset and being properly maintained, or they go ahead with selling the land.'

'The rest of this year?' Craig said. 'That's less than six months.'

'Yes. So we really need to get the community on board with this. Not just using the park more, but supporting the pet show and the fundraising in general and joining the Friends of Furzewell Park.'

'Will they at least remove the old play equipment *if* we take over management of the park?' Simon asked quietly.

'I've been thinking: if we can raise the money for materials, we could propose replacing the play equipment with an adventure playground made of natural materials: wood, with rope swings and so on.'

'Oh, I've seen something like that in a park somewhere else,' I said. 'Much nicer for kids to play on than these old metal structures.'

'Great idea,' Sara said.

'And we could include a properly planted nature walk,' Simon went on, his enthusiasm showing. 'With shrubs that attract butterflies, and different types of trees and wildflowers.'

'That sounds really nice,' I agreed.

'And a designated dog-walking route,' Simon added. 'And a kids' cycle track or skateboard ramps.'

'I'd like to see the old paddling pool enlarged and made into a proper lake,' Sara said. 'With an area for children to play with their boats, and the rest left to nature. And suitable safety precautions, of course: lifebelts, warning signs...'

'If only we had the money to do all this,' Craig pointed out.

'So we have to make sure we raise it,' Sara said. 'We need to drum up support, especially with the new families on the High Meadow estate. We need to get as many people as possible signed up as Friends of the Park. I propose we send out a newsletter, telling everyone about these ideas, so that they're all as enthusiastic as us, whether they're dog walkers, families with kids or just people who like to walk and enjoy nature. We need to make them all aware: if we're going to keep the park open, if we're going to provide these new amenities, we need funds, and we need helpers.'

We all nodded agreement, each of us, I suspect, more determined than ever to do our bit to help.

'I don't mind knocking on doors to talk to people about becoming Friends,' I said. 'And I'll have a word with Louise – I'm sure she'll help too. She lives on High Meadow so between us we can cover the new houses there as well as my side of the village.'

'Thanks, Nic,' Sara said – and Craig, behind her back, gave me another wink, making me blush and grin. We were at the far side of the park by now and I let Smartie off his lead to run and play with the other three dogs. He was growing up fast, happy now to respond to my commands, to *come*, to *sit*, and *stay*, so that I felt much more confident about letting him have a run like this. He followed Craig's Judy faithfully, seeming to admire her the most of all the dogs, looking up at her and wagging his tail as if to ask to be her friend. But for a good romp, he liked to gambol after Simon's big Max, trying to keep up with him, and turning to trot back to me when, inevitably, he got left behind, giving me a little whimper of disappointment.

'You'll catch him one day,' I would promise him with a laugh. 'You're still only a little boy, yet. Wait till your legs have got a bit longer!'

But in some ways I wished I could keep him this size forever. He was so cute at this half-grown puppy stage, so cuddly and fluffy and yet so intelligent, with his big black eyes, shiny nose and waggy tail. I just wanted to hug him all the time.

Louise came round that afternoon, ostensibly bringing Eddie to play with Mia, but, as soon as the children had run off into the garden, she sat down next to me and demanded to know how my date with Craig had gone.

'It was nice,' I said, with a smile.

'*Nice*? Is that all?' She looked disappointed. 'Come on, what was he like? Did he kiss you? Did you go back to his place?'

'*No*, Lou, I didn't,' I laughed. 'Yes, we had a kiss—' I ignored her squeal of excitement, 'but it was just, like I said, nice. We went for dinner, we chatted. He was … quite a gentleman, actually.'

'That doesn't exactly tally with what you've told me about him!' She looked at me with her head on one side. 'So are you going to see him again?'

'Yes. Well, I hope so. He said he wants to.'

'You sound … a bit *lukewarm*, Nic. Are you having second thoughts?'

'No. Not most of the time, anyway. I do want to go out with him, and I don't see why I shouldn't. After all, Josh and I are separated. I'm a single girl, as my mum keeps reminding me.' I paused, not quite sure what I was trying to say.

'But you're still feeling a bit guilty? About Josh?' Louise suggested gently.

I shrugged. 'I keep trying to talk myself *out* of feeling guilty. I *shouldn't* feel guilty, should I?'

'Well, no, but...'

'But what?' I looked at her, immediately on the defensive. 'You think I'm rushing into this? I should wait till Josh and I are actually divorced?'

'That's not what I'm saying. But look, from what you've told me, you haven't been with anyone except Josh, and you started dating him when you were just teenagers. I'd say you're bound to feel a bit weird about it, that's all. It's only natural.' She hesitated. 'As for whether it's too soon: only you can decide that.'

'I enjoyed the date. Just being out with him, having a meal together. Josh and I ... well, we just weren't doing anything like that in the end. Not for years, actually. He was hardly ever home. We just didn't spend time together. And Craig ... he was attentive and paid me compliments. Made me feel better about myself.'

'So enjoy it, Nic. Enjoy going out with him. As you say, why not? But don't take it any further until you're sure it's what you want. The days of men having to be rewarded in the bedroom for taking us out for a meal are long gone.'

'Yes, you're right. I've said I'll pay next time, anyway. And I'll just see how it goes – how I feel about it.'

Mia and Eddie came tumbling back into the room just then, closely followed by Smartie who was barking and wagging his tail in excitement.

'Can we have a drink and a biscuit please? And can we have the football goals up?' Mia said.

I'd taken them down to mow the lawn.

'We'll talk some more later,' Louise said. 'Shall I put the goals up while you get their drinks and snacks? It looks like Smartie wants to join in the game!'

'He does.' Eddie laughed. 'He's been running after the ball!'

'Come on, then. After you've had your drinks maybe Louise and I will come out and play with you.'

So it wasn't until we finally stopped, worn out from running around outside with the kids and Smartie, that we resumed our conversation. And even then, we didn't get back to talking about Craig, because Louise had something else to tell me about.

'I forgot to say earlier,' she said, collapsing onto the garden bench outside the kitchen door. 'There's another cat missing. I was talking to another of my neighbours, Jane, and she told me her Siamese has disappeared. She's frantic with worry. She's seen all the alerts and notices about the missing cats, of course, and she was trying to keep Suki indoors but, well, you know what cats are like.'

'Yes, I do. You can lock the cat-flap, keep all the windows closed and still they can slink out of the door when you only open it a fraction to take something off the doorstep.' I sighed. 'I was beginning to think that, whatever has happened to all our cats, at least the disappearances had stopped.'

'Now it seems not. I've told Jane that we'll add her Suki to our list. She's already told the vets about it, because

Suki has been microchipped – but it's hard to know what else anyone can do that we haven't already done.'

'I know. It's frustrating, isn't it, that none of our appeals have worked. Nobody's come forward to say they've seen any of the cats. Not even after the big write-up in the paper.'

Louise nodded. 'I'm not saying this to Jane, of course, but to be honest, I can't see any of these cats turning up after all this time. And the fact that there's another one missing now – unless it's just a coincidence – means that if there really is someone in the village with a vendetta against cats, doing them some harm, then they're still out there, doing it.'

'Despite all the publicity,' I agreed. 'It's a horrible thought, isn't it? Well, I'll tell the others. We ought to put out another warning, in case cat owners were thinking it had stopped, and were starting to let their cats out again. Maybe the vet could put another big notice up, warning people this is still going on.'

'Local radio is a good bet, too,' Louise suggested. 'And social media – the local paper could post about it on there too.'

'Yes. I'll put an alert on the Furzewell Village Facebook group, too. And by the way,' I remembered, 'I've kind-of volunteered you to help with a door-to-door blitz around the village.' I told her about the conversation that morning with Sara, the need for urgent fundraising for the park. 'We could use that opportunity to warn people about the cat situation too.'

I contacted the rest of the group on WhatsApp, telling them about the new missing cat and asking them all to spread the word, warning people to keep their cats indoors. Soon afterwards, Louise and Eddie went home. And I felt like the enjoyment of the day had been spoilt by the thought that someone was still, apparently, prowling around our village, preying on people's innocent pet cats. What sort of person would do that? It was hard to imagine; but there didn't seem to be any other possible explanation for so many disappearances.

CHAPTER 24

The end of term was only a week away now, and my little charges in the reception class were becoming more and more restless. The weather was warm, they were tired and ready for their holiday. Learning progressed more slowly, and the only thing really keeping their interest was the prospect of the talent show to be held on the last-but-one day.

Mia was excited about it too.

'I'm going to sing a song,' she'd announced over dinner a few weeks earlier.

Mum and I had looked at each other in surprise. This was a huge stretch from the shy, unhappy little girl who'd started at the school in February.

'You're going to sing, up on the stage in front of everyone?' I said, wondering whether she'd actually realised what was involved.

'Yes. We've been practising.'

'Oh, you're not doing it on your own, then?'

'No,' she smiled happily, 'it's me and Eddie. We're going to sing 'This is Me' together.'

I shouldn't have been surprised. They'd been singing that song together ever since they watched the film, *The Greatest Showman*. I wasn't convinced they knew all the correct words, though.

'It doesn't matter,' Mia said with a shrug. 'Eddie knows the words better than me, but Mr Gregory says we can have the music playing, and we'll just sing the bits we know.'

I'd had a chat with Mr Gregory about it the following day in the staffroom.

'I'd never have imagined Mia having the courage to get up on stage in front of the whole school like this,' I said.

'I know: isn't it great?' he said. 'Those two kids both had a difficult start here, but look how far they've come. They're both so much happier and more confident now.'

'I hope they'll be OK, though. I mean, what if one of them gets cold feet when it actually comes to it?'

'Don't worry, Nicola. I'll be at the side of the stage, and I'll join in and sing it with them if necessary. But honestly, it really is amazing how different Mia is now.'

Two days later I'd been reading her school report, struggling to hold back the tears, as the grades and comments for every subject – reading, writing, maths, science, art, even PE – showed how much she'd improved. The comment from Mr Gregory at the end of the report, saying that despite a shaky start, Mia had now caught up and was back where she should be in every area, finished with the words: '*Mia is now a confident, pleasant and hard-working member of the class. Well done, Mia!*'

On the day of the talent show, I was sitting with my own class at the front of the school hall and feeling far more nervous about Mia's performance than she'd seemed to be herself when we'd parted company that morning. Only two children from my own class were taking part. Lucy, who had ballet lessons outside of school, had opted to show off some steps. And Alfie had elected to sing 'I'm a Little Teapot' – but when it came to the moment for him to go on the stage, he got stage fright and ran back to his place in the audience. Nobody minded, of course, and we gave him another chance later, but he stayed resolutely sitting still with his thumb in his mouth. I couldn't help feeling even more anxious about Mia. Would she do the same? Would Eddie?

I sat through the two Olivias singing 'Somewhere Over the Rainbow' somewhat shakily together, and a boy in their class playing a squeaky version of 'Three Blind Mice' on the recorder. All the time I was becoming more and more fidgety with nerves and when, finally, Mr Gregory ushered Mia and Eddie onto the stage I almost wanted to get up and leave, I was so keyed up and anxious for them. They stood up there together, holding hands, Mia looking so small and solemn I could hardly bear it. And then, as the headmaster called for quiet, Eddie looked up and announced:

'We are going to sing "This Is Me", because we like this song and it's about people who feel like nobody likes them.'

I gasped out loud, almost missing Mia adding:

'And in the end, though, they didn't even care, because they liked *themselves*.'

I was so busy swallowing back tears, I forgot about feeling nervous for them. Instead, I listened with awe as these two previously lonely, shy children sang along to as many of the lyrics as they could manage, smiling at each other from time to time, not caring when they got some words wrong or when they didn't stay in time with the music. At the end, there was a storm of applause and cheering. The audience consisted of the entire school population, right up to the eleven-year-olds in Year 6 who'd soon be leaving us for senior school, with parents filling the back half of the hall. Because I was sitting right at the front with the reception class, I had to turn round to watch Eddie and Mia going back to their seats behind me, so that I could give them a smile and a thumbs-up. And it was then that I suddenly caught sight of someone standing right at the very back of the hall – standing, either because he hadn't been able to find a seat, or ... because he was applauding Mia and Eddie so frantically and excitedly. It was Josh. For a moment I felt myself go hot and cold, as if I was about to faint. *Josh*, watching our daughter in a school show? What was he doing here? It was so unlike him, he'd never come to anything before – not even when she was an angel in her very first nativity play at the age of four. He'd never been to a parents' evening. He'd never even taken her to school or picked her up. Suddenly he caught my eye and even from that distance, right across the hall, I could see he was looking awkward. He gave me a quick little wave and sat down, and I turned back, forcing my attention back to the show and my own class.

More acts followed, with a magic trick performed next by a Year 2 boy and then some more recorder playing by a group of girls, but I found it almost impossible to concentrate. My head was spinning with the shock of seeing Josh there, combined with the emotion of seeing Mia, up there on the stage and reciting those words about liking yourself. At the end of the show, the headmaster asked the parents to please wait in their seats while we took the children back to their classrooms. I stood up to walk out with my class, who were the first to leave, giving Mia another smile as I passed and whispering 'Well done'. But there was now no sign, at the back of the hall, of her father. I began to wonder if I had actually dreamt it.

Once we were back in our classroom it was almost school finishing time, and as soon as I'd helped to see the reception children off with their parents, I hurried to Mia's class.

'Hello, Nic,' said a familiar voice from behind me as I approached the classroom door.

'Josh!' I turned and gave him a smile. So I hadn't been dreaming! And although it had been such a shock to see him there at a school event, I was pleased, naturally – for Mia's sake. 'This is a surprise,' I added.

'I know.' He shrugged, looking awkward again. 'I didn't say anything before about coming, because I wasn't sure if I'd be able to get the afternoon off. But I'm glad I did. It was great, wasn't it?'

'Yes – fantastic.' Despite the strangeness of being here with Josh, I couldn't keep the happiness out of my voice, I was so excited about how well Mia and Eddie had done. Just then the classroom door opened and Mr Gregory started to shepherd the children out to the waiting parents.

'Didn't they do well?' he enthused as soon as he saw me.

'I was amazed!' I admitted. 'What they said up there, about the song: was that ... something you suggested?'

'No. They came up with it themselves. I thought it was great. You should be very proud.'

'Thank you,' I said. 'Oh – this is Josh – my, um ... Mia's father.'

'Ah! Pleased to meet you.' Mr Gregory smiled. 'Here she is now.'

I watched, fighting a mixture of emotions, as Mia threw herself into Josh's arms, chatting excitedly about the talent show, and grabbing Eddie's arm as he followed her out of the classroom to tell him proudly that this was her daddy.

'This is Eddie, Mia's friend,' I explained to Josh as we began to walk away across the playground. 'And this is Louise, his mum – *my* friend,' I added, smiling at Louise, who'd been giving me and Josh surprised looks.

'Pleased to meet you, Louise,' Josh said. 'And well done to both of you, Mia and Eddie. Your song was by far the best act in the whole show. You were brilliant!'

'Can Daddy come with us to the café?' Mia asked, tugging at my arm. 'Please, Mummy?' She turned back to Josh again, her little face flushed with the unexpected joy of having him there at school. 'We're all going to Smiths for an ice cream, Daddy. Can you come?'

He glanced at me, hesitating.

'You'd be welcome to join us,' I said, unsure whether I really meant it or not. It would have felt mean not to invite him, since he'd made the effort to come to the concert. But at the same time I felt slightly uncomfortable and a little bit resentful about the idea of him tagging along for the special treat Louise and I had planned.

Perhaps he picked up on this, because he bent to kiss Mia, giving her a quick hug, and said, 'No – thank you, that sounds like a great idea but I really ought to get back. I've got some work to finish off. I'm parked just round the corner here, so I'll say goodbye now. But well done again, kids. And Mia, next time I see you, we'll be going off to Lanzarote.'

Fortunately this was enough to take the disappointed look off Mia's face. She gave Josh another hug, and then the rest of us carried on to Smiths, Eddie and Mia walking in front of us singing 'This is Me' again at the tops of their voices.

'That was unexpected, wasn't it?' Louise said quietly as we settled down at a table.

'Yes.' I hadn't recovered from the surprise yet, or worked out quite how I felt about it. Although I was pleased he'd made the effort, it had felt so odd, seeing Josh here in

Furzewell, at the school – on what I'd thought of as my territory – and I suspected it had felt odd for him, too. 'I wonder if he's going to start turning up for more things like this now,' I added, thinking aloud.

'Mia would love that,' Louise said, putting a hand over mine and giving me an understanding look. And I knew she was right. It had been a fantastic ending to the school year for Mia – and that was all that mattered.

As arranged, Louise brought Eddie to play with Mia every day for the first two weeks of the school holiday while she was at work. The weather was warm and sunny, and they played in the garden almost the entire time, wearing shorts, sunhats and sun cream, making up their own games, climbing trees, kicking balls about, firing water at each other, laughing and having the kind of fun we all want our kids to have, before they grow up and retreat into the teenage world of gaming and social media. In the afternoons, Mum and I would often sit on the bench, watching them play, smiling as Smartie trotted around after them, wanting to join in.

'Mia's having such a lovely time with Eddie,' I said wistfully to Mum one afternoon. 'I wish I could keep her this age forever.'

'We all wish that,' she replied, smiling: 'Sleepless nights, teething, nappies, toddler tantrums, school problems – they're nothing, compared with the worries they bring when they get older.'

'I hope *I* never worried you like that when I was a teenager,' I said.

'Not when you were a teenager, no,' she responded. She paused for a moment and then added: 'But I worry about you now.'

'Sorry,' I whispered, grabbing her hand and squeezing it. 'Please don't worry. I'm fine.'

After all, here we were, on a lovely sunny day in the garden of Eagle House, drinking tea together – mother and daughter – watching the children and the little dog play together. I *was* fine. I didn't want Mum to be burdened by my issues. As it happened, there was no time to discuss it any further anyway, because just then there was a shout of 'Hello!' from the gate at the side of the garden, and Gran came in to join us, looking unusually tired and a bit grumpy.

'What's wrong?' I asked her, making room for her on the garden seat, as Mum went indoors to make more tea. 'You don't look very happy.'

'Oh, I don't know, Nicky.' She closed her eyes. 'I'm beginning to think your mother was right. Why did I ever think I was going to be able to manage on my own?'

'At Nightingale Court? But you *are* managing, perfectly well. What on earth is all this about?'

She opened her eyes again, looking at me and shaking her head.

'I really think I'm losing my mind,' she said. 'I think I'll probably end up being moved to one of those care homes.'

I took hold of her hand. 'Gran, we've already been through this, haven't we? Just because you've forgotten things a few times, it doesn't mean—'

'But it's not just forgetting things. I'm hearing things now. Imagining things.'

'What sort of things?' Mum had come back out now with Gran's mug of tea, and sat down on the other side of her, frowning at her.

'Noises in the night. People crying, mostly. Screaming, sometimes.'

'You've probably just been dreaming,' Mum said.

'Dreaming?' Gran shot back. 'I might be old, Ros, I might be losing my mind, but I know when I'm awake and when I'm bloody dreaming.'

'Well, have you talked to Lizzie about it?'

Lizzie Barnes was the warden of Nightingale Court. She was about fifty, lived in one of the bungalows herself and was supposed to keep an eye on all the elderly residents, but we'd never seen much evidence of it.

'Huh!' Gran snorted. 'No point talking to *her*. She sits around all day with music blaring, and from what Mary next-door to her says, she has it blaring all night too while she's in bed. She wouldn't hear if there was an earthquake under her own bungalow, never mind if any of us screamed for help.'

'Surely she hears if anyone presses their alarm buttons?' I pointed out. 'She has the control panel, doesn't she?'

'So she says. Not that I've ever needed to push the bloody button and if I did I'd probably be better off dead than waiting for her to respond – lazy cow.'

'Gran, this really isn't like you, to sound so fed up,' I said. Mum and I were exchanging worried looks. 'How many times do you think you've heard someone screaming? Perhaps it's kids outside in the street.'

'It's been happening every night,' she said. 'And sometimes during the day too. At first I thought it was someone's TV. They all have it up loud, you know – most of them are deaf. Josie in the bungalow opposite mine has hers blaring out those American comedy programmes, with all the windows open. It's a wonder I can hear myself think, never mind hear these screams and crying.'

'Well, I think we should talk to Lizzie,' Mum insisted. 'If someone in the complex is crying every night—'

'Not just *someone*,' Gran corrected her irritably. 'Lots of people. It sounds like … the end of the world, everyone screaming and wailing.'

'Then it *must* be someone's TV,' I said. 'Honestly, Gran, you said yourself, they all have their volume up loud, and perhaps someone's watching a box set of some terrible horror series.'

She shook her head. 'I don't know, Nicky. I've spoken to some of the other residents, and no-one else has heard it. Is it me? Am I hearing voices in my head? They say it's one of the signs of madness, don't they?'

I squeezed her hand. 'You don't sound mad in the slightest. Anyone who was losing their mind would just take it as a normal everyday occurrence to hear screams in the night.'

She didn't look at all reassured. I was upset, too, to hear her talking so negatively about Nightingale Court and its other residents. She'd been so happy there, so pleased with her little bungalow and the fact that it was all hers, and that she could live safely and independently there on her own.

'We'll find out what's going on,' Mum said gently. 'I'll come back with you, and we'll knock on all the doors and ask everyone if they're playing scary films late at night. If it's not that, then maybe Nicky and I should walk round at night-time and listen outside your bungalow. As Nicky says, it could just be teenagers screaming in the street. You know what they're like if they've been sitting outside the pub drinking cider—'

'Thank you, Ros.' Gran nodded. 'I don't *want* to think I'm losing my mind. But what with all the forgetfulness. . .'

'Maybe you're forgetting things because you're tired,' I suggested. 'Because of being kept awake at night by these noises?'

'If it makes you feel better,' Mum added, 'go and talk to Dr Osborne about your memory. I'm sure he'll tell you it's perfectly normal to get a bit forgetful as you get older.'

'Huh.' Gran shook her head. 'The way I'm going, I'll probably forget what I've gone to see him for.'

I laughed and squeezed her hand again. 'At least you haven't lost your sense of humour Gran.'

But it wasn't funny, not at all. I'd already started feeling concerned about Gran's forgetfulness – not because I thought it was anything out of the ordinary, but because it was upsetting her. Now this new issue was just adding to her worries.

As promised, Mum walked back to Nightingale Court with her a little later. She was gone for quite some time, and when she came back she was looking relieved.

'I talked to most of the other residents – those who were home, and could hear me ringing their doorbells, anyway,' she said. 'Most of them didn't have a clue what I was talking about, hadn't heard anything, and claimed to be always tucked up in bed by ten o'clock, But one old boy admitted he'd been watching a Netflix series *Zombie Flesh Eaters* until late at night. Honestly!' She chuckled. 'What these old folk get up to!'

'*Zombie Flesh Eaters*?' I repeated, shuddering. 'Sounds horrible! So does Gran accept that this is what she's been hearing?'

'Yes. He said there was quite a lot of screaming in it, and he apologised for having his TV up so loud with the windows open because it's been so warm. Bloodthirsty old sod!'

'Well, let's hope he turns the volume down, now he knows he's frightened her.'

'Oh, he's done more than that. He's invited her in to have a glass of sherry and watch it with him!'

I burst out laughing. 'Surely she's not going to?'

'I should hope not! But at least it's made her laugh too, and taken the worry out of the situation.' Mum raised her eyes and tutted. 'What were we saying earlier, about worrying about your kids? Just when you think you can *stop* worrying about them, it starts all over again – about your parents.'

I smiled, but didn't respond. I wasn't about to admit that I was already worried enough about *her* – my own mother – gadding about at night with the Gruesome Twosome, dressed to kill and made up to the nines. Who knew what they got up to in the bars and pubs they went to, and wasn't it about time they acted their age? But then again, if at the age of about eighty it was all right for that old boy in Nightingale Court to binge-watch zombie movies, and invite his frightened neighbour in to watch it with him with a glass of sherry, what the hell did I know about what was normal?

CHAPTER 25

Our warm, sultry July ended with another thunderstorm, but then August began with the heat returning and creeping up another notch. There were news reports of an unprecedented heatwave in some parts of England and even here in Devon, where the climate was normally more temperate, some of us were beginning to complain that it was too hot. The grass in the garden of Eagle House, in the park and along the roadside verges had turned dry and brown, flowers wilted, and Mum's shop sold out of ice cream and sun lotion. But I was grateful that the children could enjoy being out of doors during their school holiday.

My days were filled with activities for Mia and Eddie, and walking Smartie early in the mornings and late in the evenings, when it was cooler. I'd also now been out on two more dates with Craig, asking Mum to babysit and using Amber or Louise as alibis.

'I don't really understand why you're keeping it a secret from your mum,' Craig said, with a puzzled smile when he picked me up from the end of Pump Lane, as arranged, for our third date. 'It's not like you're a teenager. Would she disapprove of me?'

'No, of course not,' I said, flushing slightly. To be honest, I *did* feel like a teenager, sneaking out on these dates. It was awkward and embarrassing, being thirty-five and a mother myself, but living back with my mum and having to lie to her. 'I just … don't really want anyone gossiping about us just yet – do you?'

'Well, not the dog-walking group, no,' he said, equally quickly. 'I think it'd be a mistake for them to know we're seeing each other. It could make the others feel awkward. But surely your mum doesn't gossip?'

'You don't know her! Working in the shop is fatal. If I said anything about it to her, she'd have told half of Furzewell by lunchtime the next day.'

'Fair enough.' He smiled again as I reached over to grab my seatbelt, inadvertently showing off most of my thighs as my skirt rode up, and probably too much of my cleavage as I leant over. Louise had lent me her short denim skirt, as I didn't think I'd get away with wearing the red dress yet again, and I'd teemed it with a new stripy top I'd bought online.

'Can I help with that?' he asked, as he took the seatbelt out of my hand, let it go, and instead put one hand on my leg, the other around the back of my head and began to kiss me. It was several minutes before he took a deep breath and suggested, 'Shall we just forget the meal and go straight back to my place?'

'Oh, well,' I said, flustered – wanting to say yes, but feeling like I should say no – 'I'm actually quite hungry...'

'Fair enough,' he said, starting the car and giving me a smile. 'Let's eat first then!'

In fact, after the meal, we did go back to his place. It was a ground-floor apartment in a converted old mansion on the outskirts of the village and inside it was a typical bachelor pad, with modern, minimalist furniture, straight edges, black-and-white décor and a few stylish framed prints on the plain walls. Feeling awkward, I sat on the edge of the black leather sofa, absent-mindedly stroking Judy, who'd rushed to greet us when we walked in. While Craig made coffee in the little white kitchen, I stared at the bedroom, which was directly opposite the lounge. From where I was sitting I was looking straight at his king-size bed, which was draped with black linen and looked . . . tousled . . . as if he'd just got out of it.

I shivered at the thought. Was I ready for this? Another man – already – after spending so many years with just the one, my only one? I'd thought it would help to make me feel better, restore my self-esteem a little, but now it had come to it, I wasn't so sure.

'Actually, Craig,' I called out, getting to my feet, feeling shaky with indecision, 'I think I'd better go.'

'Already?' He appeared in the kitchen doorway, a coffeepot in his hand, disappointment evident in his voice. 'No coffee? No . . . anything else?'

'I'm sorry.' I was regretting it, even as I was saying it. But it was no good, was it, if I wasn't sure. 'I'm not being fair to you. Maybe we shouldn't keep seeing each other.'

He put down the coffeepot and, wiping his hands on his trousers, came over and enfolded me in his arms.

'Don't be silly. Of course I was hoping you'd stay. But only when you're ready.' He kissed me, slowly and tenderly. I felt myself melting, wondering if even now I could change my mind. But then he let me go, holding me at arm's length and looking into my eyes. 'Maybe another time, Nic?'

'If you still want another time.' I smiled. 'It's not that I don't want to, Craig. I do, but—'

'I understand. You don't have to explain.'

All the way home, all the time we were saying goodnight in the car, I cursed myself for my stupid indecision. Craig had turned out to be so different from what I'd expected. His reputation, and even the way he behaved in the group, cast him as some kind of Jack-the-lad, but in fact he seemed to be a genuinely decent guy, giving every appearance of actually *caring* about me, rather than just wanting a quick one-night-stand and moving on, as Amber had implied.

'Ooh!' Louise gasped when I whispered to her the next day, when she came to collect Eddie, that I'd gone back to Craig's place for coffee. 'Come on, tell me all.'

I gave a weak little smile as I led her into the kitchen, away from the children. 'Nothing to tell, unfortunately. I bottled it.'

'Didn't like the coffee?' she quipped.

'Didn't even have it. I just wasn't sure if I was ready. And he was lovely about it. I don't think he deserves his reputation, you know.'

'Sounds like you regret not staying now.'

I sighed. 'Yes, I do. But if I'd stayed, would I have had regretted that instead?'

'Well, only you can answer that, love,' she laughed.

'I know. I feel so mixed up. I did want to stay. But I still feel bad, about Josh. About still being married.'

'Hurry up and get divorced, then,' she said with a chuckle. 'Look, you're separated. You've told him it's definitely over. You don't wear your ring. You don't even see him anymore, apart from for handovers. You've said often enough that you want to get on with your life.'

'Yes. But I'm not sure Josh would feel the same about it.'

She looked at me, her head on one side.

'You still care what he thinks?'

'No! Well ... not really ... only about this. I mean, if I found out *he* was seeing someone else, I don't quite know how *I'd* feel about it, if I'm honest. I realise it's inevitable, but I'd just prefer not to know about it.'

She gave me a careful look. 'Are you sure you don't still have feelings for him?' she asked quietly.

I shrugged. 'A mixture of feelings, I suppose. After so long together, it's not like you can just switch off completely, is it? I'm disappointed in him, and I feel annoyed with him a lot of the time. But he's still ... *was* still ... the only man

I've ever loved. I guess it's going to take longer than this, to move on. I thought dating Craig would help with the process. Now I'm not so sure.'

Louise gave me a hug. 'I understand what you're going through, and you're right, it does take time. But sooner or later you *will* both move on, and if that involves either of you having new relationships, well yes, it'll feel weird at first, but you will get used to it.'

'Thanks, Lou.' I hugged her back. 'I'm glad I can talk to you.'

She smiled. 'And meanwhile, why not just keep dating Craig and see how it goes.'

'Yes, I'm sure you're right.' I smiled back at her. 'And I'll have to try not think about Josh, if things do move on. I'm sure *he* won't be thinking about me.'

But in fact, he was still, annoyingly, occupying my thoughts more than I wanted. For a start, I still couldn't get over the fact that he'd turned up at the school talent show. That following weekend, he was picking Mia up to take her to Lanzarote for ten days, and I was determined to talk to him about it then.

His parents were going on the holiday too, and although I couldn't help feeling horribly excluded by this little family jaunt, I was comforted by the thought that they'd be there for Mia's first trip abroad. It would be nice for Mia to spend time with her paternal grandparents. I'd always got on well with Sue and Steve, back when we all lived here in Furzewell, before Josh and I married and moved to

Plymouth. But since they'd moved away too, to a village in Hampshire, we hadn't seen them so often.

'Nana Sue and Grandpa are having one room, and Daddy and me are having another one,' Mia told me happily as I helped her pack her little panda case on wheels. 'And there's a swimming pool, and Daddy's going to teach me to do a sitting-down dive.'

I bit back all the warnings buzzing like wasps in my head: *'Be careful'*, *'Don't go near the pool without Daddy'*, *'Make sure you put sun cream on'*. I had to trust him now or I couldn't let her go. It was hard though.

'I can't wait to go on the plane,' she added, giving herself a little hug of excitement. Then she suddenly stopped and looked at me, her smile fading. 'I wish you could come too, Mummy. Will you be lonely?'

I put my arms round her, breathing in the scent of her strawberry shampoo.

'No, sweetheart. I'll miss you, but I've got lots to do, helping to get ready for the pet show. And when you get back, we'll be going to Cornwall with Louise and Eddie.'

'Oh yes. Wow!' She jumped up and did a little dance on the spot. 'I'm going on *two* holidays, aren't I?'

'Yes, you are.' I smiled at her. I could have added that it made up for the times I'd just taken her to Torquay or Teignmouth for a week on our own because Daddy couldn't be bothered to come anywhere with us. But I wasn't going to burst her bubble. She was happy, that was all that mattered.

I kept the smile fixed to my face when Josh arrived to pick her up for the drive to Exeter airport, where they'd be meeting his parents.

'Come in for a moment – if you've got time?' I suggested. 'Mia's just getting her shoes on.'

'OK,' he said, sounding surprised. 'Yes, I've allowed loads of time.' He came in and stood in the hallway, looking a little awkward. I hadn't asked him in before. In fact, it struck me that it must be the first time he'd set foot inside Eagle House for years.

'Is everything all right?' he went on. 'You've got Mia's passport for me? She's not upset about being away from you, is she? She'll be fine, Nic: I'll take good care of her.'

'I know you will. And I . . . well, I just wanted to say, it was good of you to turn up for the school talent show the other week. A bit of a surprise,' I couldn't help adding.

'Oh. Well, Mia had told me all about it, about the song she was going to sing with her friend, and . . . I decided I'd like to be there. I know I've never been to anything before,' he added quietly, meeting my eyes now, 'but I wish I had. It was amazing.'

'Yes, it was,' I said, fighting feelings of irritation again. It wasn't as if there had ever been anything stopping him from coming before. But I was determined not to turn this into an argument. We'd never be able to move on, either of us, if I kept looking back to how things used to be. 'Mia was so chuffed that you came,' I said, keeping my voice steady. 'And you didn't need to have rushed off afterwards. She'd have loved it if you'd joined us for ice creams.'

'To be honest, Nic, I didn't want to intrude – it was your time with her. Your school, your input in her life that's helped her to do so well here. I can't take that away from you.' He hesitated, and then went on in a rush: 'Nothing I do with Mia – the holidays, the outings, the presents – can ever come close to the fact that you've made her what she is: the child with the confidence to stand up on that stage and sing like that.'

'Oh,' I said, blinking at him, completely taken aback. 'Well, it hasn't been easy—'

'I know. It wasn't ever easy for you, was it, even when we were together. You've pretty much brought her up on your own.'

We stared at each other in silence for a moment. I couldn't respond, I was too stunned. Josh had never before admitted his lack of input into Mia's upbringing, even though he could hardly have denied it. Then Mia suddenly burst out of the kitchen where she'd been saying goodbye to Mum and Smartie.

'Are we going now, Daddy?' she said excitedly, adding as she threw herself at me for a hug: 'Bye, Mummy. Don't be sad.'

'I won't,' I reassured her, forcing a smile. 'Have a brilliant time, sweetheart.' But I felt terribly unsettled after they'd gone. And it was only partly because of saying goodbye to Mia.

For the first few days she was away, I felt so bereft, I threw myself into the pet-show preparations with a vengeance, to take my mind off her empty bedroom and the unnatural silence in the house. Simon had organised another gardening weekend in the park to keep it tidy, and Louise, who'd taken this week off work to be at home with Eddie, had spent some time organising a working party to clean the toilet block. We'd had the water turned back on, but the building had been padlocked up for so long, there were cobwebs draped across the insides and outsides of the windows, some of the locks on the cubicle doors were broken and we had to call a plumber to fix a dripping tap.

'I feel like locking them up again, now they're clean,' Amber said, when we finally stood back, with our group of helpers, and surveyed the sparkling windows, clean floors and fully working toilets, bleached to shining perfection and supplied with a fresh supply of loo rolls.

'Sara suggested putting up one of those signs that asks people to leave the facilities the way they'd like to find them,' I said. We exchanged a smile, both of us aware that although Sara was certainly putting in more work than anyone else on this project she was never likely to turn up on toilet-cleaning day. 'It shouldn't be necessary, but—'

'But some people are dirty and lazy, unfortunately,' Amber said with a shrug. 'Well, let's hope they'll be more considerate now that it's all being funded by the community. By ourselves.'

The plumber, a local guy who'd joined the Friends himself, had waived his bill, and Simon had got the new plants and shrubs for the flowerbeds at trade price, but the incidental costs were adding up. Apart from what we'd spent that weekend on cleaning materials, loo rolls, bins, soap dispensers, mirrors, hand dryers to replace the ancient rusty ones that had made enough noise to wake the dead and didn't even dry properly, and new bolts for the doors, there had already been the expense of advertising the pet show, buying prizes for the winners and printing the programmes.

'We've got money coming back from the businesses that've advertised in the programmes, though,' Amber pointed out, as we started to walk to the pub together. 'And none of the pet-show judges want a fee. Craig's used his charms to get the boarding kennels woman on-side and we've now got both vets.'

'That's true. Well done for sorting that out,' I said.

'Oh, it's thanks to Kelly, really.'

'Kelly?' I queried.

'The nurse at the vet's – I told you, didn't I? She was the one who suggested Mr Brent and persuaded him and the other vet, Andrew Gordon.'

I giggled. 'Which of them is she sleeping with?'

Amber stopped dead in the street and rounded on me, her face flushed with annoyance. 'Oh, sure, bring it down to your level, Nic. She's not sleeping with *either* of them. They're just decent guys who want to help out.'

'It was a joke,' I said, staring at her. 'Keep your knickers on!'

'Maybe *I* should be saying that to *you*.'

'What's that supposed to mean?'

She shrugged. 'You know perfectly well what I mean. I've noticed what's been going on with you and Craig, how you shamelessly flirt with him. You might as well just stand up in the pub and announce that you're having sex with him.'

'I'm *not*, actually. But so what if I was?' I shot back, cross and upset now. 'It's nothing to do with you, or anyone else.'

'Isn't it? Not even Sara?'

'No. Why should it be anything to do with Sara?' I said. 'Just because he flirts with her too? That's just the way he is. You told me yourself that they weren't seeing each other.'

'I said *not as far as I knew*. But maybe you should ask *her*. Look, I don't want either of you to get hurt, Nic – you and Sara are both my friends, and although I do like Craig, I know exactly what he's like. And I'm sorry, but you're really vulnerable at the moment, so soon after separating from Josh. I've tried to warn you—'

'Well, maybe you should just keep your nose out of it,' I retorted. 'Forget about that drink, Amber. I'm going home.'

'Suit yourself!'

We both turned and walked in opposite directions. All the way home, I was feeling furious with Amber, furious that Craig and I had – apparently – not been anywhere near as discreet as we'd thought, and furious most of all with myself for reacting so childishly. It wasn't until I'd made myself a cup of tea and calmed down a bit that I started, seriously, to wonder what she'd meant about Sara.

CHAPTER 26

Missing Mia was like a continual ache, somewhere deep inside my chest. However hard I tried to think about other things, it nagged away at me constantly. I imagined all the worst things possible: her tripping and falling into the pool, hitting her head; or paddling in the sea, being knocked over by a wave; or going out too far with her over-confident beginner's version of doggy paddle and getting swept away by the tide. Or lying in a strange bed, in an unfamiliar hotel room, missing me, and being upset.

When my phone warbled suddenly one day, snapping me out of imagining one of these scenarios playing out, I nearly jumped out of my skin. *Josh* said the display as I swiped to answer the call. I almost dropped it in fright.

'What's wrong?' I said, without even a hello. My chest tightened with fear as all those horrible possibilities I'd been imagining flashed through my brain again.

'Eh? Nothing,' he said. 'Everything's fine. Oh I'm really sorry, we did say we wouldn't call unless it was an emergency. But I just thought you might like to have a chat with Mia.'

'Oh. Is she upset? Has she been missing me? Perhaps you could bring her back early if she's really unhappy—'

'Nic, calm down, she's fine. She's having a brilliant time.' He paused. 'It's you we were thinking of.'

We? I smiled now, picturing Sue and Steve nagging Josh to call me, reminding him that I'd be missing Mia and worrying about her.

'That was nice of them,' I said, thinking aloud.

'Them?' He paused again. 'It was Mia's idea, actually. She thinks you might be lonely.'

'Ah, bless her. Put her on, then.'

And seconds later, I was listening to my baby girl's voice bubbling over with happiness as she described the beach, the sea, the ice creams she'd been having, the pool where, as promised, Daddy had taught her to do a sitting dive and bought her a lilo in the shape of a flamingo.

I listened, and smiled, and pictured her little face, flushed with excitement.

'And are you remembering your sun cream?' I said when she paused for breath. 'And your hat?'

'Yes. And Mummy, Daddy's bought me a new swimming costume, and a towel with mermaids on it. And I wish you were here too, Mummy.'

'Oh, are you missing me?'

'Not really.' The cruel honesty of childhood! 'But are you lonely?'

'I'm fine, sweetheart. I've got Smartie for company, haven't I? And Nanny. And all my friends.'

Not that any of them helped to fill the gaping hole in my life. But I did feel better for speaking to her.

'Bye bye, Mummy. I love you.'

'I love you too, baby. Take care, and enjoy the rest of your holiday.'

It was nice of Josh to get her to call me, I thought to myself as I sat back in my chair, my phone still in my hand. But then I remembered: it was Mia's suggestion, not his. I doubted whether he'd have thought of it otherwise. I could count the times on one hand that he'd called me since we split up – only ever about handover arrangements. But then I thought again about what he'd said to me on the day he picked Mia up for the airport. About all his treats being nothing compared with my own input in her life. It had shocked me to hear him talking like that. I supposed that now he was spending time with his daughter, he'd finally begun to realise what he'd missed. I'd tried to put the conversation out of my mind and not dwell on it but it did make me wonder if he was really starting to have regrets about not being there for us, especially Mia, in the past. I sighed. He might be behaving differently, and appreciating Mia more now, but he obviously still couldn't care less about me. So why did I still worry what he might think if I went out with another man, a man who really seemed to appreciate me and desire me? Josh didn't even have to know. But if he found out, and it bothered him – it was tough. He was my past. And Craig ... just might be my future.

I was still hoping, though, to talk to Sara. I was ninety-nine per cent positive Amber's little hints about her and Craig were nonsense. Yes, Sara did flirt with him, but surely that was all it was. And although Craig and I had agreed it was best not to let the rest of the group know we were seeing each other, I was beginning to think now that it wouldn't hurt to mention it to Sara. Apart from anything else, it might just stop her fluttering her eyelashes, shaking her hair and talking to him in that different, annoying voice she reserved for him instead of the bossy, business-like one she used for the rest of us. But when I took Smartie to the park that same evening, Simon was the only one waiting there.

'Apparently Sara's away for a few days,' he said. 'Not sure where the others are.'

'Oh, right. Well, Amber's still not walking Benji, of course.'

'No, of course, that's right. Poor old Benj.'

'And I think Craig's busy with work – he's having to stay late in the office,' I added, looking away and trying to sound completely disinterested. Craig had already told me he might not be joining many dog walks this week for that reason.

We set off on our own, heading across the park, Smartie chasing playfully after Max, wagging his tail happily. I was chatting away to Simon, telling him how much better the flowerbeds looked since his latest gardening weekend, how pleased I was to see so many children playing in the park and older people enjoying an evening stroll now the heat of the day was dying down – so it was a while before I realised how quiet he was.

'Are you OK?' I asked him, stopping and giving him an anxious look.

'Me? Yes, I'm fine.' He smiled, but his eyes didn't seem to be agreeing. 'Nic, while we're on our own, there's something I've been wanting to say,' he started, and then shook his head and fell silent again.

'What?' I watched his face, wondering what it was he was struggling with. 'What's wrong, Si? You can tell me.'

Again, he hesitated, looking away and up into the trees as if something within their branches might help him.

'Look, I know it's none of my business,' he began eventually, still not looking at me. 'But – I'm sorry – it's pretty obvious Craig has been, well, making a play for you.'

'Oh.' I felt myself flush. 'Um, well, it's just, you know, a bit of silly flirting—'

'OK. As I said, it's nothing to do with me, of course. But … just be careful. I mean, don't get me wrong, I'm sure you know what you're doing, you don't need me to nanny you, but, well, Craig's a nice enough boy—'

Boy, I thought, trying not to smile. Well, yes, of course, he was more than twenty years younger than Simon!

'—but he's got something of a reputation,' Simon was finishing, sounding so awkward and unhappy I could only feel sorry for him. 'I'd hate to see you get involved … and get hurt. That's all.' He turned back to me now, tried to give an uncomfortable little laugh and added, 'I expect you'll just tell me to shut up and mind my own business.'

'No,' I said, patting his arm. 'I'm sure you're only trying to look out for me.'

Surely Simon wasn't interested in me himself? It seemed unlikely, but at the same time I couldn't help feeling quite flattered by the thought. And for that reason, as well as the fact that poor Simon obviously felt so awkward having this conversation with me – I wasn't annoyed by his interference, the way I'd been by Amber's.

'Yes,' he said, managing another smile now. 'I am looking out for you, of course. But I won't say any more. Sorry.'

'It's fine. I appreciate the warning, but honestly, even if I do, at some point ... get involved with someone ... I won't take it too seriously. I'm not looking to settle down with anyone again. Not this soon. If ever.'

There. That should put paid to any misunderstanding. He didn't need to know, any more than Amber did, that Craig and I were, in fact, already seeing each other, and well on the way to becoming an item. Everyone would find out soon enough. But to my surprise Simon went on, without looking at me now:

'Not unless you were to get back together with Josh, eh?'

'What?' I stared at him. This wasn't the first time he'd said something like this. I'd surely made it clear enough, hadn't I? 'There's no way that's going to happen, Si.'

'I suppose not. It's sad, isn't it? After you were together for so long. And it sounds like he was the love of your life, at one time. I wonder what changed.'

I just shook my head. I didn't want to talk about Josh, and I couldn't understand why Simon seemed determined to bring him into the conversation, considering he didn't even know him. Perhaps he felt kind of maudlin about my marriage breakdown because he himself had been happily married to his own wife for so long. Or perhaps he was checking I really was going to remain single – and available...

I quickly changed the subject – and we spent the rest of the walk chatting about other things – mostly the plans for the pet show, of course. He was such a lovely man, I reminded myself yet again when by mutual agreement we eventually turned back, at the far end of the park, to retrace our steps. It was still warm and humid, despite being halfway through the evening, and both dogs were looking too hot and tired for a longer walk. It was a pity, if he really did think of me as more than a friend, that I didn't return his feelings. It wasn't because of his age: in fact, in some ways I felt a bit daft for being attracted to someone as young and immature as Craig, but from my point of view, there just wasn't that same spark with Simon that I felt with Craig.

If I hadn't been so consumed with these thoughts of Craig and how attracted I was to him, what followed would never have happened – which is why I was totally mortified and overcome with guilt afterwards.

*

Smartie was very good by now at coming back to me when I called him, so I wasn't overly concerned by the fact that, when Simon and I approached the area of the park where there tended to be more people, and where we always put the dogs back on their leads, we'd lost sight of them for a moment.

'Max!' Simon was calling. He whistled, and called again: 'Come on, Max. Here, boy!'

'I thought they were right with us!' I exclaimed. 'Smartie! Here, Smartie!'

Two seconds later, we heard them both barking, and Max came bounding towards us, only to stop in front of Simon, barking loudly, and turn around to run back again.

'What's the matter, boy?' Simon said, starting to follow him.

I could still hear Smartie barking, but I couldn't see him.

'Smartie!' I called again, beginning to worry. I ran, following Simon and Max, who suddenly stopped by the fencing surrounding the disused children's playground. My heart was banging against my ribs. Something was wrong. Max was standing at the fence, barking insistently, and now I could hear Smartie giving frightened little yelps and then whining and whimpering as though in pain.

'He's inside the fence,' Simon said. 'He must have wriggled through this hole. OK, Max, good boy, well done.' He fastened Max's lead. 'Quiet, now.'

Max, of course, would have been too big to follow his little friend through the small hole, where a couple of the wooden fence stakes seemed to have been vandalised.

'There's a cat in there,' I said. 'I can hear it yowling. Smartie must have gone in there after it. Give me a leg up, Si – I'll have to get over the fence—'

'No,' he said immediately, handing me Max's lead. 'I'll go. You stay there with Max.'

Before I could even argue the point, he'd thrown his weight against the makeshift fence, pushing out the damaged stakes, and was squeezing himself through the gap.

'I'll repair it tomorrow,' he gasped as he straightened himself up on the other side and ran towards the sound of Smartie's cries.

Too worried now to stay put, I was on the point of following him with Max when he reappeared, carrying Smartie in his arms.

'He's caught his leg on the edge of that slide,' he said, passing Smartie gently over to me before squeezing himself back through the fence. 'Let's get him straight to the vet's, Nic. He's going to need stitches.' He shook his head, sighing. 'The damaged edge of that slide is razor sharp. The council need to dismantle that before someone gets badly hurt—'

'Someone *has* got badly hurt,' I protested, before bursting into tears as I tried, ineffectively, to staunch the bleeding from poor Smartie's leg with a tissue from my pocket.

'Here.' Simon stripped off the loose cotton shirt he'd been wearing over his T-shirt and gently wrapped it around the wound. 'Come on, it's probably quicker to walk to the vet's from here, than go back for one of our cars. Shall I carry him?'

'No!' I cuddled Smartie protectively closer to my heart. 'I've got him.' I wiped my tears with the back of my hand. How had I let my attention wander like that, so that my poor puppy had ended up getting hurt? I knew the answer, of course. And although Simon was right, that it was the council's responsibility to remove the damaged equipment rather than just fencing it off with a pathetically inadequate wooden fence, and we needed to let them know how dangerous the slide was before a child injured themselves in the same way as Smartie had done, I couldn't help feeling ashamed of myself for losing sight of my little pup while I wandered along daydreaming about Craig like a lovesick teenager.

'Hush, baby,' I whispered to the whimpering little dog. 'I've got you now. The vet's going to make you better.'

Simon was calling their emergency number as we walked out of the park.

'Mr Brent's still at the surgery. He's only just finished his evening clinic,' he said, sounding relieved. 'Come on, Max, we're going with them.' He put his free arm briefly around my shoulders. 'Don't worry, Nic, I don't think the wound's very deep. It'll probably only need cleaning, and a few stitches. Smartie will be fine, I'm sure.'

I nodded, sniffing, and we walked together to the vet clinic in silence. I guess we were both thinking how easily, how quickly, the accident had happened – how careful we'd both thought we were with our pets, and what a lesson it was to us, to take even more care.

'But it was just an accident,' Simon said eventually, as if I'd spoken aloud. We were sitting in the empty waiting room while Kelly, the nurse, went to tell Mr Brent we were there.

'I know,' I said. 'And thank you for helping, Simon. You don't need to wait for us.'

'Of course I do,' he responded immediately. He leaned across me and stroked Smartie's fluffy little head. He gave me a sad little smile. 'What are friends for?'

CHAPTER 27

As Simon had predicted, fortunately Smartie's wound wasn't too serious, but because it was quite a long tear, it did need suturing. I waited, nervously biting my lip, while Mr Brent sedated him, clipped his fur away from the wound, cleaned it and stitched it closed.

'There's no need for me to keep him in,' he told me when he'd finished. 'But he's lucky; the wound was superficial so it should heal well. I'm giving you antibiotics and anti-inflammatories for him, and we'll put him into a collar, to stop him from licking the wound. I'd like to check him in two days, then the stitches will need to come out a week later. And no exercise until after that. He'll be too sore for walks anyway.'

'Thank you so much.'

'You're welcome.' He frowned. 'Did you say this was caused by the old play equipment in the park?'

'Yes. There's a sharp edge on the side of the slide,' Simon said.

I sighed. 'We think he wriggled through the fence, after a cat. It was my fault—'

'Actually, I'd say it was the council's fault,' Mr Brent said at once. 'They were supposed to have removed all that equipment, weren't they? I'm sure at your public meeting Sara Buckingham said they'd placed great emphasis on the fact that it was dangerous. It was supposed to be one of the reasons they wanted the park closed.'

'That's right. And now they've agreed to keep the park open for the rest of this year, to give us time to get them to change their minds, but yes – they were still supposed to remove the old equipment. You know how slowly they work, though.'

'Well, it's not good enough, is it? Something like this was bound to happen, with only that rickety fence around the area. It's lucky it wasn't more serious. You could probably sue them!'

'Oh, I wouldn't want to do that,' I said hastily. 'As I said, I should have been more careful – I didn't see Smartie go through the fence—'

'I'm not sure that's the point. And somebody else *will* sue them if their pet, or their child, gets injured. Would you like me to write to them, and say how concerned I am that Smartie's cut his leg? Suggest that they're very lucky his owner – you – aren't going to sue?'

I glanced at Simon, who'd been listening to this exchange with interest.

'That could be useful, couldn't it, Si,' I said.

'Very useful,' he agreed. 'It ought to push them into some action. Once that eyesore of a play area's been demolished and removed, we can remind them we're hoping to raise the funds to replace it with a proper adventure playground.'

'That sounds a great idea,' Mr Brent said. 'My kids would love that.'

'We won't actually build it, of course, unless they do eventually agree not to close the park,' Simon added quickly. 'Anyway, it'll take a lot of fundraising, for the materials. I'd do the actual work, though, with some help.'

'We're hoping the pet show will raise some of the money we need,' I explained. 'We've already sold a lot of programmes. And if the weather stays like this, we should have a good turnout on the day. Thank you so much, by the way,' I added, 'for offering to be one of the judges.'

'Oh, you're welcome.' He grinned, nodding at the nurse, who was fastening a big Elizabethan collar around poor Smartie's little neck. 'Kelly here did a good job of talking me and Andrew into it. Anyone would think you had an ulterior motive, Kel!'

Kelly blushed, shook her head as if in protest, and they both laughed. I frowned, not understanding what he'd meant, and was about to ask, when I remembered joking with Amber about Kelly sleeping with one of the vets – and the argument that had ensued. It *had* only been a joke, but perhaps I'd inadvertently guessed the truth. I decided it would be wiser not to go there!

'Well, thanks again, for everything,' I told him, instead. 'I'll bring Smartie back in two days' time, then. And if you do feel you could write to the council that would be really helpful.'

'Would you like me to help you take him home?' Simon asked when we left the vet's. I was carrying Smartie in my arms again, of course.

'Thanks, but it's fine – it's not too far now. And you've already given up more of your time than you needed to,' I assured him.

'It was no trouble at all,' he said. 'But if you're sure you'll be OK, I think I'll just take Max home and then go straight back to the park and fix that broken fence.'

'Really? But it's getting dark.'

'I've got a lamp,' he laughed. 'I know I said I'd do it tomorrow. But if Mr Brent's going to write to the council, I think the sooner I repair those fence stakes, the better, since it was me that broke them.'

'They were already broken. Enough for Smartie to get through.'

'Yes. Don't worry, I'm going to try to replace them in a way that they can still see the hole Smartie squeezed through. They'll send someone down as soon as they get Mr Brent's letter – they'll be scared someone *will* sue them. But I don't want any other dog – or child – to get hurt in the meantime.'

I nodded. 'Makes sense.'

I wanted to tell him that he was probably the nicest, most thoughtful man I knew. But I was too worried now that any affection I showed him would give out the wrong signal and let him think I was interested in him. Instead, we said goodnight and I hurried home with poor Smartie, making sure he was comfortable and ready to sleep off the trauma of his accident, before going to bed early myself. I was tired out by the worry of it, as well as by the unusual warmth of the night.

By the time Mia was due to return, there'd been no let-up in the hot weather. Because of Furzewell's situation in a valley surrounded by the rolling Devon hills, it sometimes felt as if there was no breath of air in the village at all. It would have been cooler on the coast, but I could just imagine how crowded all the beaches would be, and at least in the garden of Eagle House we had some shade from the trees. Mum and I were worried about Gran, who was finding the higher temperatures of the afternoons completely exhausting and had taken to going to bed for a nap, with the curtains drawn against the sun and a fan going in her bedroom.

'It's the best thing she can do, while it's so warm,' Mum tried to reassure me. 'We just need to keep nagging her to drink lots of water.'

I had similar concerns about Smartie who, as soon as he'd started to recover from his injury, was missing his walks, becoming mischievous again because he was probably bored.

'The trouble is,' I explained to Gran, when I visited her on the morning before Mia was due back, 'he can't go for walks till he's had the stitches out. And anyway, it would be too hot for him. Even in the garden, all he wants to do is lie down in the shade or go indoors for a drink of water.'

'I know how he feels,' Gran complained. 'I haven't got an ounce of energy. Can't be bothered to do anything, but I'm bored to tears just sitting here with the curtains drawn.'

'Why don't you come round to Eagle House for a few days? I can pick you up in the car to save you walking round there, and you'd at least be able to talk to Mum and me, and see Mia when she comes back.'

For a second, I thought she looked tempted. But then she shook her head.

'No, thank you. I know your mum thinks I'm too old and feeble to live here on my own—'

'No, Gran, that's not what we're saying. It's just that this weather is a bit exceptional. You can't do the things you'd normally do. It's not safe for you to be outside in the heat.'

'It's all right. I'll stay put, thank you very much, even if that silly old man over the back does drive me mad playing his bloody vampire films, or whatever they are, all night when people are trying to get to sleep.'

'Is he still doing that?' I sighed. 'Shall I have another word? Ask him to turn the volume down again?'

'No, don't bother, Nicky. I don't want to remind him that he wanted me to go and watch one of the damned things with him. As if I'd be interested,' she huffed.

'Well, if it goes on, I'll mention it to what's-her-name – the warden. She can talk to him.'

'Huh. Fat lot of good Lazy Lizzie would do. Waste of space, she is.'

'OK.' I felt at a loss. Nothing I could say seemed to be cheering her up. 'Well, look, keep drinking the water, won't you. And call us if you think of anything else you need from the shop. You know Mum would prefer to cook for you—'

'Who needs to eat, in this weather? A slice of toast is all I want.'

'You're worrying me now,' I said. 'Please look after yourself Gran or you *will* have to come to Eagle House.'

'Sorry,' she conceded. 'I'm being an old misery, aren't I? Go on, thanks for coming round, love. Bring Mia round to see me tomorrow when she's back, won't you. I want to hear all about her holiday, and what that damned fool Josh has wasted his money on this time.'

It wasn't like Gran to criticise Josh. She'd been very careful up till now to keep her opinions about him to herself. I walked home slowly, worrying about her not eating, getting dehydrated, being frustrated and bored, and not getting enough sleep. I stopped off at the shop to update Mum.

'I'll take her some fruit – strawberries and grapes – when I've finished here, and some ham and salad, and maybe a bottle of that sparkling apple drink she likes,' she said. 'She just needs encouragement to eat and drink properly.'

'I'm hoping it'll cheer her up to see Mia tomorrow,' I said.

And of course it did, but not as much as it cheered me up!

*

'She enjoyed absolutely everything about the holiday,' Josh said when he accompanied her to the door of Eagle House, carrying her suitcase. 'She's even learned a few words of Spanish. She can't wait to show them off to you.'

'*Hola! Comó estás?*' Mia squealed excitedly. Her face and arms glowed, but only a gentle light golden colour. Josh had evidently taken the sun cream rules seriously. 'Mummy, I had paella! It was yummy! And we went to this water park, it had the biggest water slide ever, and Daddy put me on his lap to come down it the first time, but the second time I came down on my own. It was *amazing*!'

I hugged her so tight that she eventually struggled free, laughing.

'It does sound amazing,' I said. 'I can't wait to hear all about it. Come in, let's put your case out of the way. Nanny's waiting to hear your news too. Go in and say hello.' I turned to Josh. 'Thank you,' I said stiffly, still unable to help a slightly resentful tone to my voice, despite being assaulted again by the memory of his unexpected words when he'd picked her up for the holiday. 'It sounds like she's had a brilliant time.'

'No worries.' To be fair, he sounded a little awkward himself. 'I'm just sorry that . . . well, you know.' He shrugged, looked down at his feet. 'Never mind, no point going into it now.'

'Into what?'

'Regrets,' he said, meeting my eyes for a moment and then looking away. 'Too late, isn't it? Anyway, I'll pick her up as usual for the weekend after next.'

'No, we'll be in Cornwall, remember? Probably won't be back till the Saturday night. You agreed to skip that one—'

'Oh yes, of course.' I'd half expected a protest, but instead he just said, to my surprise, 'I hope you have a nice time, then. Bye, Mia!' he shouted into the house, where I could hear her chattering away to Mum about the water park and the paella.

'Mia!' I called. 'Daddy's going! Come and say goodbye.'

'It's all right, Nic,' he said. 'I've had her for ten days. Let her catch up with her nan.'

He walked back to the car, where I could see Sue and Steve waving. I waved back, watched the car disappearing down the road, but still I stood on the doorstep, staring after it. I felt an unexpected pang in my heart – but then I turned back to go into the house, quickly.

He was right, I told myself sternly – it *was* too late for regrets. As he'd said himself, holidays in Lanzarote were never going to make up for all those years he wasn't there for Mia. I slammed the door shut and went back inside to cuddle and chat some more to my daughter. She might have had a nice holiday with Josh, but now she was home. And her home was with me.

CHAPTER 28

Because of Smartie's healing leg, I wasn't joining the dog walks that week, and it continued to be so hot and sticky that I wasn't sorry. Mum had bought a paddling pool for the garden, and each morning I set this up in the shade, filled it with cool water, and Mia was happy jumping in and out of it for most of the day – Smartie often joining her to splash around in the water, shake himself all over her and make her giggle. Eddie was in Cornwall with his grandparents, Louise was working, and I split my time between housework, gardening and visiting Gran to make sure she was coping with the heat.

I began to wonder if I'd ever hear from Craig again. Now that I'd resolved to stop worrying about Josh, perhaps Craig was already tired of me! I thought about calling him or texting him, but as he'd warned me he was going to have a busy week with work, I didn't think that would be the right thing to do. And then – the day before we were due to go to Cornwall – he finally called.

'Sorry it's been a while,' he said breezily. 'Work's been horrendous. I haven't even had time to join the dog walkers; Judy's just had to put up with a quick run around the block every night before I fall into bed exhausted.'

'Oh, I haven't been for the walks, either.' I explained about Smartie's injury, and filled him in with the latest news about the playground equipment. I'd only heard that morning that the council had indeed panicked when they received Mr Brent's letter, and their workmen were in the process of dismantling the equipment even as we spoke.

'That's brilliant news,' Craig agreed. 'Sorry to hear about Smartie hurting himself, of course, but at least we'll be rid of that eyesore before the day of the pet show.'

'Yes, exactly.'

'So: I was wondering if you'd like to come round for dinner tomorrow night. I'll cook for you. It's one of my many talents. If it's still hot like this, we can eat outside on the terrace.'

'Oh, Craig, I'd love to, but I'm off to Cornwall tomorrow morning. Louise has invited me and Mia to stay at her mum's place for a week, with her and Eddie.'

'Oh yes – you did mention that, sorry. But that means I've got to live without you for another week. God, the only thing that's kept me going all this time I've been working like a dog was the thought of seeing you again.'

'Really?' I smiled to myself.

'Yes, and I can't make tonight, unfortunately. My parents have come down from Bath, and I haven't seen them for a while, so I've got to make an effort.'

'Of course. Don't worry. I'll definitely see you when I get back.'

'OK, I'll be looking forward to it. Have a great time in Cornwall.'

I couldn't stop smiling after I ended the call. I was *almost* wishing I wasn't going away the next day, the thought of being with Craig at his apartment was so tempting. Sitting outside with him, enjoying dinner and perhaps some wine, and then … whatever came afterwards…

I got to my feet, giving myself a little shake, and went outside to take the washing off the line. I needed to pack our bags for Cornwall. I was going to have a lovely, lovely week with my little girl, my new friend and her son. Craig, and his apartment, and his cooking skills (and the other talents he'd hinted at) would still be waiting for me when we came home!

Leaving Smartie in Mum's care, we were travelling down to Cornwall early in the morning, to avoid the heat of the day and be ahead of the holiday traffic coming from up-country. Mia was awake early anyway, bouncing around with excitement about her *second holiday*.

'It won't be quite like Lanzarote,' I warned her.

'I know,' she said, falling quiet for a moment and giving me a sad look. 'Because Daddy won't be there.'

'True,' I said, and thought better of adding anything else. 'Come on then. Say goodbye to Nanny and bring your bag out to the car.'

We picked up Louise – there was no point taking two cars – and the three of us sang along to happy holiday songs for the whole journey, which was mercifully short and trouble-free. Louise's mother's home was beautiful: a modern, chalet-style house with four bedrooms and a lovely lawned garden sloping down towards the sea. Charles and Anne were welcoming and generous hosts, refusing to allow Louise or me to do anything much in terms of helping with the catering.

'It makes a lovely change for us to have company,' Anne assured me, as Mia and Eddie, excited to be reunited, ran off to play. 'And I can't tell you how pleased we are that Louise and Eddie have made such good friends. From what she tells us, you and Mia have been absolute lifesavers for them.'

I laughed. 'Trust me, the reverse is just as true. The change in Mia since she's been friends with Eddie is unbelievable.'

I'd still been putting off talking to Mia about the fact that Eddie was going to be in a different class when they went back for the autumn term. I needed to do it, and couldn't afford to wait much longer. But in the meantime, we had a week at the seaside to enjoy. The beach was a quiet, sandy cove, and the weather remained warm and sunny, but with the benefit of a cooling breeze off the ocean. The kids played outside all day every day, running, jumping, swimming, building things in the sand, hunting for shells and fishing for crabs. Despite the enforced wearing of sunhats, Eddie's fair hair had bleached to a startling blond, and even Mia had golden highlights in her dark curls. Every day, Anne and Charles insisted we left the children in their care for an hour or so – it would have been hard for us to force them away from the beach – and Louise and I went for a walk along the coast path, or drove into the nearest town to get some shopping, or just strolled to the little café on the top of the cliff for a quiet coffee and a chat.

The week passed peacefully but quickly, and by the time we eventually loaded up the car again to drive home, we were all feeling relaxed, rested and ready to face the world again.

'Back to work on Monday,' Louise said. 'Are you sure you're still OK to have Eddie again, Nic?'

'Positive. You've seen for yourself how well they occupy each other. I don't have to do a thing when they're together.'

'Well, at least there's only a week and a half left of the school hols. They go back on the Thursday of the following week, don't they?'

'Yes. And the Monday is bank holiday, of course. The pet show.' I felt suddenly shaky with nerves, just talking about it. Were we ready? I had no idea.

'Oh yes, of course! I'm really looking forward to it.'

Louise would be one of the helpers at the park gate, selling programmes. I'd be busy, with some of the others, shepherding pets and their owners to the right places at the right time. Simon would be in charge of the public address system.

'It feels like we've been planning it for ages,' I said now. 'I can't believe it's only next week.'

And we really, really, needed it to be a success. And for it not to rain!

The next day, Sunday, I was sorting washing into piles when I heard Mia talking. At first, I thought she must be chatting to Mum, but when I put my head around the door I saw she was lying on the floor with Smartie, stroking his ears as she told him all about her holiday in Cornwall. I smiled as I watched her, remembering how I'd shared all my secrets with our dog when I was a child myself.

'I didn't want to come home,' she was telling Smartie. 'The beach was amazing, and the sea was so warm. And it was fun sharing a room with Eddie. And I don't want to go back to school next week. I'm a bit scared because I'm going to have a new teacher. But at least me and Eddie will be together. I'm not so scared when he's there.'

My heart sank and my smile disappeared. We needed to have that talk. It wasn't fair of me to keep putting it off. I waited until after dinner that night, when we were snuggled on the sofa together with a book. At the end of the story, I closed the book and said:

'Mia, I've got to explain something to you.'

She looked up at me, her eyes big and trusting. 'What?'

'You know your class at school has children from two different years?'

'Yes.' She nodded. 'My year and Eddie's year.'

'Your class is for Years 1 and 2. That *was* your year and Eddie's year. But now, when you go back, you're going to be in Year 2, and Eddie will be in Year 3.'

She frowned. 'So our class will be for Year 2 and Year 3 now?'

I smiled, despite myself, admiring her logic.

'No, sweetheart. The children in Eddie's year will move up to the next class – the class for Years 3 and 4. You'll have the new Year 1 children in your class now. They were my reception children before, and I'll get a new reception class.'

Mia was still frowning. I could see her working this out, thinking it through. It didn't take long.

'So . . . me and Eddie won't be in the same class anymore?'

'*Eddie and I*,' I corrected her automatically. 'No, you won't, sweetie. I'm sorry. I know how much you've enjoyed being together, but—'

'Why can't I move up with him?' she demanded crossly. 'It's not fair.'

'Because you're younger than he is. You know that. You'll still see him at playtimes, and lunchtime, and he'll still come and play with you after school—'

'He'll be lonely,' she said, starting to cry now. 'He'll *hate* it in that class without me.'

I gave her a hug. I loved her for thinking of her friend first, even while she was upset herself.

'I'm sure he'll be all right, Mia. He's happy at school now, like you are. It was different before, when you were both new. You'll still be best friends, of course, but you *will* make other friends too.'

'I won't!' she said, folding her arms across herself and jutting out her lip. 'I don't want any other friends. Nor does Eddie.'

I stroked her hair, and talked to her about other things, about the next few days, when Eddie would be coming to play again, and the following weekend when she'd be seeing Josh, and coming home in time for the pet show. I talked about the week in Cornwall, and her holiday in Lanzarote, and how much fun she'd had on them both. And finally I read her another story. And through it all, she maintained a mutinous silence, her thumb back in her mouth for the first time in months, her arm around Pink Bunny.

'I wish you hadn't told me,' she said accusingly when I put her to bed a little later. 'I wish I didn't know about it. You've *ruined* everything, Mummy.'

'But children always blame us for everything, don't they,' Louise said lightly when I told her about it quickly the next morning when she dropped Eddie off on her way to work. 'She'll be fine, Nic. Eddie says he'll talk to her about it.'

'You've already told him? I didn't know. He hasn't said anything to Mia about it yet.'

'No. I asked him not to, until you'd told her yourself. It only came up just before we went to Cornwall and I warned him to wait. He said once you'd told her about it, he'd help her not to be upset.'

'Ah, that was sweet of him. But wasn't he upset himself?'

'He went a bit quiet. But actually, he seems to be handling it much better than I expected. I guess he's growing up.'

As I watched them playing together that day, I realised with a start that they both *were* growing up. Eddie was seven and a half now, and Mia was nearly six and a half. The half-year that we'd now been in Furzewell had made a huge difference to her, and it must be the same for Eddie. They weren't the frightened, upset children they'd been when they first met. Surely, now, they were better prepared for this new challenge? I could only hope so.

CHAPTER 29

Smartie had had his stitches removed now, and Mum had been taking him for short walks again while I was away. He seemed fine, thank goodness, and I took him out to meet the dog walkers on that first Sunday when I arrived home. Mia was busy building a den in the garden, so I left her with Mum. I was excited at the thought of meeting up with Craig again, but when I arrived at the park gate, Sara was the only one waiting.

'Simon's messaged me to say he's seeing a potential client,' she said as we set off. 'And Craig can't make it either.'

She didn't say why. She was looking a bit fed up. I supposed she was sorry to be missing another opportunity to flirt with him.

'No Amber?' I said. I hadn't seen her for what seemed like ages. Not since we'd had that argument, in fact.

'No.' She shrugged. 'I've no idea why. She's been walking Benji again since last week – his skin's much better now. Maybe she's just busy today.'

Well, at least it gave me the opportunity to have a talk to Sara on her own. But now it had finally come to it, I felt nervous about actually announcing to her that Craig and I were seeing each other. After all, it was still only early days. We'd only had three dates, but he did seem really keen – didn't he? I walked beside Sara in silence, battling with my uncertainties. If he was *that* keen, wouldn't he have called me as soon as I got home yesterday? Wouldn't he have made the effort to turn up here this morning? Wouldn't he, in fact, have been texting and calling me during the week I was away in Cornwall? I hadn't thought too much about this until now. I'd been off the dating scene for so long – in fact, I'd never really been on it, as Josh and I started going out while we were still at school – that I suppose I'd just assumed this was how it worked in the early stages of a relationship. What did I know?

But as I was mulling over these thoughts, and trying to pluck up the courage to start the conversation with Sara, she suddenly nudged me and said:

'Isn't that Amber? Over there?'

I looked where she was pointing. A little way off, where some of the gardens of the new estate backed onto the park, I could see someone bending down, holding something. I couldn't see what it was, but the person was bending down, talking to ... what looked like ... yes, it definitely was – a *cat*.

'Yes. I think it is Amber.' I frowned. Amber, talking to a cat?

'She doesn't like cats,' Sara said, sounding equally puzzled.

'No.' I laughed. 'Perhaps she's changed her mind.'

Sara gave me a look.

'Well, let's go and say hello,' she suggested. 'No, don't call her,' she added quickly, just as I'd opened my mouth to shout. 'Let's surprise her.'

I had my doubts whether Smartie and Babette would be quiet enough to give her much of a surprise, but I shrugged agreement and we walked slowly across the grass towards Amber. As we got closer, it became clearer that she definitely *was* talking to the cat – a small black moggy – and it looked as if the object in her hand was a plate of something.

'It looks like she's *feeding* it,' Sara hissed to me. 'Good grief, Nic. She's trying to entice that cat. She's trying to *catch* it.'

I felt my heart skip a beat. *No*! I couldn't believe it, I wasn't *going* to believe it. Sara had never trusted Amber, she'd always been suspicious about her not liking cats, but I refused to accept what she was insinuating. I'd known Amber for too long. However much we might both have changed over the years, she couldn't have become that kind of person.

'Amber!' I called, before Sara could stop me. 'What are you doing?'

She looked round, surprised, dropping the plate of ... what looked suspiciously like *cat treats* ... and the cat ran off, meowing, grabbing something off the ground in its mouth as it went. Amber stood up, shaking her head, sighing, as she watched the cat disappear through a gap in the hedge.

'Damn,' she said. 'It's gone now.'

'What *were* you doing, Amber?' Sara demanded, staring at her. 'Were they *cat treats* you had there?'

'What do you think I was doing?' she retorted, evidently miffed that we'd interrupted her. 'Trying to tempt it away from that poor blackbird. I could have saved it, but the cat will finish it off now. Yes,' she added, glaring at Sara, 'I keep a box of cat treats on my kitchen windowsill. I overlook the park.' She pointed to one of the houses behind us, evidently hers. I felt bad, realising I hadn't even been to her house since I'd reconnected with her here in Furzewell. 'I try to do my bit, saving as many birds as I can.'

'So *you* say,' Sara replied. 'So where's the blackbird? In your imagination?'

'No, Sara,' I said quickly. 'I saw the cat pick it up. It's taken it off into the hedge.'

'Well, of course, you *would* defend her,' she said. 'Are you sure those cat treats aren't poisoned?'

I gasped, but Amber didn't flinch. She just stared back at Sara, her hands on her hips.

'I might not be a cat lover,' she said in a level voice, 'but I'd never hurt one. Never. I'd never hurt *any* living creature. I just try to rescue birds, that's all.'

'Funny how you've never mentioned it before,' Sara said, sounding slightly less certain now.

'Because I knew you'd be like this about it,' Amber replied. 'I knew right from the start that you were suspicious about me, just because I said I wasn't particularly a cat lover. That's why I kept right out of all the discussions about the missing cats. I'm as upset about it as everyone else, Sara! I feel really sorry for those people who've lost their cats. I just wouldn't want one myself, because I don't like what they do to the bird population. That doesn't mean I'm not sympathetic to people who do like them.'

There was silence for a moment, Sara and Amber staring at each other. The two dogs were running around our legs, their leads getting tangled, panting with excitement to get on with the walk. Then, suddenly, Sara's shoulders slumped, and she shook her head.

'OK. I'm sorry,' she admitted finally. 'I've got it all wrong, haven't I? I shouldn't have jumped to conclusions.'

'No, you shouldn't have. But you didn't really know me that well, did you. I suppose you'd have no idea what kind of person I've become since we left school.. Whereas *you* were my best friend since we were kids,' she added, giving me a hurt look.

'Yes, and I never believed for a minute that you were involved in this thing,' I said.

'No, she didn't,' Sara agreed – and I glanced back at her gratefully. 'Nic has been trying to talk me out of my suspicions all along. She did say you'd never do anything like that. I should have listened. I'm sorry,' she said again.

'OK. Let's just forget it,' Amber said brusquely.

'We'll wait for you, if you want to go and get Benji and join us for the walk,' I suggested.

'No, you go on. Smartie and Babette are getting impatient.' She forced a smile. 'Perhaps I'll join you tonight.'

Sara and I were quiet for a while as we walked on through the park and out into the lane leading to Cuckoo Copse.

'I should have listened to you,' she said eventually, shaking her head. 'I've been an idiot.'

'Well, you don't know her as well as I do,' I said. I don't know why I felt sorry for her. I suppose it was just that I'd never actually heard her sounding humble and contrite before. 'And it's true, that did look odd just now, until we understood what she was actually doing.'

'Do you think she'll forgive me? I don't want any bad feeling in the group, especially while we've got our first big event coming up.'

'I'm sure she will,' I said, although, in fact, I had no idea. I might have known Amber since we were children, but if I was honest, I didn't really know her *so* well these days. I wasn't going to tell Sara that Amber and I hadn't spoken to each other properly since we'd had an argument ourselves – over Craig.

Craig.

I sighed. I didn't feel in the least like bringing that subject up now. Sara was right: we needed to work together as a group now, more than ever. The pet show was only a week away, and if I started talking to Sara about her flirting with Craig – making it sound like he was now my property so she should keep her hands off – it could well end up with *us* falling out with each other too.

After all, I thought to myself miserably, mulling it all over again when I finally got home and let Smartie off his lead to run into the kitchen and slurp water from his bowl – after all, Craig *wasn't* my property, in any sense. I wasn't sure I could even think of myself as his girlfriend. He still hadn't called me. I pulled my phone out of my pocket now, filled with a new determination. I needed to know where I stood. This wasn't the 1950s; women didn't have to sit at home waiting to be called. I dialled his number. Voicemail. I left a message. And later in the evening, I left another one. Nothing. I was beginning to think it was over, almost as soon as it had begun.

It was probably fortunate that, for the next few days, I was kept fairly busy. Mornings were spent supervising Mia and Eddie. Sometimes I took them out for the day, but mostly they were happy enough running around in the garden at Eagle House, making up their own games, occupying themselves in the mysterious little world of six- and seven-year-olds. In the afternoons, when Mum was back from work, I left the kids in her care while I went to the park to help with anything that still needed doing for the pet show. On the Wednesday evening, the oppressive heat we'd been experiencing during the last few weeks suddenly exploded with another massive thunderstorm, following which it rained heavily for most of the night. In the morning, the air felt much fresher. Walking through the village to the park that afternoon, trying to avoid the puddles, I noticed everyone was smiling and expressing relief at the change in the weather.

'We needed the rain,' old Tommy Burrows said, leaning on his gate, nodding with satisfaction.

'Yes,' I agreed. I looked up at the sky. 'I hope it doesn't keep on raining now, though. We don't want the ground waterlogged for Monday's show.'

'Ah, it'll be fine, you'll see, my lovely. Better like this, than too hot for those animals. People wouldn't bring them along for the show else, thee knows.'

It was a good point. Although we'd hired a big marquee, to provide shelter from either the sun or rain, I knew from my own experience with Smartie that pets had been getting exhausted during the worst of the heatwave.

That Thursday evening, I finally caught up with Craig for the first time since my holiday. He'd joined the rest of the group halfway through the dog walk, and was deep in conversation with Simon about making sure the gates at both park entrances were secure, and manned, on Monday. I walked with Sara, trying not to look at him, wondering how on earth I was going to cope with these walks if he really didn't want to see me anymore. Sara didn't look any happier, either, and when – finally – Craig turned and gave me a grin and a wink, she stared at me with open hostility. This was ridiculous! Sooner or later we'd have to sort it out. But for now, I was just relieved that he wasn't completely ignoring me. And a little later, as we were all saying goodbye at the end of the walk, he leaned close to me and whispered:

'Sorry I didn't return your calls. Work has been manic again.'

'Oh, that's OK,' I whispered back, although really, I wasn't sure if it *was* OK. I had a horrible feeling I was getting myself into another situation exactly like the one I'd escaped from with Josh, where his work took priority over anything to do with me.

'I'll make it up to you,' he whispered now, his breath so hot against my ear that I couldn't help shivering. 'What about Tuesday night? I'll make sure I get away from work early.'

'Great.' I smiled. Well, I had to give him another chance, didn't I? We could have a conversation about the work thing then. 'It's a date.'

When I looked back at Sara, she was glowering again. What on earth was wrong with her? Was she *really* that jealous? Or was it simply that she was such a workaholic, she was irritated by other people having fun? Well, perhaps once I'd finally managed to tell her that Craig and I were actually dating, and not just indulging in a bit of flirtation, she'd stop the disapproving looks and be more understanding.

CHAPTER 30

To everyone's relief, Bank Holiday Monday was a sunny, breezy day – perfect weather. The pet show was opening at twelve o'clock, with a stall manned by the ladies from Smiths café, selling cold drinks and sandwiches, and an area reserved for picnics so that people could enjoy lunch before the serious part of the day began. There would be a pet-picnic stall, selling food for hungry dogs and cats, and providing bowls of drinking water throughout the day. We were also having a stall provided by a pet shop in a nearby town, selling all sorts of pet foods and accessories, and a face-painting stall where kids could have themselves decorated to look like a cat, dog or rabbit. A local photographer would be on hand too, to take pet portraits for people. The main events would kick off with a display by the dog-training class I'd taken Smartie to, when he was very little. And then, finally, the various classes of the pet show. Most of these were for different classes of dogs and cats, but there were also categories for the best rabbit, the best hamster, guinea-pig, gerbil or mouse, and the best caged bird.

By the morning of the event, most of the work had been done. The marquee had been erected the previous day, and once it was up, we'd taken it in turns to make regular checks in the park to make sure there had been no vandalism or damage to it. All the helpers were in their allotted places by the time we opened the gates. I was helping Louise at the main gate to begin with, as there was, happily, already a queue and we wanted to move people through quickly to avoid anyone getting impatient. Sara was walking around the park with a clipboard, looking important, and Simon, over the public address system, began his commentary by welcoming everyone to the first fundraising event for the Friends of Furzewell Park.

'There are drinks and snacks available for both you and your pets,' his voice boomed through the loudspeakers. 'Enjoy your picnics, but please don't forget to use the waste bins provided, or alternatively take your litter home with you. Please do keep your dogs on their leads, your cats and other small animals in their cages or baskets, and your children under control. We want you all to have a good time here today and what we really *don't* want is for anyone, two-legged or four-legged, to run off and get lost.'

I was enjoying myself, watching all the people arrive with excited dogs wagging their tails, anxious cats meowing in baskets, and children carrying an assortment of scampering little creatures in cages. I really didn't have time to worry too much about Sara, or Amber, or even about Craig.

It wasn't until the rush at the gate calmed down a little, and I left Louise to manage on her own until another helper would take a turn later, that I noticed him. We'd both come into the marquee to watch the dog-training display. He was in the crowd on the far side of the arena, chatting to a girl I didn't recognise. What I *did* recognise, though, were the looks he was giving her, the way he was leaning close to her to speak into her ear, and the way she was smiling and simpering and hanging onto his arm, as if she just couldn't keep her hands off him. Even from across the arena, this was all too familiar. I felt my mood beginning to darken.

'For God's sake,' muttered a voice from behind me. 'He's at it again.'

Sara.

I turned to face her. 'Who is?' I asked, trying to sound innocent. 'At what?'

'Don't pretend you weren't watching,' she snapped. 'Craig. Looks like he's seeing someone else. Cheating on me – *again*.'

I felt my head begin to swim.

'Cheating on *you*?' I repeated. A lady with two small children and a budgie in a cage by her feet gave me a look, and I lowered my voice. 'What do you mean?'

'As if you didn't know,' she said, in the same cross tone. She turned away, sighing. 'I'm going to go and make sure Babette is OK,' she said, walking away from me.

I didn't know who was looking after Babette, or where, but it was almost time for the contests to begin, and I needed to make sure Mum and Mia had Smartie ready, brushed and looking his best for his moment in the arena, so with difficulty I put both Craig and Sara to the back of my mind again.

Once the contests started, all of us helpers were needed in the marquee, with Craig in charge, directing operations, and Simon continuing to make announcements and talking the spectators through a running commentary as each pet in turn was paraded, or displayed, in the centre of the arena.

'Ladies and gentlemen, girls and boys,' he announced, 'please take your places now in the marquee as we start today's show with the first category in the dog section: "Cutest Puppy". Put your hands together, please, for all today's loveable furry contestants, and may the best pet win!'

Mia was entering Smartie in two categories, the maximum allowed: Best Children's Pet, and this first one, Cutest Puppy. He was the third puppy called into the arena, and Mia brought him in, looking shy but proud, slowly walked him around the edge of the arena and then stood with him while the judges made notes. Mum was close by in case Mia needed help, but Smartie was as good as gold, wagging his tail at the judges and regarding them playfully with his big black eyes.

The show continued, with four more dog categories: Best Pedigree, Best Crossbreed, Best Senior Dog and Waggiest Tail, followed by four categories for cats, and finally the various smaller pets. The whole thing was very good-natured, with lots of laughs from the audience as puppies stopped to poo or chase their tails in the middle of their turn in the arena, and one nervous little Chihuahua stood stock still in the middle of the ring and refused to move. Cat owners were warned by Simon to hold tight to their charges as they walked around the arena with them, after one kitten jumped out of his owner's arms and tried to make a dash for it. Calamity was avoided when Amber, in defiance of her reputation with cats, swooped down to catch the escapee and cradled him tenderly as she returned him to his 'mummy'.

And eventually we came to the grand finale. The winners of each category, including Smartie, wearing his rosette awarded for Cutest Puppy, paraded around the arena once again to compete for Best in Show. After much deliberation from the judges, the double rosette, a silver cup and voucher for the pet shop were presented to the owners of a beautiful Persian cat called Millie.

'It's reassuring to know there are still some lovely cats in the area, despite all those disappearances,' Louise said later, as the last people began to leave the park and we finally began clearing-up.

'Yes. Not all the contestants were from Furzewell, though,' I pointed out. 'I'm glad the show was open to surrounding areas too. It would have been a much smaller affair otherwise, and wouldn't have raised so much money.'

The takings hadn't been counted yet, of course, but we'd all been overjoyed by the turnout, and were hoping the amount raised was going to exceed our expectations.

I was taking down bunting from the far side of the park when I saw Sara, carrying a sack and checking for litter.

'We need to talk,' I said, walking across to her. 'What did you mean, earlier, about Craig cheating on you? Have you been out with him?'

She gave me an exasperated look. 'Yes, of course I have.'

'Recently?' I said. 'You've been out with him recently?'

'Well, yes, you could say that.' She sniffed, as if there was something disgusting under her nose. 'He took me away for a romantic holiday just the other week.'

I sighed, closing my eyes. So that week, when she was away, she was with Craig.

'He told me he couldn't see me that week because he was so busy with work,' I said, glaring at her. 'You must have known I was going out with him.'

'No, I didn't. I knew you were cosying up to him,' she retorted. 'I presumed *you* realised *I* was seeing him.'

'No. How was I supposed to know? He didn't act like he was going out with you. I just thought you were flirting with him.'

'Right.' She glared back at me, obviously not believing me. 'Well, he's obviously already got his sights fixed on someone else, but he *always* comes back to me eventually with his tail between his legs. So perhaps now you've got the picture you'll stay away from him.'

I stared at her. I wanted to say that I'd make up my own mind whether to stay away from him or not, rather than be told by her – it was clear she didn't have a real relationship with him, whatever she liked to think. But I couldn't seem to get the words out. I felt stupid, and used. I'd only had three dates with Craig and hadn't wanted anything serious anyway, but in my mind, if nowhere else, I'd made a complete fool of myself. The clearing up was almost finished. I pleaded a headache and went home.

So much for my new life in Furzewell. Everything was ruined. I felt so mortified and embarrassed, I had no idea how I'd be able to face any of the dog walkers again. Amber and Simon had both tried to warn me off Craig, but I wouldn't listen. I'd thought Simon was just being overprotective, and I'd suspected Amber of being jealous. I'd had a horrible argument with her over it and might have ruined our friendship – all because I was so stupidly flattered by the attention of a good-looking, smooth-talking *cheat*. And what about Sara? I'd suspected *her* of being jealous too – or that she'd just resented me having a bit of fun. Now *we'd* argued, too, and I couldn't imagine she'd want to talk to me again, even if I recovered enough to want to speak to her. I wanted to cry. All I'd tried to do was feel good about myself again, after breaking up with Josh, but now I felt worse than ever. What a complete fool I'd been. One of the best days in Furzewell's history had ended up being one of the worst in mine.

PART 4

HOME IS WHERE THE HEART IS

CHAPTER 31

September arrived, and with it the return to school for me and for Mia. The day before term began, I'd heard her talking quietly to Smartie again about her worries.

'I don't want Eddie to be in a different class,' she said as she lay on the rug in the lounge with her arms around the puppy, stroking his soft head and ears. 'Who am I going to play with at playtime?'

I pretended I hadn't heard her, but when I was chatting to her a little later, I casually reminded her that, at playtimes and lunchtimes, everyone from every class would be together so she'd still be able to play with Eddie then. Although I was worried about how she'd cope in class without his reassuring presence, in another way I was beginning to realise it might be healthier for Mia, in the long run, to have to cultivate friendships with other children, those who were in the same year group as her. Healthier for Eddie, too. And hopefully they would still stay best friends.

My concern about Mia, together with the usual busy feeling of that first week of term, was helping to keep my mind off my humiliation and – as the days went by – *anger*, about Craig. It was a relief to have something positive to focus on instead, and I was really enjoying my job. I'd always loved working with children and at this little village school I felt more than ever like an appreciated member of a small team. It was very rewarding, and getting to know the new intake of reception children was one of the nicest parts of all.

I couldn't face joining the dog-walking group for the usual walks, though. I walked Smartie early in the morning, before they'd be meeting at the park, and again late in the evening, after Mia had fallen into an exhausted sleep. Her first few days were tough, for us both. She cried at her classroom door, having to be led away from me by her new teacher, and came out of class after school looking sad and tired. As we walked home with Louise and Eddie, I noticed that Eddie, by contrast, seemed quite bright and cheerful, apparently coping better with the change than Mia was.

'It'll be OK,' he reassured her, holding her hand as we all crossed the road together. 'You'll soon make some other friends, Mia, and we'll still see each other all the time, won't we.'

Louise and I exchanged a smile.

'He's surprised me,' she admitted quietly. 'He actually seems to be relishing the new class – being with older children and starting lots of new work. But he still talks about Mia all the time. I hope she soon settles down.'

Louise was, of course, the only person I'd confided in about Craig and Sara. She'd put her arms around me, expecting me to be upset and tearful, and I had to explain that I mostly felt embarrassed, cross and stupid.

'Everyone warned me,' I said, exasperated at myself. 'But I thought I knew best. I thought I could just enjoy being with a new man who seemed to like me. To make myself feel better after the separation. Instead, I've just ended up feeling ridiculous. It was too soon, and the wrong man – what was I thinking? I'm glad I didn't sleep with him,' I added, aware of how close I'd come to doing just that.

'Well, at least you found out before it had gone on for too long,' she sympathised.

'Yes.'

Unlike Sara, perhaps. I kept wondering how long *she'd* actually been seeing Craig. I hadn't spoken to her since our brief contretemps at the pet show. It had sounded, at the time, like a very on-and-off thing with her – like she went out with him whenever he had no-one else. More fool her! Although, she had apparently had a week away with him. I felt hot all over with humiliation and anger every time I thought how Craig had lied to me about that week. And needless to say, I hadn't heard from him since. He was presumably busy with the girl we'd seen him with at the pet show. Despite myself, I kept wondering whether Sara was coping with seeing Craig for the dog walks or whether, like me, she'd stopped going out with the group.

It was Amber who got in touch with me first, a week or so into September. The weather had just begun to turn, summer melting gently into a bright but cool autumn, the colours of the horse chestnut and copper beech trees along the lanes and in the park almost achingly beautiful against the paler blue of the sky. I was walking Smartie across the park, alone as usual, one evening as the darkness deepened, when her call came through.

'We haven't seen you for a while,' she said, and waited for me to respond.

'No. I … well, it's the beginning of term. I've had a lot of school work. New kids to get used to—'

'Nic,' she interrupted me gently, 'I know what happened. Sara told me.'

'Right. Yes, well, I suppose she would have done. Probably laughing about me making a fool of myself—'

'That's hardly likely, is it? She's just as cross and upset as you are.'

'Well, it's her own fault. She should have told me she'd been going out with him.'

'I did try to warn you that she might have been,' Amber reminded me, and then she sighed. 'Anyway, you don't need to be told that now. Sorry. I actually called to talk to you about your birthday.'

'Oh!' I gave a start of surprise. My birthday, at the end of September, was the last thing on my mind. I was amazed that Amber had remembered it. Although we'd kept in touch over the years when we were living in different places, we'd never texted each other birthday greetings or sent cards. And I was aware that things had been a bit cool between us recently anyway, since our silly argument over my joke about Kelly the vet nurse, which Amber had seemed to find so offensive. 'I was looking at your Facebook profile,' she admitted now. I could hear the smile in her voice. 'Just ... browsing old photos, as you do. I noticed it then.'

'Oh.' I felt quite touched, thinking of her looking at those old pictures, noticing my birthday, calling me about it, despite everything. 'OK. Well, I wasn't planning to do anything, really. It's not a special one.'

'My mum always says every birthday is special,' she said. 'And since we need to hold as many events as possible in the park, we thought it would be nice to have a barbecue.'

'*Who* thought it?'

'Me. And Simon.' She paused again. 'We're the only ones left in the group at the moment. Sara's only been once or twice, trying to avoid seeing Craig. You're not coming, obviously for the same reason. And Craig's not coming, presumably to avoid both of you.'

I would have laughed if I hadn't felt so mortified. The thought of Simon – lovely, kind, sensible Simon – talking with Amber about me and Craig made me feel even worse than I had before.

'Have a barbecue, fine,' I said, more tersely than I intended. 'But I'm not sure I'll be there.'

'So we're going to organise it for the last Saturday of September – the day before your birthday,' she went on as if I hadn't spoken. 'Meanwhile, how about you and I have a drink one night?'

'To talk about Craig again, and how stupid I was?'

'No. To talk about other things. Better things. Anything, other than that.'

I hesitated. She was holding out an olive branch. I'd been so pleased, back in February, to meet up with her again, so grateful that I had my oldest friend here in Furzewell, but I was aware that I'd been neglecting that friendship, seeing more of Louise, deliberately avoiding Amber because I'd been irritated by what I saw as her interference in my so-called relationship with Craig. I'd been wrong, and I needed to make amends now.

'OK,' I said. 'Yes. Let's do that.'

We made a date for that Saturday, and I went home feeling slightly better.

The new term slowly moved forward and gradually, one day at a time, Mia seemed to be relaxing. The day came when she went into the classroom quite happily in the morning, and came out looking even brighter, smiling and chatting to Olivia P. The following day she asked me if Olivia could come to play at the weekend.

'Of course!' I said at once, overjoyed to see she was making friends again, but alarm bells ringing slightly as I remembered the previous problems with the two Olivias. 'But ... what about Olivia S? Will she feel left out?'

'She's gone,' Mia said with a shrug. 'She's moved to another school.'

'Oh, I didn't realise.' For a moment, I imagined a scenario where Olivia P, left alone after her soul mate had departed, had now turned in desperation to Mia – despite the fact that during the previous school year, neither of them had bothered much to be friends with her. I hoped she wasn't going to mess Mia around now. But to my surprise, my daughter was ahead of me.

'I know they didn't want to be my friends before, when they had each other,' she said, 'but do you know what, Mummy? Olivia kept getting upset at school, because the other Olivia had gone. And I know how sad I used to be, when I didn't have a friend. So I felt sorry for her, and I asked her to play with me and Eddie at lunchtime.'

'That was kind of you.' I smiled at her. 'And did Eddie mind?'

'No. Because he's got another friend too, in his new class, called Zach. So we all play together.'

I gave her a hug. At last, I could really let myself believe that Mia was settling down happily here in Furzewell. Even if I was having some trouble myself.

That weekend, Mia was with Josh, and Mum was off out with the Gruesome Twosome, so I was glad I'd arranged to have a drink with Amber instead of being at home on my own. When I arrived at the Fox and Goose, she was already at the bar waiting for me, and bought me a drink before we found a table by the window.

'I wanted to fill you in about the pet show,' she said. I was grateful that she'd avoided any preamble referring to our phone conversation about Craig and Sara.

'Well, I saw from the WhatsApp messages that the takings have been counted, and it was definitely a success.'

'A *massive* success,' she said, grinning all over her face. 'Even better than we dared to hope. And did you see the message from Sara, saying that someone came down from the council to see how it went, and actually contacted her afterwards to say they were impressed?'

'Oh, wow. I didn't see that, no. That *is* good news. So have they said they'll forget the idea of selling the park?'

'Not yet. But hopefully it's a good start, and maybe it's made them think.'

'Let's hope so,' I agreed.

'Now we just need to keep up the pressure on everyone in the village to use the park as much as they can. Several people have said they're glad the old playground equipment has gone. They were worried about their kids playing there because it was so dangerous and not very securely fenced off.'

'Yes, as poor Smartie found out.'

'Well, the council has already been given an indication of what we'd like to replace it with – if and when they agree not to sell the park, of course. We're going to have another meeting, to discuss that, and plan our next event—'

'What next event?' I asked in surprise.

'Well, of course, we haven't been getting together recently to discuss that,' she said lightly, 'but Simon and I have been talking, and we think it would be good to hold a bonfire party in November. There's a whole load of council safety regulations involved, but I called Sara just after I spoke to you, and she's up for finding out what we need to do. She needs a project,' she added quietly, 'to take her mind off things.'

I nodded. I'd been too consumed with my own hurt and embarrassment about Craig to spare much thought for Sara. Perhaps she actually had feelings for him. Was she really that daft?

'So,' Amber went on, giving me a pointed look now, 'we need everyone to come to the next meeting. Just us, the committee. The—' she hesitated, then went on with a quick little smile, 'Lonely Hearts Dog Walkers.'

'Even more appropriate now, that name,' I said, a bit sourly. 'When are you having this meeting?'

'Thursday evening.'

'Oh. I don't think I can make it, sorry.'

'Friday, then.'

'That could be tricky too.'

Amber sighed, took a gulp of her beer, and put her hand on my arm.

'Nic, you can't avoid Craig forever. I know how you must be feeling, but you're going to bump into each other sooner or later, and surely the sooner you get it over with, the better. Don't shake your head – you know it's true.'

'Well, he hasn't even called me since the pet show, when Sara and I saw him with that other woman. How humiliating, not even to be worth a call to dump me.'

She grabbed my hand. 'All the more reason to face up to him,' she said. 'For God's sake, Nic, don't let him get away with it – just expecting you to sit at home, waiting till he can fit you in, between dates with the new girl.'

'He would *not* fit me in,' I retorted. 'I'd tell him where to get off.'

'So tell him first. Use your anger, girl. It's what he deserves. He's so bloody arrogant, he still thinks he can just carry on like that, stringing Sara *and* you along for as long as he wants. He really does need a kick in the pants, metaphorically of course.'

'Yes, you're right, I know. I just – didn't want to see him or talk to him at all.' I scowled. 'And we were *not* going to talk about him tonight, remember?'

'Yes. Sorry. Drink up, let's get another one. But please come next Thursday evening. It's important. If we – the committee – fall apart now, what hope have we got of keeping the park?'

And again, I knew she was right. I knew I had to go to the meeting. And I knew I had to confront Craig. The question was, which was going to come first?

CHAPTER 32

On the Sunday, Gran came round to Eagle House for dinner as usual, and seemed strangely preoccupied. As soon as we'd finished eating, she sat in the armchair and fell fast asleep.

'I'm worried she's not well,' Mum said, watching her sleeping. 'It's not like her to be so quiet, and tired.'

'Actually, I thought she seemed a bit quiet last time I popped in to see her, too,' I agreed.

Mum was in the kitchen when Gran woke up, and I was glad to have a chance to chat to her on our own. She and Mum so often rubbed each other up the wrong way.

'Are you feeling all right, Gran?' I asked her quietly. 'You don't seem quite like your usual self.'

'And what would that be?' she muttered.

'You know. Lively. Funny. Full of lots of good stories.'

'Yes, well. Perhaps I haven't heard any good stories lately.'

'Why's that?' I pressed her.

She shrugged, and for a few moments I thought she wasn't going to say any more. Then she glanced at the kitchen door, beckoned me closer, and said:

'Don't tell your mother this. But I've become addicted to late nights with zombie films and sherry.'

'What!' I burst out laughing, and she shushed me at once, looking quickly around her again. 'Gran, what on earth do you mean?' I chuckled more quietly. 'Since when have you watched zombie films?'

'Since Sidney in the bungalow behind mine kept on asking me in to watch them with him,' she said, her voice low with conspiracy, 'to let me hear the screams.'

'Oh yes. The screams you were worried about.' I felt ashamed to realise that neither Mum nor I had asked her about this recently. Gran hadn't mentioned the screams for a while now, so I suppose we'd both presumed she was satisfied that the zombie films were the cause. But we certainly hadn't anticipated Gran watching them herself – let alone *becoming addicted,* as she'd put it. 'But, Gran – are you *enjoying* watching these films?'

'Not particularly. To be honest, I think they're daft.'

'So why do you keep going to watch them? Especially if it's so late at night.'

She looked a bit embarrassed. 'Well, it's company, isn't it. We have a couple of sherries together. And he likes watching them late at night, he says it's more atmospheric.'

'But don't you find them a bit … scary?'

'Not really. Like I say, they're all a bit daft. Dead people walking around, all that stuff. And anyway, we watch them together, so it doesn't feel scary.'

I sat back in my chair, suddenly understanding. It wasn't the films, or the sherry, Gran was getting addicted to. It was Sidney! Or at least, his company.

'Can't you suggest watching something different occasionally?' I asked her gently. 'Something more romantic? And maybe suggest watching it a bit earlier in the evening?'

'I keep thinking I might do,' she said, nodding at me. 'But, well, it's not really for me to choose, is it. It's his house.'

'You could always invite him to yours, for a change,' I suggested. 'He might like that. You might have to buy the sherry, though!'

She laughed. It was nice to hear. I wondered how long she'd been struggling to keep this secret from us. No wonder she'd been so quiet.

'It's all right for you young girls,' she said, beginning to forget to keep her voice down. I smiled. I'd always be a *young girl* to my gran! 'You're used to taking the lead. You know, asking men out.' She looked down, evidently embarrassed now. 'It wasn't like that for my generation. We just thought ourselves lucky if anyone asked us.'

'Well, it's not like that anymore, Gran. We don't have to do what they say. You go for it! Ask him round to yours for an early evening with a nice romantic comedy. Much nicer than all those zombies.'

'Will you show me how to work the video machine, Nicky? Your mum bought it for me years ago, but I never use the damned thing.'

'Of course I will,' I smiled. 'I'll come back with you this afternoon.'

Mum came back into the room then, and we tried to pretend we were talking about something else. But of course, she'd overheard a great deal of the conversation, and as soon as I got back from showing Gran how her DVD player worked, I was asked for details.

'Don't tell her I've told you,' I warned Mum, when she'd stopped laughing. 'She seems to think you won't approve.'

'Approve? Well, I don't honestly know why she wants to get involved with a man,' Mum said with a sniff. 'But I suppose, if she just wants a bit of fun, bloody good luck to her.'

I smiled a little less enthusiastically at that. If only she knew how I felt now about having *fun*. I'd rather sit at home and do a jigsaw than go out with another man, thank you very much.

But the next day, I decided I couldn't put it off any longer – I needed to talk to Sara. Amber was right, I'd have to face her – and Craig – sooner or later, and it would be better if the first time wasn't in front of everyone else. The thought of having the showdown with Craig was, at that point, even less appealing than talking to Sara. I called her that evening and, trying to sound cool and civil, suggested we had a chat.

'Come round for a drink now, if you like,' she said, without any warmth in her voice.

Sara lived in a smart little cottage in a turning off Fore Street. I'd often admired the place from the outside – it was painted a pastel pink, with a thatched roof, a brick porch and lead light windows – but I'd never been invited in before. She opened the door to me and ushered me through to the lounge without a word, before pouring two glasses of wine and putting one on the coffee table in front of me.

'Thanks. Well, look, I suppose I should say I'm sorry,' I forced out straight away. 'I honestly didn't know you and Craig were … involved.'

'We've been going out, on and off, for about four months,' she said stiffly.

'Four *months*?'

'Yes. Why are you so surprised?' She was glaring at me again. This wasn't going well.

'Because, Sara,' I snapped, 'you never told me. How was I supposed to know?'

She sighed, shaking her head, seeming to shrink back against the sofa cushions.

'Craig never wanted the rest of the group to know we were seeing each other. He thought the rest of you could feel awkward.' She sighed. 'It sounds a bit silly, now.'

'Yes, it does. Because he said the same thing to me.'

'Did he?' She looked up at me sharply. 'How long *have* you been seeing him? I thought you were still married.'

'I'm separated, pending a divorce,' I said, feeling myself flush. 'Sara, I've only had three dates with Craig. It was never going to be anything serious.' I sighed, deciding suddenly to be completely honest now – with myself as well as with Sara. 'Actually, I had mixed feelings about it all along. Being asked out by someone just made me feel a bit better about myself, after ending my marriage. But I *am* upset at being treated like this, and I'm going to tell him exactly what I think of him.' When I'd worked up the courage. 'Who does he think he is?' I added crossly.

'He thinks he's some kind of Lothario, obviously,' Sara said. She took a gulp of her wine, and I realised she'd calmed down and wasn't looking angry anymore. She just looked sad, and kind of defeated. I was glad now that I'd opened up to her. 'The thing is, he can't seem to help himself – if another girl so much as looks at him, it's a challenge he can't resist. I've dumped him twice and taken him back. I must be mad. This time, he made all kinds of promises about it not happening again. That's why he took me away that week. I had no idea he'd been seeing you at the same time.'

'I can't believe I fell for his lies about working all that week.'

'Quite. And now he's doing it again. He's obviously seeing that girl he was with at the pet show. But he's been calling me with excuses about having too much work to see me at the moment.'

'Why on earth are you putting up with it?' I said, incredulous now. Sara might not have been my favourite person up to now, but she was far too good for him: clever, elegant and beautiful. She didn't need this. 'For God's sake, he's doing it because you let him get away with it.'

'You're right. I know,' she said, flatly, 'he just ... seems to be able to overcome all my common sense, somehow. Every time he comes back to me with his apologies and his promises, I find myself believing him. Getting sucked in again.'

'Come on, Sara.' I took the wine glass away from her and grabbed both her hands. 'You're stronger than that. Amber told *me* to use my anger, to tell him where to get off – but you've got even more reason to do it. You've wasted four months of your life on him.'

Her eyes filled with tears. 'He's actually not a bad guy, Nic. He just can't—'

'Don't give me that crap again, that he *can't help it*. What is he, a two-year-old? Of course he can help it. He's behaving appallingly, and you're ... you're *enabling* him.' I sighed. 'Look, he couldn't really have hoped to get away with it for long – seeing us both, behind each other's backs – but to be honest, he didn't even care, did he. He doesn't care who he hurts. He's just another selfish, arrogant bastard, and he needs us both to stand up and tell him so.'

'I know. You're right.' She gave me a weak smile. 'Thank you, Nic. I've known it for ages, obviously. But now *you* know how pathetic I've been, I can't keep on—'

'Not pathetic,' I said. This was a new side to the usually stuck-up, bossy Sara, and I was actually feeling really sympathetic towards her now. She was just like the rest of us, after all – ready to believe a man's lies, because we want them to be true. 'Maybe just too trusting.'

'Not anymore though.' She freed her hands from mine, picked up her glass again and raised it towards me. 'Here's to us, Nic. Standing together against men's crap.'

I smiled and picked up my own glass to clink it against hers.

'Putting sisters before misters,' I agreed with a chuckle. Then I took a deep breath. 'So who's going to call him first to dump him?'

'What – *now*?' she said on a little gasping breath.

'No time like the present. We don't want to change our minds, do we?'

'You go first, then.'

I nodded. He wouldn't be too surprised to hear it from me, probably wouldn't even care very much – I was just a new potential conquest. But if Sara stuck to her word and made it clear she really meant it this time, he might be slightly more shocked. To say nothing of the realisation that we'd been talking about him together.

I picked up my phone. Craig was about to get a mouthful. And Sara and I, brought together by the recent turn of events, seemed suddenly to have become friends.

CHAPTER 33

'So what did he say?' Louise squawked with barely concealed excitement. We'd come back to Eagle House together after school the following day so that I could tell her all about it while Mia and Eddie played together. 'Did he try to make excuses for himself?'

'No, not at all.' I thought back over the conversation. I hadn't held back – I'd called him names I'd forgotten I even knew, but he hardly bothered to protest. 'He … just seemed to accept it. I'm pretty sure I wasn't the first woman to rant at him like that.'

'Probably not the last, either, from what you've said.'

'No. Well, I *wasn't* the last, because as soon as I'd finished, I told him Sara was sitting next to me, listening, and wanted a word with him too. He did sound slightly thrown by that.'

'Good.'

'Yes, but when Sara started on at him, he tried to wriggle out of it, would you believe? Told her he hadn't asked me out on any dates, he'd just taken me for a drink a couple of times *as a friend*.'

'Nooo!' Louise clapped her hand to her mouth. 'The cheek of him!'

'I know. Luckily we were on speakerphone, so I yelled back that the way he'd been snogging me in the car, and inviting me back to his flat to sleep with him, were definitely *not* what you'd do with *just a friend*.'

'Good for you, Nic. So do you think Sara will stick to her guns, or is she going to weaken and take him back again?'

'I hope not. She really gave him a hard time, shouting and crying at the same time, poor thing.'

'It sounds like you've got a bit more time for her now.'

'Yes.' I thought about how I'd held Sara, after she'd finally finished the call, and reassured her, while she wiped away her tears, that she'd done the right thing and could now move on with her life. 'She's OK, really. We're very different, but let's face it, in some ways, we're all the same, aren't we?'

'We all tend to go for the bad guys?'

I shrugged. Perhaps it was true. But on the other hand, I'd never thought of *Josh* as a bad guy. He'd just stopped loving me – that was all.

I continued to walk Smartie on my own, but Sara and I had agreed that we'd both go to the meeting that Thursday evening, so that we were facing everyone together, and after that we'd try to get back to normal.

'I don't want to break up the group,' I said.

'No. But Craig probably won't want to be part of it anymore,' Sara said, managing to sound hopeful and wistful at the same time.

'Well, look, he knows now what we think of the way he's treated us – especially you. But maybe we should be the ones to show him how to behave with maturity.'

'Meaning?'

'He ought to stay in the group, face up to us and carry on politely like a grown-up.'

'Huh! I can't see that,' she said, pulling a face.

Neither could I, unfortunately. But for the sake of the companionship of our group, to say nothing of the committee working for the wider community, I hoped, somehow, we could make it work.

I was the first to arrive at Smiths for the meeting on Thursday, but as soon as I'd got a drink and sat down, Simon joined me. He took a seat next to me and gave me a worried look.

'Are you all right, Nic? We haven't seen you since the pet show. Amber said she thought you and Sara were both suffering from some kind of bug.'

I snorted with laughter. 'You might call it that! Simon, do you really not know what's happened?'

He was shaking his head, but I wasn't sure if he was just pretending ignorance, to be kind. Or perhaps I should be thanking Amber for her diplomacy. I gave Simon a quick summary of the situation, watching him raise his eyebrows in surprise at the part where Sara and I both dumped Craig over the phone at the same time.

'He's like a stupid spoilt child,' he said dismissively, shaking his head. 'He needs to grow up. He can't go around treating women like that, especially when you're supposed to be friends.'

'Well, let's hope he's learned his lesson. I doubt it, though.'

'He needs to turn up here tonight and face the rest of us like a man,' Simon said crossly, making me smile again.

'Yes, that's what I said.'

Sara arrived just then, and I gave her a nod and a smile. 'Let's see whether he does or not.'

'He won't,' she said curtly. 'He's emailed his apologies.'

'Wimp!' Simon said.

Amber arrived and we started the meeting, just the four of us. I'd already called her to tell her about the result of my evening with Sara, and she chose, wisely, to keep off the subject apart from giving both of us a quick hug and whispering *Well done*.

'OK,' Sara began, seemingly back in control in her preferred role of leader. 'So, as you know, we're proposing to hold a fireworks evening for our next event. The council have given permission, and have emailed me a document listing the legal safety requirements. They all seem fairly common sense. We can have a bonfire, with just one person nominated to light it. And we either employ a professional company for the fireworks, or do it ourselves – following all the usual precautions, as in their document.'

'I'm happy for us to do it all ourselves,' Simon said at once. 'I can get as much wood for the bonfire as we need, from my work. And Craig and I can be responsible for the fireworks. If he's capable of anything that serious, that is.'

Amber and I exchanged looks, but Sara pressed on:

'Good idea. I agree, the cost of hiring a professional company could wipe out any profit we make. So, we need to start advertising the event right away. Questions: How much should we spend on the fireworks, to make the display last a decent length of time? And how much to charge for admission in order to make a profit? I've played with some figures you can all look at here.' She passed around copies of a spreadsheet. 'And are we going to sell food? Hot dogs and burgers, I suppose? Soft drinks only? Alcohol and bonfires don't mix. And we'll need volunteers to man the refreshments.'

We were all talking at once now, looking at the figures, making our suggestions, Sara raising her voice above the rest of us to add:

'Don't forget, whatever we can raise from this event will add to what we made from the pet show and go towards the new adventure playground – *if* the council agrees to us keeping the park open. If it's a success, there's more chance of that happening.'

By the end of the evening, our plans were coming together well. I knew Louise would help, and we would circulate an email to everyone in the village who'd signed up to the Friends of Furzewell Park, telling them about the fireworks night, asking for their support and for volunteers for the evening. I was feeling motivated and excited about it, glad to be back in the company of my friends again and actually beginning to feel pretty daft for caring about the situation with Craig at all. Even Sara seemed to be back on form, but then, she was always at her best when she was telling us all what to do. I realised now that there could be a lot going on under the surface that she wasn't allowing us to see. In fact it was Simon, with his barbed comments about Craig's immaturity, who seemed to be the most bothered about it tonight.

'Might have known he wouldn't have the guts to turn up,' he said to me as we were all preparing to leave.

'Well, I can understand it, in a way.' I nodded goodbye to Sara and Amber as they left. 'Sara and I gave him a real blasting. He'd have felt pretty mortified, getting both barrels from the pair of us at the same time – whether he admits it or not. It's going to be hard for him to face us all.'

'Nevertheless, he'll have to, sooner or later. He's a coward, as well as being a cad.'

'Well, I can't disagree with any of what you're saying.' I looked at Simon, slightly puzzled. 'But you're sounding very hostile, Si. It's not like you.'

'I'm furious about the way he's treated you. Both of you,' he amended quickly. 'But Sara should have known better. You – you're new to us, you've just come out of an unhappy marriage, so this was not what you needed.'

'Thank you.' I was touched. 'Yes, it was ... upsetting. But I'm over it already, honestly. And really, I'd like us all to be able to move on from it.'

We were outside now, on Fore Street, beginning to stroll back along the darkened road. There was a cool breeze, and it was raining, the light from the few streetlamps in the village throwing wobbly reflections back up from puddles in the street. I shivered and pulled my coat closer around me and, as I did, I felt Simon's arm go round my shoulders.

'I just hate to think of you being hurt like that,' he said. 'You don't deserve it, Nic. Look, if ever you need someone to talk to – I know it must be hard, being on your own – I'll always be here for you. I'm very fond of you. I know you probably think of me as an old man, someone of your parents' generation, but—'

'Oh!' I said, horrified and embarrassed. 'Simon, look, I don't think you're an old man at all, it's not that. You've been such a good friend, I really do appreciate your kindness and everything...'

I came to an awkward halt, shrugging and not knowing how to go on. I'd suspected before that Simon might like me – as more than a friend – but decided I'd probably just imagined it. Now I couldn't find the words to warn him off without hurting his feelings. But before I could go on, he just gave my shoulder a squeeze and said:

'Good. Well, take care, Nic, and I'll see you soon.'

And with that, he was off down the road towards his own house, leaving me feeling uncomfortable and confused.

I really should have said more, made it clear that I didn't return his feelings – however fond I was of him as a friend. But perhaps he'd got the message anyway, from my mumbling attempt there? I hoped so. The last thing I wanted was to have to avoid yet another member of the dog-walking group!

The next day, though, I got up early, determined to rejoin the group, no matter what. The sun was shining now, and everything in the park looked bright and colourful – the grass sparkling with the previous night's rain, the leaves on the trees turning through their spectrum of yellows and golds, the flowerbeds full of Simon's displays of stunning chrysanthemums and dahlias. I arrived first at the park gates, and was soon rewarded by Smartie's obvious delight at being back with his doggy friends. As soon as he saw Max, he went into a frenzy of excited barking, running around him in frantic circles with his tail wagging like crazy. Before he'd even got his breath back, he was reunited with Judy, then with Benji and Babette – each encounter prompting another bout of ecstatic barking and careering around. I couldn't stop laughing, and before long all the others were joining in. It was such a relief that the ice had been broken between us all. There didn't seem to be any awkwardness with Simon, who chatted as amicably as ever, to me and to all the others, without any reference to our conversation the previous evening. I was beginning to think I'd dreamt it or read too much into it after all.

The only one who was noticeably quiet and subdued was Craig. He had at least turned up, but didn't join in any of our chat, keeping himself to himself and very much on the edge of the group as we walked. The rest of us merely exchanged knowing looks, but I was sure Sara was just as glad as I was not to have to indulge in conversation with him.

'It was hard enough even seeing him,' she admitted to us afterwards. He'd been the first to leave, giving us all a quick nod and a wave goodbye, and she looked visibly relieved to see the back of him.

'Yes, I'm sure,' I said sympathetically. Personally, I'd felt absolutely nothing, other than a kind of mild scorn, on seeing him, but then, I hadn't been as emotionally involved as she was. 'But if it makes you feel any better, I think he found it excruciating being with us. I'm sure it will get easier.'

'Well, at least he turned up,' Simon said, somewhat grudgingly. 'I really wondered whether he'd ever come again.'

'Yes, it must have taken a bit of nerve,' Amber agreed. 'I'm sure he realised we'd all have been talking about him at the meeting last night, so he deliberately stayed away. But as you said, Simon, he had to face us sooner or later. Face Sara, and Nic, and find out whether we were all going to give him another dressing down.'

'There's no point in that,' Sara said. 'It's all been said. He knows what we think of him. I'm just glad he kept quiet. If he'd tried to talk to me today, frankly I think I'd have had to punch him.'

'Yes. Probably it was for the best,' I agreed. 'Well, at least we're all back together, guys. Even if we have one silent member who's not too popular with the rest of us.'

'He needs to earn back our friendship,' Simon said firmly. 'That's the thing.'

We all nodded agreement. But nobody seemed to have any suggestions as to how he'd be able to do it.

CHAPTER 34

Rejoining my friends had made me feel so much happier and more settled, and the next week or so passed calmly and pleasantly. School was good: I'd got to know my new intake of four-year-olds properly now, and I couldn't stop smiling when I saw how contented my little Mia was, now that she'd made a real friend of Olivia, even though she was still happiest of all when she was with Eddie. Her reading and writing were now among the best in her class, and she was doing much better at maths and spellings. It seemed there was nothing now to hold her back. Even Josh noticed the difference in her, and to my surprise he commented on it when he dropped her home the next weekend.

'She seems really settled here in Furzewell now,' he said, watching as she ran into Eagle House to play with Smartie. 'She talks all the time about school, and Eddie, and Olivia, and the park.'

'Oh!' I was surprised. Surprised, to be honest, that Mia shared the details of her Furzewell life with him, when I'd always thought her weekends with her daddy were so thrilling by comparison that she didn't even give us a thought until she came back. And surprised he'd bothered to tell me. 'Well, yes, she's settled down brilliantly. It was always going to take a bit of time.'

He nodded. 'But she's obviously happy here now. And that's down to you, of course. It must have been hard for you. You've done well.'

'Oh!' I said again, really surprised now. It was unusual enough to have more than a few words of conversation with Josh at handover, and I certainly hadn't been expecting compliments. I searched his face, wondering if he was being facetious or patronising, but in fact he looked serious – sad, if anything. 'Well, thanks. Yes, it was hard to begin with, but Mia and I have both settled down now.'

He nodded again, called goodbye to Mia, and turned to go – before suddenly swinging back to face me and adding: 'Just a thought. Next time, if you like, I could just have Mia from Friday evening till Saturday night. Then I'll bring her back early in the morning so she's with you for your birthday.'

'Oh!' It seemed to be the only thing I was capable of uttering. To say I was amazed would be an understatement. Josh had barely even remembered my birthday when we were together. Well, not during the last few years, anyway. The time when I'd really needed some support was precisely the time when he seemed to turn his back on me. So hearing him mentioning it now that we were living apart was something of a shock. And I'd certainly never have expected him to suggest changing our usual arrangement, to accommodate it. I could only assume Mia must have mentioned it to him. 'Well, yes,' I said. 'It would be nice to have her here for my birthday. Thank you.'

'Good. See you on Friday week, then.'

I watched him get into his car and drive away, and as I walked back into the house I realised I was feeling more relaxed and peaceful now than I had for years. Finally, Josh and I seemed to be getting on, better than we had in a long time.

As far as Craig was concerned, I think I'd been right to suggest he had in fact found it really difficult to face us all, particularly the first time. Knowing how self-assured – OK, arrogant – he'd always been, I'd wondered at first whether he would just brazen it out, turning up bright and breezy as if nothing had happened, even expecting to carry on the kind of banter and light flirtation he'd been so good at, without showing any remorse whatsoever. It wouldn't have surprised me. But no, he was not only quiet, to the point of being withdrawn, he was looking very obviously quite chastened. He could hardly meet my eyes, or Sara's, and if he did, he'd blink and look down quickly at the ground. Within a few days, we'd all become used to this new version of Craig, but couldn't help wondering how long it was going to last. And then, the day after my unexpected conversation with Josh on the doorstep, I was just getting Mia's tea ready when I had a very surprising phone call from Sara.

'I've just had an email from Craig,' she said. She sounded excited – which made my heart sink. I really hoped she wasn't going to let him talk her into giving him yet another chance.

'Oh yes? What does he want?' I said sourly.

'Don't worry. Nothing like that. It was very businesslike. He's offered to draw up plans for whatever we want to do in the park, after we get the council's blessing to keep it open.' She paused and corrected herself. 'I mean *if* we get their blessing. He'll do it straight away though, so that we can submit the plans to the council, showing them we are fully committed to making the park a viable community resource. Craig's suggesting we incorporate – as well as the adventure playground – a new, bigger pool, as I'd hoped, more like a lake, including a boating area. And a properly designed nature walk, and a crazy golf course.'

'Right. It all sounds very expensive, though, Sara.'

'He'll do the plans pro bono. Not through his firm. But having properly drawn-up plans will make a huge difference to how we present ourselves, how seriously the council will take us—'

'Of course, I agree. But I mean, some of those things themselves sound like they're going to be expensive to build, or install. If the council lets us keep the park open, we've got to fund the installation of any facilities ourselves, haven't we.'

'Yes. That's what we're fundraising for.' She paused again. I could almost hear the smile in her voice as she went on:

'And Craig's also persuaded his company to invest in us. A considerable sum.'

'*What?*'

'It's an advertising deal. They get to name something – perhaps the adventure playground – after their company, and they pay for it and maintain it.'

'Oh my God. Are you joking?'

'No. I'm going to forward the email to you now. And the rest of the group of course. I just thought ... you might like to hear it first.'

'You're damn right I did! Thank you, Sara, that's terrific news. I mean, I know we mustn't get ahead of ourselves, but it will really help our cause – won't it?'

'Absolutely. Councils love this type of thing, Nic. I'm feeling much more confident now about approaching them again when Craig's drawn up the plans.'

'Yes,' I said. 'Me too. I hope the rest of the committee agree.' I thought for a moment, and added, 'Craig's firm – I didn't think they were really big and well known enough to want to finance something like this. They must be doing well, though, or have a lot of faith that this advertising idea will work well for them.'

'Read the email, Nic,' she replied. 'Reading between the lines, I don't think it's *just* the company who'll be stomping up the money.'

'You think Craig's contributing ... personally?'

'I ... wouldn't be surprised. He doesn't say so. But I do get that impression, yes.'

We said goodbye, and a few seconds later my phone pinged with Sara forwarding Craig's email. When I read it, I knew exactly what she meant, although I couldn't put my finger on why. Craig certainly hadn't *said* he would be increasing his company's funding personally – I doubt he'd have wanted any of us assuming he was trying to buy our forgiveness – but there was something about the phrasing of his proposal that hinted at this. I was reading it for the second time when Amber called me.

'I'd like to say we should tell him to stick his offers where the sun doesn't shine,' she said without any preamble. 'But on the other hand...'

'We can't afford to. It's too good to turn down,' I said. 'And anyway ... I'm the last person to defend him, but don't you think he might actually be feeling *remorse*?'

'Huh!' She snorted. 'Well, I suppose it's possible. Even a dog will feel sorry after his bone's been snatched away from him.'

I laughed. 'Simon was saying after the meeting the other week that Craig needed to earn our friendship again. I think this really might be his way of trying to do just that.'

'As long as it's only friendship he's after this time,' she conceded. And then: 'Do you think Simon might have had a private word with him? Prompted him to do something like this?'

I hadn't thought of that. But I could imagine him doing it, of course.

'Possibly,' I said. 'He might have just told him to grow up and be a man – I know he wanted to.' We both laughed.

'But I hope not,' I added. 'I hope this has come from Craig himself. From his own conscience.'

'It'll benefit him too, Nic, if it goes ahead,' Amber pointed out. 'Don't make it sound like he's some kind of hippie philanthropist.'

'No, of course not.' I chuckled. He certainly didn't fit that description. 'Well, I guess I'll see you later, for the walk.'

'Yes. It'll be an interesting one.'

And it certainly was, if only for the fact that Craig finally began to speak to us all again. Sara had asked us to reply to her, with our reactions, as soon as we'd read the email, and as our responses were all broadly positive, she'd decided to grasp the nettle immediately, saying: 'The sooner we get this moving, the better.'

So once we were all assembled at the park gate, she made a kind of announcement, looking rather awkward, but beginning by thanking Craig in very formal tones for his email, and telling him we'd all read his offer and suggestions, and were pleased to accept.

'Thank you again,' she added, sounding slightly as if the words were being dragged out of her with hot pliers, but managing a tight little half-smile as she said it.

'Yes, thank you, great idea, well done,' we all chorused.

'OK.' He coughed. His voice had sounded strained, as if he hadn't used it for months. Apart from when he'd used it to call Judy, none of us had really heard him speak since the group had got back together. 'Good. I'll tell the partners to put the offer of the advertising deal in writing, so we can forward that to the council, and while that's happening, I'll make a start on the plans. Well, actually—' he looked down at his feet, '—I've started already. Draft plans, obviously. I'll share them with you all, as soon as possible, then I can amend them as much as we want to.'

We all nodded at each other, and without any further discussion, set off on our walk, as the dogs were becoming restless. Craig walked a little away from the rest of us, as usual, but – without any of us becoming aware of who was doing it – the distance between him and us gradually seemed to lessen a little that evening. The following day, there was some tentative social interaction, like you might get with a new neighbour. A *How are you,* from one of us, a *Nice morning, isn't it,* from another. And gradually, very gradually, over the rest of that week, the ice was melting.

'I wouldn't say he's redeemed himself, exactly,' Simon said one morning when he, Sara and I were waiting for the other two to turn up. 'You don't treat your friends the way he treated you two. But at least he's made an effort. I think he's tried to show he's sorry.'

'It would have been nice if he'd actually *said* it, though. To me, and to Nic,' Sara pointed out. 'That would have gone a long way.'

And when, two days later, that was exactly what happened – Craig called Sara first, and then me, and having admitted he should have done it sooner, made decent and seemingly genuine apologies to us both – I knew I'd been right. Simon had been talking to him. But, to be fair, it didn't take anything away from the fact that Craig had still found the courage to do it. And it made me feel even more warmth towards Simon. He really was a lovely man. But it was no good: I still wasn't attracted to him.

CHAPTER 35

Now that everyone seemed happier again, I was looking forward to the barbecue party that the group were planning for the evening before my birthday. Because Mia would be with Josh that night, Mum and I would both be able to go, and I was pleased when Louise told me she'd got the girl next-door to babysit so that she could come too.

'Half the village seems to be coming,' Amber told me. She looked pleased and … somehow excited. 'You've obviously made yourself popular since you've been back here.'

'Oh, I don't think so,' I laughed. 'It's probably more difficult *not* to get to know everyone in a small place like this, isn't it? Especially as I work at the school.'

It was true. The barbecue wasn't a public event, but my friends seemed to have managed to invite everyone I knew, including the staff at the school.

'You're looking very pleased with yourself about it,' I said to Amber. 'What are you plotting?'

'Nothing,' she laughed. 'It's just that I'm bringing a Plus One to the party.'

'Oh, *are* you! That's good.' I gave her a hug, and she pushed me away, laughing back.

'All right, Nic, calm down.' She smiled, and added. 'I don't want a big fuss made about it.'

'Fair enough. But at least tell me who he is.'

'No! Wait till Saturday.'

I was intrigued, obviously. Amber hadn't mentioned that she was seeing anyone at any time during the seven months or so that I'd now been back in Furzewell. In fact, she always seemed so determined to turn the conversation away from dating and boyfriends that I'd given up. Why was she being so secretive about it? I wondered if this guy was married. Or someone we knew.

'It's not Craig, is it?' I teased her – and she thumped me and shouted an obscenity in response. So not him, at least!

Ah well. I'd find out on Saturday night. Something else to look forward to.

On the Thursday, though, we had a different concern. Gran had apparently turned up at Eagle House at lunchtime, when Mum was home from the shop, looking flustered and anxious.

'She said she'd finally plucked up courage to invite this Sidney round last night to watch a rom com or whatever you call it,' Mum told me when I got in from school.

'Oh, good,' I smiled. But Mum was shaking her head.

'No, it wasn't good. Well, I don't know, it might have been good as far as Sidney goes, or the film, but she's now more scared than she was when she was watching the bloody zombie films, for God's sake.'

'How come?' I stared at Mum. 'Was it something Sidney said? Or did?'

'No, no, no. I said, it wasn't Sidney. It was the screams, Nicky.'

'Screams, in a rom com? What the hell film were they watching?'

Mum sighed, as if I was being deliberately thick.

'That's the whole point. They weren't watching films with screaming in, but they could still hear screams. Well,' she amended, 'your gran heard them. Sidney, apparently, is too deaf. He normally turns the zombie films right up loud, but she forgot, and had this *Love in Paris* or whatever it was, playing at a more normal level, and he didn't like to ask for it to be turned up.' Mum raised her eyebrows as if in exasperation. 'She says he's shy.'

I smiled again, but Mum was apparently taking it all more seriously than I'd realised, so I tried to keep a straight face.

'And is she absolutely sure the screams weren't on the love-story film?' I said. 'They could have been,' I added, trying not to smirk, 'screams of passion.'

'Nicky, this isn't funny. Your gran is worried all over again now. Whenever she's heard the screams since we found out about Sidney's viewing habits, she's assumed it's just him watching more films, morning, noon and night. But apparently he denies it now. If the man can even be believed – he sounds such an oddball – she's hearing screams when he's not watching anything.'

'Sorry, Mum. But I don't understand. If the screams aren't coming from his sci-fi films, why don't *other* residents on the complex hear them?'

'Because they're all too deaf, obviously,' Mum said, getting impatient now. 'Your gran's got unusually good hearing for someone in her eighties. I'm beginning to wish she didn't. But I really do need to find out what's going on, once and for all. So that's where I'm going.'

'Where?'

'To her bungalow, of course. To sit with her all evening with no TV or music on, and listen. And sleep there all night, if necessary. I should have done it in the first place. It would have avoided all this worry. All this . . . zombie and Sidney nonsense.'

'I think she likes Sidney, actually,' I pointed out. 'He's company for her.'

'Company? She could have stayed living here, if company's all she wanted,' she retorted.

I knew I wasn't going to get anywhere if we started going down that particular road again.

'Well, if you're going round there, I'll come too,' I said instead.

'Don't be silly, you can't. Mia will be in bed.'

'We can *all* sleep there tonight. We can take Smartie.'

She hesitated. 'Actually, the dog is a good idea. He'll bark if there's anything spooky going on. But you stay here with Mia. I don't want her being disturbed and upset.'

'*You* stay here with her then,' I insisted. 'Seriously, Mum, I think it's best if I go. Yes, I'll take Smartie. If there's anything going on – which I seriously doubt – Smartie and I will find out. Agreed?'

'Well, OK, then,' she said, looking at me doubtfully as if she wasn't sure I'd be up to it. 'If you insist. But don't tell Mia you're going out on some kind of ghost hunt, will you. She'll be frightened.'

'Of course I won't. And anyway, it isn't a ghost hunt, for heaven's sake. I bet it's just one of the old boys there, snoring like a steam train, with all his windows open. Something perfectly innocuous like that.'

I waited until Mia was tucked up in bed, telling her a little white lie about going out with one of my friends.

'I'll set the alarm on my phone, so that I'll be back early in the morning, before she's awake, whatever happens,' I whispered to Mum.

'Be careful, love,' she warned me, looking worried. 'You don't think we should just talk to Lizzie Barnes again? Or the police?'

'No, Mum. As Gran says, Lizzie's useless, she won't do anything. Nor will the police – unless I find someone murdered!'

'That's not funny,' Mum protested, shuddering.

I was smiling to myself as I set off with Smartie to walk round the corner to Nightingale Court. I just couldn't believe there was really anything to worry about. But it was a breezy night, the clouds scudding across the darkened sky, hiding the moon, and the shapes of trees looming up out of the blackness, branches waving, dry leaves rustling and jumping along the ground. When a frog hopped out of the hedgerow onto the road just in front of us, Smartie and I both nearly jumped out of our skins, and I began to wish I hadn't joked with Mum about ghosts and murderers. To be fair, it wasn't funny for Gran, sitting on her own in her little bungalow, hearing these noises – even if she was imagining them. Mum was right, it needed sorting out. And if we didn't get anywhere with it tonight, I'd *have* to get Lazy Lizzie on the case again, or come round here myself every night until we'd solved the mystery.

Gran was pleased to see me.

'I'd rather it was you than your mum, she makes such a fuss,' she said, pouring me a sherry from the bottle she'd evidently bought for her previous evening with Sidney. 'And I'm glad you've brought Smartie. He's got more sense than all of us put together. If there's anything out there, he'll hear it, right enough, won't he.'

'Yes, he will. Smartie, lie down, there's a good boy. Have you heard any noises tonight yet, Gran?'

'Tonight? I've heard them on and off all day, Nicky. It's like I keep saying, I hear them every day, and every night, especially when it's quiet like this. I stopped worrying about it when we all thought it was Sidney watching his damned silly films – although, truth to tell, the zombie screams weren't really the same as the screams I hear.' She gave me a worried look. 'You don't think I'm imagining it, do you, love? You don't think I've gone completely gaga?'

'No, Gran, of course I don't—' I began, but the conversation never got any further. Because at that moment, Smartie jumped to his feet, running to the door, barking his head off. 'What is it, boy?' I said, putting my sherry glass down. 'Come on, there's nothing there. Come and lie back down, that's right.'

He'd started to pad back towards us, looking around at the door, giving a suspicious growl deep in his throat. But just as he was going to lie down, we heard it – both Gran and I – a horrible, wailing crescendo that made the hairs on the back of my neck stand up.

'What the—?' I began, jumping up, as Smartie, barking fit to burst again, ran over to the door and pawed at it, growling and barking and looking back at us, as if to say we needed to let him go out and investigate, right away.

'That's it,' Gran said, surprisingly calmly. I suppose she'd got used to it. 'That's the screaming I keep hearing. I'm *not* imagining it, am I?'

'No, you're not.' The bloodcurdling sound came again, and without another word I pulled my coat back on and fastened Smartie's lead. 'Right. Let's see what's going on.'

'Let me come with you,' Gran said, getting out of her armchair. 'It might be dangerous.'

'Absolutely not. And it can't be anything dangerous, not if it's been going on for as long as you've been saying. It's probably just some teenagers, playing around.' I hesitated, checking my pocket for my phone, taking it out and turning on the torch. 'We'll be fine. OK, Smartie, yes, I know you can still hear it, let's go.'

I didn't have to worry about following the sounds. Smartie's hearing was obviously so much better than mine, and he was pulling me hard, still growling, so that I had to run to keep up with him. Two bungalows from Gran's, he stopped dead, his head low, looking up at one of the windows. They were all closed, with the curtains drawn, but I thought I noticed movement, a slight twitching of one of the curtains at the window Smartie was staring at. Despite myself, despite all my no-nonsense talk about it being nothing – teenagers screaming, somebody's TV, some perfectly rational explanation – my heart was pounding, and not just from running to keep up with Smartie. And then the blood-curdling noise came again. Smartie let out the loudest and longest series of excited barks he'd ever made, and at the same time, I knew exactly what was in that bungalow, exactly why it was making so much noise, and why Smartie was so desperate to get at it. And two mysteries were solved at once.

'*Cats*,' I muttered. 'Yes, Smartie – it's cats, isn't it.'

Cats – it sounded like lots of them – screaming, squealing and howling, presumably all desperate to get out of there. When one started, they all joined in, which was why the noise rose in such a fearsome crescendo – like someone being murdered. No wonder Gran could hear them at all times of day and night. The other residents must have been even deafer than they thought, or had their TVs turned on twenty-four hours a day, at a deafening volume, if they couldn't hear this. The sound was going right through me.

It was a terrible chorus of anguished wailing, like nothing I'd ever heard. Poor Smartie was beside himself.

'OK, boy. It's all right. Calm down now.' I bent to stroke him. 'Good dog, Smartie. I'm pretty sure you've just found the Furzewell Cat Napper.'

CHAPTER 36

'So have all the cats been returned to their owners now?' Mum asked.

We were sitting in the lounge the following afternoon after school, Monty curled up on Mum's lap. I'd asked Mia to take Smartie out into the garden to run off his excitement. He'd scared the life out of the poor cat when he first arrived home, but to my surprise, his tail had been wagging and he seemed to instinctively recognise that Monty wasn't just any cat, one that needed a good telling-off and chasing off our territory, but a rather sad-looking, undernourished and nervous member of our own family. I was fairly confident he was going to accept him.

'Yes.'

I smiled, remembering the excitement in the voices of the various cat owners when I'd worked my way down the list, calling them, telling them to collect their missing cats from the vet's, where the RSPCA had taken them that morning. Mr Brent had been so moved by the whole thing, he'd promised to check over all the cats free of charge, to make sure their health hadn't been compromised during their captivity, and to confirm those who had identity chips were being returned to the correct owners. They were mostly, he said, going to be absolutely fine once they'd been well fed and groomed and given lots of TLC.

'And that poor woman's been taken into care,' I added to Mum now.

'Poor woman?' Mum scoffed. 'She sounds like a complete nutcase. Stealing all those cats and hiding them in that tiny bungalow? No wonder the poor things were howling. If the residents of the complex weren't all so deaf, playing their TVs at top volume—'

'I know, Mum. But at least Gran heard them. I just wish one of us had gone round there at night-time before – with Smartie! And anyway, I *do* feel sorry for that Maggie – the cat napper – she's got dementia. She honestly believed she was rescuing stray cats. Any that came near her bungalow, she took them in, and kept them in, thinking she was saving them from "straying" again.'

'She might have at least looked after them properly.'

'She thought she did. She just got muddled.'

I'd called the police, the night before, as soon as I'd realised the cats were in her bungalow. Maggie looked at us all in complete confusion when we tried to explain that the cats were other people's pets. She'd had them all shut in one room, 'for their own safety'. It was horrendous – I won't begin to describe it. The RSPCA were called out as a matter of emergency, but as we knew the cats were all local, Mr Brent intervened and took over their care.

'So wasn't anyone looking after her – Maggie?' Mum said. 'Did her family not realise what was going on, for God's sake?'

'She only has one son, who lives in America,' I said. I did feel really sad for her, despite the horror of the previous evening. 'The police managed to rouse Lazy Lizzie to get the son's phone number – Lizzie's being replaced, by the way, with immediate effect.'

'Good. About time too.'

'Yes. So they spoke to the son, who was absolutely mortified, had no idea his mum had deteriorated to that extent, and had believed she was being looked after. He obviously hadn't paid much attention to her situation, sadly – he thought she was in a care home, not in a sheltered complex, looking after herself. He's flying over as a matter of urgency to sort out a decent home for her.'

Mum sighed. 'I suppose she couldn't help it. It's that Lizzie's fault. If she'd ever stepped foot inside that woman's bungalow to check on her, she'd have known straight away—'

'Exactly.'

We sat in companionable silence for a while. Monty began to purr, and we both smiled. Mia had been even more excited than Smartie when she heard he was coming home. I remembered how upset she'd been, the first day we arrived back in Furzewell, to find out he'd disappeared – it had seemed as if all her anxiety became bound up in the loss of the cat. She didn't need him as a comfort blanket anymore, but of course, she was still pleased to bits that he was back. She even shouted out the news to Josh when he came to pick her up that evening.

'Guess what, Daddy!' She ran out to greet him as he got out of the car. 'Monty's back! Mummy and Smartie found him last night.'

'Oh, that *is* good news,' he said, giving me a smile as I watched from the doorway. 'I'm pleased to hear that. So you're all back together now, then.'

There was something about the way he said that, the way he looked at me as he waved goodbye after he'd strapped Mia into her car seat that made me wonder if he was lonely. But I gave myself a little shake. He'd never be lonely while he had his work – his only real love in life. And to be honest, if he was, it was his own fault. But despite myself I felt a strange little ache of sympathy and sadness for him after he'd driven off. He seemed … a bit different these days, with his recent talk of regrets, remembering my birthday and being more … thoughtful. What a shame he hadn't been more like that when we were still together.

On the Saturday evening, Mum and I walked round to the park together. We'd asked Gran to come along, but she said she'd see me for my birthday the next day and anyway, 'after all the fuss' and now she knew she wouldn't be disturbed by spooky noises, she just wanted to enjoy the peace and quiet on her own. I suspected Sidney might be keeping her company!

'I'm glad she's found someone to spend some time with,' I said to Mum.

'Huh!' was the response. 'Why does she want to bother with men, at her age?'

'*You* do!' I laughed.

'Well, yes, but only for – occasional entertainment,' she blustered. 'Just for fun.'

'And Gran probably just thinks of Sidney as a friend. A companion. What's wrong with that?'

'Nothing, as long as she doesn't get carried away. Men are useless as friends, and even worse at relationships. As we both know,' she added pointedly. 'That's why it's much better to have fun with our girlfriends.'

I sighed. Mum was still so determined to blame every man on the planet for the way Dad had treated her.

'It was twenty-five years ago, Mum,' I said gently.

'Yes, I do know that, Nicky. And it's never stopped hurting.'

I couldn't really blame her. My father's betrayal had been so cruel, so without any hint of remorse or care, at the time or ever since. I linked my arm through hers.

'OK. I do get it. But come on, let's have a good time tonight and not worry about men at all.'

'Too right.' She smiled back at me. 'I'm always up for having a good time, Nicky, you know me.'

It was a dry, clear evening, and by the time we arrived in the park, Simon and Sara already had the barbecues fired up and were cooking what looked like a mountain of sausages, kebabs and corn-on-the-cob. There were fairy lights hung in the trees and it all looked so pretty and welcoming.

'Here's the birthday girl!' Louise called out, and everyone cheered. 'Great work with the cats, Nic,' she added, and they all cheered again.

I laughed, shouting back that it was mostly due to Smartie that the cats had been found. Leaving Mum talking to someone she knew, I walked over to say hello to Amber and Louise. They were with another girl who I recognised, but for a minute I couldn't place her, until Amber said:

'Nic, you know Kelly, don't you? From the vet's?'

'Yes, of course.' I smiled at her. 'Hi, Kelly. Nice of you to come tonight.'

'She's with me,' Amber said. Her face looked unusually flushed. I'd assumed it was from the heat of the barbecues.

'OK,' I smiled again, completely missing the point, assuming they were neighbours on the estate, or had bumped into each other and walked round together.

'I mean,' she said, looking at me more directly, 'Kelly is *with* me, Nic. We're together. She's the Plus One I told you I was bringing.'

'Oh!' I said, the light finally dawning. 'Oh, I see. I'm sorry, I didn't ... I mean, I wasn't aware...'

I tailed off. It was no good pretending I wasn't stunned. I'd known Amber since we were children. We'd been through our teenage years together, as close as sisters, having crushes on various boys at school, fantasising about pop stars, giggling in our bedrooms about sex … about boys, only ever boys. I'd been in touch with her over the years, but never picked up any hint that she now preferred girls. Not even since I'd been back here in Furzewell, admittedly wondering why she was so reluctant now to talk about men or to discuss relationships at all, had it ever occurred to me that this might be the reason.

'It was a gradual thing,' she admitted with a smile as, a little later, we talked quietly together while Kelly chatted with Louise. 'Not a blinding flash of light or anything like that. I just started, gradually, to admit to myself that, despite the boys in the past, I'd never really felt as excited by it all as I used to pretend. And I realised the way I sometimes felt about girls was different. But until I met Kelly –' I noticed she couldn't resist looking at her, and her face lit up as she did so, '—I've never felt like this. Never once in my life.'

I hugged her, feeling tearful with emotion.

'I'm so pleased for you,' I said. 'I wish you'd talked to me about it, though – before.'

'Oh, I was going to. When we met up again, that first day you were back in the village, I was desperate to talk to you about how I'd been feeling. Kelly and I hadn't got together then, but we'd been chatting, whenever I took Benji to the vet's, and…' She smiled at Kelly again. 'Well, I was obviously hoping…! But as soon as you told me you'd split from Josh, well, I realised you had enough on your plate. It wasn't fair to start going on to you about my own issues. And then you started that thing with Craig,' she added, pulling a face, 'and I was so frustrated with you.'

'Yes, well, I don't blame you, now. I was an idiot. Just flattered by the attention, obviously. After being ignored for so long.'

'Poor you.' She hugged me back. 'But you deserve so much better.'

'Thanks, love. Now, come on, let's get something to eat before this lot devour it all!'

We sat in small groups to eat our food, most of us on folding garden chairs we'd brought with us, others sitting on blankets spread on the ground. The talk among our own little group was mostly about the retrieval of the missing cats. Kelly had been on duty at the vet clinic when they were being returned to their owners, and she described how old Tommy Burrows had tears in his eyes when he was reunited with Ginger, how the Reverend Timms had fallen to his knees in the middle of the waiting room and given thanks to God, and the young guy with all the tattoos had actually burst out crying when he saw his little Petal was safe.

'It moved me to tears myself,' she admitted. 'And Mr Brent looked pretty choked up too.'

'Well,' Simon said, 'as this is now a *double* celebration, Craig and I thought it was appropriate to open a few bottles.'

'Oh, Mum's brought some wine as well. And some plastic glasses,' I said. 'And I think a few other people have, too.'

'But it has to be fizz, surely, for a birthday,' he said, producing some bottles of prosecco from a cool bag. 'Hand the glasses round, Craig.'

I laughed and thanked them, and after they'd opened the bottles – which got everyone's attention – and poured the fizzing wine, Simon raised his own glass and said:

'Happy birthday, Nic. We're all really glad you chose to come back to Furzewell.'

'That was a nice thought,' Louise said quietly, after the fuss had died down. 'He thinks a lot of you, doesn't he – Simon.'

'Mm.' I frowned into my glass. I glanced up at him and back at Louise, adding softly, 'In fact I got quite worried a couple of weeks ago. He seemed to be saying . . . well, hinting, that—'

'That he liked you? Aw. He's such a nice guy, Nic.'

'I know, but Lou, I don't feel like that about him. I did try to warn him off, but it was all really awkward. It's been fine since, but you know, I'd hate to hurt his feelings, or lose him as a friend.'

'You'll have to make sure he got the message, then. Good grief, woman, you've only been separated for a few months and you've got men falling at your feet all over the place.'

'No I haven't!' I retorted, laughing. 'And anyway, I've come round to my mum's way of thinking, since the fiasco with Craig. Men just aren't worth the hassle.'

'I think you're right. Frankly I haven't got the time, anyway. I'm waiting till Eddie's grown up and left home, then maybe I'll have a series of flings, to make up for lost time.'

'Sounds good to me!'

We clunked our plastic glasses together and, laughing, drank deeply to the idea.

'Meanwhile,' she added, giving me a happy smile, 'I'm getting a dog.'

'Oh, how lovely! You can join the Lonely Hearts Dog Walkers!'

'I was hoping you'd say that!' She laughed again. 'Eddie and I have chosen her already – from the rescue centre in Plymouth. She's a sweet little thing, two years old, mixed breed, and very friendly.'

'Perfect. I'm so pleased for you both. Mia will be thrilled, too.'

We'd finished our food now, and I got up to put our paper plates into the rubbish sack. Louise got into conversation with my mum, and I drifted off to chat to the teachers from my school who'd come along. Everyone wanted to hear more about the cat rescue, and by the time we'd finished talking I was ready for another drink. I went over to the trestle table next to the barbecue where Craig and Simon had left the wine, poured myself a glass and sank down into a nearby chair, looking around the park, full of amazement that all these friends and neighbours had come here tonight for my benefit. I had no doubts anymore, I realised – no doubt at all – that this was where my future was. Where I belonged. Everyone here felt almost like family. In fact, I was actually beginning to *think* of the dog-walking group as my extended family. Even Sara and I, since we'd bonded over our dumping of Craig, had got along together so much better, I couldn't really understand why I'd disliked her so much before. Amber had told me earlier that evening that Sara had fronted up to her and admitted she'd been terribly wrong to suspect her of having anything to do with the disappearance of the cats, making no excuses for herself and saying she should have known Amber would never hurt animals. I was pleased that particular falsehood had been put to rest, and I respected Sara for making the apology.

'Hello!'

I jumped, sloshing some of my wine over my jeans. Simon had suddenly come up behind me and sat down in the chair next to mine.

'What are you doing, sitting here all on your own in the dark? You looked as if you were miles away.'

'Not at all.' I smiled. 'In fact I was just thinking that I never want to *be* miles away, ever again. I'm staying in Furzewell forever, until they carry me out.'

'No need to leave, even then,' he pointed out. 'We've got a perfectly good graveyard behind the church.'

I laughed. 'I know. My grandad's buried there.'

'Ah. Sorry.'

'It's fine. We were both joking.'

We sat in companionable silence for a few minutes. If I was ever going to say anything, I realised – ever going to make absolutely sure that, as Louise had said, he'd really got the message – I'd probably never get a better moment. I took a deep breath.

'Simon, there's something I need to … get straight with you.'

'Oh God. What have I done?'

'Nothing.' I smiled. 'But I keep thinking about a conversation we had a while ago. After ... well, when Sara and I were both still feeling a bit sore, you know, about Craig.'

'OK,' he said. 'Did I say something wrong?'

'Of course not. You were very kind, as always. You said, I don't know, something about always being there for me, if I wanted to talk—'

'There's something worrying you now? Tell me.'

'No, no there's nothing. It's just—' I shook my head, searching for the right words. 'Simon, I got the impression – sorry if I got the wrong end of the stick – but you said something about being very fond of me and, well, I need you to understand, before it gets too awkward between us.' It couldn't have been much more awkward than it was right at that minute. I closed my eyes and said the last part all in a rush: 'I'm sorry but I just don't think of you in quite that kind of way.'

There was a horrible, empty silence. I knew, straight away, that I'd got it all wrong. Either that or I'd offended him terribly. Or both. Probably both. I could feel him staring at me, and was only glad we couldn't see each other's faces properly in the dark.

'What kind of way?' he said eventually. 'You didn't think I meant ... that I was *interested* in you?'

'Oh. God. I'm sorry,' I blustered. 'No, of course not. I just—'

'You did, didn't you?' He sounded as wretched as I felt. 'Nic, honestly, I didn't mean ... Look, I think of you more like . . . well, almost like a *daughter*, as well as a friend, of course. I just, you know, feel like I want to help you, because you're on your own, and, well, I see you as being a bit vulnerable. . .'

He tailed off.

'Not that you're not, obviously, very attractive,' he added quickly, sounding almost panicked now. There was another excruciating pause. I wished I could just get up and walk away, away from the mess I'd made of this.

'I'm really sorry,' I said. 'I didn't mean to offend you.'

'You haven't. Not at all. But, well, the thing is,' he went on, 'it's not your fault, because I've never told you the truth. I suppose I thought you might have guessed, and you'd been kind enough not to mention it, as it's, well, a sort of embarrassing situation really, us being friends like this, but it seems you hadn't guessed, hadn't realised at all, otherwise you wouldn't have thought I was implying anything other than—'

'What truth?' I interrupted him, as it seemed he was going to gabble on awkwardly like this indefinitely. 'What haven't I guessed?'

It flashed through my mind now that he might be gay. That would explain it, wouldn't it? Why he was so embarrassed that I'd thought he fancied me. Perhaps that was even why he'd been so furiously angry with Craig about the way he'd behaved – almost angrier than Sara or I had been. Maybe he'd been interested in Craig himself. Surely not? I stared back at him, through the darkness, trying to make out the expression on his face as he still, apparently, struggled to explain himself.

'It's like this, Nic,' he began again more slowly. 'I'm quite a bit older than you.'

'I know,' I said, with a little nervous laugh. 'What's that got to do with it?'

'Well, I'm closer to your mum's age than yours. Just a couple of years younger than she is, in fact.'

'OK,' I said, frowning. Where on earth was he going with this? And how did he know exactly how old my mum was?

'Nic, I don't mean any disrespect,' he went on. 'You're gorgeous, I think the world of you. But I don't fancy you, and there's a very good reason for that.'

'Go on,' I said weakly. He was going to tell me he was gay, for sure. But why the big build up? Why hadn't he been upfront about it in the first place?

There was a long pause. I began to think he'd changed his mind and wasn't going to tell me after all. But then he sighed, shifted in his chair and said quietly, in a voice flat with his own disappointment:

'It's because I'm in love with someone else. I have been for years.' He paused, and then added even more quietly: 'The thing is, Nic, it's your mum.'

CHAPTER 37

The prosecco had gone to my head slightly by the time we started to tidy up. A few people had already headed off home and when Amber came to say goodnight, she was hand-in-hand with Kelly. I gave them both a hug, and possibly told them I loved them. I'd found myself saying it to nearly everyone as the evening progressed.

'Come on, birthday girl.' My mum appeared through the dispersing crowd and grabbed my arm. 'Time to go. Are you sober enough to walk?'

'Cheek!' I retorted. 'I'm no worse than you.'

Calling out goodnight to the last few stragglers, and carrying our garden chairs, we strolled back out of the park and down the road.

'Mum,' I said, after we'd walked in silence for a few minutes, 'why haven't you told me about Simon?'

'What about him?'

'Come on. You were going out with him, weren't you? For almost a year, he said.'

'So?'

'Well, it must have been pretty serious. He gave me that impression, anyway. He still seems very keen on you. And he's such a lovely man—'

She stopped dead in the street.

'I hope you're not going to start telling me who I should or shouldn't go out with?'

'Of course not,' I soothed her quickly. 'But you've always led me to believe you haven't had any serious relationships – just "fun" things. So I was naturally quite surprised when he said—'

'I can't help what he said.' She started to walk on again, briskly now, so that I had to rush to catch her up. 'But as far as I'm concerned, it *was* just a bit of fun. I told you before that I had one boyfriend who got too serious. Well, now you know, it was him – Simon. That's why I finished it. I'm not interested in a serious relationship, with him, or anyone. You know that. And that's the end of it.'

I could see I wasn't going to get any further with her on the subject. And really, it was none of my business. I'd just felt so sad for Simon when he'd described how Mum had been the first woman he'd really liked since his wife died, but that he realised she enjoyed her single life too much to settle down with anyone.

'She was badly hurt by my dad,' I'd explained to him.

'I know. She told me – what a terrible story. I can't blame her for losing her trust in men, in relationships. I just wish she'd have let me prove to her that we men are not all like that.'

I'd kissed him on the cheek and said I wished it too. I'd ended up feeling glad, after all, that we'd had that difficult talk. But sorry that I couldn't do anything about it.

The next day was my birthday. Mum had bought me two lovely new warm jumpers, ready for the winter ahead, but my best present was the ring at the doorbell that signalled my daughter being returned to me.

'Happy birthday, Mummy!' she squealed, giving me a hug right there on the doorstep, and then producing a rather squashed package from her coat pocket. 'It's your favourite,' she said excitedly, obviously unable to keep the secret a moment longer. 'Chocolate fudge.'

'Ooh, lovely,' I said, hugging her back. 'Thank you, baby.'

Then I looked up. Josh was following her up the path, carrying a small parcel himself. It was even gift-wrapped. For a moment, I wondered if it must be for someone else. But no – looking slightly awkward, he handed it to me and wished me a happy birthday.

'Just a small token,' he said. 'You don't have to unwrap it right now.'

But I wanted to, because I could feel that it was a book, and I was hoping it might be the new novel by my favourite thriller writer.

'Why don't you come in for a moment,' I found myself suggesting before I could regret it. Even Mia looked at me in surprise. Josh hesitated briefly and then, with a little cough of something like embarrassment, followed me into the hallway. We both must have been aware that this was the second time he'd been in here since the separation. We weren't exactly making a habit of it, but it was twice more than I'd ever expected.

'Let's just sit in the kitchen while I open this,' I said, feeling as awkward as he appeared to. We sat down at the kitchen table and I ripped off the paper. 'Oh! Brilliant, I've been wanting to read this. Thank you. But I certainly didn't expect—'

'Of course you didn't,' he said, looking down at the table. 'Why would you? I never bothered before, did I? Well, not for a long time. Not since…' He tailed off, and we stared at each other. 'Since what happened,' he finished uncomfortably. For a moment we were both silent, and then he added, 'Nothing was ever right after that, was it? Not for either of us.'

'No, well, that's water under the bridge now, isn't it,' I said briskly. 'But thanks anyway. And for bringing Mia back.'

'We should have talked about it, Nic,' he said, his voice now sounding shaky with urgency. 'If there's one thing I've realised, since you left, it's that we never talked about it, and we should have done. We let it fester, and it ended up killing our marriage.'

I got to my feet, almost knocking over my chair. My heart was racing with panic and there was a burning in my head, behind my eyes.

'I think you should go now,' I heard myself saying, ushering him towards the door. 'See you in two weeks.'

'Sorry,' he said quietly as I opened the front door to see him out. 'I didn't mean to upset you. I just think—'

'Well, I *don't*,' I returned. 'It's too late, Josh.'

He looked so dejected as he walked back to his car, I *almost* called him back. If only he hadn't started talking like that – bringing up the one thing he knew I could never even *think* about, much less start talking about now – if he hadn't done that, I might have suggested he stayed a little longer, had a coffee, played with Mia in the garden. But perhaps it was just as well, I thought, closing the door and turning to catch up with my daughter. What would be the point? It was nice of him to buy me a birthday present. Nice that he knew who my favourite author was. But it didn't mean I had to start spending more time with him, talking about things I'd successfully buried. That ship had sailed.

I'd forced myself to put the episode with Josh behind me by the time Gran came round for Sunday dinner. She seemed much more like her usual self, chattering away about how Lazy Lizzie had been pretty much marched off the premises, her bungalow (according to Gran) having to be 'fumigated, because she'd left it in such a filthy state', and telling us that the new, temporary, replacement warden was a nice 'young lady' of about fifty who had already called on all the residents to introduce herself and assure them that they could turn to her whenever they needed help with anything.

'I hope she stays on,' she said. 'She's already fixed Sidney's curtain rail. I tried, but I couldn't reach it, and he wouldn't let me stand on a chair.'

'I should think not!' Mum said, horrified – but I was just amused to think of Gran being ready and willing to get stuck in with the curtain-rail fixing.

'You could probably do that warden job yourself, Gran,' I teased her – and then regretted it instantly when she nodded thoughtfully and said she might apply, if the new 'nice young woman' didn't stay on.

'Gran,' I said a little later, while Mum was in the kitchen, turning the roast potatoes and refusing to let me help because it was my birthday, 'can I ask you something?'

''Course you can, sweetheart. Not that I know much about anything, these days, mind. But fire away.'

'Well, it's just about Mum,' I said more quietly, sitting down closer to her on the sofa. 'Mia,' I added, seeing her looking up with interest, 'why don't you go and help Nanny? She might let you stand up on a stool and peel the carrots.'

'So what is it about your mother?' Gran said as soon as Mia had skipped off into the kitchen. 'Is she driving you mad?'

'No.' I laughed. 'We get on pretty well, you know that. But I do worry about her. Do you think she'll *ever* move on, from what happened in Ireland? Not that I blame her, but—'

'No, Nicky,' Gran said before I could get any further. 'I don't think she ever will.'

'Oh.'

'But it's her own silly fault, if you ask me.'

'What do you mean? None of it was her fault,' I protested.

'Not the stupid man – your father – leaving her, of course not. He was always a bloody idiot, that Phil. Sorry, I know he was your dad, but I warned her when she first set her sights on him: *That one will never be faithful, Ros*, I said. He always had his eye on every pretty girl, weighing up his chances.'

This was all news to me, of course. Nobody ever talked about my dad, especially not if Mum was in the vicinity.

'He got her pregnant, so fair enough, he married her,' she went on – and I sat up, staring at her.

'She wasn't pregnant with me before they got married,' I said. The dates didn't add up.

'No, no. She lost that first baby. Miscarried at three months or so.'

'Oh.' I looked away. 'I didn't know.'

Gran gave me a look.

'No, well, there are subjects we don't talk about in our family, aren't there. Subjects some of us might feel better about, if we *did* talk about them, if you ask me, but—'

'We're talking about Mum at the moment,' I said, turning away, the conversation with Josh coming back at me in a rush all over again. 'Not me.'

She sighed. 'Yes. Well, she lost the baby just after they got back from honeymoon. I wished it had happened before the wedding – then he might have not bothered marrying her.'

'Gran!' I said, shocked.

'Well, let's be honest, it would've saved her a whole load of misery. But then again, we wouldn't have had you,' she added with a sudden smile. 'You made everything all right for her again.'

'That's nice.' I managed to say, still feeling somewhat shell-shocked.

'Well, it would be, if only she'd pull herself together and get over it – your father and that woman. That's what I meant about it being her own fault. She's always *wallowed*.'

'But … OK, I know she's still bitter about it, and I suppose she always will be. I don't really blame her, Gran. But at least she's enjoying her life now, isn't she? She likes being single. She likes going out with her friends and having fun—'

'Does she hell!' Gran said vehemently. 'Don't tell me you're really taken in by all that *girls having fun* nonsense? It's all a big act, Nicky. It's … her *armour*.'

'Armour against what?'

'Against the world. Anyone getting too close – men in particular. Anyone finding out that really she's not having fun at all. She's lonely. She might be happy enough now, singing around the house, cooking for you, having you and Mia to look after again. Having you for company.' Gran paused, giving me a warning look. 'But it's not good, Nicky. It's not healthy. She won't let you go, you know. She won't want you to have a life of your own again, now you're back here in Eagle House.'

'Of course she will!' I laughed. 'She'll be glad to see us go, eventually. Not that I've got any idea yet how I'm going to afford it—'

'And the longer you're here, the less she'll want you to go. Trust me, I'm her mother, I know her. Before you came back, she was lonely, but she won't ever admit it, because it might mean dropping the big act and admitting she liked someone enough to share her life with them. And she's too scared to do that.'

'Someone?' I said. 'Anyone in particular?'

'Oh, you know who I mean. What's-his-name: Simon. Nicest man you could hope to meet. Would have laid down his life for Ros, but she sent him packing rather than admit she felt the same way.' Gran shook her head again. 'I told her at the time she'd live to regret it. She lost her chance. She'll never meet anyone better than him. Not going out to bloody clubs and bars and whatnot with that Gruesome Twosome, she won't.'

'He's told me he still loves her,' I whispered. I could hear Mum coming back from the kitchen, Mia chatting excitedly to her about the dessert she'd been helping to make. 'I just wish she'd give him another chance.'

Gran shrugged. 'Waste of time talking to her,' she said. 'She's in denial.'

We had roast beef with all the trimmings, followed by apple and blackberry crumble with custard, and the conversation around the table was light and easy, all of us laughing, Mum telling Gran about the barbecue, the prosecco, and how one of our neighbours, who was a bit overweight, had sat on a rather flimsy garden chair and fallen straight through it. Mia, giggly and excited, told us about her weekend with Josh, how he'd taken her to the park near our old home, and she'd seen Polly and Jamila and how 'It was funny: it was nice to see them, but it didn't really feel like they were my best friends anymore, they seemed . . . just like ordinary people.'

But every time she mentioned Josh, I remembered the look of sadness on his face earlier, the way he'd handed me that carefully wrapped birthday present, and most of all the way he'd tried to raise the one subject we never, ever discussed. To keep my mind from dwelling on it, I kept sneaking looks at Mum – so rosy and contented-looking, serving up the food, carrying in the dessert, looking after us all as usual – and wondering if Gran was right, that underneath it all she'd be lonely and miserable if Mia and I left again. And if so, was there anything any of us could do about it? Perhaps I was destined to stay at Eagle House forever. I could think of worse fates. But no, it probably wouldn't be the right thing – for any of us.

CHAPTER 38

October arrived, with a flurry of sunshine and showers that made it feel more like April. The evenings were dark earlier, the lanes and footpaths muddy again, and there was a chill in the air that made us all start to think about the winter ahead.

'If I hear one more person talking about how many weeks it is till Christmas—' Louise began as we walked home from school towards the middle of the month.

'Or if I see one more TV advert for the latest toys, encouraging children to start talking about what they want already…' I joined in.

And we both laughed, because – annoying though it was – we knew it would always be the same. As soon as summer was over, the marketing for Christmas began. Personally, though, I had enough to think about without getting started on that already.

School was busy, with most of my reception class now settled in, fewer tears and upsets to deal with, which was always a step in the right direction, but still a long way to go before the random little selection of four-year-olds became fully confident and integrated into school life. Mia, though, was going from strength to strength, getting all sorts of commendations for her work and coming out of her classroom every afternoon beaming, holding hands with Olivia and looking out for Eddie. Her popularity with other children in her class seemed finally to be growing too, and her teacher told me she was particularly good with the younger ones – my previous reception class – who'd joined them this year.

Smartie too was growing up. Still a puppy, but bigger and stronger now and loving our long walks more than ever, he was good company, especially during the weekends when Mia was with Josh. He seemed to have accepted Monty the cat surprisingly well, and we often found them curled up asleep together, Monty with his paws across Smartie's back. If Smartie even recognised that Monty was a cat, he certainly didn't treat him like one, but more like a fellow dog with a few strange habits. Monty liked trying to lick Smartie clean, for instance, and after a while Smartie seemed to give in, and put up with it.

Gran still seemed to be enjoying her occasional evenings with Sidney, taking it in turns to choose what kind of film they watched together, and sometimes playing cards instead.

'Why don't you bring him round to dinner one Sunday so we can meet him?' I suggested. But she just laughed and said she didn't want Mum terrifying the poor man.

A week or so later, she also told us she'd been to see the doctor about her memory. Although there hadn't been any further incidents that had particularly worried her, she'd still been feeling a little anxious about the fact that she'd become, as she put it, *daft as a brush*, forgetting where she'd put things, or why she'd walked from one room to the other.

'The doctor said it's just my age,' she said indignantly – but at the same time she sounded quite obviously relieved. 'I told him it was not as bad as before, when I was awake half the night listening to those cats screaming and wondering what it was. He said that the lack of sleep would have made things worse.'

'Well, of course it would. You're better now, aren't you, Gran?'

'Yes. Still daft as a brush, though. I made a cake the other day and put it in the fridge instead of the oven to cook. When it was due to come out of the oven, I couldn't believe it wasn't in there. Anyway, I'm glad the doctor doesn't think it's dementia. He asked me a lot of silly questions about who the queen's oldest son is, and who the prime minister is, and what day it was. I told him it was the twenty-first of October, Trafalgar Day, and he said 'Is it?' So I'm not sure who was testing whom, to be honest.'

I laughed. 'Well, I'm glad you feel better about it now, Gran. I didn't know it was Trafalgar Day, either, so you know more than me *and* the doctor.'

I was actually far more concerned with the plans for the fifth of November than with the current day's date or its significance. Everything was coming together well for our Guy Fawkes party. The fireworks had been purchased, Simon had been saving wood for the bonfire for weeks now, and we had a good number of volunteers, some of whom would be building the bonfire during the last days before the event, and covering it with a tarpaulin. Other volunteers would be manning the gate, and selling food and drinks on the night. Finally, we were canvassing the whole village again, reminding them about the evening and asking them to please make sure their pets were kept safely indoors.

At our final planning meeting, the week before, Craig had some good news for us.

'I've heard back from the council about my draft plans,' he said, a huge grin on his face. 'They've said in their letter that they're very impressed. And of course, they're particularly interested in my firm's proposal – the advertising deal. I spoke to someone on the phone about it today, and he said there would be a further meeting soon about whether they're likely to drop the proposal to sell the land. He wouldn't commit himself on that yet, needless to say. But we'll be told the outcome of the meeting.'

'Oh, that's marvellous,' Sara exclaimed. 'It sounds pretty encouraging, doesn't it?'

'Let's not get our hopes too high,' Simon warned. But he was having trouble keeping the smile off his face too. 'Well done, Craig.'

It was good to see the two guys back on amicable terms. To be fair, Craig had been completely different ever since the showdown with Sara and myself. He'd dropped the whole flirtatious routine, and although he'd gradually recovered his usual confident manner and was enjoying a joke again, he now had a far more polite, respectful attitude. Of course, whether his behaviour with other women, apart from us, had changed, we had no idea. But it would be nice to think he might have grown up a bit because of what had happened. Drawing up the plans for the park, getting the advertising deal from his company, and now having had a good reaction from the council, had at least shown he was on board with the rest of us and was trying hard to redeem himself in our eyes. And that was without us even knowing for sure whether he was in fact putting up some of the funding himself. We'd probably never know.

The weather on the fifth of November was, fortunately, dry, and not too cold. Once Mum was home from work, I left Mia with her so that I could go along to the park, where a large group of volunteers had convened to finish the preparations. A young man called Oliver Prentice turned up from the council, holding a clipboard, to check we'd followed all the necessary safety regulations. At first he seemed rather officious, but having done his tour and saying he was satisfied, his manner changed completely.

'This all looks great, guys,' he enthused. 'I'm looking forward to it.'

'Oh – you're coming back this evening?' Sara said.

''Course I am. Wouldn't miss it for anything. Nothing like this happens in my village.' He mentioned a small hamlet about five miles away. 'It's brilliant what you're doing here. There's a whole crowd of us coming tonight.'

'Great!' We all grinned at each other, pleased that our efforts at promoting the event to surrounding areas seemed to have worked. 'We'll see you later, then.'

We were starting at seven o'clock, so once we were satisfied that there was nothing more to be done for now, we all headed home for a quick break to have something to eat. Simon and I walked out of the park together.

'Mum's coming tonight,' I said, giving him a pointed look. 'A chance for you to chat, at least?'

He sighed. 'I see her around the village all the time, Nic – it's not as if we wouldn't get a chance to chat, but she never wants to. At your birthday barbecue she was sitting just yards away from me, and still managed to ignore me. It's no good, she made it perfectly clear when she finished with me: she'll come out with me occasionally for lunch, as a friend, but she doesn't want anything more than that. She enjoys the single life too much.'

'That's not what my gran says, and she reckons she knows Mum better than anyone.'

'Why? What does she say?'

'That it's all a big act. That really, she's lonely. Or at least, she was, until Mia and I moved back in with her. Gran thinks she won't want us ever to move out, now.'

'If she was lonely, why did she turn me away?' Simon said, frowning. 'It doesn't make sense. I always made it clear I'd be happy with just friendship – companionship – if that was all she wanted. I'd never have pushed her into anything more serious unless she was ready for it.'

'She's still got trust issues, Si. Even after all this time. She's never got over what my dad did to her. If you ask me, she must have felt a lot for you, even if she won't admit it. That's why she couldn't keep seeing you. I reckon she was frightened of her own feelings.'

He shook his head. 'She gave me the impression she was bored with me. She kept saying she just wanted to have fun.'

'I know. It's what she says all the time. But the longer I've been back in the house with her, the more I'm beginning to wonder about this *fun* she keeps on about. I think it's just an excuse. Gran calls it her *armour*. Mum pretends she's enjoying this single girl thing, but . . . to be honest I think it's just sad, and desperate. They never seem to actually meet any men – her and her friends. They dress up, go out, all giggly and excited, and come home pretending they've had a ball.' As I was saying this, the truth of it was becoming more and more obvious to me. 'It never rings true,' I said, feeling suddenly terribly sad as I turned to him and added: 'There's . . . no light in her eyes. No *joy* in her smile. It's fake.'

He stared back at me. 'You don't think she's happy?'

'I think she's happy having me and Mia with her. But we won't be there forever.' I paused. 'Try talking to her tonight, Si. Don't tell her I've said all this, though, will you.'

'Of course not. Thanks, Nic.' He gave me a quick peck on the cheek. 'I don't feel particularly hopeful. But it'd be nice if she'd at least talk to me about it.'

'I'll try to send her in your direction, if I can,' I promised him. 'See you later.'

The evening was a huge success. The number of people who crowded into the park far exceeded all our hopes. Everyone was in a great party mood: family groups, with young children wrapped up in their coats and gloves, holding the light sticks we were selling at the gates; groups of teenagers queuing for burgers even before the event started; adults enjoying an evening out, looking forward to the firework display. Sara was the MC this time, using the PA system to welcome everyone, to announce the lighting of the bonfire and the commencement of the fireworks.

'Fabulous,' Amber breathed as, eventually, the final burst of colour lit up the sky. 'It's been just fabulous, hasn't it?'

'Yes.' I smiled at her. She'd worked hard all day, helping with the preparations, but now, watching the display, she was huddled close to Kelly, who had an arm slung around her shoulder. 'Even better than I dared hope.'

'And that guy from the council – Oliver – is here somewhere with his mates. I saw them come in. So let's hope he reports back to his colleagues.'

'Yes. It all helps, doesn't it. If they trust us to run events like this, and if they see how successful we can be, they'll be more inclined to believe we can raise the money we need.'

Sara was on the PA system again, letting everyone know the fireworks had now finished but the catering stall was still open for another fifteen minutes, serving hot dogs and burgers, and asking everyone to please take any litter home with them. Just as she finished talking, I caught sight of Mum, with Louise and our two children.

'Mum!' I called her, worried that she was about to leave and I'd have missed my chance. 'Could I ask you a favour? Take the kids over and get them a hot dog each? Louise and I are going to help with the clearing up.'

'Thanks, Ros,' Louise said at once. I'd already told her about my plan to get Mum talking to Simon.

'No problem.' Mum smiled. 'Come on Mia, Eddie. I'll take them back to Eagle House afterwards, girls. Louise, you can come and collect Eddie when you've finished. No rush.'

'Thanks, Mum,' I said – and watched her walk across the park to where Simon and one of the other volunteers were now serving the few remaining customers waiting for food. I couldn't do any more. I just hoped it might be enough to get them talking again.

'Not exactly subtle, were you,' Mum remarked when, finally, we'd all returned back from the park, and Louise had collected Eddie and taken him home.

'What do you mean?' I'd poured myself a glass of wine and collapsed, exhausted, on the sofa while Mia had been sent upstairs to get ready for bed.

'Oh, come off it, Nicky. Sending me over to the food stall, where a certain person just happened to be serving.

He got the kids their hot dogs and then, surprise, surprise, immediately handed over to his mate and suggested we had a little chat while they were busy eating.'

'So what? I thought you were still friends, at least. Nothing wrong with having a chat, is there?'

'Except that, as you surely know, having a *chat* with someone who still hopes you might change your mind and want more, is really not fair. Raising their hopes. And a waste of both our time.'

'Sorry,' I said. 'I couldn't help who was serving the food. The kids did want hot dogs.' I paused. 'So *was* it a waste of time, then?'

'Of course it was.' She'd turned away from me so that I couldn't see her face. 'And I don't appreciate being manipulated like that.'

'Oh, Mum, I *am* sorry. I didn't mean to manipulate you. It just seems such a shame. There's no harm in being friends, is there?'

'We *are* still friends. I like seeing him occasionally. We go out for lunch from time to time. Now, shall we talk about something else? The fireworks were amazing, weren't they?'

I sighed. I'd done my best. If I pushed it, I would probably just make matters worse. I hoped Simon wasn't too disappointed. Maybe Mum was right, it had been unfair to raise his hopes. What did I know, after all, about people's relationships? I hadn't exactly had much luck with my own.

CHAPTER 39

I'd never particularly liked November. The nicer aspects of autumn – the colours of the trees, the freshness and breeziness after the heat of summer, the crackling of leaves underfoot – were mostly past, but it didn't yet feel properly like winter either. The weather was damp and dismal, with heavy grey clouds hanging in the sky and frequent bursts of drizzly, miserable rain sweeping into our valley.

'What do you want to do about Christmas?' Josh asked me when he returned Mia after her next weekend with him. He always came right up to the front door with her now, and always found something to talk to me about. It was a far cry from the earlier days when he just watched her until I opened the door, and then drove off without a word. I was glad he was less hostile now, of course, but in some ways I found it unsettling.

'Christmas?' I said. 'Give over, it's too early to think about it yet. It's still at least six weeks off.'

'Sorry.' That was something new, too – Josh apologising. I stared at him, confused. 'It's just that I'd obviously like to see Mia at some point over the holiday,' he went on. 'If that's OK with you, of course. But I realise she'll want to be here with you and your mum most of the time. Just let me know what would work best for you.'

I should have just said yes, of course, and that I'd think about it and let him know. He was being reasonable: I should have been glad. But perhaps it was just my own November mood, or perhaps I was simply irritated by the very idea of him being reasonable, after all the years I'd spent asking him to be and getting nowhere. I snapped.

'So you're actually planning on being at home *at some point over the holiday*, are you? Well, that's a first. Since when did you care about Mia, or anyone else, at Christmas? It was as much as you could do last year to call me from work and ask me to save you some turkey.'

He'd closed his eyes, looking down at his feet. I half expected him to turn and walk off. Mia, fortunately, had already run off to play with Smartie as usual.

'OK. I deserved that,' he said quietly. He looked back up at me and I blinked in surprise at the bleakness in his eyes. But it was too late for him to be sorry, to admit he'd been wrong, to start talking about *the holiday*, as if he'd even understood, in recent years, what the word meant.

I swallowed. 'Well, I'll talk to Mia and let you know what she wants to do.'

'Thank you.' He took a deep breath. 'I *am* sorry, Nic.'

'OK. Bye, then.'

He turned to go, and I closed the door. He was *sorry*? Sorry, *now*? Now he knew how it felt to be left on his own, he was suddenly sorry for the way he'd treated me, neglected me and been so cold and uncaring towards me? Well, it was too late! He must realise that. Too late to start wanting to chat, to apologise and look at me with those sad eyes. It wasn't going to help. It just made me feel confused, and I didn't need it. I was happier now than I'd been for years, and I wasn't going to let Josh mess with my head.

But, of course, it wasn't that easy. I was next to Simon for the dog walk the following evening, and after commiserating with him about the way Mum had brushed off his attempts to be friendly, I found myself telling him about Josh.

'I don't know how to react to him being like this – considerate, and even remorseful,' I said, after I'd described the talk on the doorstep. 'I can't help thinking he's just putting on an act.'

'Why?'

'Well, if he's capable of being considerate and remorseful, why wasn't he like it before? I mean, I get that he might have realised now how lonely it is, being on his own, so of course he wishes I hadn't left him. What is it he misses, though? Obviously not me, or my company. He stopped caring about me too long ago. I suppose it's just having someone to cook his meals and wash his clothes—'

'I don't think he's that shallow really, Nic.'

I stopped dead, staring at him. Smartie, who'd run ahead a little way but was still on his extendable lead, came to a jerking halt and turned round, barking at me to get moving again.

'You don't even know him.'

Simon sighed, looking a bit shamefaced. 'Actually, I do. I wasn't going to tell you this – he asked me not to – but, well, it was a bit of a coincidence, that's all. We were doing some landscaping at his company's offices, back in the summer. He saw from the logo on the side of my van that we're based in Furzewell, and one evening as he was leaving, we got chatting. He asked if I knew you.'

'Oh my God. I can't believe you didn't tell me this, Simon.'

'I've wanted to, but . . . I didn't think it would be helpful. He's been confiding in me a bit, you see,' he added, sounding uncomfortable now.

'You're still in touch with him?' I asked, stunned. 'I *thought* it was odd, that a couple of times when I talked about him you seemed to defend him. I presumed it was just male loyalty.'

He laughed. 'No, I don't necessarily go in for that. It depends on the male. But in Josh's case. . .' He shrugged. 'Well, anyway, what happened was, he wanted his garden – um, your old garden – re-turfed, and a small patio laid. So—'

'Josh was having work done at home? Are we talking about the same Josh? He never even used to *look* at the garden. Or the house, really,' I added half under my breath. 'He was hardly ever there.'

'I know. He told me. We talked a lot, while I was working in his garden.'

'Hang on, hang on.' I rubbed my temples. My head was throbbing. 'You're saying he was actually *there*, at home, while you were working?'

'Yes. I fitted a lot of the work in over a weekend. He made me quite a few cups of tea,' he added with a smile. 'I … know you won't want to hear me say this, Nic, but he seems like a really nice bloke. Of course, it's one thing chatting to someone in their garden, and quite another thing being married to them, I realise that, but we've actually kept in touch. Just the odd text, from time to time, you know—'

'Wait, I'm struggling with this, Simon.' I felt like I needed to sit down. We were still standing in the middle of the park, the rest of the group now disappearing into the distance, Smartie and Max tangling themselves round our legs with their leads. 'The weekend you were working on the garden – it must have been one of the weekends Josh had Mia, otherwise he'd have been at work. Mia didn't mention—'

'No, Mia wasn't there. Apparently Josh doesn't work *any* weekends now.' He turned to me in sudden realisation. 'Hasn't he told you he's changed his job?'

'*What*?' This time I actually did sit down – not so much in shock, although that was certainly part of it, but because Smartie had finally managed to trip me over. The ground was wet and muddy, and I could see Simon was struggling between concern and laughter as he helped me to my feet.

'Your coat – and your jeans – they're soaked with mud. We'd better turn back,' he said.

'No. We'd better go over to the quiet side of the park, let the dogs off to have a run, and find a bench to sit down and finish this conversation,' I said firmly.

'I'm sorry. I shouldn't have told you—'

'Yes you should! I'm glad you did. But he should have told me himself.'

I tailed off, thinking about all the times recently when Josh had tried to engage me in conversation, and how clear I'd made it that I didn't want to chat. How cynical I'd been about his taking time off for holidays with Mia, and about his plan to see her over Christmas.

'*When* did he change his job?' I demanded, as soon as Simon and I had sat down. I was ignoring the cold damp seeping through the legs of my jeans. It was a small price to pay.

'Early on in the summer. It was at his new company that I was doing the landscaping work when I met him. He'd just started there. He seemed relieved. He was telling me he'd got close to a breakdown while he was working at the other place. He'd been promised all sorts – a higher salary, a new car, shares in the company, a partnership one day in the future – to keep him working like a slave, all hours, taking hardly any holiday—'

'*No* holiday. He seemed to love it, to thrive on it. He had no interest in being at home, at all.'

'He told me he'd felt like a zombie,' Simon said, with a sigh, 'just going through the motions, getting up, going to work, working, working, working, coming home exhausted, falling asleep, getting up again – it had taken him over. He needed the money, he said. He couldn't see any way out. You had a big mortgage on the house—'

'Yes, we did,' I admitted. 'But we could manage. He only worked like that because he couldn't face being with me.'

'That doesn't make sense, Nic. He was devastated when you left. He told me he misses you terribly. He still loves you.'

'Huh,' I retorted. But my voice was shaking, and I had to wipe away tears. 'He's never told *me* he still loves me. He never even said it while we were together. Not since ... well, not for years.'

Simon put his arm around my shoulders. It didn't feel threatening, or creepy, anymore. It felt like – as he'd said – he was just being fatherly. I found myself wishing Simon actually *was* my father. He couldn't have made any worse a job of it than my real one had.

'You can go on telling yourself whatever you like, Nic. And I know how much he's hurt you. But I think, deep down, you still love him too, don't you.'

'Huh,' I said again. I was too confused to even speak, now.

'Why don't you just talk to him?' Simon suggested gently. 'It can't do any harm – can it?'

It can't do any harm – can it? I repeated it to myself, over and over, during the rest of that week. It played on my mind while I was walking Smartie with the group, so that

I lost track of conversations and forgot what I was saying mid-sentence. And it distracted me at home, cooking dinner, so that I overcooked the vegetables and let the meat burn. Even at work, I started calling children by the wrong names, making them laugh and call me *Mrs Muddle*. I knew I had to sort myself out. And Simon was right, there was only one way to do it. I'd have to talk to Josh, calmly and sensibly. Find out what the hell was going on. Changing his job? Having the garden landscaped? Taking all his weekends off? What else didn't I know about? But I'd have to wait till the next time he collected Mia. It felt like ages away.

In the meantime, though, something rather wonderful happened, to take my mind off my own concerns. Sara turned up one evening at the park gates with a smile on her face, so wide it looked as if her teeth were going to pop out.

'We've won!' she screamed at the rest of us who were there waiting for her. 'We've done it, guys, we've actually done it!' She waved a letter at us. 'I've heard from the council: they're not selling the park. We can keep it open, and from the first of January we can call it *Furzewell Community Park*.'

'Oh my God!'

'Wow!'

'Fantastic!'

We were all yelling at once, making the dogs bark with excitement.

'Apparently they've been so impressed by our efforts, with the pet show and the bonfire party. And of course, the proposed deal with Craig's company, together with Craig's plans for the new features in the park, have clinched it,' Sara added, nodding at Craig. 'They've also finally conceded our point that another new housing development in the village would stretch the infrastructure too far. We've been invited to a meeting at the council offices next Friday – if any of you can be free? – to go through it all, and get a proper legal contract drawn up. But basically, the land will still be owned by the council, but management and maintenance of the park will now be the responsibility of the Friends of Furzewell Community Park, and will remain so as long as they're satisfied it's being used and maintained for the community.'

'We need to let everyone know,' I said. 'All the people in Furzewell who've signed up to be Friends of the Park.'

'Absolutely.' Sara nodded. 'I'll draft out a letter tonight. It'll go by email wherever possible, of course.'

'And I think we should let the local media know about it, too,' Amber pointed out. 'Let's shout it out – not just locally, but countywide! Nationwide! We should tell people everywhere that it *is* possible to fight things like this, if a community is determined enough.'

'Good idea,' Sara agreed. 'Although probably we ought to just wait till the paperwork's signed next week. But isn't it great news? Well done, everyone. It's all been worthwhile.'

'Even the dogs are excited!' I laughed, as we set off for our walk. 'Perhaps they understand. Their favourite walking place has been saved.'

We went to the pub as soon as we'd finished the walk. Nobody could have disagreed that we had cause to celebrate that evening. We were so noisy and animated as we raised our glasses and congratulated each other that the barmaid and other drinkers in the pub were asking us what had happened, and were soon queuing up to shake our hands and buy us drinks.

'Never mind waiting for the contracts to be signed,' Amber whispered to me. 'It'll be all over Furzewell by tomorrow.'

And, of course, as in any good small, gossipy village, in Devon or anywhere else – it was.

CHAPTER 40

By the time Josh's next weekend with Mia came around, I still hadn't worked out how to initiate the conversation I needed to have with him. In the end, I decided to wait until he brought her home on the Sunday evening. I then spent the whole weekend feeling ridiculously nervous, so that as soon as he rang the doorbell and Mia kissed me and skipped straight indoors to find Smartie, I gabbled, in a half-whisper in case Mum was listening:

'Um, can we have ... a talk? There are some things, I kind of, thought we should discuss.'

'Sure.' He gave me his new, sad little smile. 'Is it about Christmas? If Mia would prefer to spend it all with you and Ros, I understand—'

'No, it's not that. Can we...?' I glanced over my shoulder and came to a sudden decision. 'Mum!' I yelled. 'Could you look after Mia for a little while? I've just got to pop out.'

And before she could ask any questions, I pulled on my coat, stepped outside and slammed the door shut.

'Let's go for a walk,' I suggested. 'The park?'

He'd been looking at me, understandably, in amazement. From refusing to say more than a few words to him, to suddenly wanting to go for a walk, must have seemed quite a jump. But now he smiled and said, as we started to walk down the lane:

'Oh, the park! Mia told me something about it all being *yours* now. Does she mean it's been agreed by the council – the Friends of the Park have got control of it?'

'Yes.' Despite everything, I couldn't help smiling myself. 'Yes, it's brilliant news. We're so chuffed.'

'I bet you are. I've been following the story,' he added, looking a bit sheepish. 'Online – the Friends of Furzewell Park Facebook page. And – talking to someone else I know who's been involved,' he added, trying to sound vague.

'Simon. That's what I wanted to talk to you about.'

'Oh.' There was a silence. 'I asked him not to tell you he knew me.'

'He didn't. Well, not deliberately. I kind of got it out of him,' I said. Talking about the park had broken the ice, and it felt easier now, more natural, to be chatting to him like this. I'd made up my mind to stay in control, not to get angry or throw up old arguments. I just wanted to find out what had been going on, and why. 'He mentioned a couple of things that surprised me.'

That was putting it mildly.

'Go on,' he said.

We were walking faster than we were talking. We were halfway down Fore Street already. It was cold, and dark, and the lights of the Fox and Goose loomed welcomingly ahead of us.

'Look, shall we have a quick drink?' I suggested. 'It'll be warmer in there than the park.'

'Good idea.' I could feel him giving me sidelong looks, probably wondering what the hell I was leading up to. 'And *I'm* buying *you* a drink, to congratulate you. I'm very proud of you, Nic.'

'It wasn't just me,' I protested, unnerved by his tone, his congratulations, his *pride*. 'There's a whole bunch of us who've been working for the park. Plus all the other supporters and volunteers.'

'But I didn't just mean about the park. I'm proud of you for the way you've settled back into the community here. Made a new life for yourself and Mia. I'll be honest, I didn't think you'd make it work at first. I thought you'd end up coming back again. I hoped so, obviously – whatever you might think,' he added quickly. 'However I might have acted to the contrary.'

'Oh,' I said, quietly. I didn't know what else to say. I felt more confused than ever. We were at the pub now, and he held the door open for me as I went in, frowning to myself. Simon had implied that Josh had regrets, and missed me – and yet here he was, saying he was proud of me for leaving him, for getting on with my life without him!

While Josh bought our drinks, I sat at the quietest table, in a dark corner near the back of the bar. Sunday evenings didn't tend to be very busy here, but I didn't particularly want anyone noticing us out together and starting any rumours flying.

'Well,' he said, putting my glass of wine down in front of me. 'This is … a bit like old times, isn't it?'

I shook my head. I didn't want him to start reminiscing about our younger days together here in the village. That wasn't what we were here for.

'I wanted to ask about your new job,' I said instead, coming straight to the point. 'Why did you resign from Matthews & Pavitt?'

'Oh. He told you. Well, I resigned because it was killing me,' he said simply. 'I was making myself ill. And anyway—' He screwed up his eyes suddenly, as if he was trying not to cry. It brought a lump to my throat, against my better judgement. 'It was all for nothing.'

'For nothing?' I shot back. 'I thought it was all for the money. That, and for the sake of being out of the house. Away from me, and Mia.'

I hadn't intended to say that. But how could I not? That pain was a part of me, always there, twisting me up inside. How could it not come out?

'It *was* for the money. For the mortgage, the bills, the endless struggle to make ends meet. You know that, Nic. But mostly for the promise that it was going to end. That soon, one day, eventually, I wouldn't have to work like a dog anymore because they were going to make me a director. Give me shares in the company. Then make me a partner. I was so sure it would happen, that they'd keep their promises, if I worked all the hours God sent, showed them how committed I was…'

'But they didn't, did they,' I said flatly. 'They took advantage of you. They let you make yourself ill, let you *break up our marriage*, Josh – and didn't give you a goddamned thank you for it.'

He hung his head. I wanted to feel sorry for him – I even felt, at that moment, like hugging him. He'd been used, driven to make himself ill, wasted years of his life for that company. It had taken its toll, I could see that – of him, as well as of our marriage. But I still couldn't forgive him. Because it wasn't *just* for the money that he'd worked the way he had. And I needed him to admit it, now, if we were ever going to even be friends again.

'You're right,' he said eventually, his voice quivery with emotion. 'I made a fool of myself, and I should have seen it, long before now. I'm no worse off financially, now I've left them, but I've saved my sanity.' He nodded. 'But the other thing you said – that I worked like that to stay away from you, and from Mia, that's not how it was.'

'You see?' I said, exasperated. 'Even now, you can't admit it! You didn't care about us, Josh. You stopped loving me – I don't know when...'

I paused. If I wanted him to be honest, I had to be, too. I sat up straight, met his eyes, and for the first time, I said it out loud.

'You stopped loving me after I had Mia.' And then, tears spurting to my eyes, almost overcome by the pain of knowing what I was going to say, that I was going to speak her name at last, I added with a gasp: 'After Mia was born; after we lost Mae.'

'Oh, Nicky!' Josh said, his voice catching on a sob. 'I didn't stop loving you!'

He pulled me towards him, held me close, and to my surprise I didn't even struggle. I just wept – silently at first, and then beginning to cry properly, my chest heaving, my nose running, as if everything was pouring out of me in a torrent: the agony of my second twin being alive for only half an hour after birth. The shock, the horror, the *unfairness* of it. It had taken me so long to get pregnant in the first place: years of trying, and tests, and eventually such excitement, when we'd almost given up hope: we were having *twins*! Only to come home from hospital with just our one, precious, baby girl.

I'd dealt with the tragedy of her twin by refusing to talk about her or even allow myself to think about her. Refusing to consider that Josh must have been grieving too, that he wanted to share his grief with me. Reacting with fury and disbelief when he started to suggest, after a couple of years of this, that we might consider having another child.

'Another child?' I'd stormed. 'What for? We have Mia. Our perfect little girl. Why would we risk having another one, when it could just be *taken from us*?'

'We need to talk about this, Nic,' he'd tried, more than once. 'We've never been able to *talk*. Perhaps we should see someone. A doctor, a counsellor—'

'What for?' I'd screamed. 'I don't *want* to talk about it. I don't need to. I want to forget it ever happened. What I *don't* want is you suggesting I go through it all again!'

He'd given up. I suppose I'd left him no choice. I knew, deep down, what I did: I shut myself away, in my mind, in my heart – just me and my remaining child. Josh didn't get it. He didn't seem to care. Well, he could do what he liked. I didn't need him, badgering me to talk, badgering me to think about having another child. He *didn't understand.*

'Did I drive you away?' I said, now, breathless but finally quiet. 'Is that it? I *pushed* you into staying away from us? Because of how I was? Six years, and I never grieved properly for Mae – I know – Mum, and Gran, have kept telling me ever since, but I've always refused to listen. I … just acted as if she never existed.'

I started to cry again, and once more he held me until I wiped my eyes and sat up, shaking my head.

'This is awful. I'm sorry. This isn't what I had in mind when I said we needed to talk.'

'Maybe not. But it *was* what we needed to talk about. I did hate coming home, seeing you the way you were back then – so quiet, so *shut away*. You only wanted Mia. You didn't want me around.'

'That wasn't how it felt to me,' I said quietly. 'It felt as if you didn't care.' Then I shook my head and added, 'But I suppose … well, if that's how I came across, then I'm sorry.'

'You were in denial,' he said. 'But I was no help to you either, was I. Neither of us got it right. I was just as bad – I buried myself in work.' He paused. 'I wish I hadn't let you down. I wish we could both go back and do it differently.'

I nodded. 'Me too.'

'I still do love you, whatever you might think. Since you've been gone – since I realised you really weren't coming back this time – the bottom's dropped out of my world. Work stopped mattering. I've just lived for my weekends with Mia. I finally realised what I'd been missing, by staying away, not spending time with her, all those years. I was angry with you at first, but then I realised it was my own fault. I should have tried harder, shouldn't have given up on you. I must have been mad, to let you go.' He gave me a weak little smile. 'But it's too late now, I understand that. You've made a new life for yourself here in Furzewell. You don't need me. Why would you?'

'Perhaps I do, though,' I said, surprising myself. How did I not see it before? We'd needed each other but pushed each other away. 'Perhaps being apart for a year was what we needed, both of us.'

'To get some perspective?' he suggested.

'Yes.' I hesitated. 'It hasn't been a year yet, though. And ... maybe it doesn't have to be?'

'Nic, I'd like nothing better than for you to come back. But you're happy here. Happier than I've seen you, since—'

'Since we left Furzewell in the first place. Yes, I am. I don't want to come back to Plymouth, Josh.' I looked up at him. His dark eyes were gazing into mine, just as they used to, years back, when we'd sat here together in this pub as teenagers, newly in love, planning our future. Couldn't we still try again? Couldn't we manage, now, to make it work? 'We both need to think this over, obviously, but I have got a suggestion. You could come and live here in Furzewell. It's an easy drive into town for your work. We could sell the house.'

'You want me to come and live with your mum?' he said, raising his eyebrows.

I managed to laugh. 'No.' I thought for a minute, and then went on: 'The new houses on High Meadow are so much cheaper than houses in town. And they're nice. I've been looking, ever since I've been back here, wondering if I'd ever be able to afford one. Apparently the developers have a scheme where they purchase your existing home so that you can buy and move in really quickly.'

He was listening carefully, nodding. 'It does make sense. If I moved here, I'd have a lower mortgage. And I'd be closer to you, and Mia.'

'And you'd save even more money, Josh, if you'd stop spending so much on her when you see her. There's no need. We're not in competition. And anyway, there's nothing to spend money on, here in Furzewell!'

'Point taken,' he agreed, looking sheepish. 'I guess I just wanted her to enjoy being with me.'

'She does anyway. And . . . perhaps, eventually, she'll be able to see us both together again.'

He looked up at me. 'You need to be sure, this time, Nic.'

'I know.' I couldn't rush into this. Apart from the fact that, only an hour ago, the very idea of getting back together with Josh would have horrified me, I couldn't risk changing my mind again – not this time. It wouldn't be fair on him, or Mia. 'Let's take it slowly. One step at a time.'

'Yes. I really hope...' he began, looking at me with those soulful eyes again. 'I *really* hope... this isn't just a reaction to tonight. The emotion of, well, finally talking about Mae.'

I swallowed. 'Of course. We both need time to process all this. I'm glad, though, Josh – glad we're at least back on speaking terms.'

'Me too.'

'I promise we'll talk properly, now, about Mae. We need to. I know it won't be easy, but I've left it far too long. I'm OK, now,' I reassured him quickly, 'but I realise it's been festering away, all this time, and it's not healthy. A good cry was what I needed, obviously.'

'We'll talk,' he agreed softly. 'And I'm coming back next weekend anyway. To look at those houses on High Meadow!'

We drained our glasses and made our way out of the pub, into the cold, dark street we both knew so well. We didn't hold hands. It was enough that we were walking closely together, talking, amicably, making plans about the possibility of selling the house.

Mum looked up as I walked in.

'There you are,' she said. 'Mia's in bed, but she's still awake. She was worried, wondering where you were. Where you *both* were,' she added meaningfully, 'Josh's car still being outside.'

'I'll pop up and see her in a sec,' I said. 'But Mum: Josh and I have been talking.'

'I can tell.' She forced a smile. 'I can see it all over your face. Well, I hope you're not going to rush into anything. Don't go giving that child false hope, will you, unless you're sure, this time.'

'No. We won't. I won't say anything to Mia yet. But whatever happens, I'll be staying here in the village. It's where I belong, where Mia belongs. I might move out of Eagle House one day, but you won't be getting rid of me or Mia completely. We'll still be around.' With Josh – or without him. That was the one thing I was sure of. 'I'm staying in Furzewell,' I added firmly. 'Forever.'

EPILOGUE

LONELY HEARTS NO MORE

The wind is howling around us, cold needles of sleety rain in the air, as we walk through the park, wrapped up in our warm coats, hats and gloves – Mia running ahead with Smartie. There are areas of the park fenced off now, where Simon and Craig, together with their team of volunteers, have started work on the new adventure playground and nature walk. These first features should be ready, we hope, for the spring, but the lake, and the crazy golf, will take a little longer. We've got a company potentially interested in running the golf course: they run a similar one in Paignton. Mia and her friends are already very excited, though, about the new playground. I laughed when she told me earnestly the other day that there's no need, ever, for her to go back to Plymouth now, because not only is Daddy here, but also Furzewell is getting more exciting!

'I'd forgotten how much worse the winter always feels in the countryside,' Josh says, pulling me closer to him. 'February always was a dire month in this valley.'

'You're not starting to regret moving back, are you?' I tease him.

He laughs. 'What do you think? I've never been happier, Nic, you know that. And I'm sure spring will come eventually!'

'Yes.' I smile up at him. He looks so much better these days – relaxed, calm, *settled.* The new job's going well, and he has a lot more free time to spend with us. The salary's a little lower than he was used to, but the mortgage on the new house is a lot less, too. We're managing. We're happy. 'Do you realise,' I say thoughtfully, 'It's exactly a year since I moved back here.'

'Yes, of course. Best thing you could have done – even if it did take me a long while to realise it.'

'No. The best thing was when you agreed to come back and join me here.'

Everything has moved so fast, since that day in November when Josh agreed to think about moving back here. Within weeks we'd chosen a new house on the High Meadow estate, and looking back, even at that stage I think we both knew it was a fairly safe bet that Mia and I would soon be moving in with him there. We spent the Christmas holiday with Mum at Eagle House, and just after New Year, Josh moved into our new little house, bringing Bella the cat in her basket. The first weekend he was there, I helped him unpack the crockery, put up curtains and arrange the furniture. The second weekend, Mia and I moved in too. It seemed ridiculous not to. Smartie, having already been used to Monty, behaved perfectly with Bella, and to our delight the two pets both settled down as quickly as we did. And already, it's as if we've never been apart.

'Shall we catch up with the others?' Josh is saying now. 'It's too cold to dawdle – and Smartie's obviously doing his best to keep up with his doggy friends.'

I laugh, watching Mia running after the little dog, who's gambolling excitedly in pursuit of Max, Benji, Babette and Judy. The rest of the group, seeing Josh and I strolling together with our arms around each other and deep in conversation, have tactfully moved on ahead of us. I watch them now from behind as we walk on. Louise joins us for the walks now, with Eddie and their new little dog, Jet. And Kelly often comes along with Amber and Benji. She's moved in with Amber now and they seem to be blissfully happy together. Craig – still the joker of the group – is laughing with Simon as he tells him some kind of tall story. Craig's the one who's changed the most, of course. He does have a new girlfriend, a stunning brunette called India. When he introduced her to the rest of us he looked pretty nervous, as if he thought we might warn her about his reputation. I just hope he's really learnt his lesson and will treat India with more respect. Sara, as always, is leading the group and talking loudly about the next meeting of the Friends of the Park committee, has given us all quite a surprise recently by turning up to our New Year's Day walk with a guy she introduced as Keith – the ex she'd always refused to talk about. She told me they were seeing each other again, but just as friends, until they could be sure whether it would work out this time.

'Sometimes a long break from each other changes everything,' I'd said at the time, looking pointedly at Josh, and she nodded in understanding. They were now spending every weekend together, so I was keeping my fingers crossed for her.

'Perhaps we won't be able to call ourselves the *Lonely Hearts* Dog Walkers for much longer,' I say now to Josh, with a smile. Even Louise, who's still insisting she isn't ready yet for another relationship, and might never be, at least has her new little dog for company now.

'Especially now Simon's so much happier,' Josh agrees, giving me a hug.

Simon is, of course, the *ex*-Lonely Heart that I'm most pleased about. It was on Christmas Eve, when a crowd of us had gathered at the pub, that I decided I'd finally had enough of seeing him looking sad and wistful, while Mum sat at home in Eagle House on her own, telling everyone she was having such fun as a *single girl*. I took Simon to one side and told him the situation was ridiculous, that Mum wasn't the happy socialite she pretended to be, that she was lonely and only resisted his company – *any* man's company – because she'd never got over what happened with my dad.

'She needs someone who understands that, and who'd be patient with her and just be friends, for as long as it takes,' I said. 'I know she likes you, Simon – she wouldn't have kept seeing you for as long as she did, and she wouldn't be *refusing* to see you now, otherwise – it's only because she's so afraid of getting hurt that she's still turning you away.'

He nodded. 'I understand that, Nic. I always did. I'd never hurt her, you know that. Or rush her into anything she wasn't ready for.'

'*I* know that,' I agreed. 'But does she? Isn't it worth sitting her down and spelling it out, loudly and clearly, once and for all – instead of just hoping and praying that she'll change her mind one day? She needs you to be straight with her,' I said softly.

I was taking a risk. He might have told me to butt out and mind my own business. He might have said he'd tried already, he wasn't going to put himself through another rejection. But he didn't. He put down his drink, gave me a little smile and a shrug, and said:

'Well, I guess the worst she can do is bite my head off. You say she's at home now?' And when I went back to Eagle House, they were sitting in the lounge talking quietly together. I'd done what I could, and only hoped Mum wouldn't tell me off again for interfering.

To my amazement, she invited him round to Eagle House on Boxing Day. They were friendly but quiet with each other, as if they were both made of china and were nervous of touching each other. But on New Year's Eve, she told me they were going out for dinner together. It's progressed slowly, cautiously, from there: but now, at the end of February, they're still seeing each other, and Mum seems, at last, to have dropped the big brave act about being a good-time single girl. I'm daring to hope, now, that neither of them will be lonely forever. I'm sure the lovely Simon could be the one to bring about the happy ending Mum deserves. With Gran still enjoying her film-and-sherry evenings with Sidney, it's nice to know *she* isn't going to be lonely either.

We've nearly caught the others up now, but I pull Josh back, grabbing hold of both his hands and turning him to face me.

'There's something I need to tell you,' I say softly, 'before we rejoin them.'

'Oh.' He looks a little wary. 'This sounds ominous.'

'Not at all. It's ... good news, Josh.' I take a deep breath. 'You know what we said – after we went for those sessions with the bereavement counsellor during December?'

'Which part?'

The sessions were Josh's idea, but in the end I was glad I agreed. It was exactly what we both needed. Being able to talk about Mae, and how we both handled our grief so badly, with a sympathetic outsider, made such a difference. After three sessions, we both felt as if a huge weight had been lifted from our shoulders, leaving us ready to move forward.

'The part where we agreed it wasn't too late to think about trying for another baby,' I say, watching his face.

'Yes?' He looks back at me hopefully through the rain. 'And ... *have* you thought about it?'

'Actually, it's a bit too late to just be thinking,' I say, my voice trembling a little. I'm not sure how he's going to react. 'Josh, we ... haven't been too careful, since we've been back together. Not every time. And, well, I've just done a test. Two tests, in fact, because I couldn't quite believe the first one – considering how long it took us before. Yes, I'm pregnant! I think it'll be due in October. I hope you're all right with it ... we didn't exactly have a chance to discuss—'

'Oh my God!' He grabs hold of me, almost hoisting me off my feet, and – with the rain pouring off both our coats, dripping off our faces – kisses me so fiercely I eventually have to break free, laughing, protesting that Mia's staring at us in surprise. 'I'm over the moon,' he says, unnecessarily, his own voice shivering with emotion. He lets me go, and brushes me down as if he might have spoilt me in some way. 'I'm going to look after you so well,' he says, fiercely now. 'I won't let you do a thing. You're going to rest, and be spoilt, and—'

'No, Josh,' I say gently. 'I'm going to carry on as normal, as best I can. We mustn't spend the whole of this pregnancy worrying about ... what might happen. We need to assume that nothing will. Nothing, apart from it ending with a healthy little baby brother – or sister – for Mia.'

'You're right. You're so much stronger now,' he says. 'And I love you more than ever.'

'Good!' I joke. 'So – maybe we ought to tell Mia what all this public display of affection is about, as she and Smartie are both looking at us with disgust!'

'Are you having a *baby*?' Mia asks, in tones of disbelief.

I'd forgotten how good her hearing is.

'Would you like that?' I ask her. 'A baby brother or sister?'

'YEAH!' she screams. 'Hooray! I thought I was *never* going to have one. Can it sleep in my room? Can I push it in the pram? Can I tell all my friends about it? I can't *wait*!'

'I think that's a *yes*!' Josh says, laughing. Even Smartie's barking with excitement now, and all the rest of the group – all our lovely friends here in Furzewell, and their dogs! – are turning to look at us, smiling and asking what's going on.

And, despite the rain dripping down our necks, the cold wind freezing our fingers and toes, and the mud coating our boots and trouser legs, it feels, right now, that Furzewell is the best place on earth, and Josh is the best person to be here with. I'm so glad we both came home. So glad we're a family again. And I truly believe neither of us will have to be *Lonely Hearts* again now – ever again.

ACKNOWLEDGEMENTS

With thanks to my agent Juliet, my editor Katie and all the team at Ebury for all their help and hard work, as always. And thanks to helpful vet Sharon Whelan who once again gave me advice on a couple of pet care queries. Also to my puppy-owning friends and family for advice about buying a new pup from a breeder.

If you enjoyed

THE LONELY HEARTS DOG WALKERS

Leave a review online

Follow Sheila on Facebook/SheilaNortonAuthor and on Twitter @NortonSheilaann

Keep up to date with Sheila's latest news on her website www.sheilanorton.com

Make sure you've read Sheila's other novels …

Sam has always dreamed of working with animals...

But her receptionist job in a London vets is not hitting the spot. Unsure whether a busy city life is for her, she flees to her Nana Peggy's idyllic country village.

But despite the rolling hills and its charming feel, life in Hope Green is far from peaceful. On first meeting Joe, the abrupt and bad-tempered local vet, Sam knows she must get him on side, but that is easier said than done...

With her dream close enough to touch, will she get there, or will events conspire against her... ?

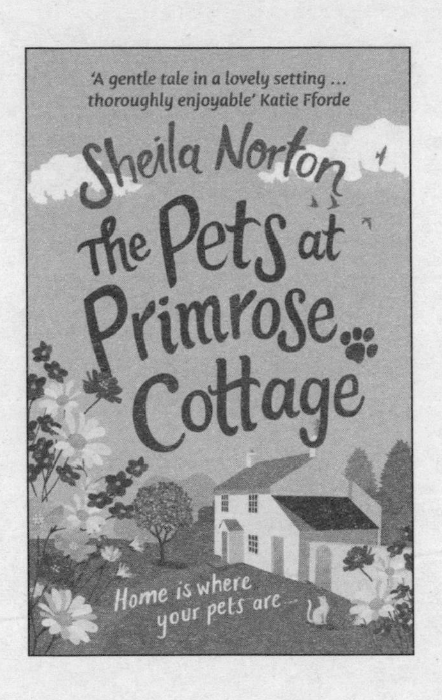

Emma Nightingale needs a place to hide away...

Fresh from the heartbreak of a failed relationship, she takes refuge in quiet Crickleford. And not before long – and quite accidentally too – Emma finds herself the town's favourite pet-sitter, a role she isn't certain of at first, but soon her heart is warmed by the animals; they expect nothing more of her than she is able to give.

The last thing Emma wants is for people to discover the *real* reason she is lying low, but then the handsome reporter from the local paper takes an interest in her story. Can Emma keep her secret *and* follow her heart's desire...?

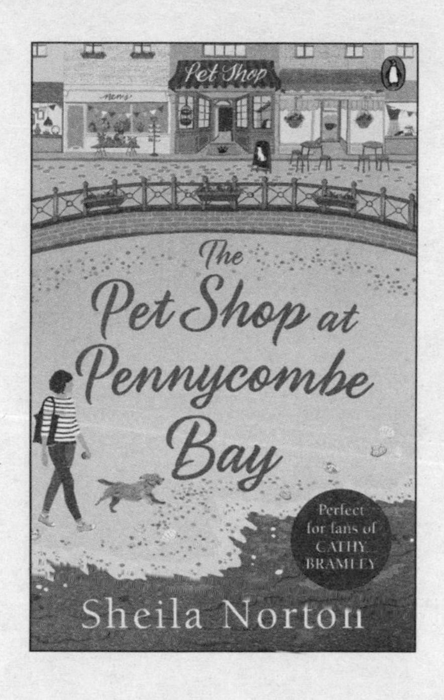

When the going gets ruff, it's time to make a change...

In need of a fresh start, Jess has moved to the beautiful Devon seaside town of Pennycombe Bay. However it isn't the new beginning she was hoping for – she enjoys her new job at the local pet shop but feels like she's treading on eggshells living with her moody cousin Ruth.

When she meets handsome stranger, Nick, on the beach, she thinks she's made a new friend or something more. Although her hopes of romance are quickly dashed when she finds out he's seeing another woman...

Can Jess make Pennycombe feel like home?

Keep reading for an exclusive preview...

CHAPTER 1

I first met Nick Abbott on a lovely morning in the middle of May. I'd been standing on the beach, the gentle waves just lapping my toes, gazing out to sea. It was my favourite time of year in Pennycombe Bay, still relatively quiet before the main onslaught of holidaymakers but with the possibility of sunny days and long, light evenings. My cocker spaniel Prudence was splashing madly in the shallow waves, full of the joy of being alive, when suddenly a big shaggy brown dog dived into the sea next to her, completely submerging her for a few seconds before she shook herself and bounded after him.

'Sorry!' called a voice from behind me. 'He's a bit too exuberant!'

'It's fine.' I turned, smiling in my usual hesitant way at the tall, blond, good-looking guy approaching me down the beach. 'Look, they're friends already.'

'So easy for dogs, isn't it,' he commented, laughing. 'No awkward introductions, no bothering with hearing each other's life histories. Just jump straight in and start playing.'

I nodded, struck dumb now with shyness. He was right, I thought sadly. If only I could be as easy and carefree as these dogs and, come to that, as easy and relaxed as this handsome stranger seemed to be. Ignoring my silence, he was already going on to talk about his dog – Buddy – how long he'd had him, how nice the weather had been, and how long he'd lived in Pennycombe Bay.

'Are you local yourself?' he asked eventually as I was still struggling to think of anything to say in response.

'Yes. I've been living here for about four years now.'

'Oh, right. I haven't seen you down here before,' he remarked.

'Well, during the winter I usually take Prudence to West Beach.'

'Oh, right. Of course. Dogs aren't allowed there from May to September, are they?' he said. 'I prefer it here anyway, myself.'

I nodded. West Beach, closer to the centre of town, was where all the holidaymakers went, but this smaller, rockier beach at Stony Cove was prettier, as well as being quieter. The only reason I chose West Beach, outside of the peak season when dogs were allowed there, was that it was a slightly shorter walk from my home, and time was at a premium. I checked my watch now, quickly, and gave a little start of surprise.

'Sorry,' I said. 'Um, it was nice to meet you but I need to get going.' I shrugged self-consciously. 'Come on, Prudence.'

As usual I was trying hard not to let my natural shyness come across as downright rudeness. It was a difficult balancing act. I could already feel myself starting to blush. But he was still smiling, as if he hadn't even noticed how awkward I was.

'Work?' he asked, sympathetically. 'Luckily I've got a day off today.' He grimaced. 'Back to the grind tomorrow, then I'll be walking Buddy a lot earlier, as usual.'

'Right.' I nodded, and managed to give him a smile in return. 'Well, sorry, but I really must dash, I'm running late.'

Prudence bounded out of the sea towards me, ears bouncing, tail waving, her eyes bright with excitement. I stepped away from her a little as she shook herself vigorously, sea water flying in all directions, then I fastened her lead. I looked up at the guy, gave him a flustered little wave and turned to go.

'Nice to meet you too,' he called after me. 'Hope I didn't hold you up! I'm Nick, by the way.'

'Oh, I'm Jess,' I mumbled, without looking back. 'Bye, then!'

I walked quickly back along the beach towards the steps up to the road, embarrassed and annoyed with myself. What was wrong with me? I couldn't even manage to have an ordinary conversation with a man without being so shy that I was in danger of coming across as downright rude. And now I'd probably made myself late for work. I looked at my watch again and tried to force myself to relax. It was OK. If Prudence and I walked at a decent pace we could be home from here in about ten minutes – if you could call it home. Then I shook myself. Now I was just being ungrateful! Ungrateful to my cousin, whose house I lived in. Ungrateful for my nice life here in the place I'd loved ever since I was a child, when my dad used to bring me here for days out from our home in Exeter. And, of course, I knew I should have been thankful for the fact that I had a job, even if it *wasn't* exactly what I'd imagined myself doing as a career. It was a nice little job, and it was better than being unemployed, I told myself sharply. Better than having to sweep the roads or clean toilets for a living. I was *lucky*, I reminded myself yet again. *Snap out of it, girl!*

The fact was that I loved living here in Pennycombe Bay, I loved being able to walk on the beach with Prudence every morning before work and, later in the summer, to swim in the sea during the evenings, when the water was at its warmest and most of the tourists had packed up and left the beach. The quaint, narrow, cobbled little streets that made up the town centre, the quirky shops and cheerful, friendly cafés were all part of the reason I felt so at home in the little town. I was so lucky to be living here, I reminded myself again. So why did I sometimes feel so unsettled? Why couldn't I shake off this niggling feeling that life had cheated me, that everybody else was more fulfilled and happy than I was?

'Why can't I be more like you?' I said out loud to Prudence. 'Why can't I just enjoy my nice life, and be grateful for it?'

Prudence looked up at me, her head on one side as if she'd like to help, if only she could.

Don't worry, Mum, she seemed to be saying. *At least you've got me!*

I laughed at the expression on her little face. As long as I had her, why should I worry about anyone else? A chance encounter with a good-looking stranger on the beach didn't matter in the least. I'd have forgotten all about it by the next day.

Home was number five, West View Villas, and was just one street back from the seafront, up a short but quite steep hill that had Prudence and me puffing from the climb. A three-storey pink-painted house, built during the rise in popularity of British seaside resorts in the 1930s, it was at the top end of a terrace of similar houses. They were all painted in different pastel colours, and had been used as B&Bs for decades, but were now mostly owned by well-off young professionals like my cousin, or as second homes by Londoners who brought their families down to stay during the summer. Because of its history as a B&B, the house was a lot bigger than it looked from the outside, with five bedrooms and two bathrooms, a big fitted kitchen that had been knocked through to the dining room, and a separate lounge at the front. It was too big for one person – my cousin – on her own; I had no idea how she'd afforded to buy it. Too big even for the two of us, but needless to say, I wasn't about to complain. Being on the end of the terrace had also given the house the advantage of space for a garage – a rarity in the tight little streets of this town – with a utility room built onto the back. The garden was small but at least gave Prudence somewhere to run around.

And best of all, because we were at the top of a hill, the back bedrooms had balconies looking over the rooftops of the houses in the next street and down to the sea.

By the time I let myself into the house that morning, my cousin had already left. Ruth was an accountant, working for a practice in Exeter where she'd been all but promised, if she stayed with them, a partnership by the time she was forty. She was counting down the years: four to go. I couldn't even begin to imagine what it was like to be Ruth: to have to put on a smart suit every day, commute on the train and spend her life in an office, dealing with spreadsheets and figures, profits and losses, assets and liabilities and all the other things she talked about, which I didn't understand or even want to. Going out for business lunches and meetings with clients; bringing work home to do at weekends. We were so different, it was hard to believe we were closely related. For a start, she was tall, slender and beautiful, with long straight dark hair that gleamed as if it were silk. I was much shorter, making me look a bit dumpy, and although my hair was the same colour, to my endless chagrin I hadn't inherited the straight, shiny look. Mine was an unruly mop of curls that I'd finally given in and had cut short – it was the only way to manage it. Six years older than me, Ruth had been like a big sister to me when we were children. I'd looked up to her then. Now, it was definitely more a case of her looking down on me.

I washed Prudence, gave her a rub down with a warm towel, filled her water bowl and watched her settle down in her bed.

'There you go, Pru,' I said, giving her a quick stroke before I left. 'Have a nice rest, and I'll see you later.'

She wagged her tail at me. *OK, Mum. Off you go to work, I'll be fine!*

'Don't give me that look,' I warned her, smiling. 'I know you're probably plotting to get all your little doggy friends round here as soon as my back's turned. I suppose you'll have a party here and finish off all the drink in the cupboard!'

It was a little joke we shared. Well, I suppose I shared it with myself. That's what happens when a dog is your closest friend – you not only talk to them, you imagine them replying, and make up imaginary lives for them too. Of course, Prudence knew I'd be coming home at lunchtime, as I did most days, to let her out in the garden. That was another reason to appreciate my nice life, I reminded myself: working locally, only a short walk into town from here. It wouldn't have been fair to have a dog if I'd worked long hours in the city like Ruth did. Not that Ruth would want a dog, anyway. She just about tolerated Prudence, as long as I kept her clean and quiet, which wasn't always easy.

I walked quickly into town, enjoying the breeze on my face, the blue sky and sunshine. As usual, I stopped off at the newsagent's, which was the shop next door to ours, where Mr Patel had my paper ready and waiting for me.

'Anything else for you today, Jess?' he asked, smiling at me.

'No thanks, Mr P.' I fumbled in my purse for the right change. 'Have a good day.'

'You too, love.'

It was pretty much the same quick, uncomplicated conversation we had every morning, and it suited me perfectly, not having to worry about what to say or how to say it. Mr Patel was a nice guy who knew all his customers by name, and he stocked a few convenience items like tea, coffee and biscuits alongside his newspaper business. So I was often sent next door to his shop for supplies during my working day too.

'Here you are, then, Jess,' said my boss, Jim Meacham, looking up with a smile when the door chimes alerted him to my arrival in the pet shop.

He said the same thing every day – as if I'd turned up unexpectedly an hour late, or as if he'd been wondering whether I was coming in at all. In fact, I was there on the dot of eight forty-five every morning, giving us fifteen minutes to have coffee and a chat before I turned the *Closed* sign on the door round to *Open.* Every day I performed the same small ritual, watched by Jim with an expression of genuine anticipation, hands on the counter, poised ready for his first customer. Actually, we both knew it could be hours before anyone came in to buy anything. Sometimes we'd have a rush – two or three sales within the first hour of opening. Other days, we'd close for an hour for lunch without having served a single customer.

Jim was getting on a bit now, but he'd owned *Paws4Thought* for over thirty years, and worked there as an assistant to his father before that – ever since he was a young boy. Back then, it had been a traditional pet shop called simply *Pennycombe Bay Pets and Supplies*, selling kittens and puppies as well as smaller animals like mice, hamsters and gerbils. I remembered being brought as a child to the shop on rainy seaside day trips, to coo over the cute kittens and fluffy bunnies, while we sheltered from the weather and my dad chatted to Jim about the latest scandal in the town. They were old friends; Dad knew everyone around here in those days. He was born and grew up in Pennycombe Bay, only moving to Exeter when he married my mum, so he always enjoyed bringing me back here for our days out together.

Of course, pet shops didn't tend to sell puppies or kittens any more, and Jim had changed the shop's name about ten years earlier to reflect the changing times. He apparently asked the local school to hold a competition for the kids to come up with a quirky new name, and no doubt it was actually the parents who put forward their suggestions. *Paws4Thought* was the result. We now stocked pet food – every brand under the sun – and flea powders and shampoos, toys and beds, leads and collars for dogs, scratching posts and litter trays for cats, cages for mice and birds, books on pet care – you get the picture. Everything but the animals, who would have made the job halfway interesting and fun.

But again, I knew I should appreciate what I had. It was a nice job, after all, and Jim was lovely. I was pretty sure he didn't even really need me, but he'd stepped in when he heard I needed a break, probably out of loyalty to my dad. And I worked as hard as I could to make his life easier and repay him for his kindness. I stacked the shelves, did the stock ordering, balanced the books, did the banking – letting him sit in his chair behind the counter chatting to his regular customers. Sometimes I felt that we were as much a meeting place of pet owners as a shop, but that was Pennycombe Bay for you. Longstanding friendships going back for generations; old-fashioned slot machines on the pier and boat trips from the harbour; traditional fish and chips, and cream teas. The British seaside at its best. Some of my friends back in Exeter wouldn't have come near the place. They thought it was dull. I wasn't sure what it said about me that I loved it so much.

'Two sugars and a digestive biscuit as usual, Jim?' I called out now, as I finished making our morning coffees in the little kitchen at the back of the shop.

'Lovely, Jess.' He came to take the steaming mug out of my hands, and as we both went back through to the shop to start another day, the stranger on the beach slipped to the back of my mind.